CATALYST

By
Michael C. Grumley

i.iii

1

Books by Michael C. Grumley

BREAKTHROUGH

LEAP

CATALYST

AMID THE SHADOWS

THROUGH THE FOG

THE UNEXPECTED HERO

ACKNOWLEDGEMENTS

Special thanks to Frank, Tim, and Les, for all of their expert and valuable advice.

Prologue

With a painful wince, Steve Caesare brushed back his shirt and slid a hand down over the handle of his gun. The hallway he stood in was richly decorated with white marble walls and thick beige carpeting, allowing him to approach the door with very little sound.

Caesare glanced up at one of the overhead chandeliers, scanning the ceiling and walls for cameras. Too well hidden. His hotel uniform was bulging at the seams, barely containing his broad frame beneath. Anyone taking a close look at a monitor would notice something wrong with his appearance.

The Tivioli Mofarrej was one of the most elegant hotels in São Paulo, and certainly the most expensive. Used by the wealthiest clientele, the hotel emanated a raw sense of power and prestige, towering among the cityscape of Brazil's richest city.

It had taken him two weeks. Two weeks following the man he had now tracked to the room at the end of the hall. Miguel Blanco was living large off the money he had stolen from Mateus Alves, his previous employer and one of the richest men in South America. After killing his former boss, Blanco had successfully stolen nearly one hundred million Brazilian reales from Alves' various accounts and trusts. It was only a fraction of the old man's wealth, but it was more than enough — enough to become one of the very elites Blanco had spent much of his life protecting.

And it had been no easy task. Gaining access to Alves' accounts was one thing. Blanco already had help with that. The hard part was covering his tracks. For that he needed the help of several others, compadres who were discreet and also stood to gain handsomely from the disassembling of

Alves' vast fortune.

Caesare, however, didn't care about the money. He was there for a very different reason. The old man had been as corrupt as his murderer and Caesare held no sympathy for either of them. He was there for one thing and one thing only: retribution.

He was there because if it had been up to Blanco, Caesare would have been just as dead, lying next to the old man on top of that mountain. But Blanco didn't know he had survived. And after two weeks of searching, Caesare was about to pay him the mother of all surprise visits.

The absence of anyone guarding the door left Caesare a bit wary as he crept closer. Guests staying in a presidential suite usually had a security detail. Where was Blanco's? The man had previously been an officer in the Brazilian Intelligence Agency, which typically left men overconfident or completely paranoid. *But if he was paranoid, where was his detail?*

Blanco was definitely in the room. At least he had been thirty minutes ago. They had zeroed in on the target's cell phone signal, and pinpointed it to thirty meters from where Caesare was now standing before it was abruptly switched off. Now, ten feet from the door, he silently slid the .40 caliber Glock out from its concealed holster and laid his index finger along the side, just above the trigger guard. He turned his head slightly, using his peripheral vision to check the hall behind him one last time.

When he reached the door, Caesare kept to the side and brought the gun around his right hip. He raised it smoothly and leaned in closer, listening. There was no sound at all. No voices. No television. Nothing.

Blanco hadn't left Rio de Janeiro with anyone except the one person Caesare knew would be with him: Alves' young and longtime personal assistant, Carolina Sosa. She was the one person who had access to many of the old man's accounts and other verifiable information. *She* was the gateway to Alves' riches.

Caesare withdrew a small magnetic card, a used but very valuable card. It came from the hotel, which took only a few hours to find in São Paulo. From a person who could encode a master keycard for almost any hotel in the city.

He held it in his left hand and twisted his wrist to peer at his watch, waiting.

Anytime, Will.

When Caesare heard the phone finally ring inside the room, he moved quickly, inserting the card into the door's lock and pulling it back out. The loud click was masked by the telephone's ring and Caesare immediately pushed the door ajar — just enough to prevent the lock from reengaging. In the same motion, he brought the tip of his left shoe forward to prop the door open by half an inch.

The phone rang again, echoing through the room. The third ring was the last, immediately plunging the room back into silence. With another quick glance over his shoulder, Caesare pressed his ear close to the cracked door. No footsteps. No movement at all that he could hear.

He pushed the door in further and was met by a cool draft of air escaping past him. The door opened further without any noise, allowing Caesare a look inside. Down the entrance hallway, he spotted a dark polished table with chairs perfectly arranged.

He stepped inside, keeping the gun low but in front. The pain in his ribs screamed as he twisted around to ease the door closed — a result of the near fatal wound Blanco had given him.

The door gave a muted click shut and Caesare eased forward over the spotless marble flooring. He stepped away from the wall and gradually edged himself around the corner.

Then he froze.

The scene before him was not what he was expecting. The room seemed pristine except for two dining room chairs positioned in the middle. In each chair sat a motionless figure, bound and bloodied. Both gagged, with their heads down upon their chests.

The first was a woman, barely recognizable through the dark brunette hair dangling in front of her face. Carolina Sosa. The second was Miguel Blanco himself, his body slumping but held in place by the ropes around his waist.

Neither was moving.

Caesare immediately stepped back out of sight, leaving only the gun and half of his face exposed. The scene looked fresh enough that the murderer could still be inside the suite. After waiting a minute, he slowly eased himself back away from the wall and moved at a wedged angle, slowly peering back into the main room. He crept forward onto soft carpet. Caesare rounded the next doorway, staying well away from the corner, providing him maximum visibility.

It took several minutes to ensure the entire suite was clear, after which Caesare returned to the front room. He gazed at the two lifeless bodies.

Approaching the pair, he stared into Carolina's hair-strewn face. Beneath the dark strands, he could see her badly bruised skin. He passed by her and stopped in front of Blanco. The man's face was entirely black and blue, his gag now fallen halfway off.

He stared at Blanco for a long time, finally shaking his head. Living a life of deceit often ended abruptly, and sometimes violently. The small rubber tourniquet hanging from the man's arm told Caesare that whatever secrets Blanco had now belonged to someone else. They had literally beaten and drugged it out of him.

It was too bad Caesare hadn't gotten to him first. At least he would have lived. He scanned the room one last time before returning the gun smoothly to its holster.

Caesare began to turn for the door when something suddenly caught his eye, startling him. His gun was back out before his brain even registered what it was.

Blanco had moved.

7

It was slight, but it was movement. Blanco's eyes remained closed, but the movement was more than just residual muscle twitching. Caesare waited with his gun lowered but gripped firmly between both hands. Then it happened again.

With one hand, he reached up and eased the Brazilian's head back before pulling the rest of the cloth gag out of his mouth. The swollen eyelids struggled, but finally managed to crack themselves open. Dark, unfocused eyes peered out.

"Blanco," Caesare whispered.

It took time for the eyes to focus on Caesare. When they did, the recognition came quickly. They opened wider in disbelief.

Caesare managed to refrain from smiling at Blanco and vindictively muttering the word "surpresa." Instead he rose and turned toward the phone. He had picked up the handset when Blanco blurted something behind him.

"Não!" A moment later he mumbled again, switching to English. "Don't call."

"I'm calling for help."

Blanco's eyes dropped to his arm, where a small drop of blood was drying over the remains of an insertion point. "There is...no help...for me," he said weakly.

Caesare knelt in front of him. "Who did it?"

"Otero," he whispered.

Caesare knelt down next to him. "What did he want?"

"Please." Blanco's voice grew fainter. "Please...save them."

Caesare glanced around the room. "Save who?"

Blanco was now struggling just to make his lips move. "My family."

Admiral Langford looked up as John Clay opened the wide door to his office with Will Borger standing behind him. The Admiral quickly waved them in as he pushed a button on his phone and dropped the handset back onto the cradle.

"Okay, Clay and Borger are here. Go ahead, Steve."

"Bom dia, gents," Caesare called through the speaker. "You're missing some beautiful weather down here. Sweltering and muggy."

Clay smiled. "Sounds lovely."

"Yeah, unfortunately it's not all sunshine and roses."

"Did you find Blanco?"

"Oh, I found him all right. But I'm afraid he's not in the best of moods. He's dead."

Clay and Borger looked at Langford with surprise.

"Dead?" Borger repeated, confused. "But we traced that call he made right before he turned his cell off just an hour ago."

"Yeah well, I don't think he was the one who turned it off. I found him in his room beaten to a pulp. The Sosa woman was already gone and Blanco was just minutes away. I couldn't do anything."

"Was he conscious?"

"Barely. I got a little out of him, but it was brief."

Clay noticed an echo in Caesare's voice. "Where are you?"

On the other end, Caesare scanned up and down the metal stairs, working quickly to get his stolen uniform off. "I'm in a stairwell, at the hotel."

Langford looked at the phone. "Any idea who did it?"

"Someone named Otero. Ring a bell with anyone?"

They all shook their heads. "No."

Caesare nodded on his end. "I suspect he was someone involved with Mateus Alves."

"What makes you say that?"

"Because that's what they were after," replied Caesare.

"What do you mean?"

"What I mean is, they weren't after the money. They wanted *answers*."

"What kind of answers?"

"As far as I can tell, answers about Alves. Whoever this Otero is, he was looking for something specific. Money is easy to trace, but Blanco and his girlfriend looked like they were subjected to some serious narco-interrogation, followed by a lethal cocktail. Either way, I'm sure Otero didn't expect someone like me to show up before Blanco was dead."

Langford's brows remained furrowed as he leaned in closer to the speakerphone. "So what did you get out of Blanco?"

"Not much," Caesare replied. "He was pretty far gone. But one of his last words was clear: *macaco*."

"Macaco?"

Caesare peeled off the last of the uniform. "It's Portuguese for monkey, Admiral. Otero knows about Alves' preserve in Brazil, and he knows about the monkey."

Langford watched Clay and Borger exchange looks. The monkey was a small capuchin discovered by a team of "researchers" who had been employed by the old man before he was murdered. In actuality, they were all poachers, except one. One was a genuine researcher and had stumbled upon a very special capuchin monkey almost entirely by accident — a monkey very different from the others they had caught.

This particular one was highly intelligent and while the average lifespan of most wild capuchins was roughly twenty-five years, this one was discovered to be profoundly older. So much older, in fact, that the billionaire Mateus Alves threw every resource he had into two goals: finding out where the monkey had come from and doing it as quietly as possible.

Langford could see the gears turning in Clay's head. "Clay?"

He glanced up at the Admiral before turning back to the speakerphone. "How did this Otero know about the monkey? Or even that Alves was searching for it?"

"Or why someone like Alves would voluntarily abandon a billion dollar empire and completely disappear from public view."

"Otero must have known something," Clay mused. "But how?"

"Blanco had been talking to a lot of people," said Caesare. "Maybe he was trying to capitalize on what Alves had already discovered. And maybe he finally found someone crazy enough to listen."

Clay nodded absently. It was certainly plausible. Except for the crazy part. They all knew that what Alves was after wasn't crazy at all. Tracing the origins of the capuchin was one thing, but what Alves really wanted was its DNA. Some primate DNA was almost 99% identical to humans. If a primate could live more than four times its normal life span, it wasn't much of a stretch for that DNA to be isolated, and potentially applied to humans.

Alves was old, in his eighties, and wanted more than anything to extend his own life. And he believed he'd finally found just the miracle to help him do it.

Clay continued thinking. "But someone wouldn't just murder Blanco on a whim…over the word 'monkey.' They'd have to have gotten more. Maybe a lot more. And maybe enough to justify killing Blanco on the spot, to shut him up."

Langford rubbed his chin. "Then we have to assume that this Otero now knows everything." After a deep breath, he leaned forward again. "Let's table that for the moment. It seems we have an even bigger problem to deal with. I just received a report from the salvage team near Guyana. They have recovered fragments of the torpedo and enough of its Comp-B explosive signature for a positive identification." Langford paused, looking at Clay and Borger. "The Bowditch wasn't sunk by the Russians like we thought. It was sunk by the Chinese."

Clay and Borger may have been visibly surprised at the news over Blanco being dead, but now they were absolutely *stunned*.

Two weeks before, the sinking of one of the Navy's most modern research ships had seemed to be a completely separate event. But it wasn't. It was connected to the billionaire Alves' death in a way that none of them could have foreseen. The U.S.S. Bowditch was investigating a Chinese warship quietly docked along the northern coast of South America, in the small country of Guyana.

However, what they discovered next was a revelation. The ship's Chinese crew was making mysterious trips into the jungle under the cover of darkness. The Chinese had made a startling discovery on the very same mountain to which Mateus Alves had traced the capuchin monkey's origins.

Over the speaker, Caesare was the first to reply. "Admiral, did you say the Bowditch was sunk by the Chinese?"

"That's right."

"But the only sub in the area was Russian."

"The only one we were aware of."

"Wait a minute." Clay suddenly looked at Langford. "That means a Chinese sub may have been there all along."

"It looks that way."

"And it waited to attack the Bowditch until their warship was leaving with its cargo."

Langford nodded. Clay knew as well as anyone how the events unfolded. *He was onboard the Bowditch when it was struck.*

"So, that's it!" exclaimed Clay. "That's why the warship

itself never attacked…because it couldn't. And that's why their sub was there. For protection. They were there to make sure the warship and its cargo made it out."

"So they gutted the thing."

Clay nodded, as the pieces fell into place. "They'd been bringing those crates out of the jungle for months. But there was no way they could have fit it into just one warship. It's too small. Unless they gutted the ship. Removing everything inside gave them the storage they needed, which meant it also left the ship defenseless. Their submarine was simply waiting, ready to clear a path for it."

Langford watched the expression on Clay's face. The guy never forgot anything. Given enough time, he could figure damn near anything out.

"Well, that was clever," Caesare said.

Langford frowned. "The Russians were bad enough. But the Chinese are a whole new problem."

Clay was thinking the same thing. Russia's relationship with the U.S. had reached new lows over the fiasco in the Ukraine. And Washington's relationship with the Chinese was also deteriorating, assisted by the Chinese coming out publicly in support of Russia's position. Until then, China had remained a reluctant geopolitical partner of the U.S., primarily due to many decades of economic trading history. But in recent years China had been taking steps of their own, inching closer and closer to an adversarial position. When news leaked out that they'd actually attacked and sunk a large United States naval ship, things were bound to escalate, and badly.

"What happens now?" asked Clay.

Langford shook his head. "Nothing good. What the Chinese found on that mountain was worth starting a war over. But make no mistake, we would have done the same thing."

Langford rubbed his eyes. The U.S. State Department had already begun condemning Russia for the destruction of the Bowditch. Now they would have to downplay their previous remarks and redirect their accusations at China. Yet they could not risk the trade relationship with China. If it collapsed, all hell would break loose, and there would be no winner on either side. The best the Administration could manage would be to corral the issue and turn it into a more subtle and very strategic counterattack. Langford knew the U.S. politicians were not going to rest until they had their pound of flesh, no matter what the long term ramifications were. The unfortunate truth was that politicians started wars but relied on men like Langford to fight them.

Langford blinked and found himself staring at the phone. The room remained silent. He straightened in his chair. "For the time being, I want you three to find out what you can about Otero. Alves had his connections and I'm sure this thug does too. And the last thing we need is the Brazilian government finding out and getting involved."

"Yes, sir," all three answered almost simultaneously.

Langford promptly ended the call with Caesare. He then watched Clay and Borger open the door, stepping out of the room.

The situation was unraveling quickly.

Langford let out a quick sigh. Soon he would have to tell the men what had happened to the Chinese warship immediately after it escaped Guyana with its precious cargo. Something that made absolutely no sense at all.

2

Clay followed Will Borger into his darkened office, which was a generous word to describe the space where Will worked. Located on one of the subfloors of the Pentagon building, the room was in dire need of some windows and sunlight. And a maid. The room was filled with racks of computer and signaling equipment which few people would recognize. A few pieces looked to be as old as Borger himself, who would soon be pushing fifty.

Will Borger approached his desk, with a screen that was three monitors wide. Clay closed the door behind them.

With a loud squeak from his chair, Borger sat down and reached out to pull another forward for Clay. "Have a seat."

"I could use the stretch."

Borger nodded and spun back around to the monitors. "I need to show you something. Something I haven't told anyone yet."

Clay watched him open a new window on the screen and begin typing. A moment later a map filled the center screen. He raised his hand and briefly tapped a large hard drive resting below the same monitor.

"This is the hard drive I had on the Bowditch. Fortunately, I had it in my backpack when we were ordered to abandon ship."

Clay peered at Borger. "The one with the video footage?"

"Correct." He motioned to the map and reached for his mouse. It was a map of South America, with Guyana centered on the screen. Borger then double-clicked several times, zooming in on the area around Georgetown. "When we got back, I wanted to see what really happened to the Bowditch. So I downloaded the video from the ARGUS

15

satellite before and after the impact."

Clay was leaning over his shoulder when Borger stopped zooming and let the image crystalize. A moment later, they could both clearly see the U.S.S. Bowditch from an aerial view.

"There she is," he said, under his breath.

The image was frozen, but the white wake behind the stern was clearly visible and showed the ship traveling full speed toward Georgetown's small harbor. It was heading directly at the Chinese warship, which was trying to leave.

Borger then zoomed back out slightly, doubling the viewing area. Both ships were now smaller, but a barely identifiable wake could be seen several hundred yards behind the Bowditch.

A torpedo.

Borger hit a button on his keyboard and the overhead images began to play as a video. He moved out of the way, giving Clay a clear view. It was only moments later when the bow of the ship could be seen beginning to move. Clay knew it was the moment Captain Krogstad had given the order to do the unthinkable. *To bring the ship around.*

"Geez," Clay muttered.

"It's hard to watch."

"It is."

Over the next few minutes, they watched in silence at the agonizingly slow turn of the ship, finally coming about just moments before the torpedo's impact.

The Bowditch was a science vessel, which meant it had no real weapons to speak of — certainly nothing with which to fight off a torpedo attack. The only offensive capability lay in the Oceanhawk helicopter housed on the main deck. In the video, they watched the rotors of the chopper gaining speed, desperately trying to lift off in time. But the torpedo struck first. Even in the video, the explosion against the port side of the bow was breathtaking. Most of the forward deck was destroyed instantly. On what deck remained, the

16

Oceanhawk's desperate attempt to escape came to an end. Clay and Borger watched in eerie silence as the blast caused the helicopter to roll and slice its spinning rotors into the deck's twisted metal. The fragments burst into dozens of giant pieces of shrapnel just seconds before the Oceanhawk fell over the side, engulfed in an orange ball of flame.

The rest of the video played out exactly as the two men remembered it. They could see everyone, including themselves, huddled on the stern of the ship where Krogstad had ordered them. If he couldn't outrun the torpedo, his only other option would be to save as many as he could. On the stern, survivors had the best chance of deploying the lifeboats. The rest of the ship was sacrificed to take as much of the blow as possible.

When it was over, Borger stopped the video and leaned back. "That's only the second time I've seen it."

Clay nodded, his eyes still on the screen. "I can see why."

With a deep breath, Borger turned back to him. "There's something else I wanted to show you."

Clay raised his eyebrows and waited.

Borger clasped his hands in front of his protruding stomach. "So, I've been picking through the rest of the satellite video. I'm not sure if you know this, but the attack was big enough that most commercial aircraft in the area were immediately grounded, even as far away as Venezuela."

"I didn't know that."

"Yep. Everything. Down. Kaput." Borger then began to grin. It was a look John Clay had come to know well.

"You found something."

"All aircraft were grounded," he repeated. "All *commercial* aircraft."

Clay raised an eyebrow. "But not…"

"But not *military* aircraft."

"Meaning what?"

"Meaning…," Borger replied, "military flights were not

17

grounded. Or should I say…the *only* military flight." He began typing again in a new window, which brought up a second map. The second map was fixed on Georgetown. Borger pointed to one frame, then to the other. "This one is the international airport in Guyana. Note the timestamp on both screens."

"They're both the same."

"Exactly. Same time, in two places. The first picture is the Bowditch after it was struck. The second, the Georgetown airport."

Borger zoomed closer in on the airport and sped up the video. Both feeds accelerated, still in sync. After almost a minute, he froze them both. "That's it. Right there."

Clay studied the image. An airplane could be seen taxiing onto one of the airport's runways.

"What is that?"

Borger zoomed in closer and waited a moment for the image to sharpen again at the new resolution. The turboprop engines were clear, jutting out beneath the craft's high wing. Borger zoomed in still further.

"It's a Y-12," Clay said, under his breath.

Borger nodded. "Correct. Chinese made, utility design, and able to carry upwards of twenty passengers."

"Was it there the whole time?"

"No. It flew in three days before the attack. At night."

Clay frowned. Of course it was at night. Nightfall seemed to be the preferred time for everything the Chinese were up to in Guyana.

Borger rolled the video again and they both watched as the plane paused briefly then accelerated down the runway and lifted into the air. As it climbed, the aircraft banked and headed due west.

Clay straightened behind Borger and folded his arms.

"Care to guess where it's headed?"

There was only one country to the west that was within the plane's range. And it was another country with whom the U.S. had a strained relationship. "Venezuela."

"Correct again." Borger continued typing on his keyboard and skipped to another location. "But not just any airport in Venezuela. It flew directly to El Libertador Air Force Base in Maracay and landed three hours and thirty-seven minutes later. Upon landing, a single person exited the plane and boarded another." He scrolled the map and stopped on another aircraft. One that was much bigger.

This time, Clay recognized the plane without having to enlarge the picture again. Both its design and enormous size were unmistakable. It was a Xian Y-20. One of the largest aircraft in the Chinese Air Force.

"I'm guessing that's a transport."

"It sure is," nodded Clay. "But it's still in development. That one is a prototype they revealed a couple years ago."

"A prototype?"

"Yes."

Clay's frown was deepening. The El Libertador base in Venezuela was infamous for the coup attempt in 1992 when General Visconti seized control of the base and launched an aerial attack on the capitol city. But it wasn't the reputation that concerned Clay. It was the fact that the Chinese planes had landed at a military base and not a commercial airport. It meant the Venezuelan government was partially involved, or at the very least, aware of the activities of the Chinese. Having the Xian Y-20 there most likely meant the Venezuelan government already knew more than they would ever admit.

"Did it fly straight back?" Clay asked.

"It did. It refueled once in Hawaii before continuing on to Beijing." Borger peered at Clay. "But why would they send a prototype all the way to South America? That's risky."

"The Y-20 has the longest range of any of their transport planes. Sending an armed aircraft would have attracted far more attention. But they still needed something *secure* that could fly back almost nonstop."

"For one person? That's one hell of an expensive trip."

"Which means it was either a very important person," he looked at Borger, still seated in front of him, "or the person was carrying something important."

"Or both."

Clay nodded. "Or both."

Together, the two continued staring at the frozen screen where a tiny figure could be seen crossing the tarmac to the larger plane.

Clay's phone suddenly rang, snapping them out of it. He looked at it and answered, putting the call on speakerphone. "Where are you, Steve?"

"Outside, near Santos. Where are you?"

"We're in Borger's office."

"Good. I hope you're helping him clean it."

Clay grinned while Borger pretended to look offended.

"You two alone?"

"Yes."

On the other end, Caesare looked out at the ocean from a shaded spot beneath a large Brazilian rosewood tree. The beach was less than two blocks away and he stood scanning the area as he spoke, looking for anyone paying too much attention to him.

By the time Langford had ended their call, Caesare had already reached the first floor of the hotel and was off the property entirely inside of three minutes. It wouldn't be long before someone discovered the bodies of Blanco and Sosa, and Caesare had no intention of being nearby.

"So what did I miss?"

Clay glanced again at the monitors on Borger's desk. "It looks like Will may have found something."

"Your voice doesn't exactly sound exuberant."

"I'll try harder next time."

"I bet. I'm going to guess there's bad news coming."

"Maybe. It seems someone got clearance and flew out of

Georgetown just after the Bowditch was hit. On a Chinese turbo-prop to Venezuela, and from there a transport straight back to Beijing."

"You're kidding."

"I wish we were." Clay leaned in, peering closer at the screen. "Just one person. Carrying some kind of a case."

Caesare sighed. "That's not good."

"Now who's not exuberant?"

"I say we blame Borger."

Will Borger's eyes opened wide with surprise, and then narrowed.

"We were actually getting ready to blame you."

In spite of the jokes, they all knew how serious it was. If Borger was right, then it looked like something had been taken off that ship before it departed. Something important enough to fly directly to Beijing, the political epicenter of China. Clay already had a guess as to what the man was carrying.

"Any idea who the person was, Will?"

"Not yet. But I'll find out."

From under the tree, Caesare nodded, absently watching an attractive woman cross the street. "Well, I'm afraid my news isn't much better. There's something I didn't mention on the phone with Langford."

Without moving his head, Clay exchanged a curious look with Borger. "What's that?"

"I got a little more out of Blanco before he took his long ride into the sunset. He told me about Otero, and that he knows about the monkey. But it seems he knows more than that. Blanco managed to spit out what Otero was asking him about. He said *Acarai*. The name of the mountain."

Clay sighed. "Crap."

"Yeah. How much he knows, I'm not sure. But it's a lot more than just the monkey."

"If that's true," Borger said, "then he's gonna be going back up there."

21

"Exactly. And if he pokes around long enough, he may just stumble across something he's not supposed to find."

Without a word, Clay stepped forward and sat down in the chair next to Borger. "That means we need to get there before he does." He stopped to think. "And we're going to need help."

"I was thinking the same thing."

"How would you like to make a stopover during your flight back?"

From under the giant rosewood, Caesare couldn't help but smile. "Are you kidding? I love Puerto Rico."

Next to Clay, Borger raised an eyebrow and spoke loud enough for Caesare to hear. "You do understand we actually need DeeAnn *on our side*."

"Piece of cake."

Clay wasn't so sure it would be that easy. "All right then. Borger and I will see what else we can find out on this end. When are you leaving?"

"I'm not sure," Caesare replied. He wiped a bead of sweat from his forehead. With the phone still to his ear, he turned back to face the glimmering skyscrapers of São Paulo in the distance. "I need something first. I need to know where Miguel Blanco's family is."

From his chair, Borger stared at Clay's phone with a puzzled look. "You want to know where Blanco's family lives?"

"No," he replied dryly. "I need to know where they are right now."

3

The bright Puerto Rican sun shimmered over the top of the salt water tank, creating a curtain of glistening sunlight waving gently through the water.

On the other side of the thick glass stood Alison Shaw, watching as the two dolphins, Dirk and Sally, occupied the far end of the tank. A group of children stood packed together there. Both dolphins floated close, playfully bumping their noses against the glass at the spots where the children were pressing their hands. They screamed with excitement when Dirk impulsively turned sideways, placing one of his flippers against the glass.

Alison was happy. Really happy. She looked down and gently rubbed the bandage wrapped around her wrist. They had returned from their harrowing trip through the Caribbean, all in one piece, with only scrapes and bruises. Chris Ramirez and Lee Kenwood had taken the worst of it, but they were home and healing quickly.

Dirk and Sally had returned with them, even though they were free to come and go as they pleased. Dirk was especially eager to return to the lab in Puerto Rico, which surprised Alison. She was sure it had something to do with how much he was fed. Without having to spend any effort hunting for fish, she suspected her lab was becoming something akin to a vacation for Dirk.

Best of all, Alison was in love. She had found the man of her dreams. John Clay was the most amazing man she'd ever met, even if the men she previously dated had set that bar fairly low. But John was nothing short of a phenomenon. Handsome, strong, smart, and a man who could really communicate. He was every woman's dream.

"It's almost feeding time," came Chris's voice from behind her. "Which means it's time for us to start arguing about lunch."

Alison turned and eyed the mug in his hand. "Isn't it getting a little late for coffee?"

Chris smiled. Most of the bruising along the left side of his face was gone. "It's never too late for coffee." His obsession had now become an ongoing joke between them. It stuck from the early days of their working together, sometimes spending all night at work. Like her, Chris's specialty was marine biology and he'd joined her team early in its formation.

Chris emptied the rest of the cup and set it down on his cluttered desk. "I'll see if the IT boys want to go. Are you in?"

"No, you guys go ahead."

Alison watched him cross the room and climb the wide stairs up to the second floor. When he disappeared around the corner, she turned back to the tank. The children were waving now, saying their goodbyes and being pulled gently away from the glass by their teachers. Another class visit was scheduled for that afternoon.

She took a deep breath and let it out slowly. There was only one thing that kept her from full contentment. And Alison was trying to remain in denial about it for as long as she could.

She glanced at the far end of the room where their massive, and now infamous, IMIS computer system covered the entire wall. Short for "Inter Mammal Interpretive System," the original version was what allowed for the incredible breakthrough back in their Miami research center. Since relocating to Puerto Rico, and closer to Dirk and Sally's natural habitat, the IMIS system had been radically improved. What that improvement led to next was a leap forward that not even they were prepared for. It not only expanded IMIS's translation capabilities beyond dolphins to primates, but it had done so in a way that surprised even their computer experts, Lee and Juan. And on top of it all, during a near crisis, IMIS had successfully translated pieces of language in a way that none of them had ever anticipated, or even programmed for.

She stared at the massive wall of servers, humming quietly with its hundreds of green lights blinking away. The system was silently crunching data and looking for more relationships between already established language patterns.

Alison looked away as she spotted a familiar face entering from the long hallway which connected the lab to their outdoor habitat. DeeAnn Draper smiled and looked curiously around the silent room.

"Must be lunch time."

Alison grinned. "How'd you guess?"

"I love predictable men." DeeAnn smiled and watched the last of the children wave goodbye to the dolphins at the other end of the tank.

Alison's face took on a worried expression. She frowned and lowered her voice. "Are you still sure?"

"Yes," DeeAnn nodded. "I talked to Penny again this morning. They're getting things ready at the Foundation."

Alison sighed. She understood why DeeAnn was leaving. The last month had been devastating for her, both emotionally and physically. She had embarked on a trip that began as a cause to help find a friend, only to end up nearly perishing herself. If it weren't for Steve Caesare single-handedly saving her, she wouldn't have been standing in front of Alison now.

A serious brush with death had a habit of changing people. Alison understood that. And DeeAnn was one of them. She was alive and grateful, but she was done with adventure. She wanted nothing now but to live a simple life and to keep a single person safe. At least to her it was a person. And now, thanks to the IMIS system, she was absolutely sure about that.

"So..."

DeeAnn answered the question before she could finish.

"We leave a week from Friday."

Alison pressed her lips together and nodded. She reached out and hugged DeeAnn. Over the last several months, the woman had become her mentor. An amazing woman in so many ways, who also had changed the world as much as Alison and her team ever had. The world just didn't know it yet.

"When are you going to tell the guys?"

DeeAnn cleared her throat. "Today or tomorrow." She managed another smile and glanced over Alison's shoulder to see Dirk and Sally approaching. They glided smoothly up to the glass, watching the two women.

Hello D Ann.

She blinked a tear away and turned her smile to them. "Hi, Sally. Hi, Dirk."

Dirk stared at her, quizzically. *D Ann sad.*

"A little." DeeAnn still couldn't quite get used to the way IMIS pronounced her name during a translation. According to Lee, the computers seemed to have trouble resolving a double "e" following the letter "d." He didn't understand it either, but the resulting pronunciation sounded more like "D-an" with a stutter. It wasn't a big deal, but it always reminded her that a machine was ultimately behind the translations.

Why sad.

DeeAnn looked at Alison. "It's a long story."

A loud buzz sounded from a monitor on the main desk. On the screen, a red error message displayed "unable to translate – story."

"It's all right," Alison said. She changed the subject. "Are you ready for food?"

Dirk became noticeably excited once Alison's words were translated into a series of clicks and whistles. *Yes, food now.*

Alison turned to Sally, who was hovering slightly closer than Dirk. "How about you, Sally? Are you hungry?"

The women heard their translation emitted from the

underwater speaker, but Sally did not answer. Instead, she simply stared at them with her dolphin's perpetual smile.

"Sally?"

Again the speaker sounded. After a long silence Sally finally replied.

You leaving.

Both Alison and DeeAnn's eyes widened in surprise.

"That's…right, Sally." DeeAnn answered. "How did you know that?"

Why you leave?

She frowned. *How could she explain human emotion to a dolphin?* It was a lot of things. Depression. Grief. Fear. Fear of somehow losing the purest thing she had ever known. And the love of finally feeling like a mother.

"It's…complicated."

The translation system buzzed again, unable to translate "complicated."

DeeAnn tried again. "It's hard to tell you."

Her response was successful, but Sally didn't answer. DeeAnn wasn't sure whether that meant Sally was satisfied with the answer or not. Dolphins were not human, but even with her limited time speaking with Dirk and Sally, she was surprised at how human-like some of the communication felt. She wondered if much of what we considered unique human communication actually had more underlying commonalities with other forms than we knew.

How you Alison?

"I'm good," she smiled. "How are you?"

How you hurt?

Alison glanced down at her bandage. "I'm getting better. Thank you." Since they had returned, both Dirk and Sally were surprisingly curious of their injuries, including those of Chris and Lee. In fact, curious wasn't quite the right term. They were more "attentive." She was very touched by their concern and wondered if they were somehow feeling responsible. They may have been there when it happened, but they certainly were in no way responsible. Still, at times it left her with a distinct feeling of not only sympathy from the dolphins but a sense of *empathy*. It prompted her to ask them on multiple occasions if they had been hurt by the explosion. They insisted they hadn't, but she wasn't so sure.

Where man?

Alison gave Sally a sly grin. The dolphin was asking about John. He had spent a few days with her on the island after their return and spent some time talking to Dirk and Sally. Being an expert in technology, he continued to marvel at what they had done with IMIS. He was particularly impressed with the vests Lee and Juan designed. Clay warned her that it was just a matter of time before the world truly understood what she and her team had achieved. He warned her to prepare for that. The wave of publicity they'd received in Miami after the first breakthrough would be nothing compared to what was coming.

Alison brushed her dark brown hair back behind an ear and answered Sally with a girlish chuckle. "John had to leave. He had to go home."

Sally made the familiar sound that IMIS had long ago identified as laughter. *He come back.*

Alison sure hoped so. And maybe one day he'd be back to stay.

Upstairs, Chris was sitting with Lee Kenwood and Juan Diaz in the computer lab. It was comfortably sized and well organized with metal tables along the wall. Neatly stacked shelves hung above them, filled with books, a wide range of computer parts, and mounds of magnetic backup tapes. Another larger table rested in the center of the room, illuminated by a bright lamp overhead. On the table lay a new vest with various cables strung to a nearby computer.

Positioned in the middle of the vest was a large speaker

with a much smaller microphone and digital camera embedded just a few inches above it. It was a replacement for the damaged unit that DeeAnn had brought back from South America. The system data had still been intact, but the small motherboard and processor were not worth salvaging.

Chris watched Lee and Juan, patiently waiting for an answer on lunch. Both were distracted and staring intently at the monitor atop Lee's desk.

"I take it you're still looking for the ghost in the system."

"It's not a ghost," Lee mumbled, moving the mouse and scrolling down.

"Sorry, I mean "anomaly."

"It's not an anomaly either."

"Riddle?"

Juan turned and rolled his eyes while Lee, still facing forward, shook his head.

"Come on! I'm joking." Chris reached down and picked up a thick textbook from Lee's desk. He thumbed through it. It advertised itself as the bible of computer algorithms. He believed it. The contents looked completely unreadable. "So what's wrong exactly?"

Lee took a break and turned his chair around. "It's not that something is necessarily wrong. It's more that something isn't right."

"Is it part of the log problem?"

"I think so."

The log problem to which Chris referred had in fact been a serious problem. Before their harrowing trip to the Caribbean, Lee discovered that the IMIS translations and the related video feeds were falling increasingly out of sync. The logs on the servers showed the frequency of errors to be increasing rapidly, leaving Lee worrying that thousands of new lines of computer code had seriously broken something.

But after several sleepless nights, they discovered that IMIS was actually picking up on very subtle cues outside commonly recognized audible patterns. In other words, IMIS, a machine, was literally learning "nonverbal" communication.

However, Lee and Juan couldn't figure out how it was doing it. The vests were working almost *too* well.

Chris listened as Lee explained what they were looking for. "So, you're saying IMIS shouldn't be as effective as it is?"

"More or less." Lee walked over to the table and held up their new vest. "When IMIS detects speech patterns from Dirk and Sally, it digitizes the signal and compares it to the database of words it has identified. When it has a match, it sends those translated words back through the speaker."

"And then in reverse order when *we* speak, right?"

"Exactly. It works as expected with the dolphins because their language is mostly verbal. But that changes with a primate. Remember, DeeAnn says primate communication involves a lot of nonverbal communication like gestures and facial expressions."

"Right."

"Well, that's where it's not making sense," Lee shrugged, looking at Juan. "IMIS is now picking up on nonverbal cues — we've already established that. We're not exactly sure on how that's happening. But the more obvious problem is that while IMIS is picking up on those nonverbal cues, it has no way to *convey* them."

"That we can see," corrected Juan.

Chris squinted. "I'm not sure I'm following."

Lee thought for a moment. "Let's say, for example, that a nonverbal cue IMIS picks up from Dulce is a shrug. It sees that from the video feed and matches it with the audio. But how does it convey that?"

Now Chris understood. "I see. So while IMIS can *observe* a shrug, it has no way to actually transmit that gesture through the vest's speaker."

"Bingo!"

"Wow. That *is* weird."

"It shouldn't be able to translate gestures in both directions, but it does. And we don't know how."

Chris thought it over. He didn't know the answer either. He had a suspicion but nothing concrete. It was a topic that Alison and he had discussed several times over the last couple years and were sure others had too. After years in the field, working with different creatures, they had eventually come to the same conclusion: there was something deeper and unknown happening when it came to communication. Especially in less cognizant brains. It was something many people had wondered about at one time or another. How animals knew so much instinctively, even things they had never been taught by a parent.

Communication was the means to knowledge. But Chris and Alison, as well as other researchers, even veterinarians, were sure there was something else happening at a deeper level. A level that humans could not yet understand or measure.

But maybe IMIS was doing just that.

4

Tiago Otero raised his head upon hearing a soft knock on the door. A moment later it was slowly pushed open and one of Otero's assistants apologetically poked his head inside, interrupting the discussion.

Otero displayed a pained expression and apologized to the man across the small table. With dark eyes topped by a head of stark white hair, the other man appeared older than Otero. He was dressed in the familiar dark green and brown fatigues of the Brazilian Army. Silently, he watched as Otero rose from his leather chair and followed the assistant out.

They stood in the hallway, waiting for the door to click shut. When it did, Otero's eyes became cold.

"What is it?"

"I'm very sorry to interrupt," whispered the younger man. "But you wanted me to alert you if there was a problem."

Otero looked at him expectantly.

"Lieutenant Russo has lost contact with his men."

Otero's expression barely changed. He stared intently, twisting his lips in a manner that made his assistant nervous. Otero's unpredictability was well-known, and his wrath legendary. It was a look his assistant had seen many times and hoped would never be directed at him. He was emphatically hoping that now.

Otero had no friends. Only enemies and fearful acquaintances. Which is how he preferred it. Everyone nervous and afraid. Fear was the ultimate motivator. It stripped the strong of their confidence and made the meek obey. Otero scoffed at those who claimed power was about money. True power was about *fear*. Power through money was for the weak. Power through fear was for rulers.

"Why didn't he tell me himself?"

"H-he's still trying to reach them, sir."

Otero stared at him, thinking. The men his assistant referred to were the men Russo had sent to Florianópolis. It was a simple job. Easy for men of their skill.

Miguel Blanco had given him the information he sought in São Paulo. Much more than he already knew. But Blanco had already talked to too many people. He had to be silenced.

More importantly Blanco had killed one of Otero's partners. Alves was a competitor — a ruthless one — but he was still part of the group. The echelon. A fellow oligarch who shared in the control of Brazil and most of South America. A man with far more wealth than most would ever know, and with it, certain protections.

Otero had warned the man that Blanco, his head of security, could not be trusted. He wouldn't listen. Instead, he trusted the young assistant he was sleeping with far too much. A common mistake of old, desperate men, clinging to the last remnants of their virility. It left him open, vulnerable. And Blanco pounced.

Alves was foolish. But Blanco was still a dead man the moment he killed his boss. Now Blanco and his entire family would be made an example of, just like so many before him. Alves was shrewd. But Otero was unforgiving.

And then there was Alves' secret. He'd gotten close, within grasp of perhaps the greatest discovery of mankind. Too close, in fact. In the end, his eagerness had compromised his objectivity. No, not eagerness. The man was desperate. Desperate for it to be true. Desperate for it to be real. And when he found out it was everything he'd hoped for, the desperation had blinded him. It was a mistake Otero would not repeat.

Florianópolis was one of the most desirable places to live in all of Brazil. Located just over four hundred miles south of São Paulo, the large island of Florianópolis was the Brazilian capital city and held the title for having one of the highest living standards in the country. With its local population composed mostly of Brazilian and European descent, the lighter subtropical weather made it one of the most sought after cities in which to reside. Assuming one had the resources, or perhaps had *acquired* the necessary resources.

Steve Caesare examined the two bodies lying face down. Both were bound, but only one was still breathing. The other was dead. It wasn't Caesare's fault. The idiot wouldn't stop. He wouldn't give up until Caesare had no choice.

He stepped back and leaned against the wall. If he thought his side hurt before, it was practically screaming after having to drag them both from the front room.

The large closet they were now in wouldn't keep them from being found. It would only delay it. And of course, the one would survive and eventually make it back to Otero. He hoped by then Blanco's family would have heeded his warning and fled the country. He had a feeling the man named Otero wasn't going to take this well.

Miguel Blanco had been a bastard. A murderer with little conscience and even less remorse. Caesare knew that and wouldn't lose sleep over him being dead. But in his experience, the families were usually innocent and largely unaware of their father's or husband's work when he was away from them. The family didn't deserve it. And Blanco's family didn't deserve to be used as Otero's calling card.

Fortunately, Caesare had the advantage. At least this time. The thugs had shown up expecting to find Blanco's wife and children unsuspecting and defenseless. Instead they found Steve Caesare. The timing was lucky but he was sure Otero would eventually find out who he was. While Caesare caught his breath, his lips curled into a wry grin and he decided to leave the man a message.

He walked forward and pulled up the dead man's pant leg, revealing a Fallkniven A1 survival knife strapped securely to his calf. Caesare unclipped the weapon and slid it out, momentarily admiring it. He then reached down and cut a shape into the back of the man's brightly colored shirt. At least they had the sense to dress the part.

If Otero were stupid enough to pursue Caesare, he should at least know who he was dealing with.

He returned the knife and nodded approvingly. The shape was a trident, the symbol of the U.S. Navy's Sea, Air, and Land teams — more commonly known as SEALs.

5

DeeAnn Draper's office was small and conservatively decorated. Just a single framed picture on the beige wall and another on her desk were all she had ever bothered to put up. It was a reflection of both her minimalistic lifestyle as well as the limited amount of time she actually spent in her office. Chris joked that it eerily resembled an advertisement out of an office supply magazine. But she did really like it there. She felt as much at home with Alison's team as she had working at the Gorilla Foundation. And what Alison and her team had achieved was simply amazing.

DeeAnn sat in her black chair and scanned the room, now wishing she'd made a little more of an effort to decorate. But then again, maybe this would make things easier.

She glanced up at the sound of a soft knock on the door.

"Come in."

The door opened just far enough to allow Lee Kenwood's young and somewhat handsome face to peek in.

"Oh good, you're still here. I saw your light on and thought I'd check."

DeeAnn grinned. "Yep. Still here. Unfortunately."

"You got a sec?"

"Sure."

With that, Lee pushed the door open and stepped inside. He was holding the latest vest he and Juan had just built. "Good news, the new vest is ready."

DeeAnn stood up, grabbing one side of it. "Lee! You're not supposed to be lifting anything heavy."

"It's okay," he shrugged. "They're feeling a lot better."

DeeAnn gave him a dubious frown. "Ribs don't heal that fast." Together they sat it down onto the other half of her

6

6

desk. She ran her fingers over the dark nylon and the two large Velcro pockets that wrapped around the waist. "I'm sorry I broke the last one."

"It wasn't your fault. Besides, it gave us a chance to tweak a few things."

"Like what?"

"Nothing major. Just some slight improvements. More padding around the motherboard." He tapped a portion lightly to show her. "And we also removed some of the material on the back, which should improve the airflow a little."

"Music to my ears." DeeAnn stood the contraption on end and turned it around. The vest was amazing technologically, but from a non-geek standpoint it was a burden to wear in hot weather. The humidity in Puerto Rico was already more than she was used to, but it had been almost suffocating in Brazil. "It feels lighter," she observed.

"The old one had heavier batteries."

The original vest had been a big step forward. Being allowed to remain in the habitat and still have it transmit back and forth to IMIS was huge. But when Lee and Juan made better versions and included a camera, it was a game changer.

"Thank you, Lee. I really appreciate it."

DeeAnn laid the vest back down and noticed he hadn't said anything. She looked back up to find him silently staring down at the vest.

"Something on your mind?"

After a moment, he looked back at her. "Do you have time to talk about something?"

She folded her arms in front of herself. "Of course. Is this about that problem with the logs?"

Lee nodded. "We were talking to Chris about it earlier today and I had a thought. Something I wanted to ask you about."

"Okay."

"So, we've talked about the whole communication problem with the speaker."

"The nonverbal problem."

"Right. The system doesn't have the ability to translate nonverbal communication back through the speaker. At least it shouldn't. So instead of trying to troubleshoot that, it occurred to me that maybe there's a different answer. Something that we're not considering."

"Like what?"

"Well, initially I thought the log problem existed because IMIS wasn't translating correctly. I'm a believer in the fallibility of computers, so I assumed it was a fault somewhere. But it *was* translating correctly, and it took me a long time to understand it." He blinked, thinking as he spoke. "What I'm wondering now is whether I've made the wrong assumption again."

"About the speaker?"

"Yes. I've been trying to figure out what happens to the nonverbal cues when they reach the speaker. The one thing I've learned is that language is really kind of…intangible. And today it suddenly hit me. What if I'm looking for the wrong thing?"

"What do you mean?"

"Well, assuming this is all still measurable somehow, it would mean that we're missing something. Maybe our idea of nonverbal is not correct. Maybe incomplete." Lee took a breath. "What if IMIS isn't missing anything…and we are?"

DeeAnn peered at him curiously. "I get the impression you have a question coming."

"Yes, I do." He grinned again. "You said yourself that primates, particularly gorillas, are very nonverbal communicators. But to us that usually means physical movement of some kind. But what if we're wrong? What if the nonverbal stuff only explains part of the missing exchange? What if there is still more *verbal* communication taking place that we're not hearing?"

DeeAnn was fascinated. She remained still, staring at him over the desk. "You're talking about frequencies."

Lee nodded.

"So, you want to know if gorillas can hear frequencies that we can't."

"Correct."

"Something tells me you've already done some research."

"A little."

DeeAnn smiled broadly. She was really going to miss these talks with Lee. "Then you probably know the jury is still out. A lot of the older research suggests that gorillas and humans share the same audio frequencies But after the gorilla genome was successfully mapped, it revealed differences in the genes tied to hearing, and therefore to communication."

"So the answer is yes?"

She shook her head. "Not necessarily. But it's widely accepted that humans and gorillas have very different aural environments…so the answer isn't no, but it also isn't yes."

"So nobody knows."

"Nobody knows."

"So then…what is your *opinion*?"

"My opinion?" She frowned, considering the question. "Is it possible they can hear things we can't? Of course. A lot of animals can do that. *Are* gorillas doing it? I don't know. Maybe."

"It could explain a lot. Like how IMIS is able to communicate so well with Dulce through just a speaker."

DeeAnn glanced down at the vest, her arms still folded in front of her. "Well, there's only one way to find out."

The programming took almost eleven hours to write and test, leaving Lee precious few hours to rest. It didn't matter. He was too excited to sleep. IMIS was hiding a secret and he was determined to find out what it was.

The problem was that IMIS wasn't programmed to process communication beyond the frequencies of human hearing. However, IMIS *was* programmed to learn artificially; so if it was processing other frequencies, it was doing so by a mandate other than the one laid out in the original computer code.

This also meant that all of the analytical tools were set between twenty hertz to twenty thousand hertz, the range of human hearing. The dolphin language was similar, except at a very high end where their echolocation was used. What Lee had spent the night programming was a new instruction set for IMIS, instructing it to include a wider range of speech frequencies in its analytics. If there was something there, IMIS was now instructed to show it.

DeeAnn was back early in the morning, at a little past six a.m. She returned with two tall cups of coffee and a bag of donuts, which she wouldn't touch but Lee loved.

He thanked her and bit into one. "I think we should be ready soon."

"Good. Dulce should be up pretty soon." She lowered the cardboard carrier down next to Lee and withdrew one of the cups. Behind them, Juan burst into the room, causing DeeAnn to jump and nearly spill her coffee.

"What did I miss?!"

"Geez, Juan!" DeeAnn checked her shirt for any dark spots. "Some of us are a little on edge here!"

"Sorry."

Lee grinned behind his own cup. He set it down and returned to his keyboard. "Not too much yet. I'm still compiling. Did you bring it?"

"Yep." Juan reached into his pants pocket and retrieved a long silver tube.

"What is that?"

"A dog whistle."

"A dog whistle?"

Juan grinned. "It's my little sister's, but it should work."

"We need to verify this first before we do any tests with Dulce." Lee raised the lid on his laptop and opened another audio program. It looked different, but DeeAnn recognized the familiar meter running from left to right. After waiting for the program to initialize, Lee spoke into the small microphone located just above his laptop keyboard. "Testing, testing."

A yellow line danced up and down as it moved across the screen, showing the waves picked up through the microphone. "Okay, here's my voice. You can see the ranges here, including inflection and volume. We can also see the wider frequency range here, which is between one thousand and five thousand hertz. Give or take. This is the range where human speech is centered." Lee backed up his chair. "Ready, Juan?"

"Yep."

Lee restarted the recording again and moved out of the way to allow Juan to lean in closer. He blew through the dog whistle, making a quiet hissing sound. This time, the sound waves on the graph jumped dramatically. The peaks and valleys were sharper and traveled well beyond the frequency ranges that Lee had pointed out. Both the top and bottom areas outside the human ranges displayed colors of yellow, orange, and red, showing the progression *away* from the narrower human range.

"Wow. Big difference."

"And this is what you think IMIS is picking up?"

"Maybe," Lee shrugged. "But even if we find it's picking up a fraction of the extra frequencies, it could be significant."

"So, now what?"

"Now we need to wait for the compiling to finish. This was just a simple test through my laptop. When the code is done, we'll need to upgrade the monitoring software on IMIS. Then we give it a whirl."

DeeAnn smiled excitedly. She grabbed the new vest and slung it over her shoulder. "I'll go get breakfast."

Breakfast was a four-pound box of celery, kale, and apples. Dulce had developed a real affinity for apples. DeeAnn suspected the higher sugar content made apples taste like a *dessert* to the young gorilla. In fact, she had become so excited, they were the first thing she searched for in the box of food. And this morning was no different.

Once DeeAnn was inside the habitat, the three-year-old gorilla came running across a small grassy hill at which point she stopped and hugged the top of DeeAnn's legs.

Apples apples.

DeeAnn smiled, setting the box down with a thud and standing up. She watched as Dulce reached in with her lanky brown arms and brought out two apples, one in each hand. She smiled broadly at DeeAnn with a toothy grin.

"Dessert is last."

Dulce stopped with a frown before placing them back into the box and picking up a stalk of celery.

The Puerto Rican mornings were gorgeous. With temperatures routinely in the high sixties and low seventies, the air felt cool and refreshing, offsetting the island's high humidity. But the best part was the smell. Tropical islands had an unmistakable smell of dew in the morning, brought on by overnight moisture on the lush foliage. With the lightest of breezes, the combination made the mornings smell like dewy sweetness — it was a smell DeeAnn was going to miss.

Of course, sweetness had another presence in DeeAnn's mornings which made Dulce's name so fitting. She was the most loving, kind creature DeeAnn had ever known, and certainly that she had ever worked with. She had saved the gorilla at a young age from a horrible existence in Mexico, and they had been inseparable ever since.

Me love mommy.

DeeAnn grinned and playfully ruffled the fur on the back of her neck. "Mommy loves Dulce."

She barely noticed anymore as the vest picked up her words, and in less than a second, sent the data to IMIS and back where the large speaker emanated a series of squeals and soft grunts for Dulce.

DeeAnn watched Dulce quickly devour her breakfast, yet when she reached the apples, she purposely slowed down as if savoring them. A sweet tooth seemed just as popular in gorillas as they were in humans. DeeAnn was dreading the day Dulce discovered chocolate.

She sat back and continued watching Dulce, then turned and looked up at one of the high-resolution cameras overhead, surrounding the habitat. She wondered if IMIS was revealing anything interesting to Lee and Juan upstairs.

As expected, Lee and Juan were monitoring all of DeeAnn's translations with Dulce. But it took almost a full minute for IMIS to display the frequency data used during the translations. When the first feedback finally came across Lee's screen, it did so in a *flood* of colors.

"Whoa!"

6

Alison Shaw burst into the computer lab and found them all huddled around Lee's desk. "Okay, I'm here. What is it?"

DeeAnn, dressed in khaki shorts and a matching shirt, turned around. "Lee's a genius, that's what!"

"Well, I don't know about that."

He motioned Alison over and pulled out his chair for her. She crossed the room and sat down, examining the screen.

"Is this audio?"

"It sure is."

"What does it mean?"

Lee smiled at DeeAnn.

"It's the problem they've been working on. Lee came to me last night with an idea that we were missing something."

"It was a problem we couldn't figure out," he added. "No matter how much we dug into the code. Then it occurred to me that maybe there are more complexities going on that we still don't know about."

Alison turned back. "So, what is this?"

"It's what IMIS is *really* hearing."

"More sounds?"

"More frequencies. The colors represent the wider bands, much wider than we can hear."

"What does that mean? It hears more words than we thought?"

"Maybe. But I suspect it may be more about tones or inflections." He looked to DeeAnn.

"I'm sure it is. In a lot of languages it's not what you say, it's how you say it. We should expect the same pattern with gorillas and other primates. We knew some of that was in the gesturing and expressions, but I certainly never expected

44

the rest to be in sounds we couldn't hear."

Alison looked at her curiously. "So, primates can hear sounds that we can't?"

"The designs of our auditory systems are very similar, but that doesn't necessarily mean they work exactly the same. Some researchers have suggested that having more advanced brains may have caused us to *devolve* out of certain basic abilities. Like the range of our hearing."

The room fell silent. It was a powerful thought. Devolution and evolution happening together. On a certain level, it made sense. Everything in life had a balance to it. Few things could be gained without something also being lost.

"Not to take away from the moment," Lee said, "but there's something even more interesting about this."

"Like what?"

"Well, we think we know how IMIS is truly communicating with Dulce now. Which is big. But..." He looked at them with excitement. "This is *not* something we programmed IMIS to do — to listen to such a broad frequency range."

"Meaning?"

"Meaning that no one told IMIS to do it." Lee smiled, waiting for them to pick up on his suggestion. Finally, he said it. "IMIS made the decision."

At that moment, they all could have heard a pin drop.

"Whoaaa," Juan whispered.

DeeAnn looked at Lee with wide eyes and tilted her head. "Are you saying that IMIS is *thinking*?"

He grinned. "Thinking, no. At least not as we understand it. But the system does employ several algorithms that give it a certain capacity for artificial intelligence. It's not thinking...but it is getting smarter at solving problems."

One floor below, the heavy figure of Bruna Lopez, the Center's administrative assistant, hurried over the dark tiles which lined the ground floor. When she reached the bottom of the wide staircase, the admin grasped the railing with her right hand and continued her rush up the stairs.

Once at the top, she immediately covered the short distance to the double metal doors and pushed them open, looking around the room.

"Miss…Alison…"

Alison turned away from the others at Lee's desk and spotted Bruna in the doorway, breathing heavily.

"Yes, Bruna. What is it?"

"Someone…is here to see you. She said…it was urgent."

Alison turned to DeeAnn with a concerned look. The last time someone came to see them unannounced things ended very badly. "Who is it?"

"A woman. From San Juan. A Boricua."

Both women quickly followed Bruna. She led them back downstairs but stopped short upon reaching the bottom step where they spotted a middle-aged woman curiously looking around their observation area.

When the woman saw Bruna returning, she appeared relieved and quickly closed the distance between herself and the women, staring intently at Alison as she did so.

"I'm sorry," she apologized. "'I'm sorry. I was just-"

Bruna was breathing hard again but still managed an irritated glare. "I told you I would get her."

"It's fine, it's fine." Alison could see puffiness around the woman's eyes. "What can I do for you?"

"I'm very sorry. I don't mean any disrespect, but I have to speak with you."

"About what?"

The woman took a deep breath. "My name is Lara

46

Santiago. I've come to ask you for help. Not for me, for my daughter."

"Your daughter?"

"Sofia. She's eight. Her class came here recently on a field trip." The woman frowned before continuing. "My daughter couldn't come. She…she hasn't been to school for a long time. She's very sick."

All three women's faces softened.

Lara pressed her lips together firmly. She had already cried so much. But the tears still came, sometimes unexpectedly. "My daughter has leukemia. Her friends came to see her recently and told her about their field trip."

"Oh, I'm sorry," Alison said, her voice having dropped to a soft whisper.

The woman forced the next words out. "She…doesn't have much time left."

Alison placed a hand over her mouth and looked at DeeAnn.

"I'm here for her," the mother continued. "She was wondering…we were wondering if we could arrange for a visit with your dolphins." Lara was clearly struggling now. "Maybe a private visit? Sofia's embarrassed of how she looks now, but she asked to see them…before it's too late. If that's possible."

Alison dropped her hand and nodded. "Of course. Of course it is. We'd be happy to have her."

"Thank you." Lara smiled and wiped a tear from the corner of her eye. "Thank you so much. Sofia loves dolphins. She's wanted to come ever since you and your team arrived, but she's been slowly getting worse. She doesn't have much strength left. So her father and I are trying to make the rest of her time with us as happy as we can."

Now all three of the women were near tears. They stepped in closer while Bruna placed a hand gently on the woman's arm.

"How soon can you bring Sofia in?"

"Is tomorrow too soon?"

"Not at all."

"Maybe ten o'clock?"

"That would be fine. We'll make sure everything is ready."

"Thank you so much. I can't…" She stopped herself, unable to finish the sentence.

They each stepped forward and embraced Lara warmly one at a time. "You tell Sofia that we'll all be waiting for her."

Bruna then wrapped an arm around her and gently guided Lara back toward the double doors.

Alison and DeeAnn both looked at each other in silent amazement. They then glanced up, realizing Lee, Chris, and Juan were standing above them at the top of the stairs.

"I take it you heard all that?"

"We did." They nodded solemnly.

"Can we count on your help tomorrow then?"

Chris smiled. "Hell, yes."

From the inside of the tank, Sally watched Alison and the others speaking. They were talking quickly and for a long time. When it was over, the others disappeared, leaving only Alison, who remained staring at her and Dirk.

"Hello, Sally. Hello, Dirk."

Sally answered as they both drifted effortlessly toward the tank's glass wall. *Hello Alison. How you?*

"I'm good. Thank you. I need to talk to you about something."

Outside, the computer beeped with an error when translating the last word. Alison shrugged. It didn't matter. "I need to talk," she repeated. Why IMIS had long been able to translate "need" and not "something" she didn't understand. There were still a number of words the system couldn't figure out and others it could. Of course now, given what Lee and Juan had discovered, there was no telling how deep IMIS's translations went.

Yes we talk, answered Dirk.

"A young girl would like to come see you tomorrow. A child." Alison thought for a moment and added, "She's very sick."

Why girl sick?

Alison frowned. She couldn't think of a way to explain it. She knew IMIS didn't have an exact match for the word "sick." Instead, for the dolphins, the word IMIS translated it to was closer to "injury" but the context was close enough. "She's been sick for a long time." She hoped that would allow them to understand.

Girl come for talk?

"Yes. She's very excited to talk to you and Dirk."

We like talk her.

"She's a very special girl. We want to make her visit special."

They weren't sure what Sofia would be able to do, but hopefully, with Dirk and Sally's help, they were going to give her the experience of a lifetime. Even for one as short as hers.

7

When Sofia Santiago arrived at a few minutes past ten, everyone was ready, including Dirk and Sally. They both floated attentively at the end of the tank, watching as the small girl was wheeled in through the double-wide doors by her father.

Sofia looked frail in her chair, leaning slightly and wrapped in a light shawl. A beautiful pink and purple scarf was wrapped neatly around her head. Below the scarf, a set of warm brown eyes darted excitedly to Dirk and Sally on the other side of the glass. Her smile completed the picture of a beautiful young girl fighting bravely against a horrible disease. A girl who had a sickness, but the sickness clearly did not have her.

Alison and DeeAnn both stood beside the tank, amused that Sofia hadn't yet noticed them. It wasn't until her mother turned the wheelchair and introduced them that the girl's eyes were peeled away.

"Well, hello there, Sofia." Alison reached down and shook her delicate hand. "My name is Alison Shaw. We're so very happy to have you."

Sofia grinned. "I saw you on the TV."

"Is that right? Is that how you found out about us?"

She nodded proudly.

"And this is my friend DeeAnn."

"Hello, Sofia," DeeAnn said, taking the girl's hand next. "It's a pleasure to meet you. We hear you're crazy about dolphins. In fact, we have a gift for you." DeeAnn brought something out from behind her back and unfolded it. It was a small T-shirt with a picture of Dirk and Sally on the front.

Sofia smiled and took the shirt with a, "Thank you." She turned back to Dirk and Sally who were still floating in front of them. Her eyes opened wide when Dirk suddenly made a noise and bolted away. He quickly circled back and swam a tight corkscrew around Sally.

Alison laughed. "As you can see, Dirk likes to show off a little."

Sofia watched excitedly from her chair as Dirk swam up and around the tank. All the while, Sally remained, floating gently in place and watching Sofia.

Alison looked to her father. "May I?"

Ricardo Santiago stepped out from behind the chair, allowing Alison to take his place. She leaned down over Sofia's right shoulder and said, "We have something neat to show you. Are you ready?"

She grinned shyly and nodded. With that, Alison pushed the wheelchair forward and headed toward their observation room, the dolphins following alongside them in their long oval tank. As they moved along the wall, Sofia gingerly reached out and brushed her fingers against the cool glass. Sally, watching the girl closely from the other side, reached her fin out and brushed the same area of glass.

They reached the double metal doors and DeeAnn slid her card over the sensor. After she heard the loud click of the door unlocking, DeeAnn pulled one side open and held it for the others. One by one, they entered the larger room. There, Sofia and her family could see Chris, Lee, and Juan smiling and waiting for them near a large desk. The desk had been moved closer to the tank and had both a computer and large monitor sitting on top. Behind them the family noticed the high-definition cameras mounted at various points around the curvature of the tank. Thick but neatly tied cables ran from the apparatuses and converged into a larger bundle, which then ran the length of the room to the giant IMIS computer system against the far wall. The rest of the room was composed of more desks holding additional computers and equipment they didn't recognize. To the right were two video cameras, side by side and pointed at the tank. Each at a different angle. Yet even with the extra desks and equipment, the room gave off an open, comfortable feel.

Chris bent down as they approached. "Welcome, Sofia. We're very excited to have you here. My name is Chris. This is Lee and Juan. We all work together here at the center." He glanced briefly at Alison before winking at her. "But Alison here is the boss."

Sofia giggled.

Together, Chris and Alison eased her chair up to the desk. "Do you know what we do here that's so special?"

"You talk to dolphins."

"That's right. Would you like to talk to them?"

"Yes!"

Alison locked one of the wheels in place and bent down on the other side of Sofia.

"They're very excited to meet you."

Lee stepped around Alison and slid a small vertical microphone closer to Sofia before hitting a few buttons on the keyboard. "Just speak right into here. Okay?"

"Okay."

"Are you ready, Sofia?"

She looked excitedly at her mother. "What should I say?"

Her mother laughed. "What happened to the million questions you had in the car?"

With one final keystroke, Lee nodded. "Okay. Go ahead."

Sofia leaned forward. "Hello?" she asked. Unsure what to do, she turned back to Alison just as the whistles and clicks emanated through the tank's underwater speakers.

Sally was still studying her and replied immediately. *Hello. How you Sofia?*

She gasped and looked at her mother again. "They know my name!"

Alison's entire team smiled. There obviously was no

translation equivalent for the name Sofia so they made one up. Similar to their own names, they created a manual translation in the database that was tied to a random set of clicks and whistles — sounds the dolphins could repeat and IMIS would then associate with "Sofia." And now, having her so excited that the dolphins knew her name made it more than worth the effort.

Finished with his display, Dirk glided in smoothly and stopped next to Sally. *We happy meet you.*

Sofia listened to the mechanized voice of each dolphin and watched their words simultaneously appear on the screen in front of her. "I'm happy to meet you too. Do you live here?"

Dirk bobbed his head. *We live ocean. We come here. Eat much.*

Alison laughed and turned to her parents. "If you've heard teenage boys could eat a lot, you should see a teenage dolphin."

"They're teenagers?"

"Yes. They were mostly grown by the time they came to live with us. But now they can come and go whenever they like. One thing we've learned is that they definitely don't like to be in captivity."

"What's captivity?"

"It's when we keep them in the tank all the time."

Sofia thought a moment, still turned toward Alison. "Do any animals like it?"

"Mmm...We're not sure about all animals. But I doubt it."

The young girl frowned, but let it go. She spoke into the microphone again. "How far can you swim?"

Dirk responded again and thrust his tail forcefully, making a tight circle. *Very far.*

Everyone laughed. Only Lee and Juan noticed the quick change on the computer screen before the sound was heard. The actual translation was closer to "much far" but IMIS quickly corrected the grammar. Alison was paying more attention to Sally, who seemed quieter than usual. She simply remained, floating and studying Sofia in her metal chair. The girl was now grinning from ear to ear. "I can't believe I'm actually talking to dolphins!"

Her mother and father smiled. Sofia asked another question just as Alison stepped away and pulled her parents to the side. She lowered her voice.

"Is it possible she can get into the water?"

8

Sofia eyed the clear blue water with a sense of both excitement and nervousness. It had been a long time since she'd been swimming, and she had been much stronger then. Her delicate arms were wrapped tightly around her father's neck as he picked her gently up out of the chair and carried her in his arms.

Inside he was in agony, knowing the number of times he would get to hold Sofia was numbered. Soon he would yearn to do it just once more.

He loved the feel of her arms around him, clinging as they approached the edge of the tank. He stepped down into the water and onto a wide, shallow ledge at which point he carefully lowered Sofia onto the concrete lip. She immediately dropped her hands to balance herself while her father sat next to her, keeping an arm around her tiny waist.

Alison and Chris were also standing on the ledge smiling. Once Sofia relaxed, Alison took a step forward in the water. "Are you sure you're okay?"

She nodded nervously.

"Good." Alison softly patted one of Sofia's hands. "We're going to be right here next to you. Don't worry." Alison gave her another minute to relax before nodding to Lee and Juan, who brought some equipment forward and set it down.

Chris reached out and picked up the clear face mask. "Do you know what this is?"

"It's a mask," Sofia answered.

"That's right. You said you used one before, right?"

"Yes."

Chris turned it around so she could get a good look at it. The mask was a child-sized version of the one they normally used — Lee and Juan had worked through much of the night to finish it for her.

Sofia took the small mask from Chris and examined it.

"Go ahead and put it over your face. You'll see that you can breathe just as good."

She looked back at the mask and moved the black oxygen hose out of the way. She pressed it into place and took a deep breath. "Wow," she smiled. Apprehension was turning to curiosity. She promptly looked up at her mother and giggled.

"You want to dip your face in the water and try it?"

Sofia nodded and dunked herself. When she came back up, she was laughing from the inside of the glass.

"Just like the ones you wore before, right?"

"Yes. But nicer!"

Alison laughed with her. If little Sofia only knew.

Next, Lee and Juan laid a bundle down on the edge of the tank. It was a small oxygen tank wrapped in a floatation cushion with another dozen feet of tubing coiled on top. It was a simpler design used by many vacation resorts, allowing a swimmer to breathe underwater without the encumbrance of having to wear heavy scuba gear. Instead, the tank and regulator would float on the surface above the swimmer and follow as needed.

The team's plan was to accommodate Sofia in the water at least enough to *float* with Dirk and Sally. They weren't sure how much her illness would allow, but now an excited Alison found herself carefully explaining the precautions they would take to keep Sofia safe. She also tried to convey how much more exciting it was to both swim and talk with the dolphins at the same time. If at all possible, she and her team wanted Sofia to have that experience.

When Sofia pulled the mask away, her father looked at her softly. "Are you ready?"

Sofia glanced around, looking first at Alison and her team. Then she spotted Dirk and Sally, watching patiently nearby with their heads out of the water. She nodded at her father. Together they untied the scarf and pulled it gently off her small bald head.

The women continued smiling warmly at her, fighting back a sudden surge of tears. Without even looking, Alison was sure the guys were doing the same.

Sofia stared up at them nervously with her large eyes. She was so beautiful.

Chris never skipped a beat. He lowered his voice just above a whisper. "Are you ready to put it on?"

She nodded and tilted her head forward, allowing Chris to slide the soft straps over her head, pulling on each one until snug. He delicately moved his fingers around the edge of the mask, checking the seal.

"How does that feel?"

"Good," she replied, her voice distorted.

"Still breathing okay?"

"Yes."

"Excellent."

Alison watched Chris next pick up a small weight belt. He snaked it gently around her waist and secured it in front. The swimsuit Alison had bought for her was a tad loose but still a close enough fit. Now that Sofia was comfortably breathing inside the mask, Alison reached out for her own gear.

Her Hollis unit was a rebreather. A redesign of the older scuba units allowing a radically more efficient use of its breathable oxygen. Even more important was the ability to allow the diver to breathe almost silently underwater, compared to the older regulators which sent out waves of loud bubbles with every breath. Minimal noise or interference was critical for IMIS's ability to translate accurately.

Alison smoothly clipped her buckles together in front and grinned at Sofia. Next, she pulled their waterproof vest over her front, turning so that Chris could secure it around her back. Finally, she pulled her own mask over the top of her head and wiggled it into place. She leaned forward, touching her mask gently against Sofia's.

"Can you hear me?" she called out.

"Yes."

"Are you scared?"

Sofia shook her head.

"Good," Alison winked. "Nervous is okay. But if you're scared we won't do it, okay?"

"Okay."

Alison took Sofia's hand and helped her slide down onto her rear in the water. She then turned to the dolphins. "Sally. Dirk. Can you hear me?"

Their response was immediate. *Yes Alison.*

"Remember. Very slow. Okay."

Slow, Sally replied.

Sloooow, Dirk repeated playfully.

Alison smiled and shook her head. He was such a boy.

Behind her, Dirk and Sally moved in and propped themselves on the tank ledge. Sofia leaned back apprehensively but slowly reached out to pet them each on the head. Their skin felt like wet leather. Smooth but almost spongy.

Sally lowered her nose and nuzzled affectionately against one of Sofia's skinny legs.

Alison, still holding the child's other hand, spoke loudly again through her mask. "Okay, ready?"

All she got was a nervous nod. With that, Alison fell into the water and quickly bobbed up, floating in front of Sofia. She gently pulled her small, delicate hand forward until Sophia slid in next to her.

Alison secured the girl with both hands. "Still okay?"

"Yes!" Sofia felt light again in the water. Like she used to before it became too hard to walk. "I'm floating!"

"Yes, you are."

Alison guided her slowly away from the edge, watching

Dirk and Sally wiggle back into the water. Together the pair began swirling around them, gently brushing as they passed.

Sofia's eyes were as wide as she could make them. She reached out and skimmed fingers over their bodies as they passed. "WOW!"

"Look under the water."

Sofia lowered her face beneath the surface to watch the dolphins. When she lifted her head back up, Alison leaned in and examined the mask. She needed to check for leaks. Because what they were about to do was going to feel like *magic*.

"Okay, Sally." Alison rotated Sofia's frame just as Sally came up smoothly beneath her, and she helped guide the girl's tiny legs down around Sally's sides.

"Can you lean forward?"

Sofia complied and instinctively wrapped her arms around Sally.

"Are you ready for a ride, honey?"

Sofia was almost shaking but still managed to nod, even with her mask pressed against the back of Sally's light gray head.

"Okay, Sally. Nice and easy."

Come Sofia.

Sally gave a thrust of her tail and swam forward. Dirk quickly fell in beside them as Alison latched onto his tail. Together all four continued across the tank, circling at the far end and slowly returning to where Alison had checked Sofia.

"Still okay?"

"YES!"

"Here comes the best part!"

Alison patted Sally, who then took off again. Her speed was no faster but this time she ducked a few feet below the surface and swam in a tighter circle.

As the warm water enveloped them both, Sophia heard the sound abruptly disappear into the cool air above them, leaving only Dirk and Sally's mechanized voices in her ear.

Now okay Sofia?

"Yes, I'm fine!" she replied, still beaming inside the mask.

Faster? Dirk asked.

"YES! FASTER!"

The water flow surged faster around them and the pressure increased against their bodies from below, giving Sofia the sensation that she and Sally were flying together.

Sofia felt as happy as she had ever been.

9

Admiral Langford stepped out of the elevator as soon as the metal doors separated. He turned left and walked briskly down Corridor Nine on the third floor, toward the Pentagon's "A" ring, avoiding eye contact with two generals approaching from the other direction.

The military was as much about status and rank as any organization on the planet, and the Pentagon served as a prestigious symbol of that system. A building filled with colonels, admirals, and generals, all of whom were seen as the best the country's Armed Forces had to offer. Men who embodied the very image of accomplishment and greatness.

Yet deep down, these same men all shared a common secret. A dark secret. A character flaw that few would admire, let alone celebrate. Each man had long ago sacrificed the priorities of his own life, and those of his family, to attain the unattainable. Men who helped shape the most powerful government in history, who shaped the very world as much as any politician ever would. Men who inevitably chose to sacrifice what most of the world would never relinquish.

These men lived in the glow of the most prized possession of all: ultimate power. The one constant that eventually changed *all* men before enslaving them. *Power* was the greatest of all drugs. In monarchies, these men were kings. In Communism, they were dictators. In republics and democracies, they were politicians and generals.

And Langford was no exception. His family had sacrificed just like the rest, living most of their lives without a husband or father. A man who they knew more as an image than a person. Until he was saved.

It was the accident that changed it all — collision that

suddenly put his teenage daughter into the Intensive Care Unit and a single phone call that shook him free from his enslavement. That night was a turning point and became his moment of clarity. For the next month, Langford and his wife rarely left their child's bedside. His daughter eventually recovered, but Langford had been *reformed*. He remained a patriot, but he was no longer bound by a personal or political agenda. His agenda now was for his family first and then his country. And it was also why the double doors to his office read in very simple, and very small lettering: Chairman – Joint Chiefs of Staff.

Langford pushed the right side door open, nodding to Clay and Borger as they both stood up. They fell into step behind Langford, who paused only briefly to take a small stack of messages from his secretary's outstretched hand before entering his office. He closed the door behind them and rounded his desk while his men each took a chair.

Clay could see the consternation on the Admiral's face. "Everything okay?"

"No."

Langford had just returned from his morning security briefing at the White House. Things were not okay. In fact, things were unraveling at a frightening pace. He leaned back into the thick leather chair and leveled his eyes at them.

"Our Chinese friends don't give up easily. They've dispatched every single ship in the CRS, the first of which should reach Panama by tomorrow morning."

"Salvage ships?"

"That's right."

Clay and Borger looked at each other. "They're not going to recover the Bowditch?"

"No," Langford shook his head. "They're coming after the Corvette. Their warship never made it back to China."

Now Clay and Borger were genuinely confused.

Langford sighed. "Two days after the attack on the Bowditch, a large area of debris was spotted off the coast of

Rio de Janeiro. The Brazilians were the first to dispatch a salvage team, who now believes it's the remains of the Chinese Corvette *and* the Forel. It appears both boats were destroyed together."

Borger was incredulous. "Wait. First the Bowditch was sunk by the Russian Forel, then we find out it was really the Chinese?"

"Correct."

"Then the Russian sub *and* the Chinese warship are destroyed together?"

Clay raised an eyebrow. "Was it us?"

His question surprised Langford, nearly making him chuckle. "No, it wasn't us. We had no one that far south."

"Then who?"

"We believe it was the Chinese."

"The *Chinese?!* The Chinese sank their own ship?"

"We think so."

"That doesn't make any sense!" Borger exclaimed. "Knowing what was on that Corvette, why on Earth would they sink it?"

Langford glanced at Clay, who was thinking again. He could almost watch Clay figure it out.

"A coup."

Langford nodded. "We think so."

"A coup?" Borger looked at Clay. "Inside China?"

"If the Corvette was sunk by one of their own, it could mean there's a split inside the government."

"Maybe within the Politburo," Langford added.

"Or maybe the cargo wasn't really on the ship," Borger said.

Clay shook his head. "Then they wouldn't be sending such a large salvage operation. It's more likely the ship did have the plants onboard, but for some reason someone else inside their government sank it."

"Then the question is why. Why would someone intentionally destroy the greatest discovery of the century?"

"Maybe revenge."

Clay turned to Langford. "I don't think so, sir. If there *is* an internal battle going on, both would have to know how valuable the Corvette's cargo was."

"So then, they either didn't understand what exactly was on that warship, or they didn't care."

Clay leaned back in his chair. "But who wouldn't care about that?"

"Okay," Borger said, thinking out loud. "So, for whatever reason, the Chinese decide to blow up their own ship, which is packed full of a plant whose DNA is nothing short of a miracle. And now they're sending a salvage team to recover whatever they can."

"A recovery *fleet*," Langford corrected.

"They're not coming to recover a ship or a sub."

The other two men looked at Clay.

"They're coming to find any traces of that cargo."

"Well, at least if we don't have it, neither do they."

Borger gave Clay a nervous look and raised a plain manila folder he had been holding. "Actually, sir. About that…" He leaned forward out of his chair and handed the folder to Langford over the desk.

"What's this?"

"Pictures, sir."

Langford opened it and began flipping through several full-size satellite images. He stopped on one and rotated it sideways. "Is this Georgetown?"

"Yes, sir." Borger scooted forward. "It's the airport. Just a couple hours before the Bowditch was attacked. This person drove from the Chinese Corvette to the airport where he boarded a Chinese Y-12."

Langford examined the next photo. It was zoomed in to reveal more detail. "What's in the case?"

Borger took a deep breath. "Sir, when John and I were aboard the Bowditch, Commander Neely Lawton talked about that plant's DNA and what made it so valuable. It wasn't just its properties and the ability to merge it together with human DNA through a bacteria. The most amazing thing was how easily it could be extracted with the right equipment. Something called a torque transducer. Or a nano-mag for short."

Langford nodded. "Go on."

"We've already established that the Chinese Corvette most likely didn't attack the Bowditch because it couldn't. They had to have hollowed the ship out to make enough room for all the material they trucked down from the mountain." Borger shrugged. "So, if they were that prepared, they may very well have had a nano-mag onboard too."

"And probably had already begun the extraction process," added Clay.

Langford looked back at the man in the photo. "And you think that's what's in the case, the extracted DNA?"

"More specifically, the bacterial medium. It's our best guess."

"I presume you followed the path of this plane?"

"Yes, sir. And the man on it."

"And they ended up where?"

"Beijing."

Langford inhaled and leaned back again. "Perfect." He ran his finger lightly over his lips, thinking. "So, if you're right, and the Chinese already have at least some of the DNA in Beijing…why the giant recovery effort? Why send virtually every salvage ship they have?"

"The most obvious reason would be because they don't know they have it," Clay said.

"They don't know about the case?"

"It's possible. If there really is a splinter within the Politburo's Standing Committee, one side may not know about the case.

"Seems like a long shot."

Clay shrugged. "Not as much of a long shot as finding

out the Chinese destroyed their own ship."

"True." Langford turned to Borger. "So where is this man and his case now?"

"I'm not sure yet. I'm...going to need to find a way into their systems and see what I can find out."

"And how do you plan to do that?"

Borger grinned. "I'd rather not say."

Langford's lip curled. He was well aware of Borger's background. Having worked as a network security expert in his former job, he was known as a "white hat." A computer hacker who caught other "black hat" hackers. It was how they came to hire Borger. He was the only outside expert who had been able to catch two hackers trying to break into one of the Navy's computer systems.

Langford hired him on the spot. Now, sitting across from him, even if Langford wanted to know what Borger had in mind, he sure as hell wouldn't understand it.

"Fine," he said, sighing. He placed his hands on his desk. "So, it appears we have two problems. If the Chinese do have the DNA from those plants or their crews turn something up from the Corvette's wreckage, they could have the means to become the most powerful army on the planet."

"They would be unstoppable."

Langford eyed Borger. "In more ways than one."

"Well," Clay spoke up, "there is a third option."

"Which is?"

"The monkey."

Langford rubbed his forehead. "Right. The monkey. Have you gotten anything more on our new friend Otero?"

Clay nodded. "We think he's going back to finish what Alves started."

"So if the monkey is still alive, it could be a third source of the DNA."

"Correct."

Which means we'd better find it first," Langford said. He

stared at both men. "Where's Caesare?"

Steve Caesare had just reached the single story terminal building of the Mercedita Airport. With a heavy bag slung over his good side, he climbed two steps and walked through a set of automatic sliding glass doors just beneath the giant earth tone letters reading "Aeropuerto Mercedita."

It was a small airport whose runway had only recently been expanded to accommodate larger commercial jets. An expansion that now enabled the airport to process four times as many passengers to Ponce, Puerto Rico's largest city in its southern region.

However, for Caesare, the airport's importance was its convenient location, less than fifteen miles from the research center and Alison Shaw's team.

The air conditioning inside created a light chill on his arms and neck. As Caesare approached an open row of seats near the back wall, he dropped his bag to the floor with a loud thud. He eased himself into the black vinyl chair with a quiet groan and peered up at the display hanging overhead. It listed arrivals and departures in bright green and amber letters. He found the flight he was looking for and checked his watch.

Less than fifty minutes left.

10

Sofia was beaming from alongside the tank as her father gently wrapped a towel around her wet body. On her other side, Sophia's mother Lara slid a pretty scarf back over her head and tied it beneath her chin. Sophia's giant smile was pure and beautiful as Alison bent down in front of her.

"Pretty great, huh?"

"Amazing!" Sofia answered excitedly through chattering teeth. She peered past Alison to Dirk and Sally, watching her with their heads bobbing above the water. "I can't believe it!"

Alison winked. "No other kid has ever done that."

"Really?"

"Really."

The expression on Sofia's face was priceless, but one look at her parents made Alison want to cry along with them. She couldn't imagine how a parent could deal with losing a child. How they could even manage to go on, missing such a giant piece of their hearts. She was honored to have been able to make one of Sofia's last days truly special, but now that she'd met her, Alison's heart was already breaking.

She pursed her lips and straightened back up, just as DeeAnn stepped in closer. "Did you enjoy that, Sofia?"

"More than anything!"

"Excellent." DeeAnn glanced at her parents kneeling behind her. "Do you need to leave or do we have a little more time?"

Lara placed her hands lightly on her daughter's shoulders. "How do you feel, honey?"

"Really good."

Lara nodded. "We have more time."

"Good," DeeAnn smiled. "So…Sofia, do you like gorillas?"

Dulce sat up straight when she heard the others approaching, a flower stem still gripped between her large teeth. She immediately sprang up and ran to the glass wall. She peered down the sloped walkway, trying to see into the darkened tunnel, and began clapping excitedly when she spotted DeeAnn pushing a small girl in a strange metal chair.

Mommy here! Mommy here!

The words emanated from behind Sofia through the new vest donned by DeeAnn. Alison and Lara followed behind with the four men in the rear. And Lee was right. The new vest was much more comfortable.

DeeAnn stopped near the large clear door and switched places with Alison. She entered the security code, grabbing the handle when the door gave a loud "click." DeeAnn stepped in first as Dulce began jumping up and down. She raised her hands and lowered them calmly.

"Easy, Dulce. Easy."

Dulce stopped with a huge grin. *Dulce easy.*

DeeAnn eyed her for a long moment before turning and waving Alison in with the chair. They stopped less than ten feet inside and spun the chair around.

"Dulce. This is Sofia. Sofia, meet Dulce."

"Hi, Dulce."

The small dark gorilla stared at Sofia curiously. She first studied the girl's body and then her legs, following them down to the footrests of the chair. Examining the metal frame, Dulce tapped it with a finger. *What this?*

Sofia looked up to DeeAnn. "It's a chair," she replied hesitantly.

Her words took just over a second to be transmitted to IMIS before returning in translated form through DeeAnn's

69

vest speaker. Dulce listened and seemed to become even more fascinated by it. Finally, her large hazel eyes traveled back up to Sofia.

You small.

She giggled. "I am. But I think I'm still taller than you."

DeeAnn laughed as Dulce frowned after hearing the translation. The young gorilla's protruding lips quickly spread back into a grin and she took Sofia's hand to shake it.

"She's been having a lot of fun with handshaking lately," DeeAnn whispered. "She's noticed that people do it a lot when they meet."

"Oh. Okay."

When she was done, Dulce took back her hand, but quickly became curious about the colorful scarf over the girl's head. She grabbed hold of the chair and raised herself up to get a closer look, then sniffed at the scarf. Without warning, she grabbed it with one hand and pulled it down.

Sofia jumped in surprise and instinctively reached up, but it was too late. Instead, all she could do was raise her shoulders in embarrassment.

Dulce had already begun pulling the scarf over her own head when she noticed Sofia's bald skin on top. She immediately lowered the scarf and studied it. DeeAnn was about to interject when Dulce raised her hand and delicately rubbed the top of Sofia's head.

You head same Dulce head.

With a slight grin, Sofia replied, "I think you have a tiny bit more hair."

Dulce rubbed her own head, checking. She laughed with a loud whooping sound. *You come play Dulce.*

The young gorilla clasped Sofia's hand and abruptly pulled her forward, almost tugging her out of her chair.

"Whoa, whoa!" exclaimed DeeAnn. "Dulce go easy, remember?"

She looked up at DeeAnn, puzzled. *Dulce easy.*

"Easier."

70

Sofia spoke up. "What do you want to play, Dulce?"
Check.

"Check? What's-" Sofia started to ask, but stopped when she spotted an oversized checkerboard sitting idly in the shade of a Rosewood tree, one of the many native African plants in the habitat.

"Oh. You mean checkers!"

Dulce nodded and pulled again, more gently.

"Okay, hold on," DeeAnn said. "We'll move her." She helped Alison move the chair forward over the rough ground and leaned in to tell Sofia something as they moved across the short grass.

"Don't let her cuteness fool you," she said with a wink. "Sometimes she cheats."

"Really?"

"Well, it's not cheating to her. She's playing. But it may not be the same game you think you're playing."

They reached a large, square wooden box with red and black squares painted neatly on top. Round circular chips were also painted and strewn around the board. Sofia watched in amazement as Dulce carefully retrieved the pieces and grouped them into separate piles.

Chris Ramirez stood off to the side, watching with the others. His specialty was marine and aquatic life, but he found himself constantly fascinated watching DeeAnn's work with Dulce. The young gorilla was adorable but even more than that, she moved in ways that were just so...human. Of course, DeeAnn had explained how very similar primate and human DNA were, but he was sure there was something else. Apes moving similarly were one thing, but there was definitely something else. Something he hadn't quite been able to put his finger on, until now.

Lee's discovery of the extra frequencies prompted Chris to rethink his many conversations with Alison about a certain cultural element which seemed to be missing in these translations. Something that suggested another level of connection. But now, watching Dulce again, the idea suddenly crystallized. It wasn't just the movements of gorillas in general. He'd observed other primates many times before. Their actions were similar to humans but not exactly the same. With Dulce, her motions were *very* similar to their own. So close, in fact, that some of her gestures looked almost identical to a human child. And naturally the specific difference with Dulce was a superior form of *communication*. Standing there in the habitat, it finally hit Chris. Maybe what made humans *human*, was not just DNA. Maybe some of that humanity was inside the communication itself.

He continued watching Dulce and Sofia with a smile on his face, quietly pondering whether IMIS would ever discover deeper secrets within the communication of humans themselves.

He blinked and returned his focus to Dulce, who was studying the board carefully and examining every chip. Finally, she reached out and placed her chip on a new red square two spaces up.

Sofia wrinkled her brow and looked at DeeAnn again. "Is that allowed?"

"I usually just go with it."

Sofia shrugged and reached forward, moving her own piece.

For the next thirty minutes, the two played every game Dulce had in the habitat, some twice. Eventually, Lee and Juan excused themselves to head back to the lab. The rest continued watching in amusement, but it was DeeAnn who was truly surprised. Dulce could be rather reckless when she played, especially given her growing level of strength. But not once had her recklessness come out with Sofia. She was as gentle as DeeAnn had ever seen her. As if she was worried about the girl.

Dulce spontaneously looked up at DeeAnn from where the two were playing and said a single word.

Friend.

DeeAnn smiled at Alison and eased the office door closed behind her. Alison turned to sit on the edge of her desk and folded her arms. She was beaming.

"That...was amazing!"

"It certainly was."

"Did you see Sofia's face when they left? She couldn't stop smiling!"

DeeAnn laughed. "Pure happiness. You really did something incredible there, Ali."

"*We*," Alison corrected.

"Okay, we did something incredible."

She took a deep breath and turned to stare out the window. "God, it just felt so good to do that for her. To give her something really special. To make a difference..."

DeeAnn tilted her head when Alison trailed off. "You mean before it's too late."

"Yes," she replied, deflating. "Before it's too late." Her excitement was quickly tempered with the painful realization that Sofia was close to the end of her life. *It wasn't fair. It just wasn't fair at all.*

"What if...what if we could do this for other kids?" Alison's eyes glanced back up, searching DeeAnn's for her reaction.

"Now that would be something." DeeAnn couldn't tell whether Alison was using the word "we" intentionally. *Was Alison subtly trying to coax her to stay?*

"It's funny," DeeAnn said. "When I first got here, I had no idea what IMIS would be able to do. It's just a computer. But it's connecting us in ways I don't think any of us could have imagined."

Alison nodded. "Did I ever tell you that when IBM came to us with the idea of IMIS, I never thought it would work?"

"No, you didn't."

"I had no idea how far the capabilities of these supercomputers had come. I thought they were just used for beating us at chess and stuff."

DeeAnn laughed. "The irony is that in some ways I think it may just teach us how to be better humans. It sure did today."

"Who would have thought, right?"

"Just don't tell Lee I said that."

As Alison began to speak, they were suddenly interrupted.

"Good afternoon, ladies."

They both turned to see Steve Caesare's tanned and handsome face peering in through the door.

"Steve?!" Alison's eyes widened. "What are you doing here?"

He smiled and pushed the door open, stepping inside. "Ah, I was in the neighborhood." He noticed the slight flush in Alison's face. "Am I interrupting something?"

"No, no. Just an emotional day. Come on in."

She rose from her desk and covered the distance to give him a hug. Caesare then turned to DeeAnn. "How are you, Dee?"

DeeAnn gave him a friendly smirk. She hated that nickname, and he knew it. She hugged him and stepped back. "To what do we owe this *surprise?*"

Caesare grinned. He was glad their relationship hadn't changed, even after what she'd been through. "I was just flying through," he said with a shrug. "Thought I'd stop by to visit two of my favorite gals."

Alison looked suspiciously at DeeAnn. *Stopping by* wasn't something a person did easily from an airplane. "I see you've shaved off your mustache. Trying to impress anyone?"

Trying to blend in, actually. He chuckled and turned to DeeAnn. "How's Dulce?"

"Good. Bouncing back faster than I expected."

"And how about you?"

She frowned, nervously. "I'm a bit slower."

Caesare simply nodded. "And how about the guys?"

"Pretty good. They're all here if you want to stop by the lab."

"I will." He looked around the room, decorated with two large Wyland prints and a bookshelf beneath the window. When his focus came back to Alison and DeeAnn, both women were staring at him questioningly. "What?"

DeeAnn spoke to Alison without looking away. "I sense bad news coming."

"Bad news? From me? Never."

"You've never come here alone before, Steve."

Neither woman was buying it. "Fine," he relented. "I came here to talk to you two. And…more specifically, to Dee."

"About what?"

Caesare dropped the act but kept a trace of the grin. "Well, we have a wee bit of a problem."

"What kind of problem?"

He crossed his arms, trying to ignore a sudden spike of pain in his side. "It's about our old friend, Mateus Alves."

DeeAnn raised her brow curiously. "I thought he was dead."

"He is. And so is his head of security, Miguel Blanco."

"You found him?"

"I did."

DeeAnn stared at him for a moment, puzzled, then shrugged. "So he's dead. Why should I care?"

"Normally I'd say you shouldn't. But he was murdered yesterday morning. By someone who we think knew Alves pretty well."

"An eye for an eye, I guess."

Caesare glanced at Alison, who was watching DeeAnn. Blanco had nearly killed DeeAnn, and Alves had been planning to. She didn't care what happened to either of

75

them. But she couldn't hide her surprise either, no matter how hard she tried.

"Blanco died after being tortured. By someone who wanted to know everything that happened up on that mountain, including who was there."

That got both of the women's attention.

"What does that mean?"

"He knows what Mateus Alves was after. He knows how he died, and where. He probably also knows about you and Dulce, and that monkey, Dexter. We think he knows just about everything, and we think he's going back to find what Alves couldn't."

The first signs of concern appeared on DeeAnn's face. "Dulce and I aren't in danger, are we?"

"I don't think so."

"Good. So why do we even care?"

"Because if he finds that monkey, I think we all know what's going to happen."

DeeAnn stared at him, but said nothing. What happened to the damn monkey wasn't her problem. She couldn't save it — she knew that now. But her brush with death had woken her up to the ludicrousness of what she *thought* she could do. It also left her with a very real appreciation of the value of life. Life was precious. And she only had one shot at it. She was no longer interested in sacrificing hers for some hopeful ideology.

"I don't care what happens."

Caesare glanced to Alison and back. "Well, that may be. But that's not what I meant. Alves was a fanatic, obsessed with the idea of immortality. And now that we know DNA can be passed between species, what do you think is going to happen if this new guy gets a hold of that monkey's DNA?" Caesare took a small step closer to her. "Alves came damn close, and believe me, DeeAnn. Alves was bad. But this guy is a whole lot worse. Blanco and his girlfriend were tortured and literally beaten to death. For answers. What do you

76

think happens if someone like that figures out how to outlive all of us?"

"That's impossible."

"Is it?"

"I'm not stupid, Steven. It's not that easy to transfer DNA."

"It can be done."

Something on Caesare's face made her halt her reply in mid-sentence. Her eyes narrowed and she turned to Alison. "You know something."

She nodded.

"What?"

"Steve's right. It can be done. We saw it, on the Bowditch."

"The ship that sank?"

"Yes."

DeeAnn was quiet for a moment. "It doesn't matter. This guy will never find a single monkey on an entire mountain. Dexter's probably already dead anyway. Even if he's not, it would take months, maybe years, to find him."

"Not with Dulce's help."

DeeAnn's eye widened and she shook her head. "No! I can't do that to her. I won't. You don't know what was happening to her up there. She may be better now, but if she melts down again...a manic gorilla who's twice as strong as you would be the last thing you want on your hands. Believe me. We can't risk that again."

"Not even for an all-expense paid trip to the rainforest?"

DeeAnn was not amused.

"Then how about a fancy medal from the President?"

"The answer is no."

Caesare's smile faded. "Okay, look. The truth is we need your help. We need you and Dulce to help us find the monkey. To get in and out, quickly."

"Who's we?"

He didn't answer immediately. Instead, he looked at

them both and then took a few steps back to the door. He opened it, leaned outside, and motioned his head. Steve stepped back, holding the door open.

A moment later, three men appeared in the doorway and one by one stepped into Alison's office. All three were dressed in casual clothes but sported hardened, chiseled faces.

"I'd like you to meet my friends: Officers Corso, Anderson, and Tiewater."

She looked them over with her arms still crossed in front of her. "Well, at least you're not dumb enough to go alone this time." DeeAnn immediately regretted her statement the moment she said it. If Caesare hadn't gone *alone* last time, she wouldn't still be alive. It was a stupid thing to say.

Caesare let it go. She'd gone through enough trauma. Taken advantage of by both Alves and Blanco on what was supposed to be a mission of goodwill, she was literally staring down the barrel of a gun by the time Caesare got to her. She had every right not to want to go back. But they needed her and Dulce, badly.

Neither Corso, Anderson, nor Tiewater replied or even moved. What DeeAnn Draper didn't know was that these three men were handpicked from three of the best Navy SEAL Special Warfare teams on the East Coast. And they were now tasked with safely accompanying Caesare, DeeAnn, and Dulce back into the jungle — four members, including Caesare, who could protect them and still maintain a small, nimble, and fast group. From the insertion to the extraction, the priority was to get in and back out before Otero and his men. And there wasn't a lot of time.

Alison remained quiet and watched DeeAnn, standing strong in front of all four men. Their presence and stone like expressions exuded a feeling of strength throughout the room. She was sure it was supposed to be reassuring, not intimidating, but it was both.

"I appreciate what you're trying to do, Steven," DeeAnn

said. "And I applaud your courage. But I don't share it. I came as close to death as I ever want to be, for a long time. I'm not a soldier. I'm a scientist. Fearlessness is not one of my strengths. Dulce may have gotten over it, but I haven't. I don't know if I ever will." She glanced briefly at the other men. "I'm sorry."

Caesare frowned. "This isn't about fearlessness, DeeAnn. Or bravado. This is bigger than you and me. It's bigger than all of us. This is about the world being a much more frightening place to live in tomorrow if we don't do something today. And every generation after us will have to pay the price. The price of not stopping this while we could."

DeeAnn stared at him, considering his words. To her, it didn't matter what happened today. There was so much evil in the world. So much apathy. It was everywhere and the world was going to end up in a bad place regardless. Maybe this discovery would hasten it, or maybe it wouldn't, but either way she was sure that in the end things would end up the same. She wasn't ready to trade her life, or Dulce's, for a bunch of egotistical men and governments who would keep fighting with each other long after she was gone. Those men didn't care about a brighter future for everyone else. They only cared about a better today for themselves. For their secret, corrupt, elitist clubs that would do anything they could to survive. And to rule. Men like Caesare and his friends might be genuinely concerned about the future, but the men they served were not.

She slowly shook her head again. "Sorry, this is not my fight. I paid my dues, and then some. DNA or no DNA, I don't believe anything is going to change. Not the people, the politics, and certainly not the system. If we were all in this to make life better for everyone, that might be one thing. But this is just a game. Nothing will change. It will always be played by people who have never played by the rules and who now want to change the game itself. I don't think they'll be able to, but I'm not willing to die just to find out. "

Caesare inhaled and finally nodded. The last thing he wanted to do was to force her to come. It wouldn't be all that different from what happened to her the first time.

He moved slowly, and as he turned, he looked to Alison, who was still watching them both. She and Caesare knew something DeeAnn didn't. Something much bigger than trying to find a monkey. Something only he, Alison, and two other people knew and had sworn themselves to secrecy.

Caesare turned to Corso, Anderson, and Tiewater and motioned back toward the door. "Give us a minute, fellas."

One by one, the men turned for the door.

When it clicked shut, Caesare looked at Alison.

"Tell her."

"Tell me *what*?"

Alison turned to her friend solemnly. "There's more."

"More what?"

"There's more to the story. About what we found on top of that mountain."

DeeAnn's eyes moved back and forth between them. "You mean when you were outside."

"Yes."

She knew what Alison was referring to. She was on the helicopter too, with Dulce. But she hadn't wanted to know what was outside or what it was they found. Dulce had already come frighteningly close to having a complete breakdown, as had DeeAnn. The truth was she didn't want to go outside. She was done. Finished. They had survived and all she wanted to do from that moment was to go home. To get home and start over.

DeeAnn shook her head. "I don't want to know."

Alison glanced at Caesare before replying. "I don't think that's an option anymore."

"Excuse me?"

Alison straightened from the edge of her desk. "There's more to this than you realize, DeeAnn, and it's the reason

Steve's going back. It's not just about the monkey or its DNA."

"No! Whatever it is, I don't want to hear it. I don't want to know." She looked at both of them in anger. "This isn't my problem. Find someone else!"

"This could turn out bad, DeeAnn. Really, *really* bad. Not just for those at the top, but for *everyone*."

That instantly stopped DeeAnn's head shaking. "I already tried to help. I did! And what did it get me? Nightmares, that's what! I'm lucky if I sleep three hours a night. You know why? Because up there, for the first time in my life, I was completely and utterly helpless! They were about to kill me and dump my body, and there wasn't a damn thing I could do about it!"

She looked at Caesare who remained quiet. "If it weren't for you, Steve, I would be dead. Dead. Right now! I will never forget what you did. Ever. But there is no way I'm going to put myself in a position where that can happen again. I don't care how many men you bring. Bring them, bring the Marines too, bring all of them, and I still wouldn't go back! I've had enough fear to last me a lifetime. I sure as hell don't need anymore."

DeeAnn could no longer stop the tears. She quit talking and looked for an exit. With a sudden burst, she ran past Caesare, flung the door open, and rushed out.

Caesare emerged behind her and watched as DeeAnn disappeared down the stairs at the end of the hall. Once she was out of sight, he turned to the other men standing behind him.

Tiewater raised an eyebrow. "That didn't appear to go very well."

The small, white Ming Dynasty vase smashed against the wall with the force and sound of a small explosion, breaking into hundreds of pieces as it fell onto the plush carpet. Tiago Otero was furious. His eyes blazed as he looked for something else to throw but found nothing within reach.

He cursed repeatedly and glared back at Lieutenant Samuel Russo, the head of his own security, and the man delivering the news about his men. One was dead and the other hospitalized. They were instructed to burn the house down with Blanco's dead family inside. But Russo's men had failed miserably. Instead, they found the house virtually empty and someone waiting for them.

It was worse than failure, it was humiliating. Now people would know that it was Otero who had been taught the lesson — direct challenge to his power and influence over all of Brazil. A mockery.

With lips snarling, Otero looked down at the table and the cut fabric Russo had laid upon it. "What is this?!"

"A sign."

"A sign of what?!"

"Of who did this. It's in the shape of a trident. The symbol used for the U.S. Navy SEALs."

His eyes shot back to Russo. "The U.S. did this?"

"It would appear so."

Otero's gaze fell back to the shirt, blinking. "Why would Blanco be involved with the U.S.? What did they have to do with anything?" After considering the possibility, he finally shook his head, sneering. "It's a prank. A diversion. Whoever did this wanted us to think it was the Americans. But they'd just as soon kill someone like Blanco as I would."

Russo stared at him over the table. "Not his family."

"Don't be so sure."

Over the years, Otero had become familiar with many of the C.I.A.'s escapades. They were as ruthless as anyone. They simply made it appear as though it was someone else. *But the Americans would never point the finger at themselves. Would they?*

His eyes narrowed. "Find out who it was. Now. No matter how you find them, I want to know who did this!"

"I will."

Otero clenched his jaw and bared his teeth. He would track down who did it, who had publicly insulted him. And when he did, that man would find out that there were far worse things than letting some worthless family perish.

He waved Russo away and waited until he left the room. Otero then turned and walked angrily through the room to his study. Lined floor to ceiling with rare and expensive books, he continued to the center of the room where a round table sat. It was covered with a giant map of Brazil and the entire South American continent. Centered on the country's highest mountain range called *Acarai*, stood the range's highest and still unnamed peak.

He and his men were going to uncover its secret. Part of the Brazilian Army was coming with him and they weren't leaving until Otero knew everything, *including what the Chinese were after.*

It was a question he would soon regret asking.

12

Otero's impending regret would come from a man named Xinzhen, who stood motionless in the enormous pavilion atop the China Club hotel. Nestled in the traditional hutong area and well-known as one of Beijing's most lavish hotels, the China Club sprawled out over ten thousand square meters and was composed of several Qing Dynasty pavilions and secluded courtyards.

Xinzhen stood solemnly, less than a meter from the thick glass wall, and peered out at the smog covered city of Beijing. The day was clearer than expected with only a thin film of pollution obstructing the view.

He scanned the light gray cityscape, noting the eerie shadows belonging to dozens of cranes with their arms rising into the air, even now. They would be gone soon but for now they remained, serving as ghostly remnants of the largest bubble in human history. A level of greatness and grueling achievement the world would not see again for hundreds of years. The world where for decades demand had radically outpaced the supply of natural resources, only to leave the most immense economic vacuum imaginable.

Reality was starting to set in, and like all economic bubbles before it, China's delusion was now imploding in on itself. Bursting, and set to leave a wave of destruction in its wake. It was little comfort for Xinzhen knowing his country was not alone. Japan, Europe, Britain, and even the U.S., were all on their own precipice. They had each lost touch with economic reality, but none had matched the sheer insanity of mainland China. Massive amounts of mal-investment had created not just "bridges to nowhere," but entire *ghost cities* able to house more than a hundred thousand residents each. Cities which still remained completely empty as though life had simply vanished from within. Built out of a construction mania and funded by government money printing, the looming destruction brought on by China's frenzy would be epic in every sense of the word.

As Xinzhen studied the city from his pavilion, he tried to imagine what it would look like when the money, and more importantly the confidence, was gone. When all of its citizens rushed for the proverbial "exit" at once.

The collapses of other nations like Argentina and Brazil were already underway and serving as examples of what was to come. Mass shortages of food, energy, and basic staples were already rampant with citizens bartering for any amounts they could find. Pianos traded for crates of toilet paper and televisions traded for personal hygiene products were already common. The shortages in China were going to be just as bad, if not worse.

Xinzhen took a deep breath. As bad as things were about to become, he cared surprisingly little. As part of the Politburo Standing Committee of the Communist Party of China, he and the other six members had long been protected by secret plans for their evacuation and survival. They would be whisked out of the city centers to the majestic mountains of Sihanba far to the north, where vast bunkers had been constructed and stockpiled. This would allow China's elite to survive safely for decades…if only they could live that long.

If the impossible *were* to be achieved, it had to be done now. Before the technical capability was lost forever. And to do it, Xinzhen was prepared to move Heaven and Earth.

He heard the door open behind him and turned to find his secretary ushering in the man he had been waiting for. Xinzhen watched the man approach through the suite's grand entryway and stop in the middle of the expansive room. He stood erect as Xinzhen stepped away from the window and crossed the room to meet him, hands still behind his back.

85

"Agent Qin."

Li Qin bowed slightly. "Your Eminence. I am honored in your presence."

Normally Xinzhen would have left him standing, but instead motioned for the man to join him. He then lowered himself onto the wide circular couch.

He watched Qin sit and stared at him. They had never met before, but Xinzhen was well aware of the man's reputation. As part of the Ministry of State Security agency, Qin was one of the very best the Counterintelligence Bureau had ever seen. He had a keen intellect and an even keener talent for finding those who did not want to be found. And in some cases, those who couldn't be found by anyone else. Qin's latest success had been the attainment of details behind China's recent presidential scandal — one that allowed the committee to oust the one man who dared challenge them, and with little resistance. A solution much preferred over normal methods, which would only attract more attention for the committee. The last thing any of them needed before a revolution.

"Your patriotic work behind Bo Xilai's treachery has been noticed. And appreciated."

Qin bowed again. "Thank you. You are very kind." He was not surprised by the invitation. He'd found more than what he was looking for with Bo Xilai, a man who had risen through the ranks of the Communist Party and been considered a candidate for the next seat in the Standing Committee. But Bo's corruption ran deep, much deeper than any of them knew. So deep were his indiscretions that Bo had found himself stripped of his titles, assets, and freedom in less than a month.

Xinzhen leaned back gently into the plush couch. "Does it surprise you that I am alone?"

Qin grinned respectfully. "Nothing surprises me, Your Eminence."

Xinzhen smiled in return. "Of course. Do you know

why you're here?"

"I have only guesses."

"Humor me."

Qin briefly scanned the room without moving his head. "The relaxation of security suggests this is not disciplinary related. But the fact that you are alone makes it unlikely to be a congratulatory acknowledgment either. Nor are we meeting in a People's sanctioned location. I suspect Your Eminence is preparing to assign me a private task of some kind."

Xinzhen continued observing the man. Qin was purposely meeting his eyes across the table, barely blinking. Something that few would do with the head of the Committee and arguably the most powerful person in China. The man was unafraid, something for which he was known. He was also willing to do whatever it took to succeed. A trait not uncommon within the higher levels of China's government, but eventually most men had their boundaries. According to his sources, Qin had none.

"What do you know about General Wei?"

If Qin was surprised, he showed no indication.

"General Wei. Highly decorated. Perfect service record over a thirty-year career. A model leader. And a dead one. By suicide two weeks ago."

"Why did he commit suicide?"

Qin replied carefully. "I'm sure I do not know."

A trace of Xinzhen's grin returned. "Of course." He paused a moment. "Why do you *think* he killed himself?"

"It is rumored that he was given an important task by the Committee and failed."

Failed was an understatement. "What do you know of his task?"

"Only that it was in South America. I do not know of what or why. No one does," he added.

"The truth is, General Wei failed his people worse than any soldier in the history of our great country. A man who

87

will be known as China's greatest traitor."

Qin tilted his head slightly but said nothing.

"Wei is the epitome of everything that is wrong with the country and why its demise is assured. In our darkest hour, he was given the highest honor and the most critical mission in China's history. Yet, instead of honor, he chose secrecy and betrayal of his people and his country. He acted like a *capitalist*. His treachery has cost our country dearly. He murdered his own men and destroyed our ships. He deceived us from the beginning, then took his own life to keep the truth from his superiors. And still we do not know why."

Xinzhen took a breath before continuing. "Your talents and your service to China have been exceptionally faithful. You are highly trusted as a man who knows what it takes to maintain that trust. For these reasons, I have chosen you."

Qin dropped his head. "Thank you, Your Eminence. I am deeply grateful for your words. It would be my honor to serve you in whatever manner I can."

"Excellent." Xinzhen stared across the small space with his powerful dark eyes. "You are to find out why. Why Wei chose to desert his country, and most importantly, what he was hiding. What he hides still in death."

"It will be done, My Eminence. With all of my ability."

Xinzhen nodded approvingly. "And your communication is to be with me, and me alone."

Qin exited the elevator at the bottom floor. Without a word, he crossed over the marble flooring through the lobby and left the hotel, emerging back into the stale, thick air. The tops of the skyscrapers disappeared into the sickly gray sky above, giving them an eerie appearance.

The valet approached with Qin's car, a black BMW M6,

and quickly jumped out, holding the door open. Once inside, Qin turned up the air conditioner to purify the air inside. The smog was better today, but he could still taste a trace of the metallic sourness on his tongue.

Once beyond the hotel grounds, he merged with the heavier traffic and headed east toward Xinhua, recounting the details of the meeting. Xinzhen's posture had shown subtle signs of nervousness. And his seething for General Wei seemed somehow exaggerated. Qin knew of Wei. He also knew that Wei had been one of the least politically aligned military figures in the army.

He decided he was more surprised that Wei had somehow turned the tables on the Committee than he was over Wei's suicide. Wei was a smart man, which meant he clearly would have understood that crossing the Committee would only be done by someone who did not fear retribution.

Qin thought again about the oddness in the old man's seeming hatred for Wei. Particularly when considering that Xinzhen didn't know what the General had been hiding.

In the penthouse, Xinzhen was back at the window gazing outward again. There wasn't much time left. The government's façade was beginning to crumble quickly now. The propaganda and misinformation were wearing thin and would only last so long. The real question was whether someone like Qin would turn something up soon enough. And whether he could indeed be trusted.

But Xinzhen had little choice. He had to take a chance, especially now. The price was simply too high, and as much as he would like to fully trust Qin, he couldn't. He had to assume that Qin may already be loyal to one of the other Committee members, and if so, he wondered whether they somehow knew more than Xinzhen did.

It was why he didn't tell Qin everything, including the sinking of the American research vessel or the details around the destruction of their own warship.

The Committee had potentially started a war with the United States in order for their ship to escape, but it was Wei who stunned them all by suddenly sinking both their ship and its precious cargo.

Nothing made sense. *Why did Wei do it? And more importantly…why hadn't the Americans said a word about the attack on their ship?*

13

Langford looked around the table and sighed. The "war room" at the White House was in complete disarray and the situation was deteriorating rapidly. For those who believed the planning around potential military excursions was always careful and deliberate, in this case, they could not have been more wrong.

Langford watched Fred Collier, the new Chief of Naval Operations, show his frustration as he insisted that they were losing the opportunity for a swift and decisive counterattack over the loss of the Bowditch and its men. He pounded the table again, this time harder. Next to him, and not surprisingly, Sam Johnston, the Commandant of the Marine Corps, was in complete agreement.

Across the dark walnut table, however, Merl Miller, the Secretary of Defense, was not so sure. He and President Carr sat side by side, listening to the lengthening outbursts of both military heads.

Collier tried to regain his composure. "What I'm saying is that the political ramifications of us *not* acting are far greater than those if we do. They have directly challenged the sovereign power of the United States, and unless we show them clearly and definitively the repercussions of such an attack, our reputation *and* our resolve will be questioned by more than just China! Showing weakness now threatens the loss of our military supremacy. To other nations, this delay won't look like deliberation, it will look like fear!"

He lowered both hands onto the table before continuing. "We know it was the Chinese and we can prove it! We have to release the information now before they begin distancing themselves with propaganda!"

"Agreed," added Johnston. "The sooner we get NATO

behind us, the better. China is going to spin the hell out of this. We've waited too long already."

"Too long?" asked President Carr. "Too long? Do I need to remind everyone here that just days ago we thought we had been attacked by the *Russians*?!" He looked around the table. "I'd say it's a damn good thing we did wait too long."

"Mr. President," Collier replied, jabbing the table with his finger. "It was my men who verified the Comp-B signature. There is no doubt in my mind it's the Chinese. Zero!"

Carr stared intently at his Naval Chief. "Okay, let's assume it is. Tell me, Admiral, how exactly does your recommended response differ now that it's the Chinese and not the Russians?"

The question was like a dagger through Collier's argument. There was no difference, and everyone at the table knew it.

"I hope I'm not the only one at the table that remembers our foreign policy with China is different than with Russia."

Collier took a deep breath. "Mr. President, may I point out that the relationship between Russia and China continues to grow stronger by the day? It won't be long before there *is no difference* in our policies."

"Except being twice as big," Miller smirked.

Collier slapped the table. "Which only underscores the need to respond now."

Johnston nodded his head. "Agreed. The last thing we need is this turning into another mess."

"Do you know what you're saying?!" responded Miller in a raised voice. "One counter response after another, until we're on the brink of war. Where do you think this leads if this time we *start* with a counterattack?!"

"Please," Collier scoffed, "this is different. The Chinese have screwed up and they know it. They'll back down when everyone else knows it too."

"And what if they don't?" asked Carr. "What if they raise

the stakes instead? The Russians didn't back down and we had all of Europe behind us. What if the Chinese don't admit responsibility *or* back down? Are you suggesting we fight *two* wars?"

"I'm suggesting we won't have to."

Listening from the giant screen at the other end of the table, the Air Force Chief shook his head. "Trying to predict the actions of the Chinese is damn dangerous. We've been wrong before, and more than once."

Collier looked up at the screen. "There's a big difference between predicting monetary policy and military strategy, General."

"Is there?" Langford asked.

"You're kidding, right?"

Langford stared back at Collier. "I don't think we're in a position to predict anything the Chinese might do." He turned toward Carr. "With all due respect, Mr. President, I think we're losing sight here."

"Explain."

"We're thinking almost exclusively in terms of retaliation. But I think we would be better served to think more about their intent. Remember, their Corvette ship was trying to leave port and *we* were about to ram the damn thing. But it's likely the Corvette couldn't have done anything even if it wanted to. Their hidden sub fired on the Bowditch defensively. If it were an offensive attack, they could have done it sooner, not at the last second. But they were there to make sure the Corvette warship made it out in one piece because of what it was carrying."

Langford paused, making eye contact with everyone. "In fact, I'm not convinced they intended to attack the Bowditch until they had no choice. And if that's true, this posturing is going to get us nowhere. It's a sideshow with our only options being more dangerous escalations."

Langford continued. "What this is really about is that cargo. We already know what was in those plants. So unless the Chinese intended to attack all along, it was simply the value of their cargo that left them no choice but to fight their way out. The fact that their sub hadn't moved means they were prepared for more than one scenario."

"What are you suggesting, Admiral?" asked Collier. "To ignore the fact they destroyed our ship and killed a fifth of its crew?"

"What I'm suggesting is we may very well find our counterattack provokes them into an ever-increasing escalation that they never had any interest in pursuing. And in the meantime, while we prepare to burn our resources to show the world who's mightier, *they* are quietly sending over a dozen vessels into the Atlantic to search for anything left of those plants. In other words, our sabre rattling may simply end up providing them the opportunity they need to keep us busy. While they recover what was clearly important enough to start a fight over in the first place."

Carr looked at him pensively. "You're suggesting we go after it ourselves."

"Correct."

"Even though we're still not sure why they sank their own ship only hours after escaping from Georgetown."

"I'm not sure it matters, Mr. President."

The President raised an eyebrow.

"Cleary something went wrong. Whether it's a coup within their government or just a catastrophic mistake, it's crystal clear what they really care about."

"Maybe they realized there was something dangerous onboard," Collier said sarcastically.

Langford considered it. "It's possible. But they're still sending every ship they have to salvage it."

"So, we try to get there first."

"Exactly."

"And you don't think," Collier replied, "that our own salvage ships trying to get there before theirs will create an escalation?"

94

"Not if we don't *send* our salvage ships."

Miller stared at him from across the table with a puzzled expression. "I'm not following."

"Commander Lawton was the primary researcher of the plant sample we stole from the Chinese. She's confident that based on its cellular structure, and the fact that salt water is almost the perfect solvent, there isn't going to be much for China to recover in the Atlantic. Not to mention the area was still burning four days later from thousands of gallons of spilled diesel fuel."

"I'm afraid you've lost me," Carr said. "If there's nothing left to recover, how then are you proposing we go after it?"

After a deep breath, Langford turned back to the President. "There may be two other ways to grab what the Chinese are after…before they can. One is through the DNA of a small monkey. And the other may be in a box shipped to Beijing, one that the Chinese government may not even realize they have."

President Carr, who was leaning back in his black leather chair, suddenly leaned forward.

"What did you just say?"

14

Will Borger leaned back in his chair with a loud squeak. His heavyset frame filled every inch of space between the armrests. "That's our man."

Clay was studying the screen again, staring at the Chinese military photo ID. It had taken most of the night, but they finally identified the individual on the Xian Y-20 who was transporting back what they suspected was the extracted genetic material. If they were correct, the contents of that case could now be the most valuable item on the planet. But, the real question was…*where was it now?*

"Lieutenant Li of the Chinese Army. Enlisted at the age of twenty-one. Received a direct appointment to officer training after four years and has since then risen from Officer Cadet to First Lieutenant. Pretty impressive."

Borger nodded with arms crossed over his large belly, mostly hidden by a deep blue and white Hawaiian shirt. "Awarded the Medal of Outstanding Service and the Medal for Outstanding Achievement. What's the Medal of Army Brilliance for?"

Clay shook his head. "Not sure."

"Well, one thing is for sure, this guy is highly decorated."

"He is indeed."

"So why have this guy Li escort the box home, almost nonstop on a secure military plane? Anyone could have done that. An honor thing maybe?"

"Possibly. Both the Chinese political and military systems are highly class-based…but if you were trying to keep something quiet, especially something this big, would you pick one of the more recognized officers in the army?"

"Not unless I wanted someone to notice."

"Right. Then why would they want someone to notice?"

Borger shrugged. "Maybe credibility. As in 'look what I have and you don't.'"

"Maybe. But then you'd have to worry about it being intercepted." Clay moved his chair closer. "Bring up that picture of him deplaning in Beijing again."

Borger complied and brought another image up on screen. It was a satellite image, slightly grainier than the first, of Li walking from the giant Y-20 to a large hangar at the Tongxian Air Base in Beijing.

"Do you see any security around the hangar?" Clay asked.

Borger zoomed in. "No."

"And he's moving quickly."

"Yeah, he is."

"So either the place was empty, which I doubt, or there was no show or display intended here."

"Okay," frowned Borger. "Then we're back to why pick someone that a lot of people on that base might recognize?"

Clay remained quiet for a long time. Finally, the corner of his mouth curled. "Trust," he mumbled.

"What?"

"Trust," Clay repeated, louder.

"Trust?"

"Trust." Now Clay was thinking out loud. "Whoever brought it in was going to be noticed. Especially on that plane. That was unavoidable. To keep it secure meant using the Y-20, which also meant attention. There would be no way to avoid that…especially if it all had to happen *fast*."

"So you give up anonymity for speed."

"Exactly."

"But why a hero Lieutenant then?"

"Because if you need it done fast, and you're going to be seen, you better be damn sure you can *trust* the man bringing it!"

"Ahhh," Borger replied, nodding his head. "Someone you could trust not to screw you."

"Right."

"So, someone in the government was out to get the sample first, and used our friend Li to protect it."

Clay shook his head again. "Not just anyone in the government. A politician wouldn't use someone like Li. A *military* man would. A military man with a hell of a lot of clout to commandeer a new prototype like the Y-20."

"So…now we find out who he took it to. Someone in the military."

"That's right. And someone who knew *exactly* what was happening in that jungle in Guyana!"

Borger smiled, then clapped his hands and rubbed them together. "Our next challenge."

Clay stood up and stretched. "How about a caffeine break?"

"Nah, I'm good. Just bring me another."

Clay nodded and picked up the empty can of Jolt cola from Borger's desk. "Didn't they make this stuff illegal?"

"That's NOT funny!"

With a chuckle, Clay turned and left the dark room. The sun was up outside, but without any windows, there was no indication of time in Borger's "bunker." Once outside and into the light, Clay blinked and quickly made his way down the wide beige-colored hallway toward the stairs.

As he was walking, his cell phone rang in his pocket. He retrieved it and looked at the small screen with a smile.

"Well hello, beautiful."

"Good morning," Alison's voice sounded on the other end. "How are you?"

"Not too bad. How's paradise?"

Alison stopped and looked around the parking lot of her research center from where she was standing. The warm sun was well off the horizon and a refreshing breeze wafted through the palm trees overhead. "It's a beautiful morning. I tried to call you last night but got your voicemail."

Clay pulled the phone away and looked at it again. He hadn't noticed the small icon indicating a new message. "I'm sorry. I'm downstairs in Borger's lab where there's not much signal. We've been tied up most of the night."

"Most of the night?" Alison asked, a hint of concern in her voice. "Did you get any sleep?"

"Not really. I'm too nervous to fall asleep in Borger's lab. I'm afraid he'll try to put something on my head and scan me."

She laughed. "Well, you must be exhausted. I'm really sorry."

Clay reached the top of the stairs and opened a door, stepping this time into a carpeted hallway. "That's all right. Talking to you is perking me up." When he looked back at the phone, he also noticed Alison had used the special encryption application like he'd shown her. The slight delay in their conversation confirmed it.

"You're such a smooth-talker. Almost as smooth as your friend Steve who showed up here yesterday, by the way. And unannounced I might add."

"Oh, right. Sorry about that. I meant to warn you."

"Warn me is right," she teased. "We had a very interesting conversation."

"Well, Steve's an interesting guy," Clay joked, pulling open the door to the small vending room. The place was empty.

"I presume you know why he was here."

"I do." Clay closed the door behind him. He promptly punched a button on the machine for his coffee, then reached over and opened the door of a refrigerator. Inside were two cases of Jolt cola with a large piece of paper taped to the top. On the paper was a scribbled message that read: "Do not drink! Property of Will Borger!" Clay always wondered why Borger felt compelled to label his drinks when no one else on the floor would drink them. "So," he continued, "how did it go?"

"Probably not as well as Steve was hoping. DeeAnn's still having a pretty hard time. She wasn't very receptive.

But Steve didn't push her too hard. Oh, and speaking of DeeAnn, there's something else I haven't told you yet. She's leaving."

"Leaving?"

"Yes. She's taking Dulce back to the Gorilla Foundation in California. She's been really shaken up by all this, and unfortunately, I can't stop her."

Clay sighed and pulled his coffee out of the dispenser. He set it on the counter next to two cans of Borger's Jolt. "No talking her out of it, huh?"

"I've tried. Believe me. She's going and there's nothing I can do to change her mind. I think there's more going on with her than she's telling me."

Clay stared grimly at the wall. "Then I guess our visit didn't help matters much."

"Uh, no."

"I'm sorry, Ali. We should have anticipated that. We were hoping for a different reaction."

"What's happening, John?"

Clay grinned. There was always something sweet in the way she said his first name.

"Things are happening pretty quickly here. Some of our assumptions about South America and the Bowditch were not accurate. And we've uncovered a few other surprises as well."

"Steve said the man who kidnapped DeeAnn and Juan is dead. Blanco. And the person who killed him knows everything."

"It looks that way. But that's only part of the problem." Clay wished he could tell her more, but he had to keep it to things in which Alison was already involved. She had been there in Brazil with him, Caesare, and Borger. She saw the same thing they had. And she also knew about the plants the Chinese had found and were smuggling out of the jungle.

"So how were things left there?"

"DeeAnn stormed out, clearly upset. But Steve didn't

push any further. Instead, he visited the guys and played with Dulce a little before he and the other men left." She continued when Clay remained silent on the other end. "Does this mean I'm not going to see you for a while?"

"Probably not. I'm sorry. Things look like they're unraveling on us. Without DeeAnn, our job is going to be much harder. I'm sure Steve told you that we don't have a lot of time."

"He did." She tried to inject a little humor. "Maybe I could call Admiral Langford and call in my favor."

She was surprised when Clay laughed.

"I don't think you want to waste it on me," he replied.

"Oh, don't kid yourself. I'm saving it, but I'm definitely saving it for you."

"Then let's wait until your odds are better." Clay changed the subject back to DeeAnn. "So listen, there's a lot I can't tell you, but I need you to try to work on DeeAnn for me. Without her and Dulce, we're going to have a pretty big problem."

"Okay, I'll try."

"Thanks. Unfortunately, I need to get back downstairs. Can I call you tonight?"

"I'll be waiting."

"What's a good time?"

This time, he knew Alison was smiling on the other end. "Anytime is a good time."

"Okay. I'll call you as soon as I can."

"I'm holding you to it. Bye."

Clay hung up and glanced at his watch. Caesare and the other SEALs should have already arrived and began their preparations in Dam Neck, Virginia. They were running out of time and Clay hoped Alison could help bring DeeAnn around. Finding that capuchin monkey a long shot, even with DeeAnn and Dulce's help. Without them, it would be virtually impossible.

Alison may have appreciated that Caesare didn't push

DeeAnn too hard, but the truth was it was a courtesy. They would avoid forcing her if they could. But when it came right down to it, if Alison couldn't persuade DeeAnn, the only option left would be to bring her by force.

15

It was past midnight and Clay was still peering at the brightly lit laptop screen. Just a couple hours before, he and Borger had finally returned to their homes to rejuvenate with the help of a quick shower.

After finding several vulnerable state-owned servers in China, Borger began the process of worming his way inside while Clay investigated something else. A missing piece that continued to eat at him.

The Russian submarine Forel was still a mystery. The sub was supposed to have been decommissioned a few years earlier. However, since the CIA had classified the sub as a low threat, it fell off the radar of the Department of Defense and was replaced by newer R&D subs in Russia's fourth and fifth generation classes.

Yet not only had the Forel mysteriously reemerged, it did so carrying a very different technology than originally outfitted.

Something wasn't adding up. Why would the Russians keep an old submarine when the majority of its fleet was more modern and advanced? Clay suspected the capture of the Forel off the coast of South America had taken the Russians themselves by surprise.

But if the Russians found out what the Chinese were up to in Guyana and wanted to spy on them, they had better subs with which to do it. All the evidence was quickly supporting Clay's suspicion that the Russian government was *not* aware of the Forel's rebirth.

He sat back in his chair, thinking. The only light in the apartment came from the dining room chandelier above him. The darkened living room on the other side of his table was clean and neat. A leather couch and coffee table faced a broad, simply decorated wall with a wide flat-panel television fixed several feet above the fireplace. Neither the fireplace nor the television had been used in months.

Clay's eyes were still on his computer screen. If the Forel had been "recommissioned," U.S. intelligence would have found out, particularly if it was still in Russia, which suggested that it wasn't officially recommissioned. Especially according to the article Clay had just found.

The article was two years old and posted by a relatively small Norwegian publication from a town just outside of Stavanger. It appeared a small group of antiwar protesters had gathered outside a quiet shipyard. They had demanded that the government stop aiding "the global war machine" by building warships for its allies, which typically meant Russia. The group had caught wind of the construction of a warship being built in their small town. Yet once some of the group members found their way into the locked building, what they found was not a warship at all, but a submarine.

The picture in the article was centered on the protesters and only captured a piece of the vessel behind them. And from what Clay could make out, the dimensions appeared to be very close to those of the Forel. The article failed to mention, and Clay already knew that Norway didn't build submarines. At least not officially. In fact, the country's own small fleet of just six submarines was assembled in Germany. Finally, what the article did include was that the shipyard was privately owned and operated by a Russian conglomerate.

But the last piece still didn't fit since the Forel was destroyed along with the Chinese warship near Rio de Janeiro. Two boats on the same path and found in the same location. The Forel was not an adversary as they'd originally thought, but an ally to the Chinese. Slowly the pieces were lining up, but still kept bringing Clay back to the same question. *Why were the Chinese Corvette and the Forel destroyed?*

He glanced at his phone in front of him as the tiny screen

lit up, followed by the familiar ring of an incoming call. He reached forward and answered it.

"Hey, Will."

"Hi, Clay. I wake you up?"

"No. I was just sitting here wondering why we don't talk more."

Borger laughed on the other end. "Good, because we may be in for another long night. First though, I think we need to get the Admiral on."

Langford logged in from his own computer and his face promptly appeared in a video window. His short gray hair was still neat, indicating he hadn't slept yet either. On the contrary, his eyes seemed to blaze intently in the glow of his computer screen.

"What do you have?" he asked immediately.

Borger began typing on his keyboard. "Sir, I think we have some answers, but unfortunately more questions too."

"Then let's start with the answers."

"Yes, sir." An image filled the rest of their screens as Borger shared a picture from his own computer. It was a waist-high shot of a senior Chinese officer in uniform. He looked to be in his early sixties with a tight haircut similar to the Admiral's. In the picture, the man looked relaxed with dark eyes focused on the camera.

"This is General Wei. Head of China's PLA, or the People's Liberation Army, and the man I believe our Lieutenant Li delivered the DNA samples to after he left South America."

Both Langford and Clay leaned forward, studying the picture.

"How do we know?"

Borger displayed a second window on the screen, filled with numeric codes. "I found the logs from Li's cell phone

105

carrier and traced them back to the day he arrived. The triangulation from the cell towers isn't as exact as GPS, but he was in the building of China's Central Military Commission. That I'm sure of. I then searched and compared the coordinates until I found people whose phone locations were close to Li's. The most likely person out of that group was General Wei."

"Admiral, it appears General Wei was the one in charge of the Guyana find. I've found emails from him and others showing that he was giving the orders. And get this, the initial discovery was made almost nine months ago. It took them another six months to get there."

"Plenty of time to gut a warship."

"Right. And from what I can tell, they pulled it off with surprisingly few people knowing about it."

"Okay, so what happened to our briefcase?"

Borger frowned on screen. "That's a good question, sir. I just finished plotting the General's phone coordinates on a map. It's a little messy." A map appeared on the screen with thousands of blue dots all around or near the government center of Beijing. "I can clean this up a little, but I'm not sure if it's worth it."

"Why is that?" asked Clay.

"Because the coordinates of his phone are much more interesting *after* Lieutenant Li delivered the case." Another map suddenly replaced the first. One with fewer dots. "You can see here that most of the dots, or coordinates, are almost on top of each other until this." He circled some of the outlying dots with his mouse. "What this shows is that Wei left the building less than thirty minutes later on that day. And judging from the distance and speed of the coordinates after his departure, he was probably in a car."

Borger's mouse highlighted a string of dots moving in one direction. "This was his path until the tower lost signal."

"What does that mean...he drove out of range?"

"I don't think so, sir. I think he turned off his phone."

16

Langford raised an eyebrow. "He turned it off?"

"Yes, sir. There were a few towers he was still close enough to connect to. And even if he didn't have a strong enough voice signal, he should have been well inside the range of the control channel used for text messages. Text messages can be received farther away, which still would have allowed the towers to triangulate."

"So he receives the case from Li, immediately gets in his car and heads north, then turns off his phone." Langford's face was somber. "Then what?"

"That's where things go from strange to bizarre." Borger hesitated before continuing. "He disappeared from the grid for almost fourteen hours before his phone came back on, at roughly the same place as it went off."

"So he turned it back on?"

"Yes, sir."

Langford crossed his arms, thinking. "Do we have any indication whether he still had the case with him?"

"There's no way to know," Borger replied. "But my bet is that he didn't."

Langford nodded. "I wouldn't exactly call that bizarre. My guess is our good General hid it somewhere, or with someone."

"Uh, that's not actually the bizarre part. It's that General Wei's reappearance on the grid was short-lived, literally. He never returned home. Instead, he drove himself back to Beijing, found a parking lot, and killed himself in his car."

"What?!" Both Langford and Clay were stunned. "Are you kidding?"

"No, sir," Borger shook his head.

"Jesus," Langford groaned. "This just keeps getting

worse and worse." He looked at his screen with exasperation. "Any of this making sense to you, Clay?"

"I'm afraid not, Admiral. But I agree with Will. If this General Wei went to so much trouble to get that case and then disappeared just before ending his life, I think we can be pretty certain it wasn't with him when he came back."

This wasn't making sense to any of them.

"Why on Earth would a man with that kind of power, who now has something virtually every person on the planet wants, simply kill himself?"

"To keep it quiet," Clay mused. He looked back to Wei's picture on the screen and it suddenly fell into place. "That's it. That's the answer."

"What is?"

Clay's voice rose excitedly. "There is no coup in China's Standing Committee. It's in the Central Military Commission. General Wei is the coup!"

"Wei?"

"Wei was in charge of the find in Guyana. So he knew what they had. He had the authority to launch a strike on the Bowditch. And he also had the authority to order the sinking of their own ship *and* the Forel. He was trying to destroy the cargo. The last remaining piece was the DNA-infused bacteria in the case that Li flew back to him. Wei was systematically destroying any evidence of what they'd found."

"But why?" Langford asked. "Why destroy the one thing that could change everything?" He shook his head and thought it over, then looked back at Borger's image. "Will, if he wanted to destroy the samples, couldn't he have done that just about anywhere?"

"I suspect so."

"So why disappear with it while trying to avoid being tracked?"

"It doesn't make a lot of sense."

"It does," said Clay, "if Wei wasn't intending to destroy

109

it."

Border nodded. "For example if he were *hiding* it."

Langford folded his arms again with a stern expression. "He destroyed what he wasn't able to contain and hid the rest."

"It appears so."

"Which means that briefcase may still be within a seven-hour drive from his phone's last coordinates."

"Or less," added Borger. "If he had to sleep."

After a long silence, Langford looked back at the screen. "How's your Chinese, Clay?"

Clay was already searching for more on Wei when he looked back to Langford's image in surprise. "What?"

Langford checked his watch. "Pack your bags. I'll arrange for your ride. In the meantime, Borger, you have approximately thirteen hours to figure out exactly where Clay is going."

By 3:30 a.m. Clay was already at thirty-two thousand feet aboard the C-20D Gulfstream III. The model C-20D was the most common variant used by the U.S. Navy and retrofitted with special naval communication equipment. It was also the same aircraft which Clay and Caesare had taken to Brazil just a few weeks earlier. A trip which set in motion a chain of events that none of them could have anticipated.

Clay peered out of the small window to his left, into the morning darkness with twinkling stars above him. There was an eerie feeling inside the cabin, sitting alone listening only to the roar of the two Rolls Royce Turbofan engines outside as they rocketed the aircraft through freezing air at top speed.

The Gulfstream would have to make multiple stops to reach its final destination in Manila. It was as far as he could go without raising flags in a government plane. From there he would have to travel aboard commercial flights, first to Taiwan and finally in through Hong Kong. With the help of a falsified passport, it would be his best chance at entering China without too much attention from customs. Once inside, it would be another 1,200 miles to Beijing and hopefully enough time for Borger to narrow down his search area. Assuming the target was still there.

Clay tried again to relax and lay back against the chair's soft headrest. He struggled to imagine what had motivated General Wei to destroy or hide the treasure which his soldiers had worked so hard to recover in that jungle.

He closed his eyes and instead thought of Alison. He pictured her face, with long brown hair falling over her shoulders. Her beautiful eyes smiling back at him. He was falling for her and let himself smile as he began to drift off to sleep.

In the end, it was his exhaustion that had prevented Clay from figuring out Wei's motives that night. And when he finally did two days later, it would already be too late.

17

Alison sat in her office, thinking about John. She had been expecting a call the night before, but it never came. She wasn't overly concerned, but it was just another example of the challenges in trying to maintain a long-distance relationship, especially with *their* jobs. Still, she had no regrets. A man like John was a diamond in the rough. The kind of man every woman wished for but rarely found. There were certainly plenty of wonderful men out there. But someone had truly broken the mold after John Clay.

Her thoughts wandered back to the week they'd just spent together after returning from Trinidad. The walks on the beach holding hands, the feeling of safety she felt with him, and the way he spoke to her. They stirred emotions Alison hadn't experienced in a long time, if ever.

It made it all the more ironic that she hadn't yet realized her cell phone was still in her car. Nor that John Clay would be well over the Pacific before she discovered the voicemail he'd left while his plane was refueling in California.

With a sigh, Alison shook herself out of her daze and stood up from her chair. She rounded the desk and walked to the door where, with a quick pull, she stepped through and proceeded downstairs. Something had been haunting her since Trinidad. Something she'd been reluctant to pursue without really knowing why. So much had happened in the last few months. So much had been discovered that Alison was almost afraid of what they might learn next.

The breakthrough with Dirk and Sally was truly a miracle of modern technology. It had blown open the doors to a real, genuine conversation between the two most sentient species on the planet. But what they'd found was not just exciting, it was frightening. Frightening in its potential to disrupt what *they* as humans had assumed for so long: that somehow animals without familiar or recognizable communicative abilities were little more than cute creatures in a kingdom over which humans claimed dominion.

But now…now they had discovered not only a shocking level of understanding in Dirk and Sally's communication, but also exposed an almost shameful level of human hubris. And a level of disconnectedness with the world around them that left Alison worried for her own species. Even Alison's own personal connections were beginning to feel devoid of any true meaning. Instead, it felt like a detached view of the planet. Mistakenly superior. Materialistic. Clinical.

The truth was, Alison was growing fearful of finding out that humans might not be very *human* after all. That rather than contributing to the world as it really was, they were instead gradually destroying it under a veneer of "progress." The last thing she wanted to do was become even more disappointed in herself or her race.

Alison forced a smile and pushed open one of the doors into the observation area. She'd often thought that the dolphins, especially Sally, could almost sense her coming. Which made it all the eerier when Sally seemed to be waiting for her as she arrived.

Hello Alison.

"Good morning, Sally. How are you and Dirk?"

We happy. How you?

"I'm happy too." She was thankful the dolphins were not able to read human faces yet. Nevertheless, if Sally detected something different from Alison's response, she didn't show it.

Where Chris?

"Chris isn't here yet. He will come soon." She approached the tank and leaned against a desk just a few feet from the giant glass wall.

Chris funny. Dirk replied as he glided in.

"Yes, he is."

113

Alison paused, thinking how best to begin. Starting with the journey seemed a logical place. Especially since it had turned out to be much more than any of them expected.

"Sally, Dirk. I'd like to ask you some questions."

Yes Alison. We talk.

"How…often do you go on your journey?"

Many.

She frowned, suspecting IMIS had mistranslated. "I mean, how many times in a year?"

One.

Alison knew the match for "year" was what the dolphins referred to as a "cycle."

"One every cycle?"

Yes.

"Why do you go?"

Journey beautiful.

"Yes, it is."

She couldn't argue with that. Diving with them near the island of Trinidad was beyond beautiful. An underwater oasis like nothing the team had ever seen.

And the population of dolphins there was simply breathtaking. Thousands, tens of thousands, maybe even hundreds covered the surface of the ocean like a giant, moving sea blanket.

"So, you go because it's beautiful?"

We go for connect. For strong.

"For connect?"

Yes. And for strong.

It was the first time Alison had seen that word translated: connect. But it verified what she had suspected. It wasn't just a journey they carried out every year, it was a migration of some kind. A return to something deeper and more meaningful to them. And not just individually, but collectively. As a group. It was *culture!*

She stared at the screen, reading the translation again. What did "for strong" mean? To strongly connect? For a stronger connection?

"Sally," she asked. What is so special about your place?"

A beep sounded and IMIS flagged the word "special." She rephrased.

"Why do dolphins go to that place?"

Place from live.

Alison frowned, unclear on the meaning.

"I don't understand."

Place from live. Sally repeated. *One cycle.*

Alison mumbled to herself, trying to understand. "Yes, every cycle. I understand that."

Live.

"I don't understand." She shook her head. Still at a loss, she decided to try another question. "Sally. Dirk. How far back do you remember?"

The room became silent while she waited for a response. When nothing came, she glanced at the computer screen to see if there was a problem. No errors. "Sally? Dirk?"

No understand Alison. Dirk replied.

Alison opened her mouth to say it a different way but stopped abruptly. Rephrasing the question suddenly appeared more difficult than she thought.

"I mean, how do your-" she stopped again. *Dammit. How the hell would someone describe a memory?*

"Sally. Dirk. Do you know yesterday?"

Yes.

"Do you know yesterday yesterday?"

Yes. Yes. Dirk followed his response with a laugh. Alison frowned again.

"I mean, do you know yesterday's yesterday?"

Yes.

"Do you know yesterday's yesterday's yesterday?"

On the other side of the glass, Sally's dark eyes glanced at Dirk and then back at Alison. She wondered if Alison were joking herself.

Three day back. Yes.

115

From the edge of the desk, Alison smiled. "Do you know ten days back?"

This time Sally's response came quickly. *Alison you play?*

"No, I'm not playing."

Dirk edged closer to her. *Yes Alison. We know ten day. We know hundred day. We know all day. You question funny.*

Alison grinned. "How many days back do you know?"

All day.

"How many cycles back?"

All cycle.

"More than a hundred?"

Yes.

Finally, Alison asked the question she had been trying to work toward. "*How* do you know more than a hundred cycles back?"

Sally's response was exactly what Alison was hoping for.

Heads.

"You mean your elders?"

Yes. Heads.

"You know from your heads? Do they teach you?"

Yes. Heads teach all.

How many elders are there?

Many.

Alison stared at them, momentarily transfixed. Their elders taught them. And they taught them things *older* than they were. Her excitement was swelling. If what Sally and Dirk just told her was correct, it was big. Huge. It meant that dolphins had more than just language and culture. They had *history*!

Alison remained quiet, excitedly thinking through the impact of what Dirk and Sally had just said. More questions began filling her head. If there was a historical lineage, it meant a cognitive progression. More than just memories or culture, it explained why their intelligence was so much more advanced than many other animals. Real *knowledge* had many components, not the least of which were lessons or learnings passed down through multiple generations. Knowledge that could lead in so many different directions.

Alison was looking for a pen and paper when she was suddenly interrupted.

"Miss Alison!"

She spun around to find Bruna behind her, eyes wide with excitement.

"Bruna. Is something wrong?"

"Miss Alison. Come! Come quickly!"

"What is it?"

"Come! Come!"

Alison pushed away from the desk only to watch Bruna turn and rush back toward the entrance. She instinctively fell in behind her, trotting until they reached the doorway.

Bruna promptly opened one of the large doors and disappeared.

Alison caught the door before it closed, pulling it open again to peer down the hall. All she could see was Bruna hurrying away and quickly disappearing around the far corner.

When Alison caught up, coming around the same corner, she stopped dead in her tracks.

There in front of her in the lobby stood Lara and Ricardo Santiago, the parents of young Sofia. They were standing side by side. Lara's eyes were red and swollen from crying.

Alison stared at them. Her face suddenly drawn. *Oh no. Not Sofia. Not already!*

"Mr. and Mrs. Ricardo," her voice trembled. "W-what is it?"

Lara Ricardo gulped back a sob and looked at her husband. Without a word she turned slightly and took a step to the side. There was someone standing behind her. It was Sofia.

Alison was overwhelmed with relief, a feeling that was

immediately replaced by astonishment. Sofia was not just behind her parents. With the help of crutches, she was actually *standing!*

There was a loud gasp behind Alison at which point she turned to find DeeAnn, stunned and frozen with her own mouth open.

"Sofia! You're standing!"

Balancing carefully between the metal crutches, the young girl was beaming at both women. Next to Sophia, her mother began crying again.

"She's getting stronger!"

18

Minutes later, Alison was sprinting at full speed back down the hallway. She burst through the double doors and continued across the room where she raced up the wide stairs. At the top, she continued until she reached the lab. In one motion she yanked the door open and rushed in, finding all three of the guys at Lee's desk.

"Something wrong?"

She didn't respond. Instead, she quickly crossed the room. Their expressions grew more concerned as she approached.

When she reached the desk, her eyes were on Chris, gazing at his face. She examined both cheeks and stepped back. "Take off your shirt."

"What?"

"Take off your shirt!"

He blinked and shot a confused look at Lee and Juan. "Wh-why do you want me to take off my shirt?"

"TAKE IT OFF!"

Chris jumped. He promptly raised his hands and pulled his white polo shirt up and over his head, revealing his olive-colored chest and stomach. The latter was carrying about ten pounds too many.

He stood waiting. "Happy?"

Alison examined his front and then spun him sideways to see his back. "Your bruises are gone."

"Yes, Ali. It's called healing."

She turned her gaze to Lee, who was also standing. "And what about you?"

He instinctively raised his hands when she stepped toward him. "Whoa! Whoa!" he grinned. "I'm married."

"Quiet." She closed in to place her hand on his side then

pressed gently. There was no reaction. "What happened to your ribs?!"

Lee shrugged. "They're better."

"Ribs don't heal that fast!"

"Maybe I have good bones."

"It's not the bones, Lee. It's all the muscles around them. They should take months longer to heal."

"Well, I guess it wasn't as bad as they thought."

She didn't answer. Instead she glanced at the younger Juan, causing him to jump back. "I'm good!"

"Ali-" Before Chris could finish his sentence, Alison was already rushing back to the door. Once outside, she ran to the stairs and descended as fast as she could.

From the tank, Dirk and Sally noticed Alison rush back down the stairs. They continued watching as she crossed the room and grabbed her bag off a nearby table.

She rummaged through it and looked up, frustrated. She said something that IMIS couldn't translate. She was clearly upset.

Her phone was still in her car, *damn it*. Alison thought for a moment, finally raising her eyes to the tank and to Dirk and Sally on the other side. They were observing her carefully.

She stepped forward and placed her hands on her hips. "Why don't you have a word for sick?!"

It was a rhetorical question, but Sally drifted closer and replied.

We have Alison.

"No! Not injured…I mean sick! Like a cold, or a virus…or a *disease*!"

Sally stared at her.

No understand Alison. You not happy?

She folded her arms in front of her, catching her breath. "It's hard to explain."

Alison you mad?

"No, Dirk. I'm not mad. I-" She stopped when she saw an image appear in the reflection behind her and turned to face a solemn DeeAnn Draper. She reached back to turn off the voice translation.

"Something weird is happening."

DeeAnn nodded. "I'll say. Sofia is suddenly standing just two days after we saw her."

"That's not all. Chris's bruises are gone and Lee can't feel his injuries anymore either."

"What's going on here, Alison?"

"I don't know." She fell quiet, thinking. The truth was she *did* know. She knew what Clay and Caesare had found in the jungle. What the Chinese had found. Those plants. The same plants Neely Lawton was studying aboard the Bowditch when it sank. Plants with a mysterious piece of DNA that allowed them to regenerate at an accelerated rate. But she couldn't see or understand how those abilities could possibly be connected with them, or for that matter, Sofia.

None of them had come in contact with the sample Lawton had shown them in her lab. In fact, Chris and Lee hadn't even been in the lab. Which meant that Alison was the variable.

Was it possible she'd come in contact with the bacteria without realizing it? She couldn't see how.

Alison began backing herself out of her thought process. If there was no link then what was happening to them now had to be unrelated. Something different. But what else could explain it? If Sofia was suddenly healing too, what could cause it in all three of them at the same time?

She looked at her own arm again. She'd already removed the bandage but raised her wrist and yet again moved it back and forth. There was still no pain in either direction. *What was happening?!*

DeeAnn was watching her, silently. Finally, she frowned and took a deep breath. "I guess you'd better tell me what you all found up on that mountain."

"What?"

"What you and Steve wanted to tell me the other day."

"I thought you didn't want to know."

"I've changed my mind."

"Just like that?"

"Yes. Just like that."

"Does that mean you're going with Steve?"

"It means I want to know more before I decide."

"Okay," Alison nodded. "Then you may want to sit down."

DeeAnn smiled, but when she realized Alison was serious she grabbed a chair from next to the table, lowering herself into it.

Still standing and with arms crossed, Alison thought for a moment. "You remember when we were all on Alves' helicopter?"

"Of course. I woke up when John and Steve were raiding the inside."

"That's right. Unfortunately, things changed when we left the helicopter. We were able to track those compounds back to the source, where a high concentration originated near a cliff wall. But the water wasn't coming down the wall. It was coming from *within* it."

"Within the wall?"

"Yes."

"You mean like inside the rock?"

"I mean like on the other side of it. There was a cavern carved inside of the mountain, Dee. And the wall was a giant door."

"What do you mean the wall was a door?"

"I mean the wall *opened*!"

"What?"

"The cliff wall. It opened. And on the other side there

122

was a giant room. The water had leaked inside and by the time it seeped back out, it was changed."

"Changed how?"

Alison took a deep breath. "Okay, this is the part that might sound a little...hard to believe. Inside the wall were giant columns. All standing like pillars in this pitch-black cavern. They were made of some kind of glass because you could see what was inside them. It was a greenish-looking liquid and each of the columns were holding thousands of little spheres inside, like large bubbles. And inside those spheres were what looked to be seeds...and embryos."

DeeAnn raised her eyebrows and spoke slowly. "Did you say *embryos*?"

"Yes."

"You found embryos hidden inside this place?!"

"Thousands. Maybe tens of thousands. And that water was seeping inside and being changed by those things. The same water that changed those plants after seeping back outside."

From her chair, DeeAnn stared motionlessly up at Alison, her large eyes blinking repeatedly.

"The water wasn't the source. The source was the things inside that giant cave. The columns and whatever was inside them." Alison lowered her voice without realizing it. "The Chinese found the plants, Dee. They grabbed as much as they could and then burned the rest. But I don't think they knew about the water. And they sure as hell didn't know what was hidden in that cliff."

"So who put it there?"

"We don't know," Alison said. "But whoever it was ...wasn't us."

DeeAnn's eyes opened wide. "*Wasn't us?*"

"They couldn't have been. Dee, these things were advanced. I mean *really* advanced. Even Will Borger couldn't believe it. And there was enough dust on the ground to tell me that no one had been in there for a looong time."

"How long?"

"Long. Hundreds of years, at least. Maybe thousands."

DeeAnn was having as much trouble processing it as they had. "But...why? Why would someone...or something...put that there?"

"Will thinks it's some kind of vault, from another species. Put here to ensure their DNA survives forever. He said scientists have already done something like it up north, in Norway, I think."

"A vault," DeeAnn mumbled incredulously. "An embryo vault."

"Steve Caesare calls it something else...an alien ARK."

DeeAnn gasped. "Holy-"

"That puts it in a different perspective, doesn't it?"

"My God," she whispered. "An *ark*?"

Alison nodded. "But instead of sending animals, they sent embryos. And seeds. Will thinks the liquid inside the tubes is some kind of nutrient, keeping them all alive." She lowered herself onto the edge of the table. "Now you can understand why Steve is going back. Because somehow what ended up in that water, and those plants, also ended up in that little capuchin monkey."

"That's why he's so old," DeeAnn whispered, incredulous.

"That's the theory. The plants were destroyed, but the DNA strain is likely still preserved in the monkey. And since our DNA is so similar to his, it may also be transferrable."

DeeAnn dropped her gaze to the table, shaking her head. She was stunned. After several seconds, she looked back at Alison. "Okay, wait. What does all that have to do with us, and Sofia?"

"I don't know. The effects seem too similar not to be related, but I can't understand how we would have picked it up. Maybe the water was trickling down to the ocean or something?"

"Wouldn't that mean you'd then have these giant plants popping up all the way down to the coast?"

"Probably. Which means it has to be something else."

"Right. Besides, once it got into the ocean, you'd probably have everything growing like crazy underwater too. Maybe-" DeeAnn shrugged, but suddenly fell quiet when she looked back at Alison, whose jaw had dropped and her face had begun losing color.

"Oh my God!"

"What?"

"OH MY GOD!"

DeeAnn looked confused. "What? What is it?"

Alison leaped up. "It IS in the water! The ocean!" She spun around to face Dirk and Sally, who were still watching them. "I SAW it! I saw it and didn't even realize!" She peered up at the top of the enormous tank. "That's it!"

"What's it?"

"Don't you see?!" Alison cried. "Sofia! None of the guys were in the water with her. Only me. But I'm not the one who brought it back. It was DIRK AND SALLY WHO BROUGHT IT BACK!"

"Holy cow."

"Holy cow is right!" Alison grabbed her backpack again and dug into the small pocket in the front, retrieving her car keys. She then dropped the pack and began running for the door.

"Where are you going?"

"To get my phone!"

19

The Florida Everglades was truly a sight to behold for anyone seeing it for the first time. Spanning nearly half the state, the Everglades rested upon a large limestone shelf, causing water leaving enormous Lake Okeechobee to form a slow moving *river* stretching more than sixty miles wide and one hundred miles long — a river flowing steadily through vast sawgrass marshes and mangrove forests to the southern half of the state. That was where it emptied into Florida Bay and the Caribbean Sea beyond.

Now, over a century after the first large-scale projects were proposed, a network of over 1,400 miles of canals and levees were harnessing a huge portion of the Everglade's massive water supply. The result of which were dozens of modern cities that could never have existed without a huge, yet shallow, river called the Everglades.

The late morning air was growing warmer from the southwesterly wind blowing gently through the endless marshes, leaving behind only slight ripples across the clear, shallow water. Too slight, in fact, to affect the fifteen-foot-long canoe gliding smoothly in and around one of many mangrove systems.

The lone woman held her paddle steady on one side, turning back out into the small channel before switching sides and rounding another outcropping. The tangled roots jutted far out across the water, slowly making their own crossing as if trying to reunite with those on the other side.

The mysterious Everglades was her favorite place in the world after studying for four years at the nearby University of Miami. She'd spent weeks at a time deep in the Everglades studying its vastly complicated ecosystem and biological systems. And the deeper she went, the more beautiful it all became.

The woman paddled slowly among the trees, allowing the canoe to coast against the soft ripples as she examined a sprawling manchineel tree, reaching ominously from the bank. The manchineel was one of the deadliest trees in the world, native to Florida. Its leaves were highly toxic as was its small flowering fruit, resembling a small apple. The tree was legendary for its poisonous sap, used for centuries by Carib Indians to poison the tips of their arrows, ensuring a long agonizing death for their enemies. A poison which held perhaps the most tragic and ironic reputation in history, being used to kill in battle the famed explorer Juan Ponce de León, who was searching for the legendary fountain of youth.

The manchineel was also the tree on which she had done her senior thesis. She was fascinated by the sheer power of its biological design, and deadly toxins, all wrapped in a cocoon of natural beauty and innocence. A plant-based eukaryote that could destroy an animal eukaryote so quickly, from a single brush, that it was one of the closest things she'd seen to an evolutionary anomaly. It was not the only poisonous plant in the world, but its efficacy and speed of eukaryote destruction put it in a class all its own.

The universe was balanced. Of that, she was sure. There was no existence of light without darkness or heat without cold. No death without life. Contraction and expansion, amorphous and formed, the list went on and on. What truly fascinated her about the manchineel tree was the *rarity* of those toxins coming together in an evolutionary process creating something so deadly. Including some toxins which still remained unidentified.

To her, it was proof that even the longest biological odds existed somewhere. And if one organism had evolved into a nearly perfect killer, its very existence suggested there could be another, somewhere, that had evolved into the perfect healer. An organism whose existence was just as much an anomaly as the manchineel tree.

And she thought she'd found it. No, she was sure she had found it. But so had someone else and the events that unfolded as a result were devastating. She'd briefly had in her hands the greatest biological anomaly in history, just days before it all came to a violent end.

She was aboard the Bowditch when it sank in a twisted heap of fire and steel. She was one of the crewmembers who made it off in time, thanks to one man who, in the face of the worst possible situation, still managed to save most of the lives on his ship. The same man who died trying to save his chief engineer below deck. In the end, the Captain was the greatest hero she had ever seen. And he was more than just a captain, he was her *father*. A father who didn't just save his crew…but one who stood between death and his own daughter, and won.

Her eyes began to well up again as she pulled the paddle up and onto her lap, allowing the canoe to slow to a stop again, against the water's soft ebbing.

Her father was gone. Her hero. Her dad.

Neely Lawton's tears came again, as though they would never end. A week alone in the solitude of her Everglades still wasn't enough to help heal her broken heart. She knew it would take time and yet she still didn't want to let go. She didn't want him to simply become a memory, or images she thought of periodically. She didn't want him to fade.

She sat listlessly in the channel, listening to the subtle sounds of the earth around her — the chirping birds and the trickling of the water around the worn hull of her canoe. In front of her knees sat her pack and tent, neatly bundled.

Neely had remained motionless against a large mangrove shoot for nearly thirty minutes when she heard it. The sound of an engine approaching. It had a distinct pitch which told her it was an airboat, a common craft in Florida used in shallow waters. And she was surprised to hear it.

Neely was *miles* from the larger lakes and channels. She

hadn't seen a soul for days, which filled her with a sense of both curiosity and concern.

It was unlikely to just happen upon someone that far up the Watson River, but the sound of the engine told Neely that the craft was headed straight for her.

She hadn't seen anyone…but it didn't mean someone had not seen her.

Someone *had* seen her. Someone she was about to wish had not.

Sitting on tall seats atop an old and dingy airboat, Sal and Jered Hicks had grown up in the backwoods and swamps of Southern Florida. Brothers who both had spent the better part of their lives among the unpatrolled waters of the northwestern Everglades hunting anything they could sell on the black market, protected or not. Yet the Glades provided something far more important to the brothers than just a source of poached alligators. It provided obscurity. The ability to simply disappear within the jungle-like terrain for months at a time. Especially when people might be looking for them. To the Hicks brothers, the state of Florida's greatest natural treasure was the ultimate protection to its inhabitants from the world outside.

Sal and Jered spotted the red canoe earlier that morning and had been quietly following it until they were sure the woman was alone. Because once they started the engine, they had to move fast.

Neely leaned forward as the boat sped into view around a nearby embankment. Two men were aboard. Each was dressed in a T-shirt and shorts with one donning a large camouflage hat, the wide circling brim hiding much of his unshaven face. The second man looked to be wearing a similarly sized, and seemingly dirtier, straw hat.

As they roared down the channel toward her, she could hear the throttle ease up, causing the boat to dip forward and begin slowing. When the men were within two hundred feet, they dropped the engine to an idle and examined Neely as the last of their boat's momentum took them the rest of the way.

The short-bearded man at the controls smiled under his straw hat. "Howdy."

Neely's response was reserved. "Hello."

"What's a perty thing like you doing way out here? You lost?"

"No."

"You sure?"

Her eyes left the first visitor and were now watching the man whose face was partially concealed.

"I'm sure."

The pilot of the craft nodded and scooted in his seat, turning around and scanning the area. "I don't see any friends. I hope yer not alone out here all by yerself. Lot a nasty things crawling around out here, worse than gators and crocs."

"I'm fine."

"You want us to tow you in? Be a lot faster."

"Really, I'm fine. Thanks."

The pilot nodded again and scanned behind them a second time. He turned to his brother Jered, who was watching the woman with his dark eyes. Without a word, Jered lowered his hand and dropped his empty beer can onto the already littered floor of their boat. His foot was resting on the top of a dirty ice cooler, held in place by an even dirtier and fraying bungee cord.

A smile slowly spread across his thin lips. "I guess she doesn't want a tow."

"I said I was fine."

Her response caused Jered's smile to widen, exposing a set of yellowed teeth. "She says she's fine."

The larger and fatter Sal shook his head. "I don't think she knows what a dangerous place it is out here." His eyes peered intently at Neely. "Why, there's gators out here big enough to-" He suddenly stopped when he noticed her position.

Her body was leaning forward as though supporting herself with a hand on the forward seat. But her hand wasn't on the seat. Instead it was just a few inches farther, resting inside the opening to her pack.

"What you got there, girl?"

Jered noticed it too and continued smiling. "I don't think your phone is going to work out here."

She watched quietly as both men laughed. Jered nodded and stood up out of his chair, approaching the front edge of the flat-bottom boat. The engine was still idling as the craft inched slowly forward, leaving less than fifteen feet between the two boats.

Sal responded to his brother's nod by reaching down for the throttle. Another quick blast of air would push them within reach of the canoe.

But just as Sal's hand fell onto the metal knob, his entire body abruptly froze at the sight of Neely sliding a gun out of her bag, her hand wrapped firmly around the handle.

Her index finger was resting just above the trigger of a nickel-plated 9mm Sig Sauer, the 1911 her father had given her after graduating from Officer Training Command.

Her eyes remained fixed on Jered, who was now leaning toward her and had been waiting for his brother to push them forward. Instead, his eyes widened when he too noticed the bright glint of the gun's barrel. He immediately straightened and looked back up to her face where her gray-blue eyes stared at him, unblinking.

His hands shot up in front of his chest. "Whoa. Easy, sweetheart. We're just being friendly now, right?" He turned to Sal who still wasn't moving either.

"T-that's right. It's a long way back. Just thought it'd be

gentlemanly if we gave you a hand."

"I don't need a hand."

"We can see that."

Jered calmly glanced down at a large duffle bag beneath his seat. Inside was his own gun. He had put it away to avoid getting it wet. Now he wished he hadn't. He was also wondering how quickly he could retrieve it. It was loaded and ready.

The two men stared at each other with the same thought. They'd been in scrapes before…far worse than this. They exchanged a knowing look that *just because a woman had a gun didn't mean she knew how to use it*.

They were considering their options when Neely unexpectedly reached into the bag with her free hand and retrieved another item. This time, it was a piece of clothing, and it was about to put an end to any thoughts the two had of escalating this confrontation.

She calmly pulled out a dark blue baseball hat and pulled it over her head from back to front. Above the cap's bill were four large, unmistakable white letters.

N-A-V-Y.

Both men's expressions changed instantly. This woman clearly knew how to use the gun in her hand.

"She doesn't want any help, J."

Jered nodded his head and stepped back from the front edge of their boat. Behind him, his brother throttled up and turned the vertical rudders, twisting the fanboat into a hard turn. It slowly curved away from the canoe and continued a 180-degree turn, just clearing the embankment on the far side of the channel. Once clear of another mangrove patch, their engine and fan emitted a deafening roar and accelerated the craft back along the path from which they came.

The burst of hot air, coupled with the smell of grease and gasoline, washed over Neely as she watched their retreat. Her heart was pounding in her chest and a bead of sweat escaped from under the cap, running down past her left ear.

She hadn't been that frightened in a long time.

Hours later, Neely Lawton rounded the river's mouth in her canoe. She was heading for Tarpon Creek, situated on the southeast end of Whitewater Bay. She took a break and glanced at the sun, which was beginning its descent into another stunning Everglade sunset. As she stretched her back, Neely watched dozens of birds take flight into the warm, windless sky. Near the edge of the water, an alligator watched her intently with only its eyes and nose protruding above the surface.

She wasn't going to make it. It was still too far to Tarpon, which meant another night on one of the chickee platforms. Something she was trying to avoid given her inauspicious morning. The fear that the two men might still be watching her would make sleeping almost impossible. It was going to be a very long night.

Then suddenly, her cell phone rang from inside her heavy pack. She was back in range again. Neely dropped the paddle at her feet and quickly dug the phone out of her bag before it went to voicemail. The number on the screen was unknown.

"Neely Lawton."

"Neely, hi. This is Alison Shaw. We met a few weeks ago on the-"

"I remember you, Alison. How are you?"

"I'm fine. How are *you*?"

Neely gazed across the bay, its still water reflecting the azure sky above it like a mirror. "It's been a mixed day. What can I do for you?"

"Well, actually, if you have some time I need to talk to you about something. Something important."

Neely leaned back in her seat and stretched her legs out. "I have a lot of time at the moment." She paused, thinking.

"How did you get a hold of me?"

"Through Admiral Langford."

"Admiral Langford?"

"Yes."

"Wow. Okay then...shoot."

She heard Alison take a breath on the other end.

"It's about something you mentioned the last time we talked. About what happened in Guyana. More specifically, the plants you were examining aboard the ship."

"Okay."

"Well, the thing is," Alison said, "I think I'm seeing something similar here."

Neely's eyes widened. "What? Where?!"

"In Puerto Rico. Here in my lab."

"Puerto Rico?"

"Yes. At our research center."

"What kind of-"

Alison stopped her. "It's a long story, and probably too much to try to explain on the phone. But I'm wondering if you could make a trip down here. We could use your help."

"Yes," she answered immediately. "Yes, I can." Neely suddenly paused, realizing where she was. "Um, it may take a little time to get there. I'm not exactly close to an airport."

"That should not be a problem. I think Admiral Langford is dispatching a ride for you."

"Does he even know where I am?"

"He said he had Will Borger searching for you. I'm guessing that probably won't take him very long."

Neely smiled on the other end. It was the first smile in what felt like a very long time, and she had to admit it felt good. "Well, Alison. I must admit, your timing probably could not be better."

From her chair, DeeAnn watched Alison as she ended the call. "So you called in your favor."

134

"I had to."

DeeAnn nodded. She looked past Alison to the double doors leading to the lobby.

Alison followed her gaze with a curious look. "What is it?"

"Sofia." DeeAnn looked back. "I've been thinking about her since she first came here and especially after seeing her now." She looked down at the table, wiping it absently with her hand. "I keep thinking about her in that wheelchair, knowing that the end was coming and yet still fighting. She wasn't ready to give up a single moment. At least not willingly."

Alison grinned. "That's true."

DeeAnn shook her head. "Can you imagine how afraid she's been? Every hour of every day, knowing what's coming? And she's *still* fighting." She turned to Alison incredulously. "She's eight, Alison. Eight!"

"Yet here I am. At my age, afraid of what might happen by going back into that jungle. But Sofia *knows* what's going to happen. I am trying to hide…while that girl is trying to *live*. Do you know how small that makes me feel? Or how horrible?"

"We all have to live our own lives, Dee. We have to make our own decisions."

DeeAnn shrugged. "And now Steve is going back, trying to protect something that may cause almost unimaginable ramifications, both good and bad. Something that any country would probably kill over. And now what if that something was actually able to help Sofia? What if it were able to help others like her?"

Alison didn't answer.

"So, say something does happen to me, Ali. Exactly how many more lives is mine worth? And even worse, what happens to them if Steve fails…because I wouldn't help?"

"I don't think it's that easy," Alison replied softly.

"No? Then please tell me how I look someone like Sofia

in the eyes from now on, after I refused to go?"

DeeAnn remained quiet, allowing the room to fall silent before she finally leaned forward and stood up.

Alison's eyes widened. "So…are you saying, you're going with Steve?"

"Not without talking to Juan first."

20

The small base which housed the infamous Naval Special Warfare Development Group (NSWDG), also known as DEVGRU, was smaller than most would imagine. It was also quieter, located on fewer than fifteen acres, and hosted a dozen buildings of varying sizes. The legendary base was also less elaborate than its reputation suggested, but what it lacked in visual awe from the outside, it more than made up for inside.

Less than four miles due south of Virginia Beach, the home of NSWDG in Dam Neck, Virginia, was rumored to have an operational training budget almost surpassing that of the entire U.S. Marine Corps. This guaranteed that the team once known as SEAL Team Six had access to the most modern weapons and fighting technology available on the planet. And the training areas both inside and below ground proved it.

It was also here, in the base's southernmost and largely nondescript building, where Steve Caesare stared down at a large 3D tabletop image before him. Resting his hands on either side, he was shaking his head slowly. *This was going to be difficult.*

Serious missions were usually planned by multiple SEAL operators to ensure every conceivable scenario and logistical detail was considered. But this time Caesare and his men were on their own. Under direct orders from Admiral Langford, they were instructed to get in and out with the least number of people knowing, no matter what resources it took. Whatever they needed, Langford would get.

But resources weren't the problem. In fact, Caesare was sure that no material item in the world, short of an invisibility cloak, was going to help them here.

The large Italian mused at his last thought, knowing the DoD was actually working on that very idea. It was done by bending light with fiber optics, but it was still decades away. All he knew was that a cloak like that would be damn handy about now.

Another problem was their inability to rehearse the mission prior to execution. Rehearsals were something SEALs did without fail, followed by a thorough debrief. This was the first mission the three younger team members would have without the benefit of either, and the concern was obvious on their chiseled faces.

Facing Caesare on all sides, Corso, Anderson, and Tiewater stood around the table, coming to similar conclusions. Ignoring the fact that they'd never been sent to rescue a primate before, the logistics involved in getting in and out unseen were problematic at best. And that was putting it mildly.

An army from Brazil's Eighth Military Region was mobilizing at its base in Belem, the nearest base to the Acarai Mountains. According to reports from Will Borger, the Guyana government was furious over what the Chinese had done and were denying all requests asking for access to the area. And as facts inevitably began leaking out, their neighbors Venezuela and Suriname were doing the same.

Venezuela was out as an entry point for obvious reasons, and any other airport large enough for military aircraft was now asking questions too. And many of the smaller airports were as well. But even if they could make it in, ground transportation was another problem. There were only two usable roads, each on either side of the mountain, both long and treacherous. Tiago Otero and his army would be coming up the south side, leaving the only road available as the one that ended in Guyana's capital city of Georgetown. It was the same road the Chinese had carved into the mountain to get their treasure out, and it was already populated with local agencies investigating exactly what had

138

happened at Acarai.

The chances of Caesare's team getting to the top undetected were growing slimmer by the hour.

The partial 3D map in front of them displayed the area in impressive detail, including the multitude of surrounding peaks and elevations, displayed with tiny white numbers hovering over each peak.

"We'd still need two vehicles," Corso said in a deep voice. "And extra fuel to make it up."

He was right. That much uphill driving would require extra fuel. They could ditch the cans once they reached the top, but it still meant less space for gear. They'd need a second vehicle, which would provide some redundancy in case they ran into mechanical problems, but it also increased their chances of being spotted.

Standing to Caesare's right, Tiewater shook his head. "It's not gonna work. Even if we got transportation, there's no way we'd make it to the top without being stopped."

Caesare straightened and folded his arms. He was right. They wouldn't have much problem disappearing once at the top, but it wouldn't matter if they didn't make it up first.

"Maybe we need a diversion."

"Better be a damn good one," Corso shrugged. "If they're stopping flights in and out, it means they're already suspicious."

Caesare frowned. "And if they have any brains at all, they know a lot of people are already looking for other ways in."

Anderson, the youngest of the four, was still staring at the map. "Christ, we haven't even left yet and this thing's already FUBAR."

Caesare's phone rang in his pocket. He pulled it out and raised an eyebrow at the number. "Caesare here."

After a moment, he glanced up at the other men. "Well, hi there." He paused, listening. "That's good news…how soon?" He checked his watch. "Great. We'll be there."

He hung up and turned his attention back to the men around the table. "It looks like they're in."

"Draper and the monkey?"

"Gorilla," Caesare corrected. "And Juan Diaz, one of their tech guys."

"Sounds like we got ourselves a full house."

Caesare nodded pensively, his eyes back on the digital map. "Yes, it does."

They weren't expecting Diaz, but it made sense. However, given their difficulty finding a way into the jungle undetected, an extra person was going to make it that much harder.

The only option he could see was trying to get into the jungle from the West. It was a significantly longer distance though, which meant it was a long shot. Yet even if they managed to make it in, it immediately presented a much bigger problem. Getting back out.

The option was feeling like a scenario in definition only. Because he was pretty damn sure that both DeeAnn *and* Juan were going to hate the only insertion possibility he had so far.

21

At that same moment, Steve Caesare's bigger problem was sitting comfortably in a leather chair, peering out a double-paned window at the scene unfolding below him. From the air-conditioned third floor, Otero watched as over a hundred Brazilian soldiers assembled on the vast expanse of concrete outside.

So much for subtly.

Several covered trucks, all painted in the dark green colors of the Exército Brasileiro, also known as the land arm of the Brazilian Armed Forces, remained motionless nearby. Already parked beside the row of transport trucks were two medium-sized fuel trucks, with more on their way. The logistical challenges weren't so much the men, it was the supplies. Transporting food, water, fuel, and even ammunition, was a herculean task, especially over a narrow road hundreds of kilometers long.

Even Otero knew that an army's supply chain was the most critical, and most vulnerable, component of any mission. But he also knew things didn't have to take so damn long.

He had managed to obtain an entire *company*, which involved pulling out all of Otero's political stops. But now, his goal of keeping things quiet was hopelessly lost, leaving Otero shaking his head in frustration. Miraculously, most people believed that a government's "bloat" somehow failed to transfer through to its military forces. How wrong they were. All bloat ran downhill, no matter what the nation. And it was something Otero was painfully witnessing firsthand.

If the Brazilian government ever tried to run itself like a business, they would find themselves bankrupt. Otero promptly caught himself, almost laughing at his own thought. The Brazilian government was *already* bankrupt.

Russo, Otero's head of security, approached from behind. "Salazar is here."

The older man continued peering forward as if not hearing but eventually turned his head. "Wonderful."

A grin spread across Russo's face, and he moved next to the large window. He watched the soldiers outside with a sense of nostalgia. Something Otero didn't share.

Unlike his boss, Russo had himself started in the army. At that very base. It was in Belem that he had completed his training to become an infantry officer and subsequently led his first platoon during the last year of the Araguaia Guerrilla War.

But Otero had no such fondness for the base or its soldiers. He had never been in the military. To Russo, he was little more than a rich politician. Or perhaps a businessman with extremely deep pockets. Pockets, of course, that also paid Russo's rather generous salary, especially given Brazil's current economic climate.

"This is not what I wanted," Otero murmured from the chair.

Russo nodded. "It's going to make things messy."

"Messy is an understatement."

Both men heard the click of the door opening behind them, followed moments later by a louder clunk when it was closed.

Wearing his perfectly pressed uniform, a stout and balding Captain Salazar continued into the expansive meeting room, rounding the arm of a chair with a wry grin.

"Mr. Otero. So good to see you," he said in a sullen voice. He reached out and offered his hand.

Otero shook it from his position but remained seated. It was a clear gesture to the Army Captain.

The truth was that neither man liked the other. Not a surprise given both their roles within a deeply corrupted

142

government. Just as it was in neighboring countries, the military complex was quickly eroding into an "every man for himself" mentality, and Salazar was the very personification of it. Thankfully some government structure still remained, but given Otero's urgency, Salazar and his company were the only available option.

"When will we be ready?"

"About four hours," Salazar answered, between tight lips. "But it will take at least two days to arrive. Hundreds of kilometers on that road will not be fast. And once we're past Sipaliwini, we don't know the full condition of the road."

Otero nodded but said nothing. He wondered if he'd made a mistake not taking Alves' approach and flying up in a helicopter. It would have cut the trip down to a few hours, but it also would have meant taking only a very small group of men. Most likely not enough to find what they were looking for. No, Alves had held a huge advantage, which was having the monkey in his possession already. Now, finding the thing in the wild was going to require every man he could get.

Otero turned back and continued watching the soldiers loading their trucks in the sweltering heat. He had no choice but to make do. If they could leave today, they might still arrive before anyone else knew what they were up to. Then secure the area to keep everyone else out.

And if things got messy, he had a plan to clean it all up once he had what he was after. A plan that would also make this the last mission for Salazar and most of his men.

Putting his distaste for the man aside, Salazar and his men were little more than resources to Otero now. Resources that would help him seize the ultimate prize. And one which, thanks to a dead Alves and Blanco, no one else appeared to know about.

Otero took a deep breath and leaned his head back against the chair's headrest.

Standing at the glass, Salazar continued watching his men

in silence with his hands clasped behind his back. It was imperative to maintain a relaxed appearance in front of Otero. For what the billionaire didn't know was that Salazar had a plan of his own: direct orders on what to do when he had Otero alone on the mountain. The old man was about to find out that his money and influence only went so far.

22

It took six hours before the convoy of trucks was finally moving. In tight formation, they headed due south past Tucurui, crossing its half-mile-wide river. From there, their route turned northwest over highway BR-230, also known as Brazil's infamous Trans-Amazonian Highway.

Extending more than 4,000 kilometers through the heart of northern Brazil, the highway was conceived in the 1970s as a means of integrating the northern states with the rest of the country. However, the project came to an abrupt halt when later in the same decade the Brazilian Financial Crisis left behind a devastated economy and vast stretches of the new highway completely unpaved.

Salazar's lead car, a deep-green painted Humvee, was followed by Otero and Russo in a white Land Rover, driven by one of Russo's men and another ex-military type named Dutra.

One by one, the stream of powerful belching trucks bounced over the rough dirt road, attracting little attention as they passed through increasingly smaller towns. Trains of military vehicles had become almost commonplace with yet another deteriorating economy. And like many floundering governments desperate to retain control of their populations, various aspects of martial law were already common throughout much of Brazilian life.

The convoy was headed for the northwestern forests of Pará. It was Brazil's second largest state, second only to Amazonas, and spanned a massive 1.2 million kilometers. More importantly, it was the state which provided Salazar's company the only clear route into the Acarai Mountains of southern Guyana.

Otero relaxed in the back seat, checking his email and

messages on a small tablet. The device finally lost connection as they pushed deeper into the jungle, which was fine with him. He preferred no one know where he was, or better yet, where he was headed.

He slowed to read the last of his downloaded emails carefully. It was from the lead contact for an international genetics team. A team he paid to have flown quietly into Belem. In the email, his contact confirmed the team and their equipment had left Munich and were due to arrive in seventeen hours. They would be waiting when Otero and his team returned.

In a growing world of scientific privatization, the German team *Genetik Jetzt* was one of the best in the world. They were confident they could not only isolate whatever genes Otero brought back within a few weeks, but could also have a prototype retrovirus designed within three months.

The team agreed to then test the prototype on human subjects, provided they were outside any medical regulations protecting Brazilian citizens. Subjects that were in no position to complain should something go awry, which it always did. And Otero knew exactly who those subjects would be. During his years backing some of the largest mining giants in South America, there was one group he had truly come to despise. The Kayapó. A group of indigenous tribes who had been sabotaging his efforts for decades. Tribes who continually waged war against the machines they insisted were destroying their native lands. Most were cooperative, but some small pockets of the Kayapó proved to be devastating to people like Otero. But individually, they could be captured and used for a far greater good than anything their simple minds could have fathomed. One of the most incredible leaps in human development. A leap now miraculously within his own reach.

Yet despite his materialistic and opportunistic flaws, Otero was still a patriot. Even without a sense of basic compassion, he remained a man deeply rooted to his nation and its former glory. His mighty country was destined to rise again, but this time it would not be through iron ore, oil, or even soybeans. Instead, it would be through the control of perhaps the greatest evolutionary achievement in man's history. An achievement that would drive every powerful government to align with Brazil, through either desire or desperation. And he would be the one to control it all. He would be the one to help his once proud country return to greatness.

Sitting directly in front of Otero, in the Land Rover's passenger seat, Russo had a very different thought. He could clearly see the change taking place in his boss's thinking. He was growing paranoid and obsessed, with thoughts becoming more linear and one-dimensional over what may or may not lie in the mountains. It was sheer folly as far as Russo was concerned. He'd seen more than his share of desperate, aging men pursuing big dreams only to have their spirits crushed by reality in the end. Dreams forever promising to deliver a miracle to change the world. The details were different, but the quest and the conclusion were always the same.

Otero's obsession was some kind of magical DNA stored in the bones of a monkey now hiding in the jungles of Guyana. Something Russo wasn't all that worried over. He had a much more practical concern.

Someone was watching Otero, which meant they were also watching him. One of his men was dead with another still in the hospital. Both were ordered to eliminate the rest of Miguel Blanco's bloodline, but instead his men had found someone even deadlier waiting for *them*. And that someone appeared to be an American.

Russo's man in the hospital claimed they barely saw the attacker before he pounced. But how did he know? How did he know either of the men was coming?

Even worse, Russo was convinced the man waiting for them had been a U.S. Navy SEAL. The marking he left on Carlos's jacket was clear. But was it a warning...or an invitation?

The obvious link was the CIA, but Otero's attention was waning quickly as this new obsession slowly consumed him. Otero could no longer see the more pressing threat before them, nor could he conceive that it might just be the beginning. If the threat were confirmed, all the DNA in the world wouldn't help either of them in a war with the CIA.

Yet while Russo remained concerned, he was far from vulnerable. He still had contacts within Brazil's intelligence agency, the ABIN. A group who was utterly ruthless when it came to tracking down information. Eventually, they would find out who the American was. And then the predator would become the prey.

23

Russo was just approaching the Guyanese border when the man who both he and Brazil's ABIN agents were searching for stepped off a plane in Puerto Rico.

For the second time in a week, Steve Caesare hailed a cab from outside the small airport. This time, however, his team remained to supervise the transfer of their equipment aboard a Beechcraft C-12 Huron. Based on two older Beechcraft variants, the C-12 was a thirteen seat, multi-use aircraft with primary duties of general transport and small-scale medical evacuations in other countries. It was the aircraft's latter reputation that Caesare was counting on to help avoid undue attention while flying over a few unfriendly countries in South America.

Now resting on a private corner of the Mercedita Airport's tarmac, the C-12 was quickly being refueled and prepared for its nonstop flight to Iquitos, Peru. The fifth largest city in the country by size, Iquitos was the largest city inside Peru's tropical and seemingly endless rainforest.

Caesare knew their options still hadn't gotten any better as he watched the palm trees zip past him from inside the taxi. He was deliberating the best time to break things to DeeAnn and decided it was too soon, knowing they still had another seven hours before reaching Iquitos. There was still a chance another scenario could present itself, but he was no longer holding his breath. Especially when the problem was neither DeeAnn nor Juan. It was Dulce.

He reached the research center in less than fifteen minutes and found DeeAnn exactly where he expected her to be. In Dulce's man-made tropical habitat.

She was sitting with her back against the glass wall, playing a simplified game of tic-tac-toe with the gorilla.

In her hand, Dulce held a stick of bright green chalk and studied a large blackboard on the ground between them. The grid lines were preprinted on the board with X's and O's drawn inside. Not surprisingly, Dulce's X's looked like anything but X's, when compared to DeeAnn's. Her O's were drawn as perfectly as possible as an aid for Dulce, who was practicing her manual dexterity.

Dulce heard Caesare's footsteps first and tilted her small furry head, peering curiously down the concrete walkway. When she saw Caesare appear from under the shadowed overhang, the small gorilla immediately leaped to her feet and ran excitedly to the clear door.

Steve here! Steve here!

When he reached the door, Caesare smiled down at her and turned to punch the entry code into the keypad behind him. After a loud click, he pushed the heavy glass door open just in time to catch Dulce in his arms.

"There's my sweetheart." Caesare suppressed a muffled groan from the strain in his side and gingerly raised his left arm to rub her head.

The word *sweetheart* no longer produced the familiar rejection tone after Lee Kenwood had manually programmed the unknown word into IMIS's vocabulary. The giant computer now translated the literal definition of Dulce's own name as the word, but Dulce still managed to pick up on the affection in Caesare's voice.

Under his dark black hair, he glanced down at DeeAnn, who was still seated on a patch of grass. "Everything okay?"

She stood up and forced a grin. "As okay as we'll ever be."

We go find friend. Dulce announced.

Caesare tilted his head back from Dulce's wide smile. "You need a breath mint. How much celery have you eaten?"

Dulce looked at him curiously when IMIS failed to translate.

Caesare laughed and gave her a squeeze. "I'm joking." He then winked at DeeAnn. "Kind of."

DeeAnn's grin seemed to grow more sincere. "She's been practically jumping up and down since I told her."

"I bet."

She checked her watch. "Juan should be down in a few minutes. He's bringing some equipment."

"I figured as much." Caesare glanced down at Dulce, who fell silent once again comparing the hair on her lanky forearm with his. "You look more Italian than I do," he said to her.

DeeAnn watched with amusement and then answered his next question before he could ask it. "I'm not sure how she's going to do, but so far so good."

"Listen, Dee. I really appreciate you coming. I know it's not easy. Considering your last trip, I-"

"I told you I hate it when you call me Dee."

"What can I say? I have bad manners. My father seems to think I was born in a barn."

DeeAnn reached down and depressed a button on the front of her vest, muting the microphone. "I suppose it just took a little time for me to come around. But I get it. This isn't about us. Ali told me about what you guys found, and she's right, there has to be a link to Dexter."

"Let's hope so. And let's also hope he's easy to find."

She watched pensively as Caesare dropped his gaze briefly back down to Dulce and gave her a quick peck on the top of her head.

"Well, even if he is hard to find, he won't be hard to *spot* when we do."

"What do you mean?"

"Didn't you hear how Alves and his men came across Dexter?"

"I thought it was your researcher friend that found him."

"It was. But it was *how* they spotted him that made them realize there was something unique about Dexter. It was at a

151

poacher's camp. They'd caught dozens of capuchins and were packing them in cages, getting ready to ship them to the coast. Capuchins fetch a high premium on the black market."

Caesare continued listening.

"You see, Dexter wasn't caught with the others. He was caught after the fact when they spotted him in the darkness trying to get the ropes securing the cages undone. And apparently he'd almost succeeded."

"What?"

DeeAnn caught herself smiling. "That's when they knew."

"He was trying to *spring* the others?"

"Evidently. Don't get me wrong, primates are smart, but not like that. This monkey is *damn* smart, which is what I meant when I said you'd notice him when you saw him. There's something different in his eyes. Something almost eerie."

"How is it eerie?"

"More like he's watching *you*. Even more than you feel it with Dulce."

"That should help. And hopefully we'll have a little luck on our side."

DeeAnn grinned and reached out for Dulce. "Let's hope. Alves was lucky to find Dexter, *twice*. I helped him the second time, but I'm sure this time is going to be much harder. It isn't just his smarts that make him special. It's his age. He's older than he's supposed to be, a lot older, which has only added to his intelligence."

Caesare watched DeeAnn, noting a momentary change in her eyes. "What is it?"

She blinked and looked back at him. "I've been thinking. It's the DNA we're after here…but we also need to find Dexter for a very different reason too."

"And what is that?"

After a quiet moment, she continued with a question.

"Do you know who Lucy is?"

Caesare thought about it and grinned. "Like from Peanuts?"

"I mean Lucy as in the nickname for Australopithecus. The skeleton found in Ethiopia in the 70's."

"I've heard of it."

"Lucy is the skeleton of the first bipedal, small-brained hominin that lived about three million years ago. The first one found with a small brain like primates but one that walks like us. It's pretty well accepted now, at least genetically speaking, but the fact is that it's still technically a hypothesis. Of course, a lot of scientific hypotheses were like that; theories that weren't proven correct until years later. Sometimes decades." She took a deep breath. "But here's the thing. To many, Lucy is the missing link. The link in our own evolutionary path where things...changed. She represents an important threshold, a time and place where the most significant leap in human history took place. The *catalyst*."

DeeAnn paused momentarily, a thoughtful look on her face. "What I'm saying is that Lucy is arguably the most important thing to have happened to us. All of us. Imagine how profound it would have been to have witnessed that incredible evolutionary moment. The single lifespan of a primate that changed *everything*."

Caesare's face was serious as he listened intently.

"Steven," she said. "Dexter is that moment! Or at least a re-creation of it. Dexter is the modern Lucy. A primate who's made the same leap across an evolutionary gap. We'll never know exactly how it happened with Lucy, but we *can* watch it unfold with him." She watched the expression change on Caesare's face. "Do you see what I'm getting at? We have a chance to witness the equivalent of our evolutionary birth firsthand! It's a scientific opportunity of almost unimaginable significance."

Caesare was staring at her. This went way beyond

anything he'd even considered. "Wow."

DeeAnn grinned. "Wow is right. But that's not all. It's not just that we have the opportunity to observe this…but now we also have the technology to actually communicate with him *as it's happening!*"

Caesare's jaw suddenly dropped. If he had been surprised by her last point, he was now completely stunned. It was a moment Clay and Borger would have given anything to witness. Steve Caesare was…speechless.

DeeAnn continued staring at him while he processed it all. The moment reminded her of why, deep down, she liked him so much. Inside, beyond his gruff and boisterous exterior, Caesare was *smart*. Smart enough to appreciate such an earth-shattering possibility.

As they stood together in silence, the sound of voices approached from the main hallway leading out from the lab. Dulce immediately jumped from DeeAnn's arms and ran several steps back to the glass wall. She turned and spoke excitedly but nothing could be heard with the vest's speaker still off. A few seconds later, Juan Diaz and Lee Kenwood emerged into the warm sunlight.

Caesare turned and watched them approach. He spoke to DeeAnn in a lowered tone. "I take it that's why Juan agreed to go back too?"

"No," she replied. "Juan agreed to go back for a very different reason."

24

By the time they had arrived back at the airport, the late afternoon humidity had tapered off, thanks to a heavy cloud cover crawling across the Puerto Rican sky. A strong scent of dew hung in the air, warning of approaching rain. Light drops were already forming on the taxi's windshield as it came to a stop.

After putting the minivan into park, the taxi driver promptly pushed his door open and climbed out, sliding back the rear left side door. Caesare stepped out from the front passenger's seat and did the same on the passenger side, allowing DeeAnn to emerge still clutching Dulce's furry hand.

Simultaneously, Juan stepped out on the driver's side. Each took a deep breath with the same feeling of apprehension. A sense driven home when DeeAnn felt Dulce's grip tighten around her own hand. Apparently Dulce was feeling it too.

Neither she nor Juan spoke. Instead, they merely stood gazing at the small aircraft. Even Alison, after climbing out behind them, realized what it was. The C-12 Huron was in almost the exact same spot on the tarmac where Mateus Alves' private jet had been just a few weeks before. A plane both DeeAnn and Juan wished they had never boarded.

"Are you okay?" she whispered.

DeeAnn fought to suppress her anxiety before managing to nod her head. "I'm fine." She swallowed hard and then grabbed her heavy backpack, slinging it over a shoulder. She tugged Dulce's hand reassuringly and stepped forward. Behind her, Caesare leaned inside and grabbed her large bag.

Juan Diaz wasn't so eager. He reluctantly pulled his heavily padded duffel bag from the back of the taxi, placing it on the ground. He watched as the others approached the airplane and as Caesare climbed a short set of stairs, ducking his head inside the oval doorway. Several moments later a man emerged from the darkened interior.

Juan's mouth dropped. If Caesare was big, the man in the doorway was *enormous*. So large that he had to duck down and squeeze his shoulders forward just to step through. And not only was he huge, but he also looked to be made out of pure muscle.

Behind him, two more men came through the door, descending toward the tarmac behind Caesare and the hulk. The other two were both Caesare's height, or maybe slightly shorter, and had strong yet slimmer builds. The one in the rear looked like he was barely out of his teens. What struck Juan immediately as he picked up his bag again and approached was that all three men exhibited an unspoken but very distinctive edge, just as Caesare did.

At the base of the metal stairs, Caesare introduced his men. The hulk was a man named Corso and shook Juan's hand with what felt like an iron paw. The two others — Tiewater and the youngest looking SEAL, Anderson — seemed more approachable but with handshakes just as strong.

Juan watched as Corso's gaze moved between each of them, stopping on Dulce. He studied the small gorilla in DeeAnn's arms with a glowering expression, eventually turning back to Caesare when he spoke.

"We don't have a lot of time. Have we missed anything?"

"We're ready," DeeAnn said, turning back toward Alison. She and Dulce both hugged their friend, then headed promptly up the stairs.

Tiewater smiled at Juan and reached to take his duffle bag. "Can I get that for you?"

"Thank you." With heavy steps, Juan followed him up. The last thing he wanted to do was go back, but he had to admit, having Caesare and the other SEALs helped. If he had to go, he was glad it was with them.

At the base of the stairs, Alison remained next to Caesare. Together they watched Juan and DeeAnn disappear with the others, one by one, through the open door to the C-12's cabin.

"They're afraid to be going back," she offered.

"Yes, they are."

Alison looked up at him. "You're not going to let anything happen to them, right?"

A smile spread over Caesare's tanned jawline. "Not a chance."

25

Later that evening, Alison watched from inside as the Embraer 190 touched down on the single runway of Mercedita Airport. There, it slowed and eventually turned toward the small terminal, located within the Vayas barrio. Outside, the rain was finally beginning to let up. Much like Miami, the smaller rainstorms usually moved through quickly and that evening was no exception.

Flight 667 was the last for the airport that night and most of the local employees had long since headed home. Alison was one in only a handful of people — just a few small families — waiting inside the terminal. She watched with an amused expression as two young children ran back and forth giggling in a game of tag.

Once the airliner began de-boarding, it took less than five minutes for Neely Lawton to appear through the double doors, pulling a large suitcase behind her. She was dressed in shorts and a dark blue tank top with no indication she was anything other than a tourist on vacation.

Alison smiled and closed the distance, meeting her with a warm hug. "How are you, Neely?"

"I'm okay, thanks. How about you?"

"Busy but good." She glanced at the suitcase and then around the room. "Do you have any more bags?"

"Nope, this is it. Got everything I need."

"Excellent. Follow me then."

Once outside, the two walked briskly through the drizzling rain to a parking lot which appeared long overdue for repaving. Neely's mouth curled into amusement when Alison stopped and opened the back of a white Nissan Leaf.

"Electric, eh?"

"Don't tell me you're surprised. An environmental girl

like me?"

Neely chuckled and lifted her suitcase in. "Not surprised at all."

Alison grinned, closing the trunk. The rain began to pick up, prompting them both to open their doors and climb in.

Inside, Alison relaxed and turned in her seat. "Are you *sure* you're okay?"

"I guess I'm as well as can be under the circumstances. Thank you, though. To be honest, I think your call was just the distraction I needed." She leveled her eyes at Alison. "Even if a little cryptic."

"Sorry about that. I wasn't in a position to say much on the phone. There's something important I need your help with."

Neely brushed a strand of damp hair away from her face. "What kind of work? You said it was something similar to what was aboard the Bowditch."

"I think so."

Neely's voice rose with some excitement. "Where did you get it?"

"Well, that's where things get a little…interesting. I don't actually have anything per se. That's what I need your help with."

"What does that mean? You don't have anything?"

"I don't have an actual specimen. But I think there's a strong relationship here."

Alison could see the look of excitement on Neely's face begin to fade.

"I don't understand. If you don't have a specimen, what exactly do you think is related?"

Alison bit her bottom lip momentarily, thinking. "I think I need to explain a few things first. To catch you up."

"Okay."

"It's not a sample exactly. It's more like…a reaction."

"A reaction."

"Right."

"A reaction of what?"

"It's a reaction *to* something," Alison replied. "It's the reaction itself that's similar. When we were on the Bowditch, that sample you had was growing. Faster than normal, right?"

"Much faster. The growth rate was remarkable, and it had a DNA sequence we'd never seen before. But the sample was lost when we were attacked." She then looked at Alison curiously. "Where exactly is this going?"

"Neely, when you were explaining to us what the DNA did to the plant, I believe you said it was actually regenerating."

"That's right."

"Which no other plant can do."

"Not to that extent, no."

"Regenerating as in *healing*, correct?"

"It was more than just healing. The entire structure was being regenerated by cells that were lost or nearly dead."

"Like cancer cells."

Neely raised an eyebrow. *How did Alison know that?* It was a comparison she'd used on a call with Admiral Langford.

"Not exactly like cancer cells. Regeneration implies a coordinated function of cells and tissues with a goal of restoring form and function. Cancer cells don't do that. They destroy the cells. But they can, however, live for a very long time. Some even live forever under the right conditions. What *was* similar in those plants wasn't necessarily their cellular restoration but their growth rate. Those plant cells were growing almost exponentially. Faster than most cancers."

Neely stopped to consider something. "Actually, I suppose cancer cells do have a *sort* of healing effect, which is the constant creation of newly infected tumors cells. So in a strange way they could be *healing*, but they're healing the tumor, which in the end is trying to kill its host. The healing

160

properties of the plants we found were much more powerful, and they were far more constructive than destructive."

Alison nodded. "That's what I thought. And that's why I asked Admiral Langford for your help." She sighed. "Okay. Now what I'm about to tell you might sound a little strange, so hear me out."

Neely raised her eyebrows but said nothing.

"A couple weeks after I got back, a woman named Lara Santiago came to our lab. She was almost in tears. Her daughter Sofia has leukemia and asked if we could arrange to have her in for a private visit."

"That was nice."

"It was nothing," Alison shrugged. "Well, maybe not *nothing*, but arranging for her to swim with the dolphins was worth it. This is where it gets a little strange though. Sofia came back a couple days later. And when Dee and I saw her, we were shocked."

Neely's eyebrows suddenly furrowed, curious. "Shocked good or shocked bad?"

"Good! Really good," she said. "Almost…*too* good."

"What does that mean?"

"It means when she came back, she was noticeably better. And stronger."

Neely thought it over. "Well, that's not overly unusual. Partial remissions are well-documented in cancer patients. Short windows of mental clarity, improved dexterity, and even a sudden surge in strength are very common." Neely frowned. "Is this related to the healing effects you were asking about? If so, then what you saw in the girl's condition may not be what you think it is."

Alison considered Neely's point. The last thing she wanted was to be wrong on this. Eventually though, her head began to shake. "No, this is not a temporary remission. I'm sure of it. I've been doing research and this is beyond any of the similarities I've read about. She wasn't just more coordinated or clearheaded. When she came in the first time, she was in a wheelchair and had to be lifted in and out of it. But when she came back, that little girl was *standing*."

"Standing?"

"Standing," Alison confirmed. "On her own."

Neely was surprised. "Are you suggesting something happened when the girl was in the water?"

Alison absently rested a hand on her steering wheel and nodded at Neely. "I think so."

"Like what?"

"Before I answer that I need to tell you something else. Something that may actually shock you."

Amused, Neely gave a slight smirk. "Okay, let me have it."

Alison took another deep breath. "You remember what happened to our boat not too far from Trinidad?"

"Yes." Neely's nod was slow. She hadn't been there, but she'd heard what happened to Alison and her team. Pirates had savagely beaten both Chris and Lee before turning their attention to Alison and her colleague, Kelly. If it hadn't been for John Clay and Steve Caesare, things would have no doubt turned out very differently.

"The reason we were out there in the first place was because of Dirk and Sally."

"Your dolphins?"

"Yes. We were following them to a place they wanted to show us. We thought it was something nearby, like a local habitat or migration. But it wasn't. It was much bigger."

Neely continued listening.

"About a hundred miles east of Trinidad, we found something we'd never dreamed of. By then, we were expecting a large breeding ground with maybe a couple hundred dolphins. What we found was something else, and instead of hundreds there were *thousands*."

Neely Lawton's eyes widened. "Thousands?"

Alison smiled. "*Tens* of thousands. From the boat, dolphins were all we could see. Everywhere. In every

162

direction."

"My God. What-"

"I don't know exactly what it is. But there's definitely something there and it's very important to them. And now...I think it may be related not just to Sofia's sudden change, but to the plants you were studying as well."

Neely blinked. "I'm afraid I'm not seeing the connection."

"John told me about the plant he retrieved from one of those Chinese trucks. He said the sample he gave you was larger than almost anything he'd seen before."

"It was," Neely confirmed reluctantly.

"That's the connection," Alison said.

"What is? Their size?"

"Yes. When we were there in the ocean with all those dolphins, we dove under the water." She lowered her voice. "Neely, I've been diving hundreds of times and I know what underwater vegetation looks like. What we saw down there were plants several times larger than they should have been and growing out as far as I could see."

"What?"

"Some of them were giant, Neely. Giant. I think there's something in that water near Trinidad. And I think Dirk and Sally somehow brought some of it back with them."

Neely stared at her with a look of astonishment.

"And that's not all. You remember how bad Chris and Lee were injured, don't you?"

"Of course, they were in the infirmary. How are they?"

Alison began to answer but stopped to consider her words. This was all sounding so unbelievable. "They're healed, Neely."

"What?"

"*Healed.* As in...completely."

"They're healed?!"

"Yes."

Her eyes opened even wider. "In three weeks?"

Alison nodded. "There's not a mark on them. Even my wrist is better. But Lee had broken ribs, which should take months. He says his pain is gone."

Neely leaned back against her door, stunned. "And they were in the water with the little girl?"

"No!" Alison exclaimed. "But they *were* in the water at Trinidad. Before we were attacked."

Neely stared at her, blinking absently. "Maybe they weren't hurt as bad as originally thought."

"I thought of that. It's definitely possible…with me and Chris. But Lee had X-rays. He had two very real cracks."

Neely was struggling. Her world relied on proof and empirical evidence. What she was getting from Alison certainly wasn't proof, but it was very compelling. And Alison certainly didn't strike her as someone who jumped to conclusions. She was extremely intelligent and no doubt, from her own work, understood the importance of objectivity.

She raised her head and focused again on Alison. "So when do I get to meet your dolphins?"

26

Hello Alison.

"Hello, Sally. How are you?" Alison approached the glass tank. Outside, the night sky had given up the last of its light, creating a clear reflection of Alison under the bright lights of the observation room.

Me good. Who you friend?

"Her name is-" Alison stopped with a small grin. If IMIS hadn't originally been able to translate her name, it sure wasn't going to be able to translate Neely's.

She turned to Neely, who could be seen in the reflection standing behind her. "We're going to have to have Lee code a name in for you."

She turned back to the tank. "Let's call her "friend" for now."

Okay. Hello friend.

Neely stared at Sally with a look of astonishment on her face. "H-hello, Sally," she whispered.

Alison glanced around the tank. "Where's Dirk?"

He gone. Come back.

"I see."

Where DeeAnn?

"DeeAnn isn't here. She's gone on a trip." Alison quickly corrected herself for the sake of IMIS. "I mean she's gone on a journey."

Sally moved her tail but said nothing.

Alison folded her arms and glanced back at Neely. "You just missed her. They left earlier this afternoon with Steve Caesare."

Neely's gaze was on the tank but darted quickly back to Alison. "Steve Caesare was here?"

"Yes. Just a few hours ago."

Alison watched with bemusement at the obvious look of interest in Neely's eyes. She'd picked up on it before when observing the two aboard the Bowditch. Neely had a crush on Steve Caesare, even though she fought to hide it. Alison couldn't blame her. In spite of Caesare's brashness, he did have an undeniable charm to him. And a girl would be hard-pressed to find a manlier individual. Except perhaps John Clay, of course.

She continued watching Neely, who was now attempting to suppress a hint of self-consciousness before turning back around to Sally.

"Sally, I have a favor to ask you."

Me favor you.

Alison smiled. Clearly IMIS's translation still wasn't perfect.

"We'd like to take a fresh sample. Would that be okay?"

From the other side of the glass, Sally studied Alison with her perpetually fixed dolphin grin.

You happy fast.

Alison turned to Neely. "She means excited." She looked back to Sally and spoke into the microphone. "Yes, Sally. We are."

After a long silence, Sally responded. *Yes Alison. Sample now.*

Given the problems with obtaining blood samples from dolphins, the most common method for Dirk and Sally's checkups were through the collection of small skin samples. It allowed Alison's team to check for a number of contaminants and other dangerous biomarkers.

Of course, this time she and Neely were looking for something very different.

Sally continued watching them from within the tank, but said nothing. Both of the women were clearly excited, but what neither realized was that Sally had a surprise of her own.

27

Chris Ramirez looked away just as Neely leaned over him, bringing the needle in gently. Leaning forward in his chair, he kept his attention to the side until the sharp pain subsided and the needle was well into his arm.

"Man, that smarts."

"Sorry," Neely muttered. "I was never the best phlebotomist." She gently slid her hand down to support the small tube filling up with blood.

Behind them, Lee was standing several feet away with one finger holding a tiny cotton swab in place. "So what exactly are we looking for?"

"Erythrocyte behavior."

Lee glanced at Chris. "That doesn't sound good."

Neely laughed. "It sounds spookier than it is. I just want to observe the growth rate of your red blood cells, also known as erythrocytes. They're the most common cells in our bodies and have a tightly regulated lifespan before they are recycled by our macrophages. If there have been nucleic changes affecting cellular regeneration, we're likely to see it at the erythrocyte level."

"Well, I'm not sure what you just said, but I'm hoping for some kind of super power."

She grinned without looking up. "Any specific super powers you want me to look for?"

Lee thought it over. "Flying is always good. Or bulletproof skin maybe."

"Maybe we should start smaller," Chris added. "Like the ability for him to eat better."

"Very funny."

Neely slid the needle out and pressed a swab against Chris's arm. She then untied the rubber strap from around his bicep. "Should I check Mr. Kenwood's cholesterol while we're at it?"

Next to the table, Alison peered at Chris. "Someone doesn't have a whole lot of room to talk. They both need to be checked."

Chris stood up and patted his stomach with his free hand. "All muscle, baby."

She laughed and stepped forward as Neely checked the seal on the small vial. "You guys are just lucky we had human-sized syringes here. That could have been much more unpleasant." She gathered the rest of the items and returned them to the box, then handed it to Alison. "Okay. Now I just need a lab."

Following the closure of the Army's Puerto Rican general hospital in 1949, along with Fort Brooke, the Rodriguez Army Health Clinic remained the primary medical facility for all active military personnel on the island.

It was from a large secured door in Building 21 that Medical Service Corps Officer J. Prodol stepped out into the lobby where he found both women.

"Commander Lawton?"

"Here," Neely said, stepping forward.

Even though she was both indoors and out of uniform, Prodol still gave a respectful nod. At six foot three and two hundred and forty pounds, Prodol almost towered over both women.

"I've been instructed to escort you to our lab as soon as possible." He glanced at the small cooler in Neely's right hand. "Is there anything you need that I can secure for you?"

"No, thank you." She shook her head and immediately passed through the door as he held it open. Alison promptly followed as did Prodol, who then escorted them down a short white hallway. At the end, they turned and continued through a much wider hall.

Just before reaching the end, Prodol retrieved a key card attached to his belt loop and pressed it against a flat scanner. A red light turned green and the door to his left made a loud click. With that, he pulled it open and stepped through.

"It's not much, but we should have most of what you need." He crossed the room, passing two researchers perched in front of their oversized computer monitors and stopped before a larger set of double doors. He repeated the step with his access card and pulled the right-hand door open.

Inside, the Clinic's lab was larger than either was expecting, filled with three rows of familiar beige tables and shelves. The chairs were upholstered in a sharp royal blue matching the white/blue motif of the room, a common look for most modern laboratories.

Prodol motioned to the nearby equipment. "We have five microscopes — two inverted and three confocal. The centrifuge and hemocytometer are both behind you and most supplies can be found in the cabinets above them. Per my instructions, the room has been cleared for your use only, and for as long as you need."

Alison was impressed. She turned to Neely, who scanned the room.

Prodol handed her a business card with the Clinic's logo on the front. "Please take your time. If there is anything you need, feel free to ring me on my mobile. Restrooms are outside."

"Thank you. I'm sure we'll be fine."

Prodol smiled politely and excused himself from the room, closing the door behind him.

As soon as it clicked shut, Neely moved to the silver tabletop refrigerator and transferred her samples from the cooler.

She then grinned at Alison. "Let's find the coffee."

Several hours later, Neely Lawton leaned away from the confocal microscope and rolled her chair back. "I think we have something."

Alison stepped forward from behind her and peered into both eyepieces. It was filled with a sample of red blood cells, grouped together in dense pink clumps, each cell with the recognizable indentations in the middle.

"Are these from Sally?"

"Yes." She brought up an image on the screen. "These are Sally's," she said, pointing to the first. "And these are Lee's red blood cells."

"They look almost the same."

Neely nodded. "Most mammalian RBCs look pretty similar."

Alison peered harder at Lee's samples. "Are they supposed to be doing something?"

"Not necessarily. The normal life span of red blood cells is between a hundred to a hundred and twenty days. If Lee or Chris's systems were exhibiting anything similar to the plants, we should see many more cells in these clusters by now, showing a sharp acceleration in cell production. But we're not, which means their underlying DNA hasn't changed."

"You mean not like the plants."

"Exactly. And it's just as I was expecting. On the ship, it was immediately obvious that something was different about the plants, which is why we investigated deeper. Their cells were replicating at an astonishing rate. But DNA changes don't work that fast. It's evolutionary, which means it takes a number of generations, and mutations, for a change to take effect."

"So a lot of time then," Alison murmured.

"Well, yes and no. I actually have a friend who likes to argue with me, insisting that the sheer number of genes in a

171

living organism is too vast. And that even if a significant change occurred with every single generation, a billion years still isn't enough time to accommodate an evolutionary path that gets us to where we are today. But my point to him is that he's thinking too linearly. His argument is true until you consider that every second of every day, there are trillions, even quadrillions, of cells in every life form on the planet that are constantly splitting and replicating. And even if a mutation does not result in a significant biological change, there are trillions elsewhere that have. And given enough time, those changes will eventually coalesce throughout the species, and in some cases, *between* species."

"And how does that apply to us?"

"Sorry. I was just making a point that DNA changes can happen faster than most people think, but yeah, it still takes time. DNA doesn't change overnight. A lot longer than a few weeks, and the exposure would have to be very intrusive, something at a cellular level."

"So nothing with Sally either."

At that, the corner of Neely's lip curled. "I didn't say that. I was speaking only about the men's samples."

Alison looked at her with an anxious trace of excitement. "Well, what does that mean?"

"Well, I'm not intimately familiar with the biology of dolphins, but most mammals' red blood cells have replication speeds that fall within a certain range. And Sally's are well outside of that. In other words, hers are replicating significantly faster."

"Really?!"

"Really. It's not nearly as fast as I saw in the plants, but it's faster than I'm guessing it should be. And much faster than either Lee or Chris's."

"So I was right about Dirk and Sally?"

"Maybe," Neely said. "There could be several reasons for the growth rate in their cells. We won't know until I put this through a DNA sequencer. It's also a long shot that

172

we'd find the exact same base order as the plants had."

"But you found it before."

She looked up at Alison. "Only because the behavior was so similar to cancer cells. I knew where to look."

"So now what?"

"Now I need to find a sequencer. The Army doesn't have one here."

"How hard is that?"

"Not very, they're pretty common these days. Lots of small private labs have them. All we probably need is a phone book."

Alison gave her a sarcastic grin. "What's a phone book?"

28

Alison awoke to the sound of a crying child and felt a brush of air as someone walked past her. Gradually, she opened her eyes and lifted her head off a firm vinyl seat. It took a moment to recognize the large room and to recount how she had gotten there.

It was almost two a.m. before she and Neely located a sequencer in a location that was still open. Most businesses in Puerto Rico closed much earlier than in the States, so she considered it nothing short of a miracle when they found an available machine in San Juan at the Auxilio Mutuo, the largest civilian hospital in Puerto Rico. After a few phone calls, a tired and disheveled technician appeared in the parking lot to escort them to the Genetics Lab.

The process of sequencing was not fast, which was why Neely had sent her out to get some sleep. Now, in the hospital's main waiting room, Alison sat up and rubbed her eyes while a small ten-year-old girl watched curiously from another chair, next to her father.

Alison checked her watch and smiled at the girl, who smiled back. It was just past six. She was just about to stand up when someone spoke from behind her.

"Good morning."

She turned to see Neely approaching from behind a row of chairs.

"Were you up all night?"

"I couldn't sleep," Neely replied. "Besides, it feels good to get back into work."

"I can understand that. Did you find anything?"

"I did," a tired Neely nodded. "And I have good news and bad news."

Alison frowned. "Bad first."

"I don't see the base order we found in the plants in Sally's DNA. But that doesn't necessarily mean they're not there. It's possible they mutated somewhere else in the dolphin's genetic code. But finding them will take time."

"Or…it's not there at all."

"Well, that *was* my first thought."

Alison sighed and slumped back down in her chair. "I guess I got ahead of myself on this one."

"Under the circumstances, I'd probably feel the same way." Neely eased herself into a chair across from Alison. "But…I don't think you have."

Alison did a double-take back at Neely, who was now grinning. "What?"

"We haven't talked about the good news yet."

"What's the good news?"

"I may not have found the DNA order we discovered on the Bowditch…but I did find some other cells acting very differently. And it wasn't in the blood. Very small amounts of collagen cells appear to be replicating much faster than even the RBCs."

"Collagen cells are one of the primary components in blubber!"

"Exactly."

"I thought you said the DNA wasn't there."

"Well, I was speaking of the blood cells. That was the majority of the sample. But the same is true for the collagen cells. No base markers."

"But if their DNA hasn't changed, how are they replicating faster?"

"I have no idea. But normally, cell behavior is influenced by one of two triggers, either an internal or external influence. The internal stimulus would be its core DNA or something else contained within its nucleus. External stimulus, on the other hand, would be some kind of catalyst acting upon the cell's *existing* biologic or genetic code, perhaps something in its membrane. In other words, another compound that causes a reaction."

"So then there's something *in* the cells?"

"That's my guess. Perhaps something they have absorbed."

Alison almost jumped out of her seat. "I knew it!"

Even as tired as she was, Neely laughed. It was exactly the reaction she was expecting. "Now, the big question is," she said, "what is that compound?"

"And why is it in their blubber?"

"I have a theory on that, actually. Both blubber and human fat share two very similar functions. Storage and absorption."

"Absorption!" Alison's eyes shot open. "That's it! They absorbed it! They absorbed whatever is in that water near Trinidad!"

This time Neely looked surprised. "That fits, Alison."

Alison gasped. "Oh my God!"

"What?"

Alison stared at her in silence with a look of shock. "Oh my God," she whispered. "It was right in front of me the whole time. All these years, and I had no idea."

"What are you talking about?"

She leaned forward with her hands outstretched. "It's the blubber, Neely. The blubber!" Excitedly, Alison jumped out of her chair. "Listen, a few years ago, a researcher at Georgetown University submitted a paper on some studies he'd done on dolphin blubber. His name was Mike Zasloff. I exchanged emails with him afterward. In his paper he showed there was something unique in the healing properties of dolphin blubber, allowing them to recover from injury much faster than other mammals. At the time, he didn't know why. The last time I talked to him, he was searching for unseen compounds in the blubber. But what if he'd already discovered the same thing we just did, without realizing it?"

"It could explain a great deal."

"Think about it, Neely. What if the dolphins are absorbing whatever it is in the water, and the plants are actually incorporating it?"

"It's entirely possible. The plants wouldn't just absorb it; their roots would take it in where the compound becomes part of the organism."

"Wow!" Alison covered her mouth. She was thunderstruck as a major piece of the puzzle connected itself. *It wasn't the plants underwater.* They were just the byproduct. She had seen it before, at the top of the Acarai Mountains. That's the origin of the plants that Neely had been studying. *But if the plants on the bottom of the ocean near Trinidad were the same, how in the world did they get that far? How did they show up beneath the surface in an entirely different environment? And how did the plants get moved so far, without impacting anything else along the way?*

What it was…was even simpler, and it hit Alison like a ton of bricks. There was no migration of the plants. In fact, just as with the mountain, it wasn't the plants at all. It was the same compound they found up there, also in the water. *The plants didn't migrate, the compound did.*

Across from her, Neely's expression grew curious as she witnessed a strange look in Alison's eyes.

What Neely couldn't tell was that even in Alison's stunned state, she was already processing this new realization. Trying to connect the two locations, but failing. There was still something missing. How did the compound get there?

She turned absently to one of the tall windows and peered outside past the hospital's large round entrance. The excitement was nearly overwhelming, and there was one person with whom she desperately wanted to share this discovery.

One person who might be smart enough to figure out the last missing piece: John Clay.

29

At that moment, John Clay was 25,000 feet over the Balintang Channel and less than one hour from Taiwan. Staring into the blackness beyond his small window, he tried to focus despite the early stages of exhaustion which were setting in. He still couldn't turn his mind off and it was beginning to take its toll.

He had an uneasy feeling of what lay ahead in China. Neither he nor Borger had a firm grasp yet on exactly where he was headed, other than a target of roughly a thousand square miles. The more they learned, the more they became convinced that General Wei hid the case that he received from Guyana. And not just from them, but from everyone. But why?

Clay shook his head and leaned back onto the headrest. He tried again to clear his mind, coming back to an image that always relaxed him: Alison.

He'd managed to talk to her briefly after his plane left the west coast, but now he was too far. Any outside communications were a liability this close to China. And if their own NSA spying program had learned anything, it was how any conversation could eventually be recorded, especially those via commercial cell towers.

Given his location and the implications of what he was after, only Clay's Navy Inmarsat satellite phone with the strongest possible encryption could be trusted.

That same satellite phone rang ninety-three minutes later just moments after Clay had exited customs in Hong Kong International Airport.

Reaching the expansive concourse of Terminal One, Clay searched for a quiet corner among hundreds of other travelers. He ducked in next to one of the terminal's giant support pillars and unfolded the phone's external antennae.

"Hey, Will."

"Hi, Clay. How you holding up?"

"Just got through customs. So far so good."

Borger grinned knowingly on the other end. "I know. Listen, I have more on General Wei."

Clay rolled his eyes at Borger's modesty. "Go."

"Remember that Wei had a wife and a daughter? The wife was a pediatrician and died a few years ago from cancer. His daughter appears to have died last year due to a degenerative heart disease."

"I remember. It doesn't seem to leave him a whole lot of motive, does it?"

"Not really. But I've been doing some digging. His wife's funeral was pretty big. I can find a ton of news articles on it. A lot of dignitaries and military personnel. Pretty much what we would expect from the position he was in."

"Right."

"But here's the thing, I can't find hardly anything on his daughter's funeral. A few mentions in local newspapers but nothing on the scale of his wife. Not even close."

"Hmm. That matches the CIA's write up on Wei. A lot of information on his wife but not much on his daughter. Maybe an oversight?"

"Dunno. I was even able to briefly break into the MIIT, their ministry of information, but it doesn't have a whole lot on her either. They have pages and pages of background for Wei and his wife when she died, but very little on the daughter's death."

"Maybe it's deliberate."

"How do you mean?"

"A double loss like that — a wife followed by his only child — would be devastating. He probably didn't want any more publicity. If anyone could keep people away, I'm sure

179

Wei could."

"Well, I think you're right about that. But there's something else. His daughter was seventeen, and a nice-looking young lady. Don't you think she would have had some friends?"

Clay frowned. "One would think."

"Right. Well, I can't find a single mention of her funeral, even on China's social media sites. And it gets stranger. I also managed to get a copy of the register from Beijing Friendship Hospital where Li Na Wei reportedly died. And there are *no* visitors over the previous four weeks, except her father."

"And she died of degenerative heart failure," Clay added. "Which doesn't happen overnight."

"No. It doesn't."

"Are there any pictures from Li Na Wei's funeral?"

"Not that I can find."

Clay stared absently at the constant stream of passengers beneath the new six-million-square-foot airline terminal.

"Is it just me," Borger asked. "Or is all that just a little *too* private?"

Clay wasn't an expert on the Chinese, but he did know there was something far more important to most men than emotional privacy. It was family honor. Was there something about his daughter that shamed Wei into a secret funeral? It was possible, but so far everything Clay knew about Wei seemed to indicate that, if anything, he was a man of ethics. So why the subversion?

"You still there, Clay?"

"I'm here."

"I don't know about you, but this isn't making a whole lot of sense to me."

"I agree." Clay took a deep breath and looked at his watch. "Stay on it, and I'll check back with you in a few hours."

"Roger. You know where to find me."

Clay ended the call and turned his gaze out through the giant window, thinking. Through the window, another TransAsia Airways jet was being brought to a nearby gate.

Borger was right. General Wei's actions weren't making a lot of sense. Something Clay was chalking up to two possibilities: either they had some seriously bad intelligence or Wei was more clever than anyone knew.

Clay was pretty certain it was the latter.

30

Jin Tang was ordinary by almost any physical standard.   At five foot four, with straight dark hair and an inexpressive face, he was virtually invisible among the horde of people flowing in and out of Hong Kong's International Airport, the gateway to Mainland China.

He watched carefully as hundreds exited the terminal doors, towing luggage and attempting to wave down one of a dozen red-painted taxis streaming past.

Tang was waiting patiently in a small Toyota hatchback well away from the first exit door. His left hand rested on the steering wheel of the still-running car while his right was snaked casually under his heavy jacket, lightly groping a 9mm pistol tucked inside his belt. His dark eyes remained unblinking, fixed on the double doors, until his target emerged in a large black and yellow Brisbane Broncos rugby shirt beneath a wide-brimmed Akubra hat.

Tang and his car were immediately moving, rolling forward smoothly until he was close enough for a positive identification.

With a squeak of his brakes, he eased to a stop in front of the door and rolled down the passenger window.

"Let's go Broncos!" he shouted, pumping a fist in the air.

The man sporting the shirt and hat peered at him with a grin. "Ah, you watch our Broncos, yeah? Great year so far." The tall man stepped forward with a smile and bent down, resting his hand on the open windowsill of the passenger door. With a subtle glance to either side, he nodded his head. "Don't mind if I do."

He promptly stuffed his bag through the back window and pulled the front door open.

As soon as the man was inside, Tang darted out into

traffic. His hand moved away from the gun and instead pulled out a photograph to double-check. It was him.

In perfect English, Tang replied and steered toward the center lane. "No offense, but your accent is terrible."

In the passenger seat, John Clay pulled the belt across his chest. "What can I say, I've only been to Australia once. And it wasn't for leisure."

Tang slowed into a sea of brake lights and watched several people move between the cars. He smiled and extended a hand toward Clay, who shook it. "Jin Tang."

"John Clay. Thanks for the lift."

"Where we headed?"

"Beijing is as close as we have so far."

Tang glanced at Clay's large frame in the small seat. "Get as comfortable as you can. We have a long drive."

"Feels like my seat on the plane."

"We'll gear up outside of Wuhan. You need anything bigger than an AK?"

"I don't think so. I'm hoping not to be here very long."

Tang grinned. "That's what I said six years ago."

"Well, I don't think I could pull off your job."

Tang's official job was a security guard for a large company contracted with the Chinese government. He was currently, and quite strategically, assigned to the Ministry of Foreign Relations of the People's Republic of China. Specifically the Department of European and Central Asian Affairs in Guangzhou. However, Tang's true job was to glean information regarding Russia's political and economic liaisons with China after the two had recently become increasingly, and surprisingly, close.

Tang's "ordinary" appearance was intentional as required by the United States' Central Intelligence Agency. His title of "operative" within the agency was also generic. More simply put, Tang was a U.S. spy.

And even though the security agency he'd been infiltrated into as a cover was far from efficient, they did have some semblance of protocol. He had a maximum of three days before his absence would raise attention.

"I sure hope you have something better than just Beijing soon."

Clay nodded. "So do I."

31

In Beijing, Li Qin remained standing in the middle of General Wei's former dwelling. The apartment was located in the district of Dongcheng, the same district home to The Forbidden City, the Temple of Confucius, and the infamous Tian'anman Square where in 1989 Chinese soldiers opened fire on hundreds of pro-democracy demonstrators. It was the movement that was heard around the world.

Today, Dongcheng was the largest upper-class area of Beijing, housing some of Hebei Province's wealthiest aristocracy.

Yet as Qin stood in the main living room of the spacious apartment, he was struck by how simply Wei had lived. The light walls, floor to ceiling bookcases, and checkered carpeting were nice and appropriately decorative but of a somewhat simpler taste. Of all the people Qin had investigated from within the Ministry of State Security, Wei was without a doubt the least extravagant.

Xinzhen, the most senior of the Politburo's Standing Committee, had tasked him with uncovering and understanding Wei's final actions which led to a surprise revolt against the most powerful men in all of China. At least that was how Xinzhen had described it to Qin, which meant it was most certainly not accurate.

Xinzhen's reluctance to reveal too much was itself a clue. Never before had Qin been asked to work within such a vacuum of information. He was told to find information that no one had, and to do it with virtually no information to begin with. The great Xinzhen was holding back. And judging from past experience, the more a person held back information, the deeper the scandal went.

Qin moved to the windows of the apartment, where he

pulled out his cell phone and calmly dialed.

On the second ring, the call was answered by a young man barely into his twenties with jet-black hair and eyes to match. One of *the* best computer hackers in all of Eastern China.

Known only as "M0ngol," his gaunt pale face remained illuminated in the bright and eerie glow of his computer monitor.

China had grown at an astonishing pace for over four centuries, in what many would term "reckless abandon." And the young man on the other end of Qin's call was the very personification of that recklessness, now in a new and frightening digital world.

M0ngol was one of the hundreds of sophisticated hackers employed by China's infamous intelligence ministry, hired in response to the devastating level of spying initiated by the United States' National Security Agency.

Countries all over the world were first stunned to learn of the NSA's actions when finally exposed, then immediately driven to thwart what they deemed an invasion of national sovereignty. Both friends and foes rushed to establish their own counter-agencies, and not surprisingly, the one country with the resources needed to go head to head with the United States…was China.

The most populous country in the world had a plethora of exceptionally gifted computer hackers at their disposal, already motivated by curiosity and greed. The only motivator that China's Ministry of State Security needed to add…was anger.

The world of espionage had changed. Wars were now increasingly being fought on a digital battlefield of electrons. Individual hacking of emails and bank accounts were considered quaint next to nationally funded attacks on other countries. Attacks that were barely imaginable just a few years ago with capabilities that too few were even able to grasp.

War had been reborn, and with it, a new modern soldier. One that did not require physical training or battlefield fortitude. The new soldiers were young men and women, barely out of their teens, having lived and breathed computers almost since birth. Instead of rifles, they used keyboards.

M0ngol was one of China's new soldiers. One of the best, and just like the NSA, China's spying took place both internationally and *domestically*.

"What do you see?" Qin asked.

His dark eyes flickered back and forth between two of the screens before him. The algorithms used by China's banking systems were still too crude to notice the patterns that M0ngol now saw. "It's been going on for a long time. Withdrawals and transfers over the last year. Different amounts and different times to appear random. All withdrawn into cash."

"No deposits?"

"Nothing outside of his salary."

Qin crossed the carpet and approached the apartment's kitchen. It was well-kept with nothing left out on the counters. He continued to the bedroom where things were just as neat.

M0ngol switched his focus to a different screen where one of his programs was plotting locations against Wei's banking activities. Those dots suggested yet another pattern.

"Credit usage shows much heavier activity accompanying southern destinations, toward Baoding and Shijiazhuang. Several repeated trips."

Qin nodded on the other end and sat down on the edge of the large bed, scanning the room. "What kind of purchases?"

"Flights, hotels, and meals. Little else. A mistress?"

"Perhaps." *It was possible*, Qin thought. Most men that age had mistresses. But Wei was different. He was not a man of excess, and his career history showed a genuine distaste for politics and extravagance. Quite rare for a man of his rank.

Qin glanced at two large pictures positioned atop the dark sandalwood dresser. One of Wei's wife and the other of his daughter.

"There's something else," M0ngol said. "There was a maintenance service on his car a few months ago. The miles for this vehicle number significantly increased over the last year." He paused and checked another screen. "But his phone records show something entirely different."

"Explain."

"They show his phone was offline repeatedly, frequently on a weekend. But never during his trips to Baoding and Shijiazhuang."

"A problem with his phone?"

There was a long pause while more data was checked. "I don't think so. The pattern is too predictable."

Predictable, Qin thought to himself, staring at the two pictures. Predictable wasn't the word he had in mind. Everything about Wei's last months were beginning to feel like something else. His records, his communications, and now his apartment…and the two distinct photos on a dresser. No, the word that kept coming to Qin's mind was *intentional*.

He knew that Xinzhen and the rest of the Politburo had tasked Wei with a secret mission. Something highly classified and outside of official communication channels. It was also clear that it had gone very wrong.

32

The lonely, well-maintained road between Ji'an and Wuhan, China, was surrounded by sprawling farmland in every direction. Dotted by thousands of clusters of dark green metasequoia trees, the landscape passed by silently, silhouetted in a thick gray haze beneath a bright full moon.

Traffic was sporadic at best, which caused Jin Tang to nearly veer off the road when John Clay suddenly burst upright in the passenger seat next to him.

Clay looked through the front window before searching the interior of the car.

"Jesus!" Tang said. "That must have been one horrible dream."

Clay ignored the remark and finally found his satellite phone still in his left pocket. He pulled it out and quickly turned it on.

He hadn't been sleeping.

Several minutes later and seven thousand miles away, Will Borger stopped on the white granite steps of a wide stairway and pulled out his ringing phone. His chest heaving, he answered it, grateful for the interruption.

"Clay?"

"Will, where are you?"

"In a stairwell. On my way to Langford's office."

Clay raised a curious eyebrow. "You're taking the stairs?"

"I think Caesare's been feeding me subliminal messages about my lack of exercise."

"I believe it," Clay joked. His expression quickly became serious again. "Will, I need you to listen very carefully."

"Clay?" Barked Langford.

"I'm here, Admiral."

"Good.   I've got a very excited and nearly hyperventilating Will Borger in front of me, insisting I get you on the phone. What's up?"

"It's about General Wei, sir. I think I know what's he's done with the case."

Langford pointed Borger to a chair on the other side of his desk and placed the call on speakerphone. "Go ahead."

"Will and I have been trying to put the pieces together since I left. But things weren't fitting. Wei's actions before his suicide, the deaths of his wife and daughter, even his cell records were all pointing to something we kept missing. Something big."

"So what is it?"

Clay took a deep breath and glanced back over his shoulder at Tang, who was waiting by the road in the dark, next to the car. "Admiral, the only way I can get things to make sense is if we change one of the variables. Something we're assuming is true but may not be."

"Spit it out, Clay."

"Sir," Clay said. "I don't think General Wei's daughter is dead."

Langford looked at the phone on his desk with surprise. "What?"

"I don't think she's dead. It's the only thing that makes sense."

Langford peered thoughtfully at Borger.

"There is very little on his daughter's death," Clay continued. "Too little. I think he orchestrated it and had the records scrubbed."

"But if his daughter is still alive, then why kill himself?" Borger asked.

"To protect her. If she *were* suffering from a heart disease, which I do believe she was, he would have had to

190

fake her death to keep people from making a connection after he was gone. If his whole family was believed to be dead, then the investigation stops."

Langford frowned, thinking. "So, what about the case?"

"I'm betting only a few people knew about it. And that he moved his daughter to someplace safe, then carefully left a trail of clues that led *away* from her. The one thing he couldn't easily control was the cellular towers tracking his location. So he turned off his phone when he traveled to see her."

"So he hid the case with her?"

"He may have done more than that," Clay replied over the speaker. "If his daughter was dying, Wei may very well have been holding the one thing that could help her. The DNA from the plants in Guyana. And if they did find a way to transfer it to humans, he may have used the last of it on her. If he did, killing himself was the only way to prevent an investigation from finding her. A last and seemingly delusional act by the grief-stricken husband and father. But I don't think he was delusional at all."

"So he let everyone assume he was crazy and smear his name."

"Exactly." Clay switched the phone to his other ear. "Purposefully destroy his family honor to save the only family he had left."

Borger nodded. "It makes sense, except that family honor is more important to the Chinese than anything. Could he sacrifice his family's entire name for his daughter?"

The room fell silent when Clay didn't answer. He didn't need to. Whether Borger knew it or not, it wasn't a question for Clay…it was a question for Langford. Clay was one of the few people who knew what Langford had gone through with his own daughter.

Admiral Langford had grown quiet but finally nodded. "Yes, he could." With a grave face, he turned and looked out the window. "I would have."

Silence returned to the call. Clay waited almost a full minute before speaking again. "Will, we need to find where Wei hid his daughter."

"Right."

"Probably someplace remote, but still with enough medical equipment to treat her."

33

Seventeen-year-old Li Na Wei's eyelids fluttered open weakly. The darkened room around her was blurry with just a few streams of light edging in from a nearby window. The old and tattered shade gradually came into focus along with the peeled paint around the wooden window sill.

She rolled her head more to the left and traced the wall back to a small shelf with dead flowers and a few other items she didn't recognize.

From the top of her left hand, a clear IV tube ran up and over her pale arm to an old-looking machine. She looked at her hand and then raised it, gingerly wriggling her fingers.

On the other side, past her right hand, she spotted the faded chair and smiled, images of her father sitting next to her coming to mind. She often felt the warmth of his hand in hers even before waking up. But not today. He was probably back in Beijing.

Li Na took a breath and looked curiously down at the blanket on top of her. Her curiosity grew with her second breath and she took a third one, deeper this time. Something was different — she could breathe again. Still with some difficulty but better than before. And less pain.

She didn't recognize the room. How long had she been asleep? Days? Weeks? It felt like a long time.

It couldn't have been that long, she decided. Her muscles would have been even weaker.

She reached up with her right hand and tapped a small silver bell with her fingertip. A low "ding" sounded.

A minute later, a doctor leaned in. Upon seeing his patient awake, he smiled and entered.

"Hello, Li Na. How do you feel?"

"Who are you?"

"My name is Dr. Lee."

She blinked, then remembered his question. "I feel better."

"Good." He stood at the foot of her bed, touching her toes through the blanket. "Can you feel that?"

"Yes."

He nodded and removed his hands. "Can you move your toes?"

She complied. Satisfied, Lee moved to her right side and inserted the tips of his stethoscope into his ears. "Can I listen to your heart for a moment?"

"Okay."

He placed the round diaphragm lightly against her chest and listened. The beats were stronger and more regular.

"Squeeze for me," he said, placing his right hand in hers.

She squeezed.

"Excellent. Are you in any pain, Li Na?"

"A little. Not much."

"Good."

The doctor gently raised her arm and slipped it through a blood pressure cuff. He then held the diaphragm of the stethoscope against her vein and pumped several times, staring at his wristwatch.

He was stunned. A few weeks ago she'd been days away from death. Then her condition began to improve. Her body seemed to be strengthening. And now, she was awake.

He'd seen miracles before, but not like this. Li Na's heart was beating twice as strong as it was before, and faster. Her temperature was back under thirty-seven degrees Celsius, bringing a huge sigh of relief from Lee and his nurse. And it all happened after her father's final visit.

Barring a relapse, Lee was growing increasingly confident the young girl would survive. Which meant fulfilling the promise he made to her father. And soon. Because the one thing General Wei had repeatedly pressed was that if his daughter *did* survive, there would soon be people searching for her.

34

M0ngol's dark eyes sifted methodically through the computer logs of one of China Mobile's system servers. The giant file was one of several that contained the company's geolocation metadata for most of its customers in the greater Beijing area.

However, what M0ngol was searching for was not Wei's phone number. He already had that. The geo data tracked signals from the SIM cards of each cell phone and more importantly logged the signal strength of each signal as it was polled. Comparing the strength against multiple towers allowed him to discern in which direction a unit was moving, such as General Wei's just before it had been turned off.

What he'd found in the older logs showed him more of the same: a northbound direction prior to the tower losing the signal, then reestablishment of that signal days later, traveling south.

M0ngol's thin lip curled as he copied the last piece of data. He started to close the window on the server and reached for his phone but abruptly stopped, his hand frozen on the mouse. Something had caught his eye as he was looking away, and he stared back at the screen carefully. The directory of computer files was sorted by date and time, along with several other columns of information.

What M0ngol noticed was that some of the log files had a slightly different time stamp than the rest. It was a very subtle difference few would have noticed.

After studying the screen, he opened a new window and brought up the server's audit logs. He manually scrolled through the giant list. What he was searching for wasn't there. All other audit activity was listed, except for the six time-stamped files he was looking for.

M0ngol slowly leaned back in his chair without taking his eyes off the screen. He knew exactly what he was looking at.

Deleting audit logs was easy. Much easier than trying to change a file's time stamp. Doing that would require temporarily changing the server's clock, which would create a huge ripple effect that could take hours to fix. Instead, the files were opened and closed at almost precisely the same time but twenty-four hours later. And it was done to make the time stamp difference as subtle as possible.

Someone else had been looking through the cell tower files.

Will Borger was now typing feverishly on his keyboard. Manually finding a small medical building within a thousand-mile radius would take forever. He needed a faster way.

The new ARGUS satellite didn't have the right path to give him an aerial view of Beijing. But there were two other satellites that did. He didn't need a live feed like he could get from the ARGUS either. He just needed one with a good enough resolution, and both of these older birds could still read a T-shirt from space. More than strong enough to spot a car.

Of course, it was not as easy as it sounded. Even for Borger. He had to use a program like he did for the Forel that searched pixel by pixel. But this time, he had to tell it what it was looking for. More importantly, he needed it to look for the same pixel signature traveling the same direction and time for each of the days when Wei turned his phone off.

And now that Borger had the make and model of Wei's car, finding it was at least *theoretically* possible. The question was how smart could he make his program and whether it would work in time. For this, he would have to commandeer more servers.

Hours later, after testing and launching his modified program, Borger looked at his watch and opened another can of Jolt. Clay had a while before he would even be close, which Borger hoped would give him enough time.

Until then, he needed to check up on his Brazilian friends and get Caesare some more intel.

He popped open the top of the can, and from the third monitor on his desk, watched the overhead flight path of the team's C-12 Huron.

35

Steve Caesare had a serious problem. He moved forward to speak quietly to the pilots as he peered out through the cockpit's front windshield. Even from fifty miles out, it was clearly visible. A fast moving thunderstorm headed northeast, over the western half of Colombia.

Unlike other weather patterns, thunderstorms were not something to be flown through. The combination of rising warm air and sinking cold created dangerous surprises, including air pockets that could drop an aircraft's altitude by thousands of feet in just seconds. Flying around them was the only safe option.

Their problem was they didn't have enough fuel for a significant deviation. After being denied to land and refuel in both Venezuela and Colombia, their situation was quickly growing into a serious problem.

If they did fly around it, the extra distance would use up far too much of the precious fuel they had left. And trying to fly *through* the storm would present a headwind and consumption drain almost as bad as going around it.

Caesare watched the copilot finish plotting the change before turning to look at him over his shoulder. It was too far. An outside route was out of the question unless they all wanted to be buried in Colombia.

Their only remaining option was a risky one — to cut inside and hope the storm's trajectory didn't change. In other words, to pray it continued moving along its current path. Because if it changed on them, all bets were off.

Caesare nodded and turned around, moving back down the narrow aisle to his seat.

DeeAnn sat across from him in a rear-facing seat with Dulce nestled against her chest. "Everything okay?"

"Sure," Caesare said, smiling and winking at her. "I was just checking to see when the movie starts." *Worrying them at this point would serve no purpose.*

DeeAnn frowned. The problem with Steve's sense of humor was she couldn't tell what was a joke and what was a diversion. She studied him as he sat back down, but his face gave nothing away.

On her lap, Dulce was watching Corso — his huge frame sitting diagonally across from them. When he turned away from the window, their eyes met and Dulce smiled widely, exposing nearly all of her teeth.

Corso seemed less than amused.

The small plane dropped suddenly, surprising everyone but Caesare, who glanced at DeeAnn. "You're going to want to put your seatbelts on."

She nodded and stood up, still holding Dulce. DeeAnn turned and placed the gorilla back into the seat. She then fastened the belt around Dulce's small stomach and moved across the aisle to sit in the seat facing Corso. She fastened her own belt and looked back across the aisle where Dulce was now grinning at Caesare. Unlike Corso, Caesare was grinning back.

She watched them for a moment before glancing at Corso's long face. "You don't seem to like her very much."

Corso turned his heavy gaze to her. "I didn't join the Navy to babysit monkeys."

"It's a bit more complicated than that."

"True. We're bringing a monkey to find another monkey," he replied sarcastically.

"Gorilla."

Corso stared at her with a look of indifference.

"Don't worry about him," Anderson grinned from two seats back. "He's always in a bad mood. Even when he sleeps."

"And he's still a kid," Corso retorted, looking back out his window.

200

"Not according to the government." Anderson was still grinning. "I'm old enough to kill the enemy but not old enough to drink. Makes perfect sense, right?"

DeeAnn smirked. She was beginning to understand how Alison had become so disillusioned with the government. She then heard the "click" of Juan's seatbelt behind her.

So far, the flight had gone smoothly and what little turbulence they had experienced was mild. The bumps didn't seem to bother Dulce much. They didn't seem to be any bother at all to Tiewater, who could still be heard snoring from the rear of the plane.

She let herself relax, in spite of Corso. They would be on the ground in a couple hours. Perhaps the trip wouldn't be as bad as she or Juan feared. It was unfortunate they had to take a longer route, but after Caesare had explained the political problems involved, it made sense.

Her only major concern now was how easy it would be to find Dexter after they reached the mountain. Lee and Juan had captured Dexter's exact pitch from the data in her previous vest and were confident that, once close enough, they could identify him again. The question was how close did they need to get? The vest's microphone was sensitive, but the sheer amount of noise the vest had to sift through for normal communication left her wondering how effective it was going to be. And they still had to get within range for which they were relying completely on Dulce's instincts.

The small gorilla was still insisting she could find Dexter, but DeeAnn wasn't sure what that actually meant.

DeeAnn sat quietly, contemplating, while Caesare remained just as quiet next to her. This storm was another problem he didn't need. Flying through a thunderstorm was damn dangerous.

It took less than thirty minutes to get the bad news. The storm had indeed turned east, and straight into their path. The two pilots seated in front of Caesare stared through the

201

windshield with a look of dread.

Avoiding most of the storm, they would have made it with at least some fuel left. But now…their odds were fifty-fifty at best. It was growing in size and both pilots knew that no one would fly through what was ahead of them unless they had absolutely no choice. Which they now didn't.

Colombia's Medellin and Bogota airports had followed Venezuela's lead and denied them permission to land, which left Iquitos, Peru, as the only runway now long enough to accept them. They could, of course, try to force their way down using the international distress frequency — but once on the ground, Colombia would know who they were and where they were likely headed.

Now at less than ninety minutes from Iquitos and a top speed of 320 miles per hour, the C-12 Huron was four hundred and fifty miles away and burning fuel at an alarming rate.

Another sudden gust shoved the plane sideways in the air, causing everyone in the cabin to grasp something to avoid being thrown. Outside, the sky had darkened into an ominous gray as the giant storm began to envelop them.

Caesare moved back down the narrow isle to Juan and DeeAnn, the latter having stolen his seat across from Dulce. After activating the vest, she was talking to Dulce to keep her calm. Following another severe bounce, the young gorilla wrinkled her nose with concern.

No fly like bird.

DeeAnn shook her head in agreement. "No, this is not like a bird. But don't be afraid."

She and Juan looked up when Caesare motioned her to mute the vest.

"This storm isn't going our way," he said. "An emergency landing in Colombia would out us and there's a good chance they wouldn't let us leave. Which means our only option is to fight through this and get to Iquitos as fast as we can." They all grabbed hold as the aircraft plunged

202

again by several feet. "The good news is that this is a hell of a plane and Iquitos is going to be ready for us. The bad news is that conditions are going to get worse." He looked to DeeAnn. "How are you guys holding up?"

"Not great." DeeAnn looked to Dulce, who had her two long arms wrapped firmly around the metal armrests. She was talking less and less and DeeAnn could see increasing signs of anxiety.

"Juan?"

"I'm okay for the moment. But I may need a bag."

"I'll see what I can find," he said, patting the top of Juan's seat. "We're gonna make it. Just hang in there."

It was the best thing he could think to say. And it was true what he said about the durability of the plane. Even the storm's powerful winds couldn't flip it, but running out of fuel was a different matter. If they could make it to the airport, there would be only one danger remaining: landing. Because as bad the wind sheers were at altitude, they were far worse at ground level.

As Caesare turned to leave, the small satellite phone in his pocket rang. He braced himself against the low ceiling with one hand and pulled the phone out with the other.

"That you, Will?"

"It is," Borger answered. "How you guys doing?"

"Getting pretty bouncy, but we'll make it." *Hopefully,* Caesare thought.

"You've got a big storm headed right at you."

"That's very helpful, Will. Any other good news?"

"Yes. Otero and his army are about a third the way up the mountain. They've stopped for the moment, but they're moving faster than we thought. What's your ETA?"

Caesare rolled his eyes. *ETA? Chances of survival might be a better question.* He raised his voice over a sudden wave of thunder. "Soon."

"How soon?"

"VERY soon! I'll call you back when we're on the

ground."

"Okay. Be safe."

Caesare ended the call and shook his head. His estimated time of arrival on the mountain was complicated. Their situation had gotten considerably more difficult…and he still hadn't told DeeAnn the worst part.

36

The Brazilian's stop on the way up the mountain was more than momentary. Otero stood in the shade of a small rubber tree, watching the long line of Salazar's men digging along a deteriorated section of road, trying to repair it enough for their trucks to pass.

Otero lazily slapped a hand against his neck at another insect. The treelined canopy above them was not enough to block the glaring sun, which had turned their stretch of the forest into a sweltering sauna.

After being outside for even a short time, it was enough to drive Otero back to the air conditioning of his Land Rover. Russo faithfully followed and climbed in on the opposite side.

The road reconstruction was being directed by Salazar's second lieutenant. A man in his early thirties, standing out in the heat with his men while Salazar also remained inside his lead vehicle.

Sitting silently behind Salazar was a female with short dirty-blonde hair, dressed in a white sleeveless shirt. Being a civilian zoologist assigned to the mission by a much higher-ranking officer did not prevent Salazar from pushing his authority onto her. Authority she had thus far largely ignored.

Dr. Becca, as she was known, kept her head down inside the cab, reading more on the work the deceased Mr. Alves had been conducting at his so-called "preserve." A place which apparently had a number of dark secrets.

She'd read the information on the capuchin monkey several times, looking for any details or facts she may have missed. It was crucial she knew everything she could. One of the images gleaned from a security camera gave a better than average picture of the monkey — all solid gray fur, as opposed to the more common speckled colors, which meant at least some hope of ever finding the animal. But all in all, Becca was highly skeptical.

From her perspective, she had been pulled from her existing job at a prominent research center in Salvador to assist an army group of Neanderthals into the jungle in search of a mystical primate, supposedly carrying the secret to immortality. And not just human immortality but apparently all cellular life on the planet. It sounded ridiculous.

Becca had enough biology experience to know that immortality was a farce. A dream envisioned by people who never made very good use of the time they had until it was nearly up. Nothing in the biological kingdom had thus far escaped the tendrils of death, and she was sure that neither she nor any of the grunts outside were going to be the first.

Her goal was simply to find whatever they were looking for so she could return to her work in Salvador. However, she did have to admit that, while she found the immortality story absurd, she was somewhat fascinated by the more credible possibility of a capuchin having a higher level of intelligence than normal. *That* was how nature worked. Advances in small steps over long periods of time, not some magical leap. And given that capuchins were already rather intelligent, finding an outlier was far more believable...and interesting.

Becca continued reading through her thick folder, unaware that Salazar had opened his own door and climbed out until she felt the wave of heat rush past her.

Outside, he approached his lieutenant and waited for an update, even though there was little to offer. Anyone could observe the men still toiling away in sweat-soaked shirts.

"How much longer?"

His lieutenant turned away from one of the other soldiers. "At least an hour, maybe two."

Salazar pursed his lips with agitation. With hands on his hips, he spun around and looked back downhill the way they came. He spotted the Land Rover with Otero and Russo speaking inside and smirked. He wondered just how the two thought they would possibly retain control of anything they found when surrounded and outgunned by Salazar's men.

Fools.

Inside, Otero was looking forward to the look on Salazar's face when he found out who was really in charge. And where the loyalty of his men truly stood.

"The idiot still has no idea."

When there was no answer, Otero turned to find Russo gazing out at the forest.

"Christ, this isn't about your ghost again. I already told you it's not related." He shook his head. "I don't pay you to be paranoid."

Russo grinned and turned back to him momentarily. "Yes, you do."

The older man conceded. "We can't accomplish anything from up here."

"I'll still feel better when we know who it is."

"It's coincidence. When we return, we will deal with them…and *their* family."

Unless it really is the U.S. But why would they want retribution for Blanco? Russo shook his head. "Something doesn't feel right. The timing of it all." He turned back to Otero. "What if Blanco talked to the U.S. about the monkey?"

"Why would he do that?"

Russo thought about it. "He wouldn't."

"Exactly. I tell you, it's something else. We'll find out who and why. Then we will deal with them." Otero motioned outside. "But this comes first."

Russo nodded silently. It wasn't the right time or place. He simply needed more information. He was sure there was a connection between the attack on his men and the U.S. but he couldn't seem to find it.

What Russo didn't know was that soon he would be far closer to his *ghost* than he ever imagined.

37

In Beijing, Qin stood examining items in General Wei's old office when his phone rang again.

"Yes," he answered.

"I have information you're going to want to hear," M0ngol said.

Qin slid a book back into the huge bookshelf. "Go ahead."

"You wanted to know what our General Wei was involved in before his death. The answer is something very secret and very big. So big that he was reporting directly to the Politburo Standing Committee. I recovered some deleted emails that refer to a project in South America. A project they were all very careful not to mention. Instead, they referred to it as *Element*."

"Element?"

"Yes. Most of the communication appears to have been verbal, but there were some written exchanges required, particularly around authorization of resources."

"What kind of resources?"

"Men. And ships. From what I've pieced together, it looks like the project was some kind of excavation. Something they insisted that no one else know about."

Qin stared thoughtfully through the darkness of the room. "It appears they succeeded."

"Yes, it does. I can find more, but it will take time."

"If Wei was keeping their secret, why destroy him and his reputation?"

"Maybe he didn't keep it well enough."

It was possible. However, thus far every indication suggested Wei's death was indeed a suicide. It was far more likely that Wei had not compromised their secret at all but, instead, may have kept it *too well*. But why?

"If there was a split in the Politburo," Qin said, "then we should be looking for something after his last visit. Something unusual."

M0ngol smiled in the glow of his monitor. "You mean like a secret flight of a new prototype jet to South America and back?"

"What?"

"That's right. A day before Wei disappeared."

"Where?"

"It landed here in Beijing."

"What was on it?"

"I don't know yet."

Qin stood frozen, thinking. This was why Xinzhen hadn't told him everything about General Wei. There were some things Xinzhen didn't want him to uncover. "So we have an excavation in South America, and a secret flight back just before he disappears. Then he reappears to kill himself."

"Sounds strange."

"No." Qin silently crossed the room and looked out over the glowing lights of Beijing. "It sounds like a man trying to hide something. Do we know where he went yet?"

"We're still working on that. And there's something else you will want to know."

"What?"

"Someone else is trying to find out where he disappeared to. They've been accessing the same servers and records, even before we did."

Qin's eyes blazed. "Who?"

"We don't have an ID yet. We are tracing backward, one server at a time. Whoever it was is very clever. We think it came from Washington, D.C."

Finally, Qin showed genuine surprise. "Washington," he whispered. *That was it*. The piece explaining China's altercation with the Americans in the Caribbean Sea. Of

course, to the Americans it was more than an altercation —
they'd lost.

It took only moments for Qin to connect the dots. *It was
a fight over the excavation. Whatever it was, the Americans knew
General Wei had it flown home. Now they too were trying to find out
what Wei had done with it.*

"Find out who was in the system. Use the entire team if
you must."

M0ngol nodded on the other end. He was going to do
more than just find him.

Fifteen hours away in his own dark computer lab, Will
Borger had his answer.

His farm of servers had successfully found and tracked
the pixel profile of Wei's car and displayed not just the path
of the car, but where it had stopped.

And just like Clay had deduced, it was a small rural
hospital.

Borger couldn't dial the number fast enough. When Clay
answered, he almost shouted into the phone. "We have it!"

"Have what?"

"Wei's destination. And it was his only stop after leaving
with the case."

"Location?"

"Just over four hundred and sixty miles due north of
Beijing! In the mountains. Looks like it's a small hospital
for several surrounding towns and villages. I'll text you the
name and coordinates."

"Nice work, Will."

"Listen," he continued. "There's also a small airfield
about ninety miles further north. It looks usable and would
probably allow you to get there faster, but it might be
military. Just an FYI."

"Okay. We'll stick to the roads then. Should be in

211

Beijing in about twelve hours. I'll check back in three."

"Sounds good."

Clay ended the call and looked at Tang in the driver's seat. "You need a break?"

"Not yet." Tang nodded to the satellite phone. "Where we headed?"

"A small hospital about four hundred north of Beijing. We're looking for General Wei's daughter."

Tang raised an eyebrow but kept his eyes on the dark road in front of them. "The intel I got said Wei's daughter was dead."

"Yeah. Ours too."

38

At just past six a.m., Doctor Lee waited patiently by the door while his nurse helped Li Na Wei back into bed. They were both amazed at how quickly her strength was returning after being nearly motionless for three weeks. There was minimal shaking in her legs and her balance was quite good.

The nurse propped a worn pillow behind Li Na's back, allowing her to sit up straighter. Once she was settled, the nurse straightened the sheets and blanket again before nodding to Lee and leaving the room.

It was far too soon in his opinion, but a pledge was a pledge. If she awakened, Wei wanted his daughter informed immediately. A decision Lee still felt was excessive given the girl's current state of health. The last thing she needed at the moment was an emotional blow like this.

He sat down on the foot of her bed and leaned forward with a soft look on his face. "You are doing very well, Li Na. Very well. But there are things I need to tell you. Things about your father and things about how you got here."

"Okay," she said, peering at him curiously. Her body still felt weak, but her eyes were wide awake.

Lee reached inside his dingy white coat and retrieved an envelope. Without a word, he handed it to Li Na.

She took it in her right hand, examining it, and then turned it over to find a familiar seal on the back. It was her father's chop. She slid her finger under a loose section and ripped the flap open, breaking the wax seal. Several sheets of paper were folded neatly inside.

Li Na glanced at the doctor nervously as she pulled them out and unfolded the pages. Her father's handwriting covered both sides of every one.

Beneath the room's single fluorescent light, and while Dr. Lee waited, Li Na began reading.

When she finished, she was weeping.

"Is this true?"

Lee frowned. "I don't know what it says."

"My father is dead?"

The doctor nodded solemnly. "Yes. I'm very sorry, Li Na."

She covered her eyes with both hands and sobbed. "Why?!"

She knew why. It was all in the letter. Her final days of a deteriorating disease, most of which she was not conscious for. Her father's depression after losing Li Na's mother, and his utter devastation at the impending loss of his daughter. His princess.

But unlike many fathers who might be struggling with the same agony, there was something he *could* do. There was a slight chance that Wei could still save his daughter's life by giving his own. By sacrificing everything he had, including their family name. Their honor. He wrote about the many memories he had of her as a young girl. The dancing, the smiles, the laughs. And her hugs that made him feel as though there was no one else in the world but them.

He explained that in the final days, those memories were all that enabled him to get out of bed in the morning. To continue on, accompanied only by desperation and the fear that he would run out of time.

He never revealed to her that he'd been in charge of a project investigating a unique discovery deep in the jungle. One that proved to be as important as they hoped. And just as dangerous to the world as he feared. Something utterly miraculous.

Alas, to use the discovery meant erasing every link or reference to it that he could, including himself to her. It was why he sought out Dr. Lee and secretly moved Li Na from her hospital in Beijing. It was why he destroyed much of the information and falsified the rest. And ultimately, why he took his own life, returning to the eternal arms of Li Na's mother. He died just for the hope that his precious daughter might live.

Some Chinese fathers were bound by honor. Others were bound by love.

Finally, he told her to remember how much they both loved her, what an amazing young woman she was, and that one day she would change the world. The greatest honor of his life had been as her father, and he would be grateful for eternity for that distinction.

Li Na kept her head against the headboard and slowly opened her eyes. "I don't want to live," she said, shaking her head. "Not without either of them."

Lee didn't answer.

She brushed several strands of wet hair out of her face and stared at Lee. *Parents were the only true anchors a child had to the Earth. And now...now she was cast adrift. What did anything even matter now?*

As if reading her mind, Dr. Lee cleared his voice. "This might be difficult for you to hear, but your father was proud to do what he did."

She laid a hand back over one of her eyes. "I know."

"I learned something, Li Na, when my father died several years ago. He was very old, but I was happy to spend time with him before he passed. We talked for hours, and I told him the most important thing to me, as his child, was to know that he was proud of me."

She lowered her hand and blinked. "I know he was proud of me."

"Do you know what my father told me?"

She shook her head.

"He told me that the most important thing to him, as my father, was to see me live." Lee thought for a moment before his eyes returned to hers. "I've been a doctor for many years. I've seen a lot. And still it's hard to explain. Understand, Li Na, that when a man loses a spouse, it destroys his heart. But when a father loses a child it destroys his *soul*."

Across the bed, her bottom lip began to tremble.

"I can promise you, there was nothing more important to him than saving your life."

She didn't speak again for several minutes. Finally she asked, "What exactly did he do?"

Dr. Lee shook his head. "I have no idea." When she looked puzzled, he continued. "He wouldn't tell me. He said it would only make things more dangerous. That no matter how thorough he was, someone would still find out what he had done. Of that he was sure. The discovery was so important to the government that they would never give up."

"I can't stay here, can I?"

Lee was hesitant but shook his head. "Not for long."

"How long?"

"That depends on you. On when you're ready. I personally think you have a lot more healing to do, but then again, I don't know the things that your father did."

"Neither of us does."

Lee's lip curled slightly. "That's true."

The room fell quiet before Lee promptly stood up.

"I have some things for you. From your father." He left the room and returned a few minutes later. In one hand was a soft leather satchel. In the other was a square case made of metal. Lee put them both on the bed within reach of her good hand.

"Take your time. These were left for you and they have not been opened." He walked to the door where he turned back to her. "Don't try to figure everything out today. We have time, and I'll help you."

Li Na watched him pull the old wooden door closed behind him. She peered down curiously at the two items resting on her bed and picked up the leather satchel first. She began to open it but paused. Her emotions might not be ready for what was inside.

She set it back down and instead pulled the metal case closer. After studying it, she tried one of the clasps which promptly sprung open. She followed with the second, which opened just as easily.

Slowly, Li Na lifted the cold top, pushing it up and away. The contents were surprising given the bulkiness of the case's exterior. Inside were three large vials fitted neatly into a hard interior gel.

One was filled with a frozen, pinkish material. The other two were empty.

39

In South America, just over the Peruvian border, another wind shear hit the C-12 Huron hard, sending everyone in the cabin sideways and clinging desperately to the arms of their seats.

They were less than fifty miles from Iquitos and running on fumes. The pilots fought to keep the plane's altitude level as the pounding rain reduced their visibility to what was directly in front of them. They were now fighting for a controlled descent.

Communication from the small airport in Iquitos was now constant, feeding the pilots information from the ground and waiting for visual contact.

In the cabin, DeeAnn was desperately trying to maintain a grip on Dulce's hand, which was now covered in sweat. She hadn't said a word in the last thirty minutes. Instead, her young hazel eyes were wide with fear, squeezing DeeAnn with one hand and her chair with the other.

"It's okay, Dulce. We're okay." DeeAnn kept talking loudly through the speaker on her chest, trying to calm her. She lowered her face, trying to get the small gorilla to look at her. Unsuccessful, she spoke over the noise to Caesare. "How much longer?!"

"Ten minutes!"

Caesare watched DeeAnn roll her eyes and turn back to Dulce, who he realized was obviously having trouble. But he was focused on something far more critical — the sound of the engines outside, or more specifically the sound of sputtering. The fearful sound that would tell him the last of their fuel was gone. As long as he could hear their high-pitched whine, they still had a chance. But if they lost the engines at this distance, even a decent glide ratio wouldn't get them far enough. And now, deep over the rainforest, there were no open areas for an emergency landing. It was the runway at Iquitos or nothing.

Another sudden plunge tested their seatbelts, and a loud whimper was heard from Dulce. Behind DeeAnn, Juan had both eyes closed. If they crashed, he didn't want to see it coming.

Caesare tuned out the voices of the two pilots in the cockpit and pressed to find the engines again amongst the noise. But instead he heard the sound he had been dreading...a sputtering engine. The left fuel tank was now empty.

The voices of the pilots turned to shouts as they tried to restart the engine. No dice. They redirected everything to the right side, fighting even harder to keep the craft level.

Caesare felt the nervousness and fear coursing through his veins. He tried to concentrate as if to *will* the second engine to keep turning. He couldn't let everyone die.

He checked his watch again...eight minutes.

40

The right engine began to sputter. Just twelve seconds before their forceful impact onto the Iquitos runway.

The sudden reverse thrust of the right engine caused everyone to lurch forward. But the uneven reversal resulted in the aircraft veering hard to the right. Suddenly they were off the wet runway, careening into a field of tall wet grass and mud.

The soggy ground grabbed the wheels instantly and pitched the Huron sideways, causing its left wheel to buckle and its struts to smash into the black asphalt. A shower of sparks erupted under the plane as the struts dug into the asphalt, continuing over the edge and into the mud.

With a thunderous shaking, the plane slowed and its large nose crashed into the ground, plowing to a violent stop.

Caesare was instantly on his feet and across the aisle, pushing DeeAnn and then Dulce back in their seats, checking for injuries. Both stared back at him, alive but in shock.

"Is anyone hurt?" He unbuckled their belts and gently searched DeeAnn first. She shook her head and he turned to Dulce, who immediately leaped into his arms, soaking wet and clinging as tightly as she could.

No like bird.

With Tiewater already pulling Juan from the seat behind them, Caesare could only laugh.

The large wooden door burst open and Will Borger stuck his head into the conference room, interrupting Langford, who was seated with several other men.

"Sir! Steve Caesare and the others are on the ground in

Iquitos!"

Langford took a huge breath and leaned back in his chair. "Thank God. Any injuries?"

"None, sir. Everyone is fine."

Langford looked across the table with relief. Secretary of Defense, Merl Miller, smiled. "That was damn close."

All of them broke into laughter and Langford slapped the table. He then turned to Borger. "You tell him if he does that again, I'll court-martial him."

"Yes, sir!"

Langford turned to Douglas Bartman, the Secretary of State, sitting across the table and to his right. The man was smiling under a head of dark brown hair. "The Peruvian government assured us they will keep the incident quiet. And it's a hell of a lot easier to maintain our cover of a humanitarian mission now without casualties."

"Any cooperation from Guyana yet?"

"No. Not from any of them yet."

"What about Brazil?"

Bartman frowned. "Brazil has severed all communications with us. As has Venezuela."

"Well, Venezuela isn't a surprise." Miller shrugged.

"Agreed. Brazil is surprising though. Then again, their Union is coming apart at the seams so we don't know what the hell is going on in there."

"Or," Langford replied, "it could mean they know more about our involvement than we think."

"You think they know why the Bowditch was sunk?"

"They might." Langford turned to Borger, still at the door. "Keep us posted, Will, and provide whatever help you can to Caesare's team. We'll work on things from here. If you find any indication that someone knows what we're up to, tell me immediately."

"Yes, sir." Borger ducked back out and closed the door.

Langford returned to Miller. "You were saying?"

"We have three full ranger teams ready to go in if

Caesare's team fails. There will be no secrecy at that point, just a fight to take the primate back from the Brazilians, assuming they find it first. We'll get it, I can promise you that. But it will be messy, both militarily and politically."

"Let's hope it doesn't come to that."

Across the table, Bartman shrugged. "Your man Caesare is not only outmanned but taking in two civilians and an ape. I'm betting we're gonna need those Rangers."

Langford's phone rang and he leaned forward to fish it out of his pocket while replying to Bartman. "You might be surprised."

He answered his phone. "Langford."

"Admiral Langford? This is Alison Shaw."

Langford looked around the table with a mild look of surprise. "Ms. Shaw. What can I do for you? I trust Officer Lawton has arrived."

"Yes, she has," Alison answered. "She's with me on this call. We have some important information."

"Okay. I'm listening."

On the other end, Neely leaned closer to the phone. "Admiral, we think we may have a lead on another biological source."

"What kind of source?"

"Plants, sir. With similar characteristics to those in Guyana."

Langford's expression froze. "Repeat that, please."

"We may have another source, sir. Like the others. But in a different location."

Langford stood up out of his chair and stared at the other men in front of him. "What do you need?"

Leaning onto her desk, Alison glanced at Neely. "Funny you should ask, Admiral."

In a pressed white button-down shirt, Captain Emerson

was standing quietly aboard the U.S.S. Pathfinder's bridge, reviewing a report on a thin computer tablet. He calmly flicked his finger, scrolling the screen, and continued reading even after he was interrupted by his communications officer.

"Captain?"

"Yes," Emerson answered without looking up.

"Sir, I have an urgent message for you."

"From who?"

"From the Pentagon, sir."

Emerson stopped reading and looked up. The officer rose from his seat and handed the captain a folded piece of paper. Emerson lowered the tablet and took the paper, flipping it open with one hand.

He read the short message and blinked at the white paper. He read it a second time, more slowly.

"You have got to be joking."

41

"Hello, Sally."

Hello Alison. Sally's eyes moved to Neely. *Hello friend.*

Neely smiled. "Hi, Sally."

"When will Dirk be back?"

Dirk back tomorrow.

"Hmm," Alison paused, wondering how on Earth she knew that. "Sally, we'd like to ask you some questions."

Yes. Sally answered, thrusting her tail and gliding in toward the edge of the tank. *We talk.*

"Sally, we'd like to take you and Dirk back to the place you showed us. The beautiful. Will you come with us?"

Yes. We go happy.

"But we need to go quickly. On the metal. Like the first time."

Okay.

Alison opened her mouth to speak again but stopped. She waited several seconds for Sally to say something else, but there was only silence. She half expected Sally to ask why they were going back, but she didn't. Alison glanced briefly at Neely as if to say, *that was easy.*

She then turned back to the tank. "Sally, you told me that dolphins remember a lot. Like a history." Before she could continue, IMIS emitted a loud sound from the computer screen. It didn't have a translation word for "history."

"Do you remember telling me that?"

Yes Alison.

"You also told me you were happy for us to talk again."

Very happy Alison. You happy too.

"Yes, I am very happy. Just like you. But this is the first time we remember talking to dolphins. With the help of our metal. Do you remember talking to us?"

Yes. We talk Alison. Far ago. You no remember.

"No. We don't. How do you remember?"

Heads.

Alison turned to explain to Neely, who was still wearing an expression of mild amazement. "Heads means their elders. We met some near Trinidad. From what we can gather, their lineage resembles some of the early cultural histories of humans. Passing down history and knowledge through verbal communications."

"Fascinating."

"It really is. It suggests a certain evolutionary *commonality* across species. Chris thinks it's where instinct leaves off and cognition begins."

Neely nodded. "It would explain an awful lot."

"I agree." Alison continued. "Sally, do you know how long ago humans and dolphins talked?"

No. Heads know.

"Do you think we can ask them?"

Yes. Them very talk. Heads very happy for Dirk and Sally.

"Your elders are happy for you?"

Yes.

"Why are your heads happy for you?"

This time, Alison could have sworn Sally smiled. *Alison. Humans happy you and Chris make talk.*

She nodded. "Yes, they are. Chris and I are the first."

Dirk and Sally first two. A moment later IMIS changed the word "two" to "too."

Alison stood motionless, staring at Sally through the glass after her words reverberated over the computer's speaker. She was overcome by a revelation followed by an odd feeling of embarrassment. She suddenly realized how one-dimensional her thinking had been this whole time.

She should have been looking at the tank's glass as a *mirror.*

Alison, Chris, and Lee had garnered a small amount of

notoriety for being the very first and only humans to break the language barrier. What she had never considered until now was that it was exactly the same for Dirk and Sally. To their own culture, *they* were the ones who broke through to mankind. As excited as Alison was, her dolphin friends were clearly just as excited.

Alison pushed her office door open with her shoulder and stepped inside, carrying two cups of coffee. She placed one on the desk in front of Neely before stepping back and sitting in a second chair.

Neely took a sip and watched her with a bemused grin. "Quite a day, huh?"

"God, you can say that again."

"How are you feeling?"

Alison almost laughed. "Elated. Shocked. Exhausted."

"Amazed."

"That too. And maybe a little obtuse."

"That was quite a conversation to witness. I'm guessing you had no idea that was coming."

Alison shook her head. "No. But talk about *big*!"

"I would say so."

"There are so many implications to all of this — biology, evolution, anthropology. The things we're learning by finally being able to communicate with another true sentient being are staggering."

Neely sipped her coffee again. "They certainly are."

At that, Alison paused to study her colleague. "Given what we just learned, you seem a tad calm."

Neely laughed. "I know. I do. There's a reason for that. I've been thinking."

"About?"

"About something Sally said." She leaned forward and placed the cup back on the desk, then straightened in the

226

chair. "Let me start by saying how impressive that computer system is that you built. I mean, I'm skeptical by nature, but that system is turning me into a believer."

"I know the feeling."

"It's funny. There is a fine line between skepticism and optimism. Skeptics want you to prove it and optimists want you to believe it. And speaking from deep in the former's camp, I will admit there is a certain resistance there to big ideas."

Alison shrugged. "Skeptics keep optimists grounded."

Neely chuckled. "That's how a lot of us like to think of it. Some of it also comes from constant disappointment, but that's another story. The reason I'm saying this is because I've been considering some things from the other side. My first reaction when Sally said humans and dolphins used to communicate was that it was nonsense. It sounds like a plot for some kid's movie."

Alison laughed.

"But the more I think about it, the more disappointed I am with myself for dismissing it. Because, even objectively speaking, there are some aspects of science that may support it. Particularly in genetics."

"Really?"

"Yes. Think of our genetic history as a giant tree system with branches cascading down to smaller and smaller branches, all replicating millions of times, over millions of years, and eventually touching everything." Neely stopped mid-thought. "Have you ever heard the old Albert Einstein quote that, 'God doesn't play dice with the universe?'"

"I don't think so."

"Einstein was troubled by the apparent randomness of the universe and came to believe that there had to be some underlying, hidden law to explain why what appeared to be random actually wasn't. Most of his thinking had to do with particles and things like that. But it still begs the question: does God play dice?"

"When you say dice are you talking about *chance?*"

"Yes, exactly." Neely nodded. "Regardless of a person's fundamental religious belief, if we step back and ask ourselves that question, most people have to acknowledge that the answer is yes. At least to a large extent."

Alison looked confused and put her own cup down. "I'm not sure I'm following."

"Okay, look. Let's say half the population believes that life is *designed,* while the other half believes it simply evolves. Evolution being the randomness, or *chance,* that Einstein struggled with."

"Okay."

"So here's the rub. If I didn't believe the world was created by chance, then why does the entire planet currently *operate* on chance, including virtually every form of life on it?"

"Life runs on chance?"

"Yes! Think about it. Each tree, plant, and even grass all release millions of seeds and billions of pollen over their lifetime in the hope of reproducing, or spreading. This happens every day all over the planet. Animals and insects do the same. Even with humans, females produce hundreds of eggs and males produce billions of sperm, all for the *chance* of reproduction. It's the same everywhere to varying degrees. Almost all life on planet Earth operates under the rules of chance."

Alison stared at Neely. "Wow!"

"Right? Anyway, I didn't bring that up to get on a soapbox. I personally believe in God, but I think there are some big gaps in the explanation. Those who believe in intelligent design might argue the chance factor was *part* of the design, which is a valid point. What I'm trying to say is this: when you consider the sheer magnitude chance plays in our world, and the genetic cross-pollination that's been going on for millions of years, is it any surprise that much of our DNA is the same?"

228

"Well, humans had to start somewhere, right?"

"I don't just mean humans, Alison. I mean ALL life. All life on the planet shares a LOT of DNA."

Alison nodded. "Like humans and primates."

"Correct. But the genetic picture is even bigger. Our closest DNA relative is the chimpanzee. Did you know that of the three billion basepairs in the human genome, we share 99% of those with chimpanzees?"

"Wow. I didn't know it was that high."

"Most people don't. But this is where it gets interesting. We also share 97% of our DNA with all other apes, and we share 93% with mice."

"Mice?!"

Neely nodded. "Mice. And if you keep going down the line, you'll find that we share over 50% of our DNA with a banana."

Alison's eyes widened. "What? That can't be right."

"It is," Neely smiled. "Now stay with me. I'm about to explain why I started this. If life's reproduction processes operate by mathematical chance, and its DNA is like a giant tree branching out over the planet for millions of years, leading us to now share much of what we are genetically…*then how different do you think we really are from dolphins?*"

Alison eased herself back into the chair with eyes still fixed on Neely.

"Alison, Sally said we used to be able to communicate. And while I initially dismissed it, looking at it from strictly a genetic standpoint, does it still seem all that *impossible?*"

"No."

"No," agreed Neely. "And here's the kicker — most of that shared DNA is considered junk. Strands and basepairs that have long been deactivated through evolution. And there's no telling what they used to be used for. What if some of those billions of old genes tied into some of our cognitive communication? What if there were abilities that used to be active and we have simply *evolved out* of them? In other words, what if we lost the ability through evolution but dolphins didn't?"

42

"Alison, it's me."

"DeeAnn?! How are you?"

DeeAnn didn't know whether to laugh or cry. "We're okay. Even though Steve just tried to kill us. But we're in Iquitos now." She braced herself as the large SUV she was riding in turned a corner.

Known as the Capital of the Peruvian Amazon, the city was founded between the Amazon, Nanay, and Itaya rivers as far back as 1757 as a Spanish Jesuit deduction. Originally inhabited by Yameos and Iquito natives, the city eventually grew to be a lead city in the late eighteenth century during South America's "rubber boom."

Today Iquitos stood as a proud city among giant plains, dwarfed on all sides by the western Amazon jungle. None of which could be seen by DeeAnn or anyone else in the vehicle thanks to a torrential downpour.

"We got hit by the mother of all storms, and we're now trying to make our way to some place called Pebas." DeeAnn's side window was abruptly covered by a wave of water as they passed through an intersection.

"How's everyone else?"

"Good," she said, raising her voice over the beating of the windshield wipers. She looked to Dulce next to her. Her small face was plastered against the opposite window in what could only be described as fascination. "Apparently some are doing better than others."

"What does that mean?"

"It doesn't matter. We're all fine, although Steven is not exactly my favorite person at the moment."

On the other end, Alison looked playfully at Neely. "What's that? Steve Caesare's not your favorite person?"

She covered the phone's microphone with her hand and whispered excitedly to Neely. "He's still available!"

Neely Lawton stared at her, turning several shades of red from embarrassment. "Shut up!"

"What's in Pebas?" Alison asked, removing her hand.

"I don't know. Steven isn't telling me."

"That doesn't sound good."

"No, no it doesn't." DeeAnn rocked in her seat after a large dip in the road. "Anyway, I can't talk for long. I just wanted to check in."

"Thanks, DeeAnn. I'm glad you're all okay. We've had a few surprises here."

"Anything bad?"

"No. Not bad. More like…astounding."

"That's great. I look forward to hearing all about it when I get back."

"Deal."

DeeAnn smiled. "Thanks, Ali. I needed a quick pick-me-up. When Steven stops talking, I get nervous."

"I know the feeling. Hang in there and call back when you can."

"I will. Thanks."

DeeAnn hung up the phone and watched as Caesare twisted around from the seat in front of her.

"Please tell me you forgot I was in the car with you."

She gave him a devious smile. "Whoops."

The deluge continued for the entire duration of the drive. Outside, the heavy rain left little to see, even out the front windshield. The bright headlights behind them were the only evidence that the other two vehicles were still there, carrying Juan and the rest of Caesare's team.

The rain eventually began to lighten. Shortly afterwards, the Peruvian driver next to Caesare slowed and turned onto a small muddy road which was almost entirely hidden in the dense jungle. DeeAnn jumped when giant leaves began slapping the sides of the vehicle as it bounced and rattled over a trail not much wider than a set of tire tracks. After a few miles, the slapping gradually disappeared and the leaves were replaced by bright green grass on both sides, illuminated by the headlights.

Moments later they caught sight of an approaching structure with its shadowy shape rising into the darkness. Upon closer inspection, they watched the outline materialize into an old Quonset hut with dim glowing lights inside. The shadow of another unmistakable shape emerged next to the building — a large airplane sitting idle in the tall grass.

Stopping next to the old building, DeeAnn could make out the words "La Vida Del Aire" painted in large red letters on the plane's fuselage.

The driver climbed out at the same time as Caesare, who briefly ducked back in his own door and grinned at them. "Wait right here."

The door slammed shut before she could think of a reply, leaving her and Dulce sitting in silence, silhouetted in the bright glow of the vehicle's headlights directly behind them.

"Wait right here?"

Dulce didn't reply. She was trying to touch the small streams of water zigzagging down the other side of her window.

DeeAnn watched as the other three men's shadows passed her window and joined both Caesare and their driver. Together, the five climbed a short set of wooden steps. Pushing open a door to a scarcely lit room, they all disappeared inside.

The metal door banged shut behind them as the men examined what appeared to be more a living room than an office. In fact, even calling it a living room was a stretch. The only two furniture items of note consisted of a ratty leather couch in the middle and a large, dark wood table with nonmatching chairs nearby.

Along the right wall, miscellaneous crates and empty boxes were stacked neatly against the hut's metal frame which rose above them, echoing the fading raindrops outside. Underfoot, wooden planks squeaked almost as loudly as the door when the men moved forward. They stopped again when another man in his late fifties appeared from the far end. He was dressed in faded blue coveralls and a wide brimmed hat, dripping from both sides.

"Buenos dias, Ricardo." The stranger stepped forward into the light, revealing red cheeks and a thin graying beard. He motioned to the ceiling and the sound of rain picking back up. "What are you doing out in this?"

The driver, Ricardo, waved. "Buenos dias, Joe. I have some Americans come to see you."

From under his brim, Joe peered curiously at Caesare and the other men. "You don't say. And what might you boys want?"

"A little help," Caesare replied. He then cocked his head slightly. "Your accent sounds an awful lot like a Texan."

"Oklahoma," the man corrected, stepping closer. "Been an ex-pat almost as long as I spent there though. What kind of help you and your giant friend looking for?"

Corso gave Caesare a sidelong glance but remained silent. "We're hoping for a ride."

"A ride?" He closed one eye, suspiciously. "You boys in trouble?"

Caesare grinned. "Not yet."

He noticed the tattoo on Tiewater's forearm. "You military?"

"Not as far as you know."

"Then what are ya?"

"How about environmentalists?"

Joe chuckled. "Well, they sure are growing you big these days. Okay, I'll bite. What's a bunch of environmentalists

234

need a ride for on a night like this?"

"Surveying mostly. We're having trouble finding a ride in from the north."

"That's what I hear. That must be some damn important surveying."

Caesare slid a backpack off his shoulder and approached the table. He unzipped a large pocket and pulled out five stacks of one-hundred-dollar bills. "You could say that."

Joe studied the bills and slowly shook his head. "I ain't going to jail for anybody. Jail in South America is a hell of a lot different than the States. It doesn't take shipping much of anything illegal to spend the rest of your life in a place I don't wanna be in."

"That makes five of us. We just want a ride, Joe, and quickly. You're the closest and can get us the farthest."

He eyed the money again, uneasy. Men dropping money like that usually had a heap of trouble not far behind them. "What makes you think that plane outside even flies?"

"Because it would be awfully hard to make your secret drops over the border without one. Food and medical supplies don't fly themselves under the radar."

"I don't know what you're talking about."

Caesare grinned again and stepped forward in his dripping wet boots. "Humanitarian missions can be a sensitive topic. Especially in countries like Venezuela who don't like to admit they have serious problems, even when their governments are crumbling around them. They'd rather let thousands of their citizens starve than appear weak and admit they need help.

"And the aid they do receive is always highly visible. With things like documentation, customs inspections, and import clearances. Bureaucracy that slows things down and gets a lot of things *lost* in the process. Am I right?"

"How would I know?"

"Not surprisingly, some organizations take the most expedient route and simply drop supplies themselves.

Usually at dusk and in areas that aren't well monitored."

The older man folded his arms, remaining quiet.

"Joe, our goals here aren't all that different. If you don't out us, we won't out you."

"That sounds like an offer I can't refuse."

Caesare shook his head. "I've never been much for coercion. Just consider it another drop. Prepaid. And a way to help a whole lot more people."

"Yeah? How many more?"

"More than you can count."

Joe nodded, then held up his hands. "All right. Don't tell me any more. I reckon the less I know, the better."

Tiewater smiled. "You and us both."

"Well, we can't go anywhere until this storm eases up. A few hours at the very least. And I don't know where you're headed, but there ain't many places to land if you're going east. So I don't know how far you're gonna get."

Caesare opened his mouth to speak when they were interrupted by the sound of the front door opening again. They turned to see DeeAnn step inside from out of the rain, holding Dulce in her arms.

Joe's eyes opened wide with surprise at the sight of the gorilla.

"Something tells me this is one of the things I probably shouldn't know."

It was dawn before the storm began to abate and move north again. Caesare's team finished packing the plane while DeeAnn and Juan stood near a wall of the forested jungle, waiting and watching Dulce sniff and nibble on various plant leaves. They had enough food for her on the plane to last several days, but it was an opportunity for Dulce to acclimate her diet if possible.

This good.

DeeAnn examined the tree and compared it to a small

236

book that covered many of the indigenous species of the area.

"Is that one okay?" Juan asked.

"She certainly seems to think so." DeeAnn picked one of the leaves and held it next to the book. "Ipomoea something. Says it's a variant of a sweet potato."

Juan frowned. "Are you supposed to eat the leaves?"

"They're edible." She took a bite. "Tastes a little like sweetened spinach. Here."

"I'm good. Thanks."

DeeAnn laughed and caught Juan peering at the airplane over a hundred yards away. Joe was beneath it, running his checks.

"You okay?"

"I guess so. I'm just worried."

"About what?"

"Everything." Juan struggled to understand what it was exactly that was bothering him. Maybe he was overly sensitive after their last trip. Maybe he was too exhausted to think clearly. Or maybe he *was* thinking clearly and his last trip had awakened a new level of paranoia in him, or perhaps common sense.

The two were interrupted by Dulce. Without warning, she sprang to her feet and ran between them toward an approaching Steve Caesare. He caught the gorilla in mid-leap and raised her up onto his shoulder.

"Everybody ready?"

"I think so. We were just doing a little foraging. In case we run out of food."

"Good idea. How about you, Juan?"

"Yeah, I guess so."

DeeAnn reached for Dulce. "We need another potty break. There's no toilet on that plane."

She lowered Dulce to the ground and headed back toward the hut. The structure was now clearly visible in the morning light, and completely covered in rust.

As he watched them leave, Caesare turned to Juan. "You okay?"

"Yeah, I'm fine."

"Look, I know this isn't easy. But I do appreciate you coming with us."

"I guess I figured it would be better to volunteer before I was forced to come. That is what was going to happen, right?"

Caesare nodded. "More or less."

"Then no thanks necessary." He offered Caesare a meek smile.

Caesare stood, studying him. "Why *did* you volunteer, Juan?"

"I told you. It was better to-"

Caesare cut him off. "That's not it. I can read people, kid, and there's something else going on."

Juan didn't respond immediately. Instead, he looked back at the plane before answering. "It's my little sister."

"Your sister?"

"She's only six. She was a surprise to my parents when I was fourteen…and she's amazing. We have a big gap between us, but she looks up to me like I walk on water. She calls me her héroe."

"I don't think I'm following."

"My parents worked a lot so I was the one who looked after her. You know, kept her safe and all. She looks up to me."

"What's her name?"

"Angelina." Juan breathed in, struggling. "I came because she was diagnosed a few months ago with leukemia. And she's showing accelerated symptoms."

Caesare shook his head. "I'm sorry, Juan."

"If you met her, you'd know why I volunteered. She's the most incredible kid I've ever known. Always smiling. Always making everyone happy. Even when she gets disappointed, she just smiles and says it's okay." Juan's trembling lips turned into a smile. "She says her favorite part of the day is when I get home."

He glanced over Caesare's shoulder at Tiewater, who was now crossing the small field toward them.

"DeeAnn told me what you guys found on the mountain, Mr. Caesare. So if there's something out there that might help my sister, I'm willing to do whatever I can. After all, a hero doesn't give up, right?"

With a sympathetic frown, Caesare nodded and turned as Tiewater reached them.

"Sir, we're ready."

Behind them, the large propellers of a 1952 Douglas DC-3 began to turn as one engine sputtered and roared to life, followed by the second. Black smoke coughed from the massive Rolls Royce Dark Mk. 510 engines, then quickly dissipated in the warm moist breeze blowing across the open field.

As the three men approached the aircraft, Joe swung around and met them near the tail, yelling over the deafening engines. "I have a local guy who helps me with the drops but figured you wanted to keep our party small."

"The smaller, the better," Caesare yelled back.

The older man nodded before grabbing the metal ladder and climbing into the fuselage.

When DeeAnn climbed aboard, she paused at the top of the ladder, still clutching Dulce in one arm. She glanced down the inside of the fuselage to find Juan and Anderson. Both were sitting on a long, padded metal bench near the opening of the plane's cockpit where Joe was checking his instruments. Against the other wall, three large boxes were secured by orange nylon straps with giant balls of fabric on top.

The thundering roar behind them forced her inside quickly, causing her to trip and stumble into the arms of

Tiewater. He caught her and gently turned the two around at which point they managed to make it to the bench. When they sat down, Anderson handed her two worn pairs of headsets.

DeeAnn peered at them and placed one over her head. She then took the other and held it to Dulce's head, trying to determine the best way to situate them. When she finally wiggled them in place on top of Dulce's petite skull, she almost laughed.

Dulce looked surprised at the sudden reduction in noise. She scanned the cabin curiously, then pulled her headset off again.

"No. Keep it on, honey." DeeAnn grabbed Dulce's headset and pushed it precariously back into place. "It will keep things quieter."

Dulce stared at her before making a chuttering sound, and pulled them back off.

She turned to Juan. "I guess it's still too loud for the vest to work in here."

"It definitely won't work as well. Maybe if they close the door."

Anderson smiled. "There is no door."

"What?"

"It would be too hard to open in mid-flight."

"Are you saying it's going to be this loud the whole way?"

"Yep, the whole way!" he laughed.

With her mouth open, DeeAnn shook her head. There was a little less noise inside the plane, but still enough to have to raise her voice over. She stared at the open door before turning back. "Aren't we going to freeze?"

"Nah. We'll be flying low until the end."

Just then Corso's huge frame climbed into view and nodded to Tiewater, who joined them in the forward cabin. "You're going to want to belt in for takeoff. It's going to get pretty bouncy," he yelled.

"Oh geez." DeeAnn fumbled for the belt behind Dulce.

240

"What's in these big boxes?"

"Our supplies." He raised a hand and patted a small area of Dulce's head. "And her food."

"What's that on top of the boxes?"

Before she could get a reply, Tiewater turned as a large, thick pack flew through the open door, caught by Corso. He promptly dropped it behind him and caught another. This repeated until he had several packs stacked neatly on the floor.

A minute later, the engines roared louder. Caesare finally climbed up the ladder, tossing the wheel blocks toward the rear. He quickly pulled the ladder up as the plane began to move over the bumpy field, accelerating and turning the bumps into larger bounces.

DeeAnn's eyes followed Caesare as he approached, squeezing in behind her and Anderson. "I liked the last plane better," she said aloud.

He grinned.

Glancing again at the boxes, she repeated her question. "What's that cloth thing on top?"

Caesare frowned. "Listen, Dee. Remember when you told Alison you weren't a big fan of mine at the moment?"

"I was joking!"

"I know. But this isn't going to help."

"What do you mean?" It was then that she suddenly put things together. The cloth on top of the large boxes and the packs that Caesare threw to Corso through the door. "What WERE those?!"

Caesare tone became apologetic. "There was no other option, Dee. Believe me."

Her eyes widened nervously.

"If there were an easier way to get in, we would have taken it."

"Oh my God!" She began to panic. "Are those *parachutes*?!"

"Kind of."

"KIND OF?!"

"Okay. They're parachutes."

Juan leaned forward with the same look as DeeAnn. "Did you say parachutes?!"

"I was hoping we would find another option. But there isn't one. And unfortunately, there aren't any runways where we're going. Just enough fuel to make it there and back."

"Oh, God! Please tell me you're kidding!"

Caesare shook his head. "I'm sorry. There was no other way."

She covered her face with her hands, then pulled them away. "No! No! I am NOT jumping out of an airplane! Stop! Stop the plane!"

Just as she spoke, DeeAnn became aware that their bouncing from side to side had promptly dissipated. She stared out of the door, past both Caesare and Corso who were now on the end of the bench. She was just in time to see the blur of bright green grass fall away as the powerful DC-3 climbed into the air.

"Take it easy," Caesare said loudly. "It's going to be fine."

"Normal people do not equate parachutes with things going *fine*, Steven!"

Caesare winked. "Trust me. Clay and I have done hundreds of these and never had a single problem. You couldn't be in safer hands."

Hearing no further disputes, Caesare nodded and leaned back against the metal wall behind him. He was glad they didn't press him on it because that last bit wasn't entirely accurate.

43

"Hey, Clay. How you holding up?"

"Swimmingly, Will. What do you have?"

Borger was staring at a red circle on his screen, displaying the GPS location of Clay's satellite phone. From there a thin line plotted the rest of his course to the small hospital.

"Beijing was the last big city, so at your current speed you should reach it in three hours and thirty-nine minutes. Give or take."

"How much detail can you see?"

"A fair amount. But without a live feed, it's based on still shots from the last couple days. Very little activity. I only see a few old cars going in and out. It's located in a pretty dense area of forest with an elevation of 4,500 feet. The south and east sides look like they fall off a couple hundred feet from there, so the road winds in from the southwest. There's not much around it."

"How big is the place?"

"Not very. Some of the building is obscured by the trees, but I'm guessing maybe three or four thousand square feet."

"Then if she's there, she won't be hard to find."

"True," Borger smiled. "Stay on G111 until you get to 351. From there head northwest." He repeated the coordinates. "I can't tell what it looks like from ground level. It may be easy to miss."

"Thanks. Anything else?"

"Not at the moment. I'm going to work on finding an exit for you. I also need to check in with Caesare. They're getting close. In the meantime, get some sleep."

Clay smiled and pushed himself against the back of the passenger seat, trying to stretch his legs. It took over two hours from Beijing for the smog to finally lighten, but the setting sun was still shrouded in a thicker than normal orange hue.

Finding the hospital in the dark might prove difficult. At least it would make things easier getting back out. Neither he nor Tang knew what they would find, but getting the case was the priority. Unless Wei had indeed injected his daughter, which changed things considerably. Sneaking the case out was one thing — having to bring a young woman out with them was quite another. Especially depending on her level of cooperation.

Across the Pacific Ocean, Steve Caesare pressed the phone tighter against his ear. "Say again, Will!"

Borger raised his voice. "I said you're ahead of Otero. But not by much. They've passed Silpaliwini and are on their way up the Acarai Mountains now. Still about a day away but you're going to have to hurry."

"Hurry?" Caesare called back. "I hadn't considered that."

"How long until you're on the ground?"

He looked at DeeAnn and Juan, who were both watching him. "Probably a little over an hour."

"Okay, call me back when you're down. I should have-"

Borger stopped in mid-sentence with his eyes frozen on the screen in front of him. Around the edge of his largest monitor, a thin red border appeared and began flashing. His heart almost stopped. He slowly turned and peered at the other monitors. They were doing the same. Everything was flashing.

"What was that?" Caesare's voice sounded through the phone's speaker.

Borger didn't answer. Instead his hand slid up and over the phone until it found the button on top, where he powered it off without a word.

His screen continued flashing and another window appeared, also in red, displaying a live streaming column of computer code. He recognized it immediately.

It was a program he had written himself. It was an aggregator, not of data, but of threats. Borger was all too aware of the computer hacks occurring on a daily basis. More importantly, he was familiar with the various computer worms released over the last several years. Worms that weren't written by some kid at home. These attacks were written at the *state* level. By governments, including the NSA.

Clay and Caesare's teasing over Borger's paranoia wasn't a joke. He was *extremely* paranoid. He knew what could really be done using hidden computer code, and he wrote a custom program to detect it.

His program was an aggregator that collected digital signatures of the worst known worms and viruses. And applied something called heuristic modeling to look for *behaviors* of those worms, even if he couldn't find them directly on his hard drives.

Borger stopped the stream of scrolling data and studied the details. The behavior didn't look like a worm. Instead, his program detected something "unusual" in his work patterns. He traced the coded message to another file and then found it. The color drained immediately from his face.

His computer microphone had been activated. And it had been on for over twenty minutes before his program flagged it as unusual.

Borger quietly pushed himself away from his desk, sliding back in his chair. Someone was in the system. And someone just listened to everything he had said.

Borger burst out of the lab, heading directly for the stairs where he sprinted to the top. He continued, running up another flight until he reached the next floor and an outside exit. He pushed through the glass door and into an outdoor foyer before pulling his satellite phone back out and redialing.

"Clay!" he shouted between heavy breaths. "We have a breach!"

"What?"

"A breach! Someone is in the system! And they just listened to our last conversation!"

"Are you sure?!"

"Yes, I'm sure. And if they're in my system, everything could be compromised!"

"What do you mean by everything?"

"I mean, *everything*. Wei, the case, his daughter, the hospital. Everything!" Borger stopped in his tracks. "Shit. That means they probably know about you too. And where you are!"

"Dammit!" Clay growled. "Who is it?"

"I don't know. Maybe the Chinese. They might have found out I was poking around their systems. So, whatever they didn't know before, they probably know now. And if they do, they might also know where you're headed. Hurry!"

Clay shot a look at Tang. "Step on it!"

Tang grabbed the steering wheel with both hands and mashed the accelerator down. The Honda's small engine immediately surged and began picking up speed.

"Find out who it is!"

"I will." As Borger turned back toward the door, he suddenly had an idea. He immediately rushed back down the stairs as fast as he'd come up.

If someone was listening…maybe they were *still* listening.

44

The expression on M0ngol's face did not change when he heard Borger rush back into his lab. Nor was he fooled with the man's attempted misdirection. He listened with a slight smile as Borger pretended to be on the phone again, giving different information. It was quick thinking, but something M0ngol was half expecting once the man realized he was being bugged with his own system.

M0ngol had hoped it would take longer to detect his presence. Previous targets had taken days or even weeks to detect the hack, which indicated just how careful this man Will Borger was. The dearth of data M0ngol had to piece together in order to tunnel back showed Borger to be extremely savvy. The man was not to be underestimated.

Of course, if he were smart, Will Borger would immediately power down his entire system, which was exactly what it sounded like when the microphone on the other end promptly went dead.

He had been found out, but it didn't matter. M0ngol calmly reached for his phone and dialed Qin's number.

"Go ahead."

"How close are you to a computer?" M0ngol asked.

"Five minutes."

"Good. Let me know when you're online. I have something to show you. And you'd better hurry. We don't have much time."

He hung up the phone and began typing. He brought up a large map of Beijing and zoomed in, looking for G111 highway. He then switched screens and replayed the audio from Borger's microphone, listening again to his conversation with someone named Clay. M0ngol wrote down the coordinates, then looked up and typed them in.

The map on his screen jumped north, zeroing in on a small building which matched Borger's description — the hospital.

He then worked the distance back toward Beijing by three hours and thirty-nine minutes, giving him an estimate of Clay's location. Next he factored in a change in speed after hearing the car accelerate in the background.

M0ngol watched as his computer began calculating and answered his phone again when Qin called back.

"I'm on."

"Is this your laptop?"

"Yes."

"Hold on. I'll connect."

A moment later, Qin watched as a map was displayed on his own screen.

"We found who broke into our systems. It looks like we're not the only ones looking for Wei's daughter. They think they know where she is."

"Who?"

"A small group inside the U.S. Navy."

"Are you absolutely sure?"

"Yes. They just severed our connection."

Qin's map jumped to an overhead satellite picture of Washington, D.C. — with a prominent red icon identifying the Pentagon building.

Qin nodded. "So, where is she?"

"They think she's here." The map changed to an image of the small building surrounded by trees. "And two of them are almost there. They should arrive in just under three hours."

"Zoom out."

The picture shrank and Qin studied the map. "Where are they right now?"

"I'm guessing about right here." Another icon appeared further south.

"You said three hours?"

"Maybe less. They're moving faster now."

"Have you identified them?"

"Not yet."

"Find out who they are and what they're driving," was all Qin said before hanging up. After only a brief moment, he swiftly began scrolling through the address book on his phone, searching for a name. Three hours might be enough time, given the right resources.

General Wei's puzzle had just been solved. It was all about his daughter. Everything. The man had fooled everyone and now, whatever was extracted from South America, Wei had hidden it away with his daughter.

The Americans may have figured it out first, but Qin now knew everything. And he would beat them there.

Unfortunately, Qin didn't yet know that there was still more to the puzzle. And one of the missing pieces was presently scared out of her mind.

45

DeeAnn Draper wasn't just scared. She was also pissed.

She glared at Caesare with a combination of fear and anger while Anderson stood behind her, cinching two nylon straps in place. The harness was composed of two thick straps running between her legs and up the back side, with two more crossing around and fastening tightly over her chest.

The area below the center plate of her harness left barely enough room for the IMIS vest. It remained on while both Juan and Dulce went through the same ordeal. Anderson cinched hard one more time, causing her body to stumble forward. DeeAnn caught herself against the bare interior wall of the plane.

How dare he, she fumed. *How dare he hide this from her. From both of them! This wasn't some joke. These were their lives Caesare was gambling with. She knew what was involved. There was no reason for him not to tell her. She still would have done it.*

Glowering, DeeAnn looked around the cabin. The powerful rushing wind blowing through it filled her with a sense of reality and dread that she couldn't shake. *Okay. She was pretty sure she still would have done it.*

Dulce, bound in her own smaller harness, said something that couldn't be heard above the howling from the airplane's open door. She seemed to let it go and gazed up as Caesare placed a child's helmet on her head, fastening it in place. The helmet sat awkwardly atop Dulce's cone-shaped scalp and she examined the top of it with her long fingers. It wasn't until the goggles were secured that DeeAnn almost laughed out loud. With two enlarged eyes peering through her goggles, the small gorilla resembled something right out of a cartoon.

Even through her anger, DeeAnn marveled at how calm Dulce seemed to be in the presence of Caesare — a man she clearly had a strong connection to. She watched as Caesare picked Dulce up in his powerful arms and moved to the other side of the cabin. He made eye contact with Corso and Tiewater, who already had their chutes on, then motioned to the small crates and held up three fingers.

Both men nodded and began detaching the straps that secured them to the wall.

Oh God, she thought. *Three minutes!* DeeAnn could feel herself beginning to hyperventilate. She didn't know if she could go through with this. From the look in Juan's eyes next to her, he was having the same thought.

She had been hoping that somehow they wouldn't have to jump. That something would change. Maybe Joe would call back from the cockpit that they had to postpone it because of a mechanical problem or bad weather. *She couldn't believe she was hoping for bad weather in a plane!*

The last couple of hours had actually been smoother than expected. A break in the storm gave them a surprisingly clear flight and calm conditions. Now, she found herself perversely wishing for the opposite.

She stared nervously at Caesare and raised her voice. "I don't know if I can do this!"

She jumped back when Corso and Tiewater pulled one of the crates free, sliding it between them, toward the back of the plane.

"You'll do fine," Caesare replied loudly. "We're at a low altitude. We'll be on the ground before you know it."

"It's not the landing I'm afraid of. It's the part about *leaving the plane!*"

He examined her calmly. "Are you afraid of heights?"

"I am right now!"

Caesare looked at Juan. "Juan?"

Juan glanced at DeeAnn before replying. "I'm pretty freaked out too."

All he could do was nod. He understood their fear. Their inexperienced minds racing through all the things that could go wrong. But there wasn't anything he could do about it. At least not at the moment. The best he could do for them was to make the experience as short as possible. They could yell at him later when they were on the ground.

He looked at his watch and held up two fingers to his men.

DeeAnn couldn't believe how quickly those two minutes passed. The men had moved all three boxes to the door and unbundled the large parachutes on top. Suddenly, they all nodded to Caesare at once and pushed the first one out into the howling wind. They quickly followed with the next two, getting them all out within a matter of seconds from each other. She watched as Corso and Tiewater stepped back, and Caesare then made his way to the cockpit.

He slapped Joe on the shoulder and shouted something to him. Less than a minute later, DeeAnn grabbed one of the straps on the wall as the plane began to bank to the right.

"Okay. Here we go."

It seemed to happen in a blur. Tiewater and Anderson moved behind them and began attaching her and Juan's harnesses to their own. They pulled them in tight to ensure they were secure. Together, they pushed the two forward, with each pair shuffling awkwardly toward the door.

Behind them, Caesare fastened Dulce to his own harness, facing inward toward his chest. Her dark legs dangled in the air as he shuffled and joined them at the door.

Corso stood on the other side, ready to help them out. Through his goggles, he stared down at his watch. He held up one finger to the men and they nodded.

In a fog, DeeAnn yelled to Corso. "Why aren't you attached to anyone?"

"It would exceed the weight limit of the chute."

Her eyes shot open. "There's a *weight limit*?!"

Corso ignored her and motioned to the men. Tiewater

and Anderson both reached around, folding DeeAnn and Juan's arms in across their chests.

Behind them, Caesare smiled into Dulce's trusting eyes and whispered into her left ear. "This time like a bird."

DeeAnn's heart nearly froze as she peered straight out the door at the blue sky with green treetops far below. The last clear image she saw was Anderson's hands reaching past her and gripping each side of the door, followed by a hard push.

OH…MY…GOD!

A minute later, Joe leaned out from his cockpit seat and looked back through the cabin.

Everyone was out.

He banked into a hard left turn, giving him a clear view of the ground below, and counted parachutes. Satisfied, he gradually leveled the DC-3 and headed back the way they came.

He was surprised to find signs of the storm still visible on the horizon. At that distance, he shouldn't have seen anything. He didn't know yet that the storm had once again turned east toward him.

It took less than an hour to realize how much trouble he was in. With nowhere to land before the Peruvian border, he was left with just one very bad option.

He would not make it back.

Two hours later, Joe Marcionek, a sixty-three-year-old ex-Army pilot who had helped thousands of suffering souls by flying in the face of political tyrants…would reach his final twilight.

His last moments would be a fight to the very end, and without a single regret.

Echo Pier was located in San Juan, Puerto Rico. It served as the primary base of operations for all United States Coast Guard activity in the eastern Caribbean Sea.

Overlooking the Bahía de San Juan, the "Sector," as it was officially known, was the region's only Search and Rescue station. It was also the nearest marine dock both secure and large enough to accommodate most of the U.S. Navy's larger ships.

The six shore units included management of two of the nation's busiest ports and the protection of over 1.3 million square miles of open ocean. However, at that moment, the station's commanding officer had his full attention glued to the window. Captain F. D. Arthur watched the arrival at Echo Pier with a touch of anxiety, particularly after receiving a call directly from Admiral Langford only hours before.

The gleaming white hull of the arriving ship was known well at the Sector, serving as not just one of the Atlantic's primary research vessels, but perhaps its most distinguished — the U.S.S. Pathfinder.

Captain Emerson stood on the ship's bridge, stoically. He watched as it eased alongside the giant dock, its huge rubber fenders shrieking against the concrete pillars. Heavy mooring lines were lowered to where they were tied around bollards large enough for children to climb on. The dock's twelve-foot fenders gave up their final protest, permanently coming to rest, pressed against the Pathfinder's thick steel hull.

Emerson heard the Pathfinder's diesel engines disengage and nodded to his first officer, Harris. Emerson then crossed the small room and opened the metal and glass door, stepping out into the warm sun. He continued along a lightly painted gangway until he reached the end and then descended a ladder to the ship's main deck.

Emerson continued down two more levels before continuing aft. When he reached the stern, he stopped to observe the flurry of activity.

Two of the ship's winches had been removed by his crew, making just enough room on the platform for a twenty-thousand-gallon water tank. This one larger than they'd built before...and for good reason.

Lee Kenwood briefly held up a finger over his shoulder before returning it to the keyboard and resuming his typing.

"Not yet."

"It's time, Lee."

"I know, I know. I just need to finish this one module." He continued typing hastily for another minute before stopping to double-check his work. When he was sure, he saved the window and clicked another button to begin compiling. He pushed himself away from the desk, rolling backwards and twirling his chair to face an impatient Alison.

"Done?"

"For the moment," he nodded. "Enough to get things started. The rest I can do en route."

"Good. Because we're about to be late."

"Sorry." Kenwood leapt from his chair and stuffed his laptop into a backpack. "But believe me, that was something you definitely wanted me to do." He then trotted to a wide cart holding several pieces of hardware. "Locked and loaded."

Alison examined the computers stacked neatly on the cart, along with two large plastic containers packed with more equipment and peripherals.

"Fine. What were you working on?"

"I made some progress on that problem we had last time with IMIS getting confused with too many translations happening all at once. I identified the acoustical signatures for Dirk and Sally and am trying to create a filter based on those. It should help us single them out from other dolphin exchanges."

"That's great, Lee."

He shrugged. "We shouldn't get too excited yet. It's probably going to take quite a bit of tweaking."

That thought worried Alison. They were going to need to make it work sooner than that. But instead, she just nodded at his cart. "Are you sure you have everything?"

"Yep." He patted one of the servers affectionately. "Redundant servers and as much data as they can hold. More powerful too."

"Good." She stepped in front of Lee as he began to move, reaching the door first and holding it open for him. Together, they wheeled their way to the elevator.

"Is Kelly here yet?"

"Yes. She and Chris are waiting at the dock. Everything else is packed."

The elevator door opened and Lee rolled the cart inside, followed by Alison, who pressed the button for the bottom floor.

"So, about this audio signature thing." There was a slight bounce as the elevator began to move. "How much *tweaking* do you think it will take?"

"I'm not sure. I've never done it before. Probably a lot, but we can start on the way."

Alison nodded. They didn't have a lot of choice. They were in a rush, but she was worried about the trip for another reason. This wasn't like their last trip where Dirk and Sally traveled alongside their small boat. That was much slower, but they had the luxury of multiple days, which made the arrangement possible.

This time, they were transporting the dolphins in order to

get there faster. Something they had done only once before. On the same ship, as a matter of fact, but it was over a much shorter distance. This time, they were headed to Trinidad, which would take just over eight hours. The tank would be bigger, but still a very tight fit for two dolphins. And there was a finite amount of time they could remain in such a confined space with certain "needs." It was also why they were swimming alongside them now to reach the Pathfinder in San Juan. It wasn't something most people thought about, but Alison knew that without a bathroom break beforehand, they would soon have a natural problem on their hands.

The elevator reached the lower floor and opened again, where Alison and Lee wheeled out through one of the building's side exits, into the warm morning sun. A strong wind blew against them when they rounded the corner of the building. Upon reaching the wooden ramp, Lee stepped around and guided the cart down slowly from the front.

Kelly Carlson ducked her blonde head out from the boat's small cockpit when she heard the thumping over the uneven planks of the ramp. She'd been in Palmas Del Mar overseeing the purchase of another boat and the subsequent repair of its port-side engine. It still wasn't perfect, but they weren't going far, and she'd remain behind to continue the work.

She called Chris out of the salon to help Lee load the servers onboard and secure them for what was shaping up to be a short but somewhat exciting ride, given the morning chop.

Near the stern, Neely Lawton had already boarded. She was waiting, quietly staring out over the water. She didn't appear anxious or excited. Instead, it was one of apprehension, knowing they were headed back to a place not far from where her father had just died. A place where he gave his own life to save them all.

That they were going back to the same area, and for the

258

very same reason, was more than a little sobering.

A few hours later, Captain Emerson had an equally concerning thought. He didn't know exactly what they were after, but given the close proximity to where the Bowditch was lost, it wasn't exactly a stretch to suspect a relationship. And like the Coast Guard's Base Commander, his orders too had come directly from Admiral Langford, which was unusual. It made Emerson wonder just how many others were aware of their new "mission."

"They're here, sir," Harris said, sticking his head inside.

Emerson stepped back outside through the bridge door and joined his first officer at the railing. Harris handed him the binoculars and pointed out past the pier.

He spotted the Teknicraft aluminum-hulled catamaran heading directly toward them and recognized Chris Ramirez standing outside the pilothouse at one of the forward railings. He couldn't make out anyone else except the two dolphins swimming next to them, occasionally jumping between the swells.

He returned inside and grabbed the handset, raising it to his ear. When his head engineer Tay answered on the other end, he asked the same question he'd asked less than a half hour earlier.

"How close?"

From the Pathfinder's stern, Tay nodded confidently. "We're ready, Captain. We're done reinforcing the tank and it's filling now. I'd say ten minutes."

"Excellent. We'll need to transfer them as quickly as possible."

"Yes, sir." Behind Tay, the heavy, fabric sling swayed slowly in the breeze. "We're all ready for that too."

"Well done. Let us know when everyone's aboard."

"I will, sir."

Emerson hung up and placed the handset back in its

cradle in front of his communications officer. He returned outside and peered back out over the water, this time handing the binoculars back to Harris.

"Any idea behind the urgency, sir?"

"Nope."

Alison and Chris watched impatiently from the side of the metal tank while the tall orange winch moved Dirk smoothly across the open deck, lowering him into the tank beside Sally. After some difficulty unwrapping the sling, Tay's team double-checked the integrity of the tank before giving a thumbs-up.

Behind them, Kelly squeezed Alison's shoulders. "That's my cue." She winked at Chris. "You sure you have everything before I untie?"

Chris nodded, hiding his disappointment. "I think so." He started to add something to keep the conversation with Kelly going but didn't know what else to say, without it sounding corny. Instead, he tried to stand there and appear cool while she hugged Alison.

"Drop me a postcard."

Alison laughed. "Sure. I'll put it in a bottle."

Kelly turned and headed for the gangplank. "I'll be watching the store, so let me know if you need anything."

"Thanks, Kel. Will do."

Alison's eyes wasted no time. She turned to Tay, who was already on the phone confirming that they were ready.

The rest of the crew had begun pulling in the Pathfinder's giant lines from the dock when Captain Emerson appeared above and promptly descended the ladder.

He raised his voice over the ship's engines as they rumbled to life. "Dr. Shaw. It's nice to see you again."

Alison shook his extended hand. "Thank you, Captain. I guess this makes adventure number three."

He smiled. "I suggest we don't count the first two."

Alison couldn't agree more. The first time she and the team had to be evacuated from the Pathfinder by the Coast Guard. The second trip ended with the terrible fate of the Bowditch. As Steve Caesare once said, they weren't exactly batting a thousand.

Emerson turned to Chris. "Mr. Ramirez."

"Hello again, Captain."

After looking at the dolphins, Emerson said, "Are we all set here? I understand we're on a tight schedule."

"Yes, I think we're ready when you are."

"Very good. I'm afraid we have some larger swells than usual, so for safety reasons I'll need to ask you both to remain above on the main deck. You should still be able to keep an eye on your friends from there."

Alison followed the captain's gaze up one flight. "That's fine. Can we remain outside?"

Emerson nodded. "Of course. The wind is quite strong, but no one freezes in the Caribbean. Mr. Kenwood is setting up his equipment upstairs." He looked around the stern. "I presume Commander Lawton has already reported upstairs."

"Yes. She headed up as soon as we arrived."

"Very good. If you'll follow me."

They both fell in behind the captain and climbed up a white ladder, painted to match the hull. When they reached the next level, Emerson turned to face them before continuing. "I'll let Mr. Kenwood know where you are. Is there anything else we can provide for you?"

"Thank you, I don't think so."

He nodded again. "Hold on tight."

After he had departed, Alison turned to Chris. "You ready?"

He took a deep breath and wrapped his grip around the metal railing. "As ready as I'll ever be."

"You sure?"

"Yeah. I just never thought I would be back on this ship again so soon."

"Me either."

Chris looked down at Dirk and Sally, relaxed and moving slowly inside the tank. "Things are getting a little crazy, huh?"

"You could say that again."

"Kind of…scary crazy."

Alison looked at him curiously. "What do you mean?"

"I don't know. Everything just seems to be happening awfully fast. The things we're learning are way beyond what we ever expected."

"It's true. But if we're right about these plants…"

"I'm not talking about the plants, Ali. I'm talking about," he paused, shaking his head, "all of it. IMIS, the translations, Dirk, and Sally. We never dreamed of finding this much. Humans went for so long thinking dolphins were just smart mammals. A step above pets really. Now we find out they have culture, heritage, a history of their own."

Chris sighed. "It makes me think about how much history we humans have been ignoring, all around us. Every species has a history. A heritage. History isn't just what's happened or where we've been, Alison. History is about our place in the world."

Chris paused, trying to figure out how to put his feelings into words. "I guess what I'm saying is that it's all kinda scary. It's scary to find out how much exists around us that we've just been oblivious to. Or maybe apathetic. It also makes me wonder just how much more Dirk and Sally know."

"We're finding out."

"We are. But it kind of feels like we're stumbling backwards into all of it, doesn't it?"

Alison considered his question. "It does."

"It started out as exciting, but now it's beginning to feel a little eerie. Do you remember that video we saw on the internet? The one with that dive team who was approached by a bottlenose?"

"The one caught in the line?"

"Right. It was caught in a fishing line and had a hook stuck in one of its flippers."

"Of course I remember. It was amazing."

"It was, right? I saw that again the other day and if you watch the video carefully, there are so many things that indicate a much deeper level of consciousness. How slowly it matched the diver's movements. How close the dolphin was to him, like they were bound to each other. It worked together with him to get the hook out and the line removed. For those few minutes, they were partners. They just *knew* what the other was trying to do." Chris shrugged. "Anyone can see it if they look close enough. It doesn't take someone like us to show the world there's a lot more there than we think."

Alison grinned. "And that scares you?"

"No, not that. It's how *fast* it's all happening. How fast our world is changing. Just look at how fast IMIS is translating now. There's a lot happening in this world that we don't know about and it feels like it's exploding."

He shook his head. "And the world doesn't seem to do well with explosions in *anything*. What happens to us, Ali? What happens to all of us when the world realizes how deep this goes? It's like discovering extraterrestrials. Realizing that we really aren't alone in the universe. Hell, we're not even alone on the planet. We never were. And IMIS is the *catalyst* for it all."

She looked back down at Dirk and Sally, thinking. "I know what you mean. It wasn't too long ago that I thought the truth was more important than anything. That all the politics — all the cover-ups and deceit — would right themselves if there was enough truth. But now I'm not so sure. I'm beginning to think that truth, for all its virtue…is dangerous. For us and for them."

263

Chris nodded. "I think people can only absorb so much change at once. And as a society, probably even less."

"Maybe you're right." Alison's eyes glanced back to the shore where she watched Echo Pier receding behind them. "It's ironic, isn't it? We tell stories and even make movies about how great a different future would be. But we rarely think about all the consequences." Her eyes remained fixed on the horizon. "Remember when we first started this project? Remember all the research we did…and some of those crazy stories?"

"How could I forget?"

"Maybe some of them weren't so crazy."

Chris frowned. "Ali, some of those people claimed dolphins could shapeshift into mermaids."

"I'm not talking about *those*. I'm talking about some of the others."

"You mean the ones about healing."

"Right. Some of those people claimed they were healed after touching dolphins."

What was left of Chris's grin abruptly faded.

"Maybe some of those people weren't crazy, Chris. Maybe they *can* heal. If not directly then maybe indirectly." Alison took a deep breath and turned around, leaning against the rail. "Now, thinking about what you just said, I think you may be more right than you know. Society doesn't deal with change as well as we all think. At least not sudden change." She looked up into Chris's eyes. "What do you think would happen if people found out they can heal? What do you think happens to dolphins then?"

Chris sighed. "Elephant tusks come to mind."

"And shark cartilage. And that doesn't even work."

He folded his arms. "People would go crazy. When millions of those people think they can be healed from disease by getting a hold of a dolphin."

"Especially if it's true."

"Exactly."

"And then there's the plants. If they really are like what John recovered in Guyana, how in the world do you keep that secret?" She paused, thinking about John, and something he'd said just a few weeks earlier: *beware the leap*.

"Explosions," Chris said.

"Okay, you're right," she said in a lowered voice. "This is getting scary."

"And we're right in the middle of it." He watched Alison become quiet and decided to change the subject. "Anyway, now that you're sorry you asked…how's everything else? How's John?"

"I don't know." She shook her head. "I haven't talked to him in a few days." She tried to convince herself it wasn't a big deal. Just another routine mission that didn't allow him to make calls. He'd said as much when they last talked. But something didn't feel right. Something felt very wrong and she didn't know why.

48

John Clay was also feeling worried, at the lights he and Tang were now seeing in the distance, above the trees.

Helicopters.

But these helicopters were not just searching. These were bigger...and they were landing.

Apparently it was decided that stopping everyone was better than trying to find them from the air. Borger was right. Someone knew.

The lights from the two large choppers descended and disappeared behind a dense patch of trees, leaving only a faint glow overhead to indicate anything was waiting on the other side.

As Tang rounded a slight curve, both men could see three sets of brake lights shining brightly from the cars ahead.

"This isn't good."

"No, it's not." Clay looked at the map on his phone again. They were less than seven miles away. Damn close. He immediately reached into the back and grabbed his bag.

The road straightened, allowing them to see the first set of headlights shining at them. The bright white lights flashed off momentarily before resuming, indicating something had just passed in front of the distant vehicle.

"Someone's approaching on foot."

"Slow down." Clay shoved the satellite phone back into a side pocket and lifted the heavy bag onto his lap. "They'll see us if we stop." He then reached up and turned off the interior lamp.

"What are you going to do, jump?"

"Yep."

"Okay, let me get closer." Tang continued to slow the

vehicle smoothly and drifted toward the edge of the road. They were now within a quarter mile of the blockade. Up ahead, flashlights appeared next to the first stopped car.

"Keep your brights on until you get my door closed again."

Tang nodded. "Say when."

Clay quickly checked his feet and legs to make sure they were clear, then found the handles of his bag and cinched them together. "Go!"

As soon as Tang turned on the car's bright lights, Clay opened his door. In a split second, he jumped into the darkness and disappeared while Tang swiftly leaned over, fumbling for the door. His fingertips found a corner of the handle and pulled it shut, careful not to slam it. At an eighth of a mile, he turned the brights off and continued slowing behind the car in front of him.

Tang fought his instinct to look back for Clay in the mirror just as one of the powerful flashlights moved further out into the road and shone directly into his windshield. The beam remained on him as he coasted in, behind the others, where he counted five soldiers on the road. Two were holding flashlights with two more gripping QBZ-95 assault rifles tightly in their hands. The fifth and closest soldier, with a flashlight already trained on Tang, turned back down the road as another car appeared in the distance.

Tang could see the men were not in the mood for pleasantries.

"Where are you going?" a voice barked from behind a flashlight.

Tang feigned confusion and held up his hand to block the bright light. From what he could see, the man looked to be in his early twenties which probably meant he was inexperienced and hopefully unprepared for a driver taking the offensive.

"What is this? What's happening?" He kept his voice loud in an effort to mask any noise from the trees.

The soldier's pause behind the flashlight was brief. More brief than Tang had been hoping for.

The man staring down at him was not a rookie. Instead, he peered at Tang with a look of bemusement. Without a word, he checked the empty passenger's seat.

"Where are you going?" he asked again, sternly.

Tang didn't take his eyes off him, even while a second flashlight appeared and began searching the rest of his car.

"I'm going to visit a friend." He remained calm, knowing that without the bag in the back seat their flashlights wouldn't find anything...unless they opened the trunk.

"And where is your friend?"

Tang paused. His mind was racing, trying desperately to retrieve one of the towns Clay had mentioned.

"Dadonggou."

The soldier's mannerism did not change. He continued studying Tang and extended his hand. "Identification."

"What is the meaning of this?" he tried again.

"It's a security check."

"There has never been a check here before."

"How many times have you visited your friend?"

"Many times. And there is no trouble in this xian."

"That's right. And we are here to ensure it remains without trouble." The soldier nodded, examining Tang's ID. "You are a long way from Guangzhou."

Clay slid to a stop at the bottom of a steep bank. Much steeper than he was expecting, causing him to lose control and slide into a small creek with a splash.

He quickly jumped to his feet and scrambled behind a nearby tree trunk. He waited for flashlights to appear over the edge of the road, but seeing none, Clay dropped his bag on the damp earth in front of him.

Unzipping the bag, he pulled out a set of night-vision goggles and slid them over his thick dark hair. Next he retrieved a black matted .40 caliber and pushed it into the waistband of his pants before swinging the bag onto his shoulders again.

He moved smoothly through the thick layer of needles and leaves, winding away from the road above him. Once beyond the glow of lights and the muffled voices, Clay broke into a sprint.

49

Qin peered out from the small window of the Harbin Z-6 helicopter into the near pitch-blackness below. There were now only occasional lights visible from the air, which gave the darkened interior of the cabin an eerie feeling. Only the thumping of the blades and the cockpit's instruments were left to remind him that they were moving.

The last three hours had unleashed a frenzy of activity. Once M0ngol had zeroed in on the American's location, time was of the essence. They had to stop him before he reached the hospital.

The mobilization took less than thirty minutes, but it still required time to travel the several hundred kilometers. Fortunately for Qin, there was a small team of Special Operations Forces on return from maneuvers at the base of China's Guangxing Reservoir, close enough to intercept the American before he could.

Qin checked his watch impatiently. He hated having to call Xinzhen, but he had no other choice. He needed transportation immediately…and men. And being a member of the Politburo, Xinzhen had as much authority as anyone within China. A level of authority that had a fully equipped Z-6 helicopter landing in the parking lot of the MSS building a mere half hour later.

But now Xinzhen knew. Not everything, but enough to know what Wei had done and what was likely hidden in a small building in the middle of nowhere. Qin didn't mention it was a hospital, nor that it was where he believed Wei's daughter to be a patient. He'd been at the MSS long enough to learn that investigators never revealed everything, even to the Politburo.

Especially since he now possessed information Xinzhen

would kill over. He already had. And Qin was now walking a thin line between a being an asset to someone like Xinzhen and being a liability.

He glanced up when the helicopter's copilot waved to get his attention and pointed to his headphones.

Qin nodded and glanced at the two men sitting next to him. Xinzhen's men, both of whom were already aboard the chopper when it arrived at MSS.

Together the men watched him stoically without saying a word.

Qin raised the headphones and lowered them over his ears before adjusting the microphone.

"This is Qin."

"Sir, we've stopped twelve cars. But no American yet."

Qin's eyes narrowed. They should have been there by now. "Any *gweilo* at all?"

"No, mostly locals. But two are from Beijing and another from Guangzhou."

"What kind of cars are they driving?"

The soldiers on the ground paused. "Several Hyundai, GM, Nissan. And a Honda."

Qin remained, thinking, staring into the darkness with his coal-colored eyes. The man would have had to come in quietly. Unnoticed. And he'd need help to get here quickly. Which also meant help blending in.

But in China, cars were not used for blending in. Instead, they were about status and prestige. Something that was especially true in Beijing. Cars were meant to be noticed, not overlooked.

"How old?"

"Hold old are the drivers?"

"No. The cars."

The soldier on the ground turned and assessed the cars. "Most are new. Within a few years. The Honda is old. Ten, maybe fifteen years."

"Who was the driver?"

"A security guard. From Guangzhou. Says he's visiting a friend."

"From Guangzhou?"

"Yes."

Guangzhou was too far, Qin thought. Almost anyone traveling that far would have taken a plane over paying for two thousand miles worth of gasoline. Especially a lowly guard.

"Where does he work?"

"Ministry of Foreign Relations."

Qin's eyes widened. His response was instant. "He's a spy. Subdue him!"

"Subdue him?"

"Yes! Now!"

Qin leaned forward urgently and slapped the copilot on the shoulder to get his attention. When the man turned around, Qin motioned forcefully toward the windshield. The message was clear: *hurry*!

On the ground, Tang was standing nearby, watching the soldier. He couldn't hear what was said on the phone, but the sudden change in the man's expression was enough.

50

With his computer now secure, Borger was watching from his chair. The icon representing Clay's phone had suddenly jumped off the road and was now moving very slowly.

Another screen displayed the latest overhead shot from the satellite. He typed in the coordinates, which quickly zoomed the picture in. Most of the image was completely dark, except for two items.

Borger picked up his phone and dialed.

Clay was struggling up an embankment when the phone rang in his pocket. He pulled it out and answered without stopping.

"Not a good time, Will."

"Clay!" Borger shouted. "You okay?"

He rolled his eyes inside the green-tinted goggles. "That's debatable."

"I see lights coming in from the northeast. I think they're helicopters."

"You're a little late," Clay replied, between breaths. He spotted a narrow path through the trees and plowed through several large bushes to reach it, where he broke into a run again.

Borger zoomed out and examined a third light on the image. This one was further away and headed due north. "I have another one coming in."

"How far?!" Clay shouted into the phone, still pumping his other arm.

"Twenty minutes. Maybe less."

"Dammit!" Clay hung up and dug in, lowering his head. He bolted ahead with everything he had.

Li Na Wei opened her eyes and watched as the dark room sharpened around her bed. Her eyesight was as good as it had ever been, and she glanced around from item to item, scarcely recognizable beyond the soft lime-green glow of her heart rate monitor. The old machine's rhythmic beep matching itself to the beating of her heart.

It was all she could hear, but something had awakened her. She scanned and listened...waiting. But there was nothing else.

She hadn't been able to sleep much since finding out about her father. It all felt so surreal. A loneliness she had never felt before wrapped in the disbelief that it was really happening. Yet each time she awoke, no matter how long she had slept, her situation felt increasingly real.

This time, though, something was different. No pain. No chills. This time, it was a feeling. A sick, almost nauseous feeling crawling its way up her chest.

It was the feeling of danger.

She heard it before Dr. Lee, who had just bolted upright in his small cot. The storage room was almost bare, leaving plenty of room for the folding bed, where Lee had slept since Li Na regained consciousness. Now sitting alert on the flimsily-sheeted mattress, he listened carefully to make sure he wasn't mistaken. That it wasn't a dream.

It wasn't. The distant sound came again, louder. The sound of an approaching helicopter.

"Li Na!" He jumped to his feet and ran through the open door, stumbling into a rolling bed parked against the wall. He pushed it hard out of the way, knocking it into the opposite wall and toppling two unused IV stands. Finally past, Lee raced toward the room at the far end of the hall.

"Li Na!"

The teenage girl was already out of her bed. She turned from the window when she heard the doctor shouting. She was still dressed in her thin, light-blue gown.

Lee's footsteps could be heard approaching. When he finally burst into her room, his eyes focused on Li Na's shadowy figure just a few feet away and grabbed her arm. "Someone's coming!"

"Who?"

"I don't know. Perhaps the people your father feared!"

"Are you sure?"

He paused, listening again. It was much closer. "Helicopters don't come here." He ran to the small cupboard and threw the doors open. Grabbing her clothes, he pushed them into her arms in a panic. "Get dressed. Quickly!"

Li Na needed no convincing. The sickening feeling in her chest was still there, and growing stronger. She fumbled, separating her clothes and then slipping each foot into a pant leg.

Lee ran back to the door and looked back the way he came. A blinding light swept over the small building, shining in through several windows as it passed overhead. The sound of the aircraft's rotors outside became deafening.

He darted across the hall, into the small kitchen, and raised the lid of a freezer resting against the far wall. Inside, at the bottom, was Wei's strange metal case.

Lee yanked it out and returned to the room. He again pushed the case into her arms, this time grabbing one hand. "Hurry!"

He led her back down the hallway and into the storage room, throwing his cot out of the way. He yanked the small closet door open and pushed her inside, quickly closing it and pulling the cot back in place against the door.

No sooner had the Harbin touched down that one of Xinzhen's men, sitting closest to Qin, yanked the door open. The man then leapt from the helicopter with the blades still churning at full speed. His boots hit the hard ground and he tore into a run toward the building. The second man who followed was nearly as big and reached the wooden door just steps behind the first.

It was locked.

Neither bothered looking at Qin as he climbed out. Instead, the second man stepped back and promptly withdrew a large pistol from inside his coat. Without a word, he pointed it at the door and fired multiple rounds into the wooden door jam, shredding it. When the door still didn't move, he fired twice more. This time, the left side of the heavy door slumped. With one last powerful kick, it swung inward, dropping wooden splinters everywhere.

Inside, Lee ran from the storage room, barely reaching the front door before it burst open.

The first of Xinzhen's men stepped through the doorway and growled. "Where?"

"Who are you?"

"Where is she?!" he repeated.

When Lee didn't answer, the large man stepped forward and slammed him hard against the wall.

"I-I don't know," Lee groaned, "who you're talking about."

Behind them, Qin's voice was icy. "Your patient."

Sputtering, the doctor shook his head. "I have several patients."

"Wei's daughter. We know she's here."

The large man's hand gripped Lee around the throat.

"I don't know who that is."

276

Qin grinned at him, sardonically. "Oh, I think you do." He turned and examined the short hallway. He motioned to the right. The second of Xinzhen's men nodded and stormed down the narrow corridor.

An elderly male patient appeared in one of the doorways with a walker. Xinzhen's man stopped in front of him, glancing briefly into his room before placing a hand on the old man's chest and shoving him back inside. The thug moved on, indifferent as the elderly patient toppled to the cold tile.

When he reached the next room, the agent found a bald woman with weak sunken eyes and cheeks lying frail in her bed. Her tired eyes were clearly unable to comprehend what was happening.

It was the next room where he stopped and looked back down the hall at the others.

"This one's empty." He looked back inside. "But someone was here."

Qin immediately stormed toward the room, along with Xinzhen's first agent who still kept the doctor's throat gripped tightly in his huge hand.

When Qin saw the bed and its blankets thrown off, he turned back to Lee. "Who was in here?"

The man's grip tightened when the doctor didn't answer. "Where is she?!"

From inside the small closet, Li Na tried to sense what was around her. When she heard the gunshots, she froze. Her father was right. She checked the doorknob for a lock, but found it smooth and featureless. She continued searching with her hands.

There were shelves on both sides, filled with things she didn't recognize. Some she did, like small cardboard boxes and sealed plastic bags with pieces of plastic inside. Some were softer. Probably bandages.

She stepped back and stumbled into a large object on the floor, slamming it loudly against the wall. Tall, thin objects fell onto her as she scrambled to catch what she couldn't see. One of the missed items struck her in the forehead.

She cried out softly and rubbed her head. *What was the doctor thinking?* This was a terrible idea. There was nowhere to go. He must have thought he could convince them she wasn't there.

But if he couldn't, this was the worst possible place to be.

With a nervous hand, Li Na turned the knob and pushed, just enough to crack the door open.

She could see part of the bed, positioned against the door. Against the other wall, a shelf held clear tubing, boxes of latex gloves, and linens. After a moment, she leaned out and nervously peered around the closet door.

That's when she heard the voices.

Qin was eyeing the doctor with anger. He opened his mouth to speak again, but stopped when his eyes caught something behind them. The rest of the hallway was clean. Yet at the far end, two IV stands lay sprawled on the floor beneath a rolling bed that was turned at an odd angle. On the other side of the bed, a dim light reflected out through the room's doorway.

Qin's eyes moved back to the doctor, who was now watching him nervously. Without a word, Qin stepped around the agent who still held Lee and walked silently down the hall. Unlike the first two rooms, the second two had patients who hadn't woken up from the commotion.

When Qin reached the rolling bed, he pushed it carefully out of his path. He stepped over the fallen equipment and drew his gun as he inched closer to the doorway. He glanced back at the other men only briefly before stepping inside.

Qin scanned the room, noting the worn cot and small

closet with an open door. Inside the closet were stacks of cleaning supplies with several haphazardly placed brooms and mops. On the floor, a plastic bucket lay on its side.

Qin examined the rest of the room.

What he was searching for was hiding less than a meter away, directly behind him.

52

Will Borger didn't take his eyes off the screen. He watched with annoyance as the latest satellite image slowly came in, overlaying the old picture. When the transfer finally finished, the lights he had been tracking were exactly where he was afraid they would be.

"Crap!"

He zoomed in as far as he could. Even in the dark, the outline of the small building was recognizable, along with the helicopter parked less than a hundred feet away.

Borger grabbed his phone and dialed again. There was no answer. He turned to another screen and zoomed back in on Clay's satellite phone. It was still moving.

He was almost there.

Qin stood silently in the room, listening to the final whirring outside from the helicopter's rotors. He looked down at the small cot and studied the blankets. They were messy. The position of the rusted frame so near to the closet looked out of place. Intentional.

He couldn't hear Li Na's breathing behind the door, not over the rotors or Xinzhen's men continuing to shout at the doctor. But he knew she was still here in the room. He turned slowly with his raised gun and looked behind him. There was only one other place to hide.

He reached out with his left hand and fingered the doorknob, pulling it decidedly away from the wall.

The door's shadow moved with it, revealing the terrified young face of Li Na Wei standing against the wall. Her dark hair was messy, with bangs stopping just short of her wide eyes.

The resemblance to her father was unmistakable.

"Well, well, well," Qin breathed quietly. "You *are* alive after all."

He looked her up and down. Her clothes were as disheveled as her hair. "Where is it?"

She didn't answer.

Qin lowered the gun slightly, pointing it at the girl's midsection, and raised his voice over the noise from outside.

"Where is it?!"

Li Na stared at him, and in an act of unexpected defiance, shook her head from side to side.

Qin gazed at her coldly. He didn't have time for this. He didn't know where the American was, and on top of that, the fewer of Xinzhen's men who knew, the better. He stepped away and peered through the door, back down the hall. "Bring him here."

Li Na remained still, listening to the scuffle outside. The doctor was abruptly thrown into the room where he stumbled to the far wall. He turned and looked at Li Na apologetically before reluctantly facing Qin.

"Our young lady appears to have forgotten how to speak. And I have very little time, so I'll ask you once and once only. Where…is…it?"

Lee glanced at all three men, careful not to look in the direction of the closet. He knew it didn't really matter where it was. They'd find it eventually. What mattered more was that Lee had monumentally failed both Li Na and her father.

He failed to heed her father's warning as quickly as he should have. He thought he had more time. To help her. To understand exactly how Wei had saved her. And to prepare her. But it was too late. The man before him had an unmistakable look in his eyes. He was going to kill them no matter what he said. Of that, the doctor was sure. Lee might buy Li Na a few minutes, but that was all. And it wouldn't be enough to matter.

281

There was nothing else he could do. He stared at Qin's gun pointed squarely at his chest. His life was going to end there. That morning. In the tiny hospital that he had helped to build with his own hands.

Lee was surprised when a wave of emotion suddenly passed over him, squelching the fear. It was the feeling of…satisfaction. The satisfaction that if it had to happen here, there was no place more appropriate. It was in this tiny hospital that with only the barest of resources, Lee had saved hundreds of lives. And with the money General Wei had donated for helping his daughter, it would go on to save hundreds more. Maybe thousands.

In the end, his life wasn't any more important than those he'd cared for. For those he had brought into the world and for those he had helped out. It was simply-

The doctor's last thought was cut short by an explosion from Qin's gun. The bullet ripped into his chest and through one of his ventricles. He collapsed onto the floor and was dead within seconds.

Li Na screamed, horrified. She watched helplessly as the life slowly faded from the doctor's eyes. She stumbled backward against the wall, beginning to hyperventilate.

With a sickening grin, Qin turned back around and faced her.

"I'm going to ask you one…more…time."

A wave of terror welled up through her chest as Li Na tried desperately to speak through the shock. But she couldn't. Her lips wouldn't move. She tried to say something. Anything.

Suddenly, the second of Xinzhen's men, who was guarding the door, appeared to take a clumsy step forward before collapsing in front of them with nothing but a blur visible behind him. It was the blur of a rifle butt, now spinning in the air just as the larger of Xinzhen's men drew his gun.

He was fast. So fast that he managed to get off two

rounds before a flash erupted from the end of the AK-47's barrel now pointing into the room. Three bullets hit him in the chest, sending the agent into the wall and then to the floor, where the pistol rattled from his limp hand.

The barrel of the rifle immediately swept across the room and stopped against the doorjamb, angled directly at Qin.

In a flash, Qin pulled the teenage girl in front of him. He kept her between himself and the door before glancing back at Xinzhen's men, lying still in front of him.

His eyes darted back to the barrel of the AK. The American had arrived.

53

Out of breath and with his chest heaving, John Clay remained pressed against the doorjamb while peering over the top of the rifle, his aim locked in on Qin and Li Na. Even with his sweating hands and throbbing legs, the rifle remained motionless, waiting for the slightest movement from Qin.

In response, Qin twisted and managed to slouch further behind the girl's outline, leaving very little of his body exposed. His eyes peered around her with a hidden smirk.

"Ah, the American."

Clay's stonelike expression didn't change. "In the flesh."

"And who exactly might you be?"

"My name isn't important. Let her go."

Qin paused, waiting to see if there was anyone else with the American. Hearing nothing, he relaxed slightly but kept Li Na close. "My name is Qin," he said in nearly perfect English.

"Good for you."

"And as you can see," he said, gripping the girl's arm tighter, "you're too late."

Clay frowned. "Feels to me like I'm just in time."

"No." Qin shook his head. "I have her now. You don't."

Clay's eyes glanced away, double-checking the room and the men on the floor. They returned to Qin in an instant. "You may have her, but there's only one door."

Qin nodded, then slowly raised his gun and pressed it against Li Na's soft cheek. "And there's only one girl."

"Maybe you're not as smart as you look," Clay said, still hidden behind the rifle. "You obviously haven't thought about what happens to you if you kill her."

Defiantly, Qin wrapped his arm around Li Na's waist and forced her sideways, shuffling them both to the middle of the room. Exposing Clay in the doorway.

"The lapse in judgment is yours. I have a shield. You don't."

"I don't need a shield."

"Ah, there it is. The American bravado. Simple and shallow." Qin moved slightly behind Li Na, brushing his collar open with his chin and revealing a small microphone. "This is Qin. Our target is here at the hospital. Move quickly."

Well, that was a problem. Clay thought to himself. He remained steadfast, calculating how much time it would take the others to arrive. Four, maybe five minutes. Which meant he had less than two to get out and put any distance between them.

"When they take me, I'm going to take you first," Clay responded calmly.

Qin stared at him for a long moment and Clay noticed a slight change in his expression. Uncertainty.

The American was bluffing. He wouldn't sacrifice himself. *Or would he?* His mission was the girl. Which meant he'd kill her before letting Qin have her. It was exactly what Qin was prepared to do. Now he had to stall until the other soldiers arrived. But the American had the advantage: an exit. He could kill both Qin and the girl and still escape. It's what Qin would do in his place. But the man wasn't moving. How long would he wait before acting?

Clay's eyes shifted to Li Na Wei, petrified and sickened at the feel of Qin's breath on the back of her neck. She stared helplessly back at Clay.

"Do you speak English?"

"A little."

"He is going to kill you," Clay said. "No matter what you do."

"Shut up!" hissed Qin. "I just want the case. Give it to

285

me and you're free."

Li Na's eyes turned, searching for Qin but unable to see him.

"When he gets the case," Clay continued, "he will kill everyone here to keep it. Beginning with you. Your only chance to escape lies in the next sixty seconds."

"SHUT UP!" Qin yelled. He turned his gun on Clay, extending it over the girl's shoulder. "Tell me who you are or I will kill you right now."

Clay studied the gun. "You have a Norinco nine millimeter. Even at this range you have very little chance of preventing me from shooting you. Your bullet travels at thirteen-hundred-feet per second. Mine travels twice as fast. Which means a clean shot will pass straight through her and tear a giant hole through you. And guess which one of you I'm going to try to save first?"

"Your name!" Qin seethed.

Clay's grin was slight, and not at all visible from behind the rifle. "Call me...Ishmael."

Qin stared at him with grim satisfaction. "You're surrounded, *Ishmael.*" He pressed harder against Li Na. "And out of time. You *and the U.S. Navy* are too late."

Clay was still counting in his head. Qin's mention of the Navy told him exactly what he was afraid of. Qin knew everything. But the man was right, he was out of time.

Clay returned his gaze to Li Na. "Thirty seconds."

She began shaking. Scared to death, she looked helplessly at Clay before allowing her eyes to drop to the doctor's lifeless body at their feet. She closed her eyes momentarily before opening them and giving Clay the briefest of nods.

His reaction was nearly instantaneous. Pressing his index finger against the trigger and sending a single, explosive shot from his rifle.

The bullet hit the outside of Qin's outstretched hand, ripping through the top of his knuckles and tearing it away from Li Na, who covered her face and dropped to the floor.

Qin screamed and lost his grip on the girl, stumbling back to grab his bloody hand which was now missing an index finger. Clay's second shot tore into his left thigh, throwing him violently to the floor.

Li Na fell to her knees and Clay rushed forward to pick her up.

"We have to go. Now!" He helped her to the door, but stopped as Li Na suddenly pulled away. Without a word, she ran back to the closet and retrieved the metal case from inside. She then jumped past a struggling Qin and followed Clay out.

54

DeeAnn hit the moist ground with a thump. She and Anderson landed faster than expected, sliding several feet and onto their butts. Behind them, Juan and Tiewater stumbled but managed to land on their feet. Corso followed, whose boots hit the ground with a heavy thud.

Caesare arrived last, landing effortlessly with several strides and Dulce wrapped tightly in one arm. Once stopped, he disconnected the chute behind them before unbuckling her smaller harness. He lowered her to the ground only to find she was still clinging to him.

We fly! She said excitedly through DeeAnn's vest.

"Yes, we fly," he agreed laughingly and looked at DeeAnn as she approached, glaring at him. "You okay?"

"That's debatable."

He looked past her. "Juan?"

"I'm okay," the engineer nodded. "But if you all don't mind, I think I'll stay here and kiss the ground for a while."

Tiewater laughed and slapped him on the back. "Ah, that was an easy one. Try doing it at night."

"While being shot at," added Anderson.

"Uh, no thanks."

Caesare turned back to Dulce and pulled her helmet off. "How are you, Dulce?"

Me happy. Fly fun.

He wasn't the only one surprised that Dulce remained closely at his side. Both puzzled and still upset, DeeAnn stepped in and caressed her dark brown back. "Are you hurt?"

No hurt. Dulce was excited. She studied the trees and ground, sniffing the air. She was eager to find her friend. The first primate she had communicated with. Or at least the first one she remembered.

Contrary to what some pet owners might claim, Dulce *knew* she wasn't a human. She knew she was different and craved contact with others like her. And while many humans might assume their pets were content in a human world, Dulce had explained just how wrong that assumption was.

Dulce wanted to be with her own kind. She needed to be with them. And Dexter was one of them.

Standing over her, DeeAnn could see the excitement in her eyes. There was no doubt how much Dulce loved being back in the wild. Safely this time. Safely, DeeAnn observed, with Caesare.

Like the other men, Caesare stood and rolled his parachute into a compact bundle. He then stashed it inside a group of fern bushes and tossed his nylon harnesses in after it.

"Now what?" DeeAnn asked, when he turned around.

"Now we find our drops. Anderson, find us a place to settle in and establish a perimeter."

"Yes, sir." The young SEAL scanned their small landing site intently before trotting uphill and disappearing through an opening in the trees.

Caesare looked to Tiewater. "How close are we?"

"Pretty close," he replied, staring at a small GPS screen. "Maybe two miles."

It took an hour to retrieve their crates and haul them uphill to the best location they could find. Concealment and cover were their top priority. They needed a base that was well concealed and ensured that nothing could be seen from the road, which rounded the top of the mountain a half mile away. It also needed enough natural backing to avoid being mistakenly silhouetted against the horizon.

An expanse of palm trees provided a thick wall of concealment but not as much cover as they'd hoped for. However, it provided a wide view of the area below and the best field of fire they were going to find. Caesare hoped it wouldn't come to that.

Finally, they needed an escape route. In a fight, things rarely went according to plan, which could leave a fast retreat as their last viable option.

It didn't take Anderson long to find a way out through the trees and down the other side of the hill. Together, he and Tiewater relocated a small portion of their ammo and food supplies to a backup location and covered it under a pile of brush.

Coming in light meant they had enough food to keep six adults supplied for five days, but not much more. A growing gorilla ate more, requiring her own crate of vegetables. But even those wouldn't last long.

Anderson returned to camp and quietly checked their visibility from all four directions while Tiewater approached with Juan's bag over his shoulder.

"Where do you want your gear?"

Juan looked up from his work, making adjustments to DeeAnn's vest. "Um, over here, please." Tiewater nodded and dropped it with a thud next to the rock Juan was sitting on.

Juan returned his attention to DeeAnn's vest as it lay sprawled across his lap. The belt had been damaged during the jump from the airplane. The wide band was made from neoprene for comfort as well as protection of the thin batteries and circuitry inside. The damage caused one of the connections to break, leaving the unit without one of the six batteries.

Once Juan located the broken wire, he retrieved a butane-fueled soldering iron and began repairing it.

DeeAnn watched curiously, while also keeping an eye on Dulce, who was sitting nearby munching on a head of kale.

Further below, Corso emerged from the trees and climbed uphill with heavy steps. When he reached Caesare, he turned around and pointed. "There's another ascent a few hundred yards straight out. Less cover but enough for a crossfire. The road passes closer to that side then heads north, toward what looks to be an open patch. But not big enough for more than one or two choppers. I can see why they didn't airlift in. Nowhere else to land."

Caesare nodded. "That and they don't want to be noticed any more than we do." He pulled his phone out from his pant leg pocket and turned it on. After dialing Borger's number, he waited, listening. Instead of an answer, he got a busy signal. He tried again. Still busy. Caesare said nothing and dropped it back into his pocket.

Caesare watched as Tiewater retrieved four HK416 assault rifles and handed one to him. He took it, appreciating the familiar feel of hard, cool metal in his hands.

He turned to Juan. "How much longer?"

"Should be just a few minutes. It's pretty minor." Juan kept his eyes on the tip of the iron as wisps of smoke rose from inside the belt. "I do have more batteries in my bag that need to be charged."

Caesare nodded and smoothly slung the 416 over his shoulder. He unzipped the padded canvas where he found the batteries and pulled them out, along with a large solar panel. After placing the batteries on a nearby rock, he unfolded the panel into thirds and positioned them toward the sun. Finally, he attached each piece of hardware to a small charge controller and turned it on.

"That should hold it." Juan glanced at DeeAnn and stood up, resecuring the neoprene belt. "But it's not as strong as the original so we need to be careful."

"Okay." She took the vest from Juan and slipped it back over her white T-shirt, settling the belt over the top of her hips. She flipped it on and waited for it to initialize.

"Can you hear me, Dulce?"

Yes, me hear.

DeeAnn turned to Caesare. "Are we ready?"

"Yep." Caesare slid a backpack over his wide shoulders. On his hip was a holstered camouflage-colored Sig Sauer 9mm. The extra weight of another gun and its ammo was less than ideal, but carrying a second weapon had saved his life more than once. "We're about a quarter mile now from where we last saw Dexter. Once there, it's all up to you, Dee."

Anderson stepped forward, handing both DeeAnn and Juan a padded Camelbak with straps, and a long clear hose fastened to the front.

"What's this?" Juan asked.

"Water."

DeeAnn took one and slid it on her back, amused. "Juan, you and Lee really need to get out more."

His reply was sarcastic. "We're on top of a mountain, Dee. I'm pretty sure this counts."

She laughed and turned back to Caesare.

"We need to hightail it. We don't have much time before Otero and his men arrive. Stay behind Anderson and me. Tiewater and Corso will bring up the rear. Stay on our heels and do not step *anywhere* outside of our footsteps. We don't have time for any injuries or surprises. If you need us to slow down for any reason, tell us but keep your voice down. We don't know who else is up here. Questions?"

Both shook their heads. Dulce merely grinned at him from the ground with a hand inside DeeAnn's.

DeeAnn jumped suddenly at the sound of Corso slapping a magazine into his rifle. When she turned around, he peered at her with his usual stone face.

They reached their location within twenty minutes, where the smell of smoke was thick in the air, reminding both DeeAnn and Caesare of the grim circumstances of their last

292

visit. When they reached an opening in the brush, they could see the devastation still spread out before them.

A huge swath of the forest had been wiped clean. Destroyed. With the only remnants of vegetation burnt beyond recognition. Farther away and uphill, a sheer cliff wall, hundreds of feet high, towered above them and the blackened earth.

"Jesus Christ," whistled Tiewater. "What the hell happened here?"

"Destroyed," Caesare answered.

"Why?"

"To keep something quiet."

Tiewater stepped onto the burnt field and scuffed at it with his boot. "Like what?"

"You don't want to know."

Behind him, DeeAnn held up an arm, covering her mouth and coughing into her sleeve.

"I'm guessing this has to do with the monkey we're looking for."

"That's right." Caesare surveyed the area then spoke in a low voice, "The bodies are gone."

"What bodies?" Juan asked.

"Those belonging to the men who did this. Chinese soldiers. They were murdered before they finished the job."

DeeAnn peered down at Dulce, who was also staring out over the dead terrain. She wore a puzzled expression, as if not entirely understanding what she was seeing.

Smell bad.

"Yes," DeeAnn nodded, solemnly. "The smoke smells very bad."

Caesare and Tiewater stepped further out, scanning the area before motioning to the others to follow.

Once in the open, DeeAnn bent down and looked at the gorilla. "Dulce, it's time to find our friend."

She grinned excitedly. *Yes. Dulce find friend.*

Her large hazel eyes panned the hillside past the large cliff

293

face and settled on the ground at her feet. A moment later, and to everyone's surprise, she sat down in a patch of tall grass, spared from the destruction by only a few yards. She picked a wildflower and sniffed at its tiny purple petals. She picked another and another, smelling each one.

Smell. Dulce held a flower out for DeeAnn, who looked puzzled but accepted it. She sniffed and raised an eyebrow.

"What do you smell?"

Dulce grunted and shook her head. *Flower smell pretty.*

DeeAnn frowned and looked around at the others. She stopped on Corso, who was clearly not amused.

"I guess her sense of urgency isn't quite the same as ours," DeeAnn reflected out loud.

Corso didn't reply. He simply stared at her and slowly shook his head.

She was about to apologize when Dulce abruptly stood up. Her large nostrils wiggled and she turned her head, as though listening. She then walked for several yards and sat back down in the grass.

Caesare lowered his rifle and pulled the satellite phone back out of his pocket. He dialed the number again and waited. Still busy.

It was too early to be concerned, but he needed to talk to Borger, and soon. He needed to know how much time they had before Otero and his goons arrived. Watching Dulce told him their chances of finding the capuchin first were dropping dramatically.

But there was something else. He looked solemnly past the others to the cliff face in the distance and followed it down to its base.

Finding the monkey was one thing, but Caesare and Borger both knew he was also there for another reason. Something even more important. There was something inside the base of that cliff that needed to be protected at all costs. Because if it was found, especially by someone like Otero, the world was not ready for what would come next.

Caesare was there to make sure that didn't happen. Only five people knew what was hidden there. And if he had to, he would tell his men. Because if it came down to it, they needed to understand that *no one* could be allowed to find it.

No matter what.

55

The distant peak was in sight now and a frustrated Otero watched from the back of his Range Rover as their convoy made its way slowly and painfully up the narrow winding road.

His frustration was reaching new heights after multiple stops to repair the failing road. Wind and rain had eroded large sections, making it impossible for the larger trucks to pass without substantial reinforcements.

The third repair had unexpectedly given way when their trucks tried to pass, resulting in a near loss of the entire vehicle and its supplies. A loss that big would have been significant. He could live with the loss of some of his men, but fewer supplies meant less time to find the creature for which they had come.

It was becoming increasingly evident to Otero that the success of this mission was going to rely on a single person. And she was sitting in the vehicle just ahead of them, behind Captain Salazar.

Dr. Becca sat rocking back and forth with the sideways motion of the Humvee as it climbed, bouncing over what was left of the old road. Hours of driving — coupled with having to listen to Salazar spout his fascist political views — was making the trip truly deplorable. Instead, she tried to focus on the few positive aspects she could find. Like the vehicle's air conditioning.

She'd met men like Salazar before. And just like them, he was an ass, plain and simple. A bureaucrat dressed in a military uniform and nothing more. Hiding within just another large government organization that was once again buckling under its own self-serving weight.

Brazil's economy and its government were now completely imploding. Like many countries, Brazil was now in the last desperate throes of its collapse and was printing money like mad to stave off the inevitable: the long overdue cleansing of the country's elite and political class.

To Becca, Salazar was part of the problem. Unfortunately, those in power never relinquished it without a fight. But this wasn't her fight. She simply wanted to get back and save whatever career she might have left.

A career that, after reading all of the information she'd been given, just might include the zoological breakthrough of the century. She was now convinced that at least part of what Salazar and Otero were after...was real. A capuchin demonstrating a significantly higher level of cognition.

If it was true, it was the kind of discovery for the record books and one from which world renowned careers were launched.

In front of Becca, Salazar leaned forward, attempting to reach the dashboard in spite of the vehicle's bouncing. His fingers found the small vent and adjusted the angle higher, trying to cool his beading forehead. The air was gradually growing cooler the higher they climbed, but it still wasn't enough yet.

He returned his hand to the grab handle overhead, trying to steady himself after one bounce from a particularly large hole. Salazar's own satellite phone rang loudly just as it fell from its tucked position against his leg. He fumbled for it but managed to get the phone to his ear by the third ring.

"Yes," he answered, over the vehicle's revving engine.

The voice on the other end was deep. "How close are you?"

"About five or six hours."

"It's about time."

Salazar opened his mouth to explain but was cut off.

"Does anyone suspect anything?"

"No. I don't think so."

"Good. Surprise will be key. You cannot risk anyone knowing. Do you understand?"

"I do." Salazar glanced at his driver for any indications that he was listening in.

"You should also know you're going to have company."

"What do you mean?"

"There is someone else at the top."

Salazar's brow lowered. "Who?"

"We don't know. One of our AEW aircraft spotted an airplane over the area, which abruptly turned around over the mountains."

A drop. Salazar cursed silently to himself and gritted his teeth. It was exactly what he was trying to preempt.

"You know what's at stake," said the voice. "And you know what happens if you fail."

56

"This is bullshit."

Everyone turned to Corso, standing in a small patch of shade with his HK416 gripped firmly in his large hands.

"Excuse me?"

His eyes moved to DeeAnn, then to Caesare. Dulce was sitting overhead in a young aphandra tree, examining its branches.

"She's not going to find a damn thing."

DeeAnn turned to Caesare before he could reply. "We need to give it time. This isn't exactly a science. She's doing the best she can."

Corso looked up again into the tree. "Yeah, it looks it."

A moment later, a large white and yellow flower fell down onto Corso's shoulder, where he brushed it away and glared at the gorilla. Dulce returned a toothy grin.

"What the hell you expecting, Corso?" Tiewater grinned, descending from the top of a large rock. "You want the little thing to draw us a map?"

Anderson shrugged. "That would be nice."

DeeAnn was still staring at Caesare. "We need more time."

Time was a luxury they didn't have. Caesare glanced at his watch again and peered up at the sky. They had three hours of daylight left at the most. And all the while Otero was getting closer. He needed to know how close but Borger still wasn't answering his phone. Something was wrong.

"Ask her again," he said.

After a moment, DeeAnn sighed and turned back around to face Dulce. "Where is our friend, Dulce?"

No know. Me look.

"How much more time?"

Her vest unexpectedly beeped, signaling a bad translation.

"How much longer?"

Dulce peered at her curiously from the tree. She looked like she was about to reply when she stopped. The gorilla abruptly stood up in the tree and steadied herself with a branch. Her posture was stiff. Alert. After a long silence, she spoke.

Go there.

Everyone on the ground looked up with surprise.

"Go where?"

There. Dulce raised her lanky arm and pointed.

"Is that where friend is?"

Dulce scampered down and leaped from the tree, landing on Corso's broad shoulders. Her focus still in the direction she had pointed.

"Get the hell off me!" Corso violently shook his shoulders, sending Dulce jumping to Tiewater, who caught her in his arms.

"You're really something with the ladies."

"Shut up."

DeeAnn closed in and repeated. "Where, Dulce? Show us where."

She pointed again, across a large section of the burnt field. *There.*

Past the field, a wide section of trees covered the area, which sloped away from the peak. Their dull green color bore a resemblance to olive trees, with thin branches swaying gently from side to side in the breeze, now blowing over the top of the mountain. The trees continued on for as far as they could see. They became denser before rising again over another ridge, and then disappeared where the mountain continued another long descent.

Caesare immediately continued forward, leading the way over the burnt ground and into the tall grass on the other side. When he reached the edge of the trees, he stopped and turned to Dulce, who passed him and climbed another tree. She sat, listening.

Corso shook his head. "This is a waste of time."

"Not necessarily," DeeAnn replied, crossing her arms. "All primates are semi-terrestrial, meaning they live in large social groups. They don't roam very far from a home location except for foraging. Most humans are the same. Like nesting with birds."

Corso smirked. "Well, we're pretty far from home now."

"That's because we have airplanes," Juan quipped, sitting down. He unzipped his bag, pulled out several square-shaped bundles and turned to DeeAnn. "Time for a battery swap."

She nodded, twisting away from Corso and powering off the vest. Together, she and Juan removed the previous batteries and inserted a new set. Once Juan double-checked the connection and secured the Velcro flaps back over the pockets, she turned it back on.

"Can you hear me, Dulce?"

Dulce looked down from the tree and frowned. She held a dark finger over her mouth.

DeeAnn rolled her eyes while Caesare laughed.

"You might be teaching her too well."

Several minutes later, Caesare's phone rang in his pocket.

"Will, where the hell have you been?"

"Sorry, Steve. I don't have time to explain, but things are getting crazy. I see you guys are on the ground."

"We are. And looking for our friend. Where's Otero?"

"Hold on." Borger pulled up his live feed from the ARGUS satellite. "They're close. Very close. Maybe an hour or two from the summit. I'm counting…seventeen vehicles, most are large trucks. Probably carrying men or supplies."

"They're carrying both," Caesare said dryly.

"Right. The only road bears north across the top of the

peak, about a mile or so from where you are, so you should see them soon."

"Great. Anything else?"

"Not at the moment. But call me if you need any more. I'll try to ring you back if I can't answer. I need to help Clay."

Caesare's brow rose. "What's going on with Clay?

"I'm not sure yet. He reached the hospital but now it looks like he's moving again. I've been trying to reach him, but he's not answering."

"All right. I'll ring off. We're fine for the moment." Without waiting for a reply, Caesare ended the call but remained staring at the phone.

Caesare had his own problems to worry about, but he did have one guess on why Clay wasn't answering his phone.

57

Clay wasn't answering his phone because he couldn't. With a rifle in one fist and the hand of Wei's daughter in the other, he was rushing down the steep embankment, half running and half sliding. He struggled to find a smooth path, knowing the girl couldn't see what he could through his night-vision goggles.

Behind him, Li Na lost her footing several times but Clay's strong arm kept her on her feet. When they reached the bottom of the ravine, they both splashed through a shallow stream and scrambled up the other side.

Through the tall trees, the two helicopters to the south could be heard taking to the sky. Qin had apparently gotten to a radio — most likely aboard his own chopper.

He suddenly slipped in a thick pile of leaves but managed to catch himself. He regained his footing and pulled Li Na up behind him. Once they cleared the top of the incline, he continued again as fast as the girl could keep up.

Several hundred yards later they reached another drop, this one much steeper. He panned from one side to the other, looking for a way down. Almost as if on cue, the phone in the pocket of his pants rang.

His answer was immediate. "Need some help, Will."

Borger was already studying a daytime image of the area. "There's a fairly large stream in front of you. Let me see if I can find an easier way across."

"I'm not worried about the water. I need a way down."

"There's a small area to the east where it looks like it flattens out. One hundred yards upstream, or maybe two."

Clay slung the rifle over his shoulder to keep the phone in his hand. He kept a tight grip on Li Na and moved quickly along the ridge.

"The choppers are in the air," he said, panting into the phone. "And headed this way. What's ahead of us?"

"Us?" Borger raised his eyebrows. "You have Wei's daughter?"

"Well, I sure as hell hope that's who I grabbed."

Borger zoomed out, looking for something he could give them. Anything.

"There's a small house to the southeast, but it's pretty far away. Maybe a mile and a half. Everything else is in the other direction."

"Too far," Clay mumbled. He stopped on the edge of the ridge and spotted the area Borger described. Instead of a cliff, soft dirt descended at a more manageable descent. He dropped to the ground, pulling Li Na down with him and sliding down the embankment, his feet out in front of him. He dug in with the heels of his boots, sending rocks and leaves spilling down in front of him.

Directly behind him, Li Na did the same.

When they reached the bottom, Clay pulled her through the water and waded across. When they reached the other side, Clay brought the phone back up to his ear.

"You still there?"

"Yes."

"Where's the house?"

"Roughly four o'clock from your current direction."

"Okay."

Borger was now studying a different image of the same region, this one taken at night. He examined the area where the small house was situated.

"Uh, Clay. There may be a problem. I don't see any lights at that place. I'm not sure if it's occupied. I'm looking for another option."

There was no answer.

"Clay?" Borger checked his phone. The call had ended.

The terrain gradually leveled off, allowing Clay and Li Na to pick up speed. Overhead, the sound of the helicopters was followed only seconds later by searchlights.

Clay quickened his pace. A mile and a half was a long way over this kind of terrain. He ground to a halt near a tight cluster of trees and released Li Na's hand. He then removed his goggles and looked up at a bright beam of light sweeping the forest behind them.

He pulled the teenage girl in close and pressed them both against a tree trunk as the searchlight passed over them. He watched it continue on before looking down at Li Na.

"There's a house nearby, but we have to move faster or we'll never make it. Can you run on your own?"

"I think so."

"Good. Stay close to me."

Not far away, Qin's helicopter finally rose into the air once the pilot had wrapped his bloody hand in a thick bandage. He listened through his headphones to the exchange between the other two helicopters searching the ground for Li Na and the American.

"If you see them," Qin broke in, "stop them! Even if you have to *shoot*. They must not escape!"

Once above the trees, Qin could see the aircraft lights from the other two choppers. One to the southeast and the other to the northeast. The rest of the soldiers were on the ground, sweeping forward in the same directions.

Even in his panic-induced rage, Qin knew he was lucky. These men were some of the best in the Chinese Army, and he couldn't have hoped for a better group to provide aid. But it was more than coincidence. More than luck. It was fate. The message was clear. Destiny was on Qin's side.

Now the girl and the American were in the middle of nowhere. Headed in the worst possible direction. And all they could do was run.

58

That was exactly what Clay and Li Na were doing. Together they weaved in and around the dark tree trunks, stopping frequently to remain hidden. The bright curtains of light pierced the canopies overhead and bathed the ground, passing ominously back and forth.

After another pass, Clay dropped his bag and pulled out a dark thermal blanket. He wrapped it around Li Na to cover her lighter clothing. It would make it easier to blend with the ground beneath them, as long as they were not moving when spotted. It wasn't foolproof, but it was better than nothing.

If Qin had any experience, or brains, he already had men on the ground following them. Having to stop when the light approached meant they had to move even faster in the darkness. The men on the ground would be gaining. Their shrinking lead and the house ahead of them were now all that was separating them from Qin.

The sound of the helicopter's thundering blades passed over once more and had just begun to fade when they darted out together again, running for all they were worth.

It felt a hell of a lot longer than a mile and a half.

When Clay found the small house, he was expecting something more…recognizable. Instead, what Borger had spotted from the air was little more than an old shack. More than that, it looked as though it was barely standing, positioned in a small clearing and surrounded by tall tallow trees, their canopies fighting for the open sky overhead.

On the ground, near the structure, were tools and a wooden cart, its wheels appearing ready to fall off. On the ground was a pile of something Clay couldn't quite make out. But what caught his eye was the soft glow of light visible through a very old, but surprisingly clear window.

He stepped forward and looked through it. There was little to see. The view was blocked by a cloth curtain.

Without the slightest hesitation, he moved to what looked like a front door and tried the rusted knob.

Locked.

He stepped back and stared at it. All at once he raised his leg, and with a powerful kick, focused his boot against the door, just inches from the knob. In an earsplitting crack, the door exploded inward and slammed against an interior wall.

Inside, in a small room, sat a Chinese family. Ragged and sitting around a wooden table with fear in their eyes. The shock of having their front door kicked in had left them motionless, holding food to their mouths in mid bite.

The small family was composed of two school-age boys and a younger sister sitting next to their parents, with a stove fire burning behind them. On the table, flames from several homemade candles danced in the sudden burst of outside air.

The family's faces didn't change. They remained fixed at the table, unmoving. After an awkward silence, the father's eyes blinked past them, out through the door at one of the searchlights as it passed overhead.

Still heaving in the doorway, Clay turned to Li Na.

"Tell them we need help."

307

59

The man at the table listened to Li Na and looked up again as the second helicopter roared past.

His eyes moved to the tall man standing in the doorway, with one hand firmly grasping a rifle. He was clearly an American soldier, breathing heavily and with a face like stone.

The father carefully put down his wooden bowl, not taking his eyes off either one of them. Eventually, he motioned to the boy on his right — the taller of the two — and spoke softly. Nearest to the stove, the mother remained completely still.

Struggling to remain patient, Clay turned and peered back through the door. "We don't have a lot of time."

"Wait," Li Na whispered back.

The boy, not more than thirteen, rose nervously from the table. He stepped away and moved to the door where he turned, staring directly at his father.

His father nodded firmly. Even to Clay, the message was clear: *move!*

They followed the boy as he ran, zigzagging through the forest as though he had every tree memorized, and every step.

Clay was surprised to see the teenager instinctively stop when the light returned, waiting for it to pass before resuming.

They reached a worn path, barely as wide as a single footprint, and followed the boy up a steep incline, winding their way around a small, heavily covered hill. When they reached the far side, they stopped in front of a rock face protruding from the underbrush. Carved into the rock was a large dark hole, almost as tall as Clay and just as wide.

The boy spoke in a hushed tone to Li Na, who translated to Clay.

"It's a mine. An old one. He says there's another entrance at the other end, about a kilometer and a half."

She paused, listening to the boy again.

"From there, an old road leads out through a small valley where it meets the railroad tracks."

Clay stared at the opening in the rock. "Tell us about the mine."

In Chinese, she repeated what Clay had said and the boy explained.

"He says it was abandoned a long time ago. No one knows about it anymore. There are several tunnels. We need to keep to our left."

Clay didn't respond. Instead he stepped forward, examining the opening with a grim expression. Most caverns and mines were not the adventure, nor salvation, most people considered them to be. Long and winding underground tunnels were very dangerous, especially mines with multiple adits. More people lost their way, and their lives, than the public knew. And it was always in the same order. They lost their light, then their way, and finally fresh air.

This was not a good option.

Overhead, a searchlight approached. Somehow they had deduced Clay's direction, and unfortunately, the trees were not dense enough to hide them forever. The mine, even as a bad option, was better than none.

He shook his head and slid the bag off his back. He'd have to carry it in by hand. In its place, he slung the rifle. Clay placed a hand on the boy's shoulder and thanked him using one of the few Chinese words he knew.

"Xie xie."

The boy responded with something he didn't understand.

Nevertheless, the look in his eyes reinforced John Clay's long-held belief. A belief that ultimately, no matter where they lived, regular people were all the same. More than anything else, they wanted to grow old. To raise healthy children and to help one another. In the end, most people simply wanted to leave the world a better place. Distant enemies, he was convinced, were simply the product of political brainwashing.

Clay smiled at him before nodding to Li Na. He then bent over, ducking his head low, and stepped into pitch blackness.

Once inside, Clay estimated a distance of thirty feet before lowering his bag and fishing out a small compact military style flashlight. He turned it on, instantly washing the narrow walls in bright light.

"Are you okay?"

"Yes," Li Na nodded. She stepped forward carefully, using the ambient glow from Clay's light in front of her. The ground was littered with chunks of rock and large pieces of stone, some of which had fallen from the low ceiling, leaving pocks overhead.

The walls, less than a foot away on either side, bore deep scrapes in the rock and were largely covered in a dark film.

"Did the kid mention what kind of mine this was?"

Li Na paused for a moment. "Uh...coal?"

Clay fingered some of the material off a nearby wall and smelled it. "Iron ore."

"Iron ore. Yes. What is it for?"

"It's used in steel." Clay picked up his bag, holding it out in front of him as he moved forward. *Things just kept getting worse.*

60

Things *were* getting worse. Caesare studied the distant sky, which was continuing to change. The setting sun had already disappeared behind the dark horizon, cutting their light short and causing the team to turn back early. Their storm had resumed its easterly direction.

Tiewater stepped up behind Caesare, who was standing on a rocky outcropping. "That doesn't look good."

"No. It doesn't."

"How long?"

Caesare shook his head. "I'm not sure. Maybe tomorrow morning."

Tiewater scratched at the base of his lightly colored hair. He was graying prematurely, giving a distinguished contrast against his darker eyebrows. "We're going to need to find some cover. That could be a hell of a downpour."

"Agreed," Caesare nodded. *This was all they needed.*

They both turned as Anderson came rushing out from a wall of palms below and scaled the small incline. He reached them only slightly out of breath.

"I may have some good news."

"Good, we could use some."

"I found some tracks headed northwest. Tire tracks. We have company up here and it's not Otero."

Caesare and Tiewater looked at each other. "Who?"

"Poachers, most likely."

"Poachers?" Tiewater frowned. "Why is that good news?"

A wry grin appeared on Caesare's face, matching Anderson's. "Because the poachers may be looking for the same thing we are."

"And not even realize it," Anderson added.

Caesare motioned to Tiewater. "You two check it out. Corso and I will stay here and find some shelter. If nothing else, maybe these poachers can save us some time." He checked his watch. "Find out where they are, fast."

"Yes, sir." Together, both men promptly scrambled back downhill and disappeared.

Caesare stepped down and followed a small path of matted grass back to the area where the rest were seated.

Corso approached him and spoke in a low voice. "What's up?"

"Anderson may have found us a shortcut. In the meantime, we need to find some shelter. The storm isn't finished with us."

"Yeah, I saw that. I'll see what I can find." He raised a small wire microphone and earplug, then wrapped it around his left ear.

Caesare turned to DeeAnn and Juan, resting on a pair of nearby rocks. They looked exhausted.

"Where's Dulce?"

DeeAnn looked up above Caesare's head. He followed her eyes up just in time to catch the small gorilla, hanging from the tree and trying to place a small white flower on his head.

"Someone seems to be enjoying herself."

Juan finished replacing the batteries and handed the vest back to DeeAnn. "Where'd the other guys go?"

"They're checking some things out. The storm is headed our way again."

"You're kidding."

"I wish I were. Things may be about to get very wet." He scanned the ground around them. "And very muddy."

"What do we do?"

"Corso's searching for shelter. If we can find a decent place, we'll need to relocate."

"Where are the other two?"

"Looking for a shortcut."

Juan and DeeAnn both looked at each other. "What does that mean?"

He grinned at DeeAnn. "It means that even poachers may still have one redeeming quality."

61

"Poacher" was such an ugly word. Hugo preferred almost any other term. And frankly, he never understood why the practice was even illegal.

The Brazilian took another drag off his cigarette and scratched his stubbled chin absently.

As far as he was concerned, the black market was the way the world should be, pure opportunity without all the government leeching.

Poaching, like most lines of work, was simply the filling of a need for those who wanted something. To him, there was little difference between cats and dogs and the more exotic pets that some people wanted. Pets were pets. And in this case, a capuchin was simply harder to find and capture.

But more than that, it was a matter of survival. For him. The truth was that it was getting damn hard to make a living in Brazil, honest or not. He hadn't always been a poacher, but when the economy collapsed he had to find a way to feed his family. When it came to them versus an empty table, who gave a crap about a bunch of monkeys? As long as people continued to pay, he would continue to satisfy the demand.

Hugo finished his cigarette and dropped it into the moist soil, rubbing it out with his boot. He remained still, listening as the first moments of darkness enveloped the area. The evening mist rolling over and down the mountain felt cool against his sweaty neck and arms.

Not far away he could see the flicker of light from another cigarette. His partner, Vito. There were four of them in all, each fanning out in the darkness, waiting.

The monkeys were easier to hear at night.

They waited almost forty-five minutes before hearing the first whistle. It was quickly followed by another, and then another. Hugo's ears zeroed in on a direction. Roughly eleven o'clock from his position. He could see Vito's cigarette suddenly disappear.

Hugo withdrew his JM Special dart gun and checked it. The dart was chambered and ready. The tranquilizer was stronger than necessary, but given the capuchin's habit of running or climbing after being shot, a weaker dose too often made for difficult retrievals. Hugo and his partners had learned that risking the effects of a more powerful drug was an easy trade over trying to track the damn things down.

He stalked briskly into the dense forest, rolling his feet carefully from heel to toe in an effort to remain silent. The soft, damp ground helped reduce the noise as he moved delicately over the leaves.

All four were now moving in on the increasing chatter, and what was beginning to sound like a big score.

With his face painted black, Tiewater edged forward through a group of ground ferns, letting the tip of his rifle float out first before sweeping past the objects in front of him — large tents, an oversized fire pit, and stand-up tables with a propane stove and cooking utensils.

Further away were two trucks, both old and covered in mud, sitting silently. The first truck was a Ford Explorer and the other a long flatbed with dozens of wooden cages stacked on the back. Inside the cages sat several monkeys who had stopped screaming and were now curiously watching Tiewater emerge from the bushes. The abrupt silence of the capuchins made the area feel eerie, leaving only the sound of his footsteps as Tiewater eased himself out fully into the open. He was covered by Anderson, perched above him and following steadily through the sights of his HK416.

Tiewater approached one of the tents and stopped

outside, listening. Hearing nothing, he pushed the tip of his barrel through the nylon flap and moved it aside, peering in.

Nothing.

One by one, he checked the others before looking up to Anderson and shaking his head.

"No one here," he whispered into his microphone. "But it's definitely not abandoned." Tiewater moved to the larger of the trucks, where the monkeys were still watching him. He looked into the front cab.

"Judging from their supplies, I'd say four or five, tops." He moved back to the smoldering fire pit and studied it. "They've been here a few days."

"They sure are tidy."

Tiewater nodded. "Makes for a quick departure, and with minimal evidence."

"Smart."

"Or paranoid." Tiewater stopped, noticing something on the ground. Kneeling down, he retrieved his flashlight and held it close to the soil, covering it with his hand. The beam was small and focused and revealed several footprints.

He turned it off and put the light away.

"Tracks?" Anderson asked.

"Yep."

62

Hugo eased to his left, shifting more weight onto his elbow as he scanned for a source of the chattering. Dressed in full jungle camouflage and hat, he kept the brim low, covering most of his face.

Through the night scope, he checked slowly from one tree to the next, until spotting his target on a wide branch. The dark outline of the capuchin was unmistakable, moving only slightly as it chattered back and forth.

Hugo remained trained on the silhouette for a long time, giving his colleagues time to lock in on any others. Once the first shot was fired, they would all have to follow suit before the rest fled.

To make matters worse, some monkeys were surprisingly sharp, realizing something was wrong before the poachers had a chance to shoot. They still hadn't figured out what tipped off the brighter ones, which forced them to be even more cautious.

Hugo lowered his head and centered his scope on the target. He took a deep breath and slowly let it out, smoothly pulling the trigger halfway through.

A loud thump exploded from the end of his rifle, followed by two more shots nearby. The silhouette on the branch shrieked and fell from sight, hitting the ground with a thud. High-pitched screams instantly filled the air overhead. Dozens of capuchins scrambled away as Hugo and his men leaped to their feet, running for the trees.

He reached the base of the tree and grabbed the tiny figure curled on the ground. But when he held it up, the white tip of the dart dangled from its loose skin, not from the body. It wasn't a direct hit. The monkey wasn't unconscious.

Instead, it began flailing in his hands, screaming and

clawing wildly. The small creature desperately tried to free itself while Hugo struggled to hang on. One of the monkey's claws abruptly took a chunk of skin out of his soft cheek, causing a searing pain.

Hugo yelled and squeezed harder, trying to restrain the creature, but it only fought harder. After another painful gash across his mouth, Hugo's right hand withdrew his sap and brought it forward, smashing the hard metal against the monkey's tiny head.

The animal was instantly silenced. As it fell limp in the man's hands, he brought it closer, studying it in the moonlight.

"Shit," he growled. *The damn thing was dead.*

He stood up and removed the dart, angrily dropping the limp body onto the ground. He looked around for the other men and spotted the outline of Vito moving toward him.

"Yours sounded lively," the shorter man called out.

Hugo felt his lip. Even in the darkness, he could feel the blood on his fingertips. "Damn thing attacked me. I had to smash it."

The other man laughed and held up his captive's listless body. "Got mine."

Over the tops of their rifles, both Tiewater and Anderson watched the two men converge and continue talking. A few minutes later, two more arrived, both empty-handed.

Tiewater eased his head up and brought his mike in closer. "Tie here."

"Go ahead," replied Caesare.

"I think this is the place our gorilla is looking for. And you probably want to hurry."

Caesare's eyes stopped when he heard Tiewater's

message. They were moving the last of their gear under a small rock shelter, not far from where they'd been. It wasn't perfect, but it would provide at least some protection from the rain without compromising their position.

Caesare turned his head to Corso and had just began to speak when they all heard the sound they had been dreading. The distant roar from dozens of engines as the first sets of headlights crested the top of the mountain.

All four stood and watched over the trees as truck after truck appeared, steaming up the last of the incline, and approached over the dirt road.

63

Leading the procession, Salazar's vehicle continued for another half mile before stopping in the middle of the road. He promptly climbed out of his Humvee and moved off the road, watching with a smile the line of headlights as they appeared one by one. Eventually the vehicles began braking to a stop behind him.

His lieutenant climbed out of the third vehicle, a large truck carrying over a dozen men, and approached Salazar. Together, they watched the silhouettes against the long line of headlights as their men began pouring out and surrounding the trucks.

Salazar retrieved a cigarette from his shirt pocket and watched as Otero, emerged from his Range Rover with Russo close behind him.

He ignored both men and spoke directly to his lieutenant, Sosa. "Get a base set up and find some fresh water. I want a dozen men out searching for whoever or whatever was dropped off here. And tell them they're authorized to shoot first."

"Sir?"

"You heard me. Shoot anything they see unless it's a goddamn monkey."

Sosa displayed a look of concern. "Sir, if there's someone else up here, we don't know who they are."

"I don't care who they are."

The lieutenant's eyes flickered briefly to Otero and Russo before returning to his commanding officer. "Sir, what if they are Brazilians?"

Salazar looked at Sosa hard. "Then they have no business being up here."

Sosa simply stared at Salazar. The tense moment was

interrupted by footsteps from the grass. They all turned to see Becca's smaller frame emerge from the darkness.

"Dr. Becca," Salazar said. "Your men will be ready within the hour. I recommend you be as well."

"An hour?" she said, surprised. "I thought we were starting in the morning."

"The plan has changed. Someone else is already here. And they're likely searching for the same thing we are."

Otero was watching, his features barely visible in the darkness. "When was the drop?"

"This morning." Salazar turned back to his lieutenant. "Get your men moving." Then he turned to Becca. "Doctor. One hour."

With that, Salazar turned and walked back toward his vehicle. Both his lieutenant and the doctor quickly disappeared into the darkness, leaving Otero and Russo alone.

"How did he find out about the drop?" Otero muttered.

"He's communicating with someone," Russo mused. "Someone with access to Aeronautics Command. We don't have any radar stations up here, which means the drop could only have been picked up by aircraft. Probably one of the Orions."

Otero didn't answer. Instead, he stood there thinking, still watching the lieutenant's silhouette as he marched back to the trucks and began yelling orders.

For the first time, Otero felt a streak of nervousness run through him. He had secured support at the highest level. From the office of the President. And he was told Salazar was nothing but a pawn, whose sole purpose would be to help him reach the Acarai Mountains.

But something wasn't right. Such as why Salazar was notified of the air drop instead of him. It made Otero wonder. The economic collapse in Brazil had left the country teetering on the brink of civil war, with the current government in tatters. A grim realization began to wash over him.   Perhaps those Otero had aligned himself with...were no longer in control.

Which would mean neither was he.

64

Where we go?

Dulce was struggling to keep up through the dense foliage, even as DeeAnn pulled her along.

"We have to hurry." DeeAnn's breathing was labored, but she still managed to reply in a hushed tone. She gripped Dulce's furry hand tighter and tried to stay behind the figure of Steve Caesare, hacking his way through the heavy growth.

When her vest translated her words, she cringed at the speaker volume, which blared loudly.

"Jesus," growled Corso behind them. "Turn that thing down! Everyone's going to hear us."

Caesare halted in front of them and spun around. "He's right."

"Uh…" DeeAnn looked down at the blue light on her vest, searching.

"She can't," Juan answered, from behind her.

"What?"

"There's no way to turn down the volume."

"There's no volume?"

Juan turned from Corso and looked at Caesare's silhouette. "No. When we designed the vest, we didn't think we needed one. Besides, changes in amplitude complicate things with the translation."

Corso looked over the top of Juan's head to Caesare. "That's the dumbest thing I've ever heard."

"Yeah, well, communication doesn't work very well if one person can't hear the other."

Caesare stared at them, then finally nodded. He wasn't happy about it, but he understood.

From the ground, Dulce looked back and forth between them. *We stop.*

DeeAnn placed a finger over her lips. "Dulce, quiet."
Dulce quiet.

DeeAnn cringed again as the translation seemed even louder now that they were standing still.

Caesare watched Dulce, but spoke to DeeAnn. "Turn it off."

"What?"

"Turn it off."

"But…"

"We can't take any chances."

DeeAnn looked at Juan, hoping for another option, but he simply frowned.

Reluctantly, she squatted down in front of Dulce so she could see her face. She placed a hand gently on Dulce's head and again put her fingers to her lips.

Dulce watched her curiously, unsure of why they had to be quiet. No one else was talking. With a troubled expression, she watched as DeeAnn made the blue light go off.

The screaming of the capuchin monkeys from their cages began even before an angry Hugo pushed his way through the thick brush. He stormed into their small camp, followed by the other three, and dropped his gun on a fold-out table. In frustration, he then turned and kicked dirt into the smoldering embers of their fire.

Behind him, Vito approached the truck and pulled an empty cage up onto the flatbed. He pushed the limp body of his prize into the cage and closed the wooden door, securing it with a clasp and cable.

He suddenly stopped. One of the cages was empty.

"Merda."

The others looked up, including Hugo, who was now searching for something to stem the bleeding from his cheek. He grabbed a piece of cloth from his bag and pressed it in place before turning back to the truck.

Without moving his head, Vito's eyes stared across the bed. "Another one gone."

"What?!"

"Another one is gone," he repeated.

Hugo stormed over to the truck and glared at the crate in disbelief. "How the hell…" He moved around to the back, keeping the cloth pressed hard against his cheek. "I told you to lock it right this time!" he bellowed.

"I did!"

"Then it's broken." Hugo pushed him out of the way and studied the cage. Primates, even capuchins, could be stronger than they looked. Especially when locked in an enclosure and panicking.

He spun the cage around with one hand, examining it closely in the dim light of a nearby lantern. He couldn't see anything wrong. The thick wood frame still felt strong. He refastened the clasp and cable — they locked securely. Finding nothing broken, he yelled and threw the crate, sending it tumbling over the ground.

"I saw him check it," one of the others said.

Hugo shook his head, scowling. "Then you're both idiots!" He glanced at the amount of blood on his cloth and threw it away.

"What the hell is happening?" he yelled. The night had already been a waste, with only a single capture between them. Now another was lost.

He didn't know how the capuchins were escaping, but they were. Somehow.

"ETA?"

"About fifteen minutes," Caesare replied.

Tiewater nodded from his hiding spot less than sixty feet from the poacher camp. Their faces painted black, both he and Anderson watched the poacher's outburst from a

325

distance.

"What's happening?" Caesare called over the radio.

Tiewater spoke quietly. "Our friends are home and one of them seems to have gotten his panties in a wad." He continued his reconnaissance, motionlessly.

From the other side of the encampment, Anderson also lay watching, listening to Tiewater through his own headset.

"How many are there?"

"Four. The big one is in charge. Camp is probably a couple thousand square feet, with two vehicles. One small and the other larger for cargo. Observable weapons are sidearms and some tranquilizer rifles. Doesn't look like they've been here more than a few days."

"Any defenses?"

"None."

A few minutes later, Tiewater slid backward out of position and stood without a sound. Remaining low, he moved back through the trees where he found Caesare and Corso waiting in the darkness.

"What are they doing?"

Tiewater shrugged. "Eating. But it sounds like their poaching isn't going too well."

"What a shame," Caesare remarked sarcastically. "We're out of time. Otero is here. We need to find the monkey in a hurry."

"Well, I suspect these guys have a pretty good guess as to where." Tiewater motioned over his shoulder and turned back, followed by Caesare. But as Corso took a step forward, he suddenly paused. He felt something stuck in his collar and reached up to grab it.

It was soft, and only when he examined it closely could he make out the shape. One of Dulce's flowers. He shook his head. Then, glancing forward to make sure he wasn't seen, Corso raised it up and sniffed it.

Hugo was still stewing from his seat on a fold-out chair. He took another bite of dried meat and shook his head, keeping his eyes on the fire.

The other men were also seated around the fire, eating silently. They'd had a definite streak of bad luck. One that was refusing to break, leaving the last few hunting trips as complete losses.

"We need to try something else," Vito replied, after dropping his metal plate to the ground. "They're learning our ways."

"They hear us coming," Claudio, the third man, replied.

"Then what do you suggest?"

Vito turned around and faced the cages on the back of the truck. "Maybe we can use the ones we have…to catch more."

"You mean as bait?"

"Yes. Maybe we tie one up in the forest to lure the others."

"His screaming will warn the others before that."

"Not if we sedate him."

Hugo considered it. More of the powerful tranquilizer in such a short amount of time would cause problems with the animal's nervous system, but if it allowed them to catch more, the risk would be worth it. If they caught enough monkeys, they could simply kill the bait.

Hugo raised his eyes and began to nod, then suddenly froze. The rustling behind Vito had been subtle. Not enough to be heard and barely enough to be seen in the dim light. At that exact moment, the other three poachers each witnessed the same dreaded sight — figures dressed in black and hidden behind the barrels of their assault rifles.

From different directions, Caesare, Tiewater, Corso, and Anderson all stepped out in unison. Each emerging from a position visible by one of the poachers, all of whom froze in stunned silence…except one.

Claudio, the youngest of Hugo's group and an Argentinian…panicked. At the sight of Tiewater, he was immediately on his feet before anyone could stop him and drawing his weapon.

Corso, moving slowly out of the brush behind him, saw the kid draw and bolted for him. It took only a few steps at full speed for Corso to reach him and knock him out with the butt of his rifle, but not before a single shot exploded from the .45 caliber pistol.

65

Hiding less than a hundred yards away, DeeAnn, Dulce, and Juan all jumped when they heard the loud gunshot. But it was the Brazilians, even further away, who stopped in their tracks. All eyes turned north with dozens of hands instinctively gripping their own guns.

Salazar and his lieutenant looked back at each other, completely ignoring both Otero and Russo.

There was no second shot.

Salazar began yelling. "Hurry! Move!" He locked eyes with his lieutenant. "Move your men out *with* the search team. NOW!"

It was less than a minute before Caesare reappeared in the darkness and looked down at DeeAnn. "We have to move. Right now!"

They scrambled to their feet. "What the hell was that?"

"An accident."

"Did you shoot them?"

"Not exactly."

"Not exactly? What does that mean?"

"It means we're going to have company if we don't get out of here immediately."

A few minutes later they all emerged into what DeeAnn recognized as a small camp. Surrounded by four tents, several fold-out tables and chairs, they could see Anderson standing nearby, bandaging Tiewater's arm. On the ground was a large man with his arms bound behind his back. He had a deep bronze complexion and sat dressed in rumpled camouflage clothes. He watched the SEALs standing over him with a look of confusion.

"You okay?" Caesare asked Tiewater.

"Yeah. Just a graze."

"Where's Corso?"

"Here."

He turned to his left to see Corso's large frame appear, pushing through a wall of waist-high plants.

"Where are the others?"

"Sleeping."

Caesare grinned and knelt down in front of the man, resting his rifle across one arm.

"What's your name?"

The man stared at him without replying.

"Name," Caesare asked again, louder.

Hugo stared uncomprehendingly at the men.

Caesare sighed and stood back up. "Anyone speak Portuguese?"

"I can ask how much cab fare is," Tiewater said with a grimace. "But that's about it."

"Great."

"Portuguese wasn't exactly popular in high school."

Caesare looked at Corso with surprise. "Really? *Now* you get funny?"

"It takes me a while."

"No kidding."

Tiewater straightened his arm and snaked his sleeve back down over his bandage. He stared down at the poacher. "We don't need him. We know where they were."

Anderson nodded in agreement.

Steve Caesare thought for a moment before turning around to DeeAnn and pointing at her vest.

"Turn it on."

"I thought you wanted it off?"

"It doesn't matter now. Everyone heard the gunshot. Which means a company of soldiers is now headed this way."

He watched DeeAnn turn the vest back on before

kneeling down again, in front of Dulce.

From her own viewpoint, the small gorilla watched Caesare's frame lower to the ground. He was looking at her with an expression she'd come to know as worried.

She stepped forward, studying him, and wiggled her large black nostrils. She could smell his nervousness.

When he spoke, she heard his mechanical voice through DeeAnn's vest.

You hear now, Dulce?

She nodded at the mechanical sound from the vest.

"Yes. I hear you."

Me need you help.

"Yes. I help." Dulce grunted, smiling at Caesare. "How help you?"

We need find friend. Need fast. Very fast.

"Yes. I can find friend. I find friend quickly." Dulce sniffed again. It wasn't just nervousness she could smell on Caesare. Some of it was fear. They were in danger.

"I find him."

Yes Dulce. Now. Fast!

Dulce snorted confirmation. At this distance, she could already hear the monkeys. And they were close.

66

The rolling of the ship caused Alison to stumble and brace against the wall for support. A few steps in front of her, Neely seemed to have less trouble keeping her balance, but even she stumbled slightly as she reached for Alison.

"You okay?"

"Yeah." Alison stepped back into the middle of the narrow passageway and continued forward with a hand on each wall.

Together they reached the door at the end, on which Neely knocked firmly. She glanced anxiously at Alison and cleared her throat.

The door opened moments later with Captain Emerson standing on the other side. Dressed in a pressed white, short-sleeve shirt, his trim frame filled the opening. He examined them with his piercing gray eyes. After a brief moment, he pushed the door open further and stepped back.

"Commander Lawton. Dr. Shaw. Please come in."

They both entered without a word and walked into a surprisingly roomy cabin, complete with a small dining room table and leather couch. On the opposite wall stood a chest-high shelf, filled neatly with books and secured behind four small, decorative glass doors.

"Have a seat," he said, motioning to the couch.

The two women complied as they watched Emerson pull out a chair and sit facing them, wearing a dour expression. "We should be arriving in a little less than an hour. So I thought we should have a talk."

Both women nodded in silence.

"This isn't the first time Langford has commandeered my ship like this. In fact, he seems to be making a habit out of it lately. This is, however, the first time he's done so without giving me much information as to why. What he did tell me is that you two ladies are looking for something pretty damn important. And my job, and that of my crew, is to do whatever we can to help you find it." He leaned back slightly and crossed his arms. "Is there some light you two care to shed on this?"

Neely and Alison looked at each other, unsure of what to say. Emerson continued, shifting his gaze over to Neely. "I'm sure you would agree that being ordered to relinquish part of my ship to a junior officer, and a civilian, begs for a bit more explanation."

Neely cleared her throat, nervously. "Uh, well, the truth is Captain, we're under orders as well."

"From Langford?"

"Yes, sir."

"I'm not surprised." He relaxed slightly and reached up to rub an eyebrow. "Okay. Then let me go first. Some of what I'm about to tell you, you may already know, but some you may not. Our destination, from the coordinates that I believe Ms. Shaw provided, seems to be pretty damn important. And not just to us. Therefore, I've been ordered not to loiter."

Alison looked at the captain with a confused look. "What does that mean?"

"It means we are not to be here when the sun comes up."

"What? Why?!"

"Because there are dozens of satellites poised to snap pictures of this area, and someone may be watching. And if whatever you're looking for is as important as it sounds, Langford is not willing to broadcast precisely where we're looking."

"H-how long do we have then?"

Emerson glanced at his watch. "A little less than ten hours."

"Ten hours?!" She glanced nervously at Neely. "Then what?"

"Then we leave. And head for Guyana where we will anchor and appear to be examining the wreckage of the Bowditch."

Emerson watched the expression change on Neely Lawton's face.

"Guyana?"

"I'm afraid so. I'm sorry, Commander. It's the only place the Pathfinder will seem *expected*. If we need more time back here, we'll have to figure out how to do it without being noticed."

"And how will we do that?"

"Likely with something less noticeable, perhaps a fishing boat."

"We're going to steal a fishing boat?"

A smile emerged from Emerson's mouth. "No, Ms. Shaw. We'll charter one. I'm aware of your opinion of the Navy, but we're not *that* bad."

Emerson turned back to Neely. "I know this won't be easy for you, Commander. Your father managed to bring us to a draw on the first fight, but it seems the battle isn't over. So if you two are going to find what it is you're after, I suggest you do it before sun up."

Neely blinked at him, surprised. "With all due respect, sir, ten hours isn't nearly enough time."

"Then I guess we'll have to make the most of it. Which leads me to my next question. How can my ship, and my crew, assist you?"

Alison wasted no time. "Let me talk to Sally and Dirk. We need time to test with them. Otherwise, our translation system may not operate correctly in the open water."

Emerson thought it over. "You'll have to wear a harness. These swells won't get any better until we can power down. And even then only moderately."

"Fine, I'll wear a harness." Alison was growing desperate. They'd planned to use the entire trip to work out the bugs in the new software code, but outside conditions on

334

the deck had made it impossible. Instead, Lee was left trying to make some progress through loopback testing, but there was only so much he could do through simulation.

What Alison feared now was that it simply wouldn't be enough time. That a badly functioning unit would make their deadline impossible to meet. And on top of it all, if these plants *were* like those in Guyana, it wouldn't just be amazing. It would call into question something even bigger — *where exactly was the source?* And that was why she needed Dirk and Sally so badly, not to mention a working vest.

Sitting next to her, Neely Lawton felt a very different fear building up inside her. She was now quietly praying that the plants were in fact what they hoped they were — not just for the discovery, but because the last thing she was prepared for was revisiting the place of her father's death.

Emerson was still watching them from his chair. "Anything else?"

"Yes," Neely said in a low voice. "Admiral Langford ordered us not to reveal what we're looking for…to anyone."

"He informed me of that as well. Not exactly as easy as it sounds. Nevertheless, all personnel aboard have been instructed to provide whatever assistance you need, but they are not to ask any questions outside of their charge."

Alison turned curiously to Neely, who merely nodded in response to the captain.

"A question, Ms. Shaw?"

She looked puzzled. "Is that…even possible?"

"A ship-wide gag order?" The corner of Emerson's lips curled. "It happens more than you might think. Especially on this ship." He leaned forward and stood up. "All right, that should do it. The ship is yours for the next ten hours. Whatever you need, we will provide. But as of this moment, we weigh anchor at zero-five-thirty, sharp."

"Captain," Alison said, standing up with him. "I hate to say this…but I think we're going to have even less time at the site."

"And why is that?"

"Because we have to slow the ship down."

"What do you mean, slow it down?"

"We're going too fast."

"Too fast for what?"

"Captain, those coordinates you've plotted are home to the largest breeding ground for mammals I've ever seen. We're about to sail straight through an awful lot of dolphins."

Emerson stared at her. "How many are we talking about?"

Alison grinned. "More than you might think."

67

They were getting closer.

From inside the tank, Dirk and Sally could both feel it. Privately, they'd been feeling it for hours. The gradual strengthening of a sensation deep within their lipid-rich melons used for echolocation. It was a subtle but unmistakable sensation they'd known since birth. A feeling which was found only one place on Earth.

Sally spoke directly to Dirk. "We're getting closer."

Dirk nodded and lifted his head above the water in the tank. "Yes. I hear them too." He dropped back below the water. "I'm hungry."

Sally made a slight sideways movement, similar to a human shaking their head. "You're always hungry."

"Because I'm strong."

Sally laughed. A moment later, she heard something and rose above the water. From her viewpoint, she spotted Alison, moving slowly down the outside of the ship. Accompanying her was a larger human, one they recognized but didn't know a name for.

The larger human attached something to Alison's body. He then held tightly as Alison approached. She was having difficulty walking.

When she reached the tank, Alison looked down and touched the talking machine on her front. The bright blue light appeared, followed by a mechanical translation of Alison's voice.

Dirk. Sally. How you?

"We fine, Alison. How are you?"

Alison gripped the side of the tank to steady herself.

Me good. Need help.

"Yes. We are happy for help. What help do you need?"

Help fix metal. Practice talk with Alison.

"Yes," Sally replied. She watched Alison, wondering what she was trying to do. "We are happy to practice talk with you.

Alison remained staring at the dolphins for several seconds, wondering what she sounded like to Dirk and Sally. She finally turned away and used her free hand to press the earbud in tighter.

"Lee, can you hear me?"

"Loud and clear, Ali."

"Are you connected to the vest?"

"Yes, I am," Lee answered, typing diligently. Next to him inside the ship's bridge, Chris watched Lee's screen. "I'm reactivating the new code. Stand by." A few moments later, Lee slapped the enter button and double-checked the screen. "Okay, I think we're set."

"So tell me again how we're going to do this?"

"You need to have them speak at the same time but saying different things. That way I can test the filter. Let's try to filter Dirk out first, then Sally. If that works, we'll try it against more complex translations."

The ship suddenly rolled hard to starboard and Alison briefly lost her footing. Jim Lightfoot, standing several feet behind her, began to rush forward as she quickly scrambled back to her feet.

She steadied herself again and shook her head at what Lee had just said. "How on Earth am I going to communicate *that*?"

68

By the time the Pathfinder's powerful engines began to slow, Lee Kenwood had concluded that they'd gotten as much out of their testing as they were going to get. It was far from perfect, but better than nothing under the circumstances. However, without more dolphins to test it, he couldn't be sure how well his "fix" was going to work. His fear was that it wasn't going to work well at all. Tracking a single conversation was one thing, but successfully translating dozens of them simultaneously was another. And contrary to what most people believed about computers, software bugs were the norm, not the exception.

Lee leaned back and folded his arms, staring at his screen. The problem was that he had now applied the new, largely untested code and reverting back to the old code would be their only option if it didn't work. But that would take time.

Down on the stern, Alison was worried about something else entirely. Although she and Neely had come back to investigate the plant life covering the ocean bottom, she had the distinct impression Dirk and Sally had come, not just to help, but for a totally different reason. One they had yet to share with her.

If she was right, Alison had no idea what that reason was. She stared at Dirk and Sally, both watching her quietly with their heads poking out of the water.

She couldn't shake the feeling that something unexpected was coming.

Alison looked up when several more men appeared on the deck above, led by the ship's lead engineer, Elgin Tay. He was shorter than the others but moved with an air of confidence. One by one the men descended the ladder and moved aft toward her and Lightfoot, swaying back and forth with the rolling of the ship. She recognized the last figure in line as Chris.

The ship's forward momentum gradually slowed and was replaced by steep side to side rolling from the ocean swells beneath them. Lightfoot approached from behind and grasped the rim of the dolphin's tank for support. "We can take the harness off if you like. It's still going to be a little rocky though."

"Fine with me." Alison began unbuckling. "At least if I fall over now you guys aren't going far."

"Very true."

Tay and the others approached, several putting their own hands on the tank. "Everyone okay?"

Before she could answer, her vest translated Dirk's reply. *We good.*

Dirk jerked his head, laughing.

Tay laughed with him. "I guess that means he's ready to get out."

Alison's vest emitted a sharp tone.

"There's no word for *guess*," Alison replied. "But yes, I think they're more than ready."

Ready.

"Okay, but I need to warn you, this may not be easy. These winches are strong, but they can be difficult to maneuver in conditions this rough. We don't normally use them when it's this bad. Payloads are too heavy. If they start swinging around, things can get dangerous in a hurry."

Alison stared at him, nervously. "How dangerous?"

The ship suddenly pitched and everyone grabbed something for support. "Very."

"We have to get them out."

Tay gave an understanding nod. "All right, men. You heard the lady. We're bringing them out. Careful as we go."

Within minutes, the giant winch was unchained and its powerful arm extended out over the rear of the stern. A chain was then wrapped around the arm, holding it in place.

340

A large, thick sling was retrieved from a nearby compartment. One of the men tied a control line to the underside of the sling, allowing them to counter any excessive movements due to the ship's swaying.

Next, the fat cable from the winch's arm was released and secured to two large metal rings running through the sling's two center points.

As Tay's men struggled under the pitching of the ship, Chris managed to make his way to the side railing. They hadn't heard it before above the roar of the Pathfinder's engines, but as those systems were powered down, a familiar sound arose from all directions: the sound of dolphins.

Lightfoot, helping with the sling, abruptly stopped. He whirled around and spotted hundreds of moving shadows in the water. "Holy crap! You guys see that?"

Another of Tay's men edged closer. "There's a ton of dolphins surrounding the ship." He turned back just in time to see Alison's grin.

"Just wait until dawn."

Once the sling was in the tank, Sally moved forward, easing her sleek gray body into the fabric cradle. She waited while Lightfoot and another engineer ran their hands alongside, ensuring nothing was restricted and the overhead cable was taut enough to keep the dolphin secure in the event of a problem.

When they'd loaded the dolphins in Puerto Rico, it was done as carefully as possible. This time would be different. Their priority now was to get them off as quickly as possible.

Alison's expression grew increasingly nervous as she watched the men trying to work and at the same time struggling to maintain their own footing.

"Lightfoot!" Tay yelled. "Man the control line. The rest of us will help lift her out. Once she's out, it's going to be all winch."

"Aye." Lightfoot gripped it tightly. "Ready."

Tay glanced to his man, Smitty, controlling the winch. "Okay, we're going to time this with a roll to port. We lift in the middle and gravity will swing her out over the water. Lightfoot will slow her down. Everyone understand?"

Tay nodded. "All right, here we go. On my mark. Ready…wait for the roll."

The lower deck promptly began to rise again.

"UP!" he yelled.

The winch's cable lurched and immediately grabbed, hoisting Sally up while those around her steadied the sling. But the vessel rolled too quickly. Her heavy body was abruptly pulled out of their hands and swung hard toward the falling side of the ship. The swing accelerated too quickly, sending her far out over the water and back again.

"Look out!" Tay shouted. "She's coming back!"

No sooner had he yelled than the weight of the Pathfinder's enormous keel overcame the upper sway of the ship and the motion reversed. Sally's momentum increased even more rapidly, sending her swinging toward them and missing the rim of the tank by inches. Her four hundred pound body passed over the tank and smashed into Chris at full speed, throwing him careening into the winch's thick base.

"Chris!" Alison shrieked and let go of the tank, sliding across the wet deck. She scrambled to get her feet out in front of her and managed to stop herself between the winch and one of the ship's stanchions.

She grabbed Chris's limp body and pulled him closer. "Chris! CHRIS!" Seconds later, Smitty dropped into place on the other side. He wrapped an arm around Chris's frame, preventing him from moving.

"Check him!" Smitty yelled.

Alison frantically ran her hands over him until she found Chris's neck. She pressed two fingers in, searching. She felt nothing and moved to the other side of this neck.

"Get the control line!"

Standing above her and Smitty, the other men struggled to secure the control line while Sally slowed and began swinging back again. The line, now wet, whipped past them, whipping through Lightfoot's outstretched hand.

Tay watched Sally swing uncontrollably back over the water.

"Wait! Wait!" he shouted. "Let her go!" He twisted around and stared at Smitty, who was trying to right himself with one hand.

"Smitty!" Tay yelled. "Let it go!"

Smitty's eyes found Tay's and looked at him in confusion. He pushed Chris's body toward Alison and she grabbed him with both arms. He then rose onto one knee and steadied himself against the base of the winch.

"Smitty!" Tay yelled again. "Let it go!"

It took only a moment for Smitty to understand. He braced himself against the winch and grasped the metal handle controlling its motor. He watched Sally's thrashing tail as she sailed toward the water yet again.

When she was far out enough, Smitty released the tension, letting Sally's momentum catapult her out over the ocean and into the water with a splash.

Lightfoot struggled to the side, where he watched the sling billow in the water just enough for Sally to escape.

Behind him, Tay was already on the phone to the bridge. "We need medical on the main deck *now*!" He turned back to see Smitty raise the cable and empty sling back out of the water.

Within moments, the ship's doctor and medical assistant burst from a door above them on the upper deck. They sprinted down the metal grating until they reached the ladders and descended. Even with the swaying of the ship, they made it to the stern in less than a minute.

Doctor Kanna wrapped his fingers around Chris's neck, searching. He then moved to his wrists. "I'm not getting anything. Get a stretcher down here!"

Tay barked again into the phone. Two more men appeared overhead carrying a basket stretcher. They reached the ladder and slid it down to the others.

Tay's team gathered around as Kanna folded Chris's arms in over his chest. "Get him in, quick!" In a coordinated movement, they lifted and moved him into the basket where thick nylon straps were secured over him. Alison pulled herself to her feet and watched the men move smoothly to the ladder, raising him back up. Kanna followed and together they disappeared from Alison's view.

"You okay?" Tay asked.

"I don't know."

"Don't worry. Kanna's one of the best doctors in the Navy."

"It's true," Lightfoot said. "He's in good hands."

Alison nodded reluctantly and blinked. The clock was ticking and she knew it. She reluctantly turned back to the large tank. "Now what?"

Tay took a deep breath. "We have one more dolphin to get into the water."

"Not like that again, I hope."

Tay managed a smile. "Trust me. The first time's never the best."

Her eyes fell on Dirk with his head still bobbing above the water. "Are you ready, Dirk?"

Yes. Ready.

"Okay…let's do it."

A moment later, Lightfoot reached down to grab the control line, now hanging over the edge of the steel tank.

The three steadied themselves against the edge as the ship rolled through another large wave.

"This time, don't fight it."

Tay and Lightfoot pulled the sling down into the shallow water and held the sides open for Dirk, who promptly circled and slid into place. Smitty reeled in the cable just enough to pull the thick canvas closed and waited for a signal. He nodded to Tay and Alison. "Say when."

69

Their second attempt was smoother. Working with the roll of the ship, Dirk became a living pendulum, oscillating past the equilibrium position until they had enough momentum for it to carry him beyond the edge of the deck. Smitty timed the release of the cable perfectly and let Dirk fall into the dark water. Smoother than the first time, but not something any of them wanted to try again.

And while the team aboard the Pathfinder was exhausted, Dirk and Sally seemed little worse for the wear. In fact, Alison had a sneaking suspicion that Dirk had actually enjoyed his launch.

With calmer nerves, she and the others went topside to check on Chris. Standing in front of the wall of glass with Tay and Lightfoot, she was overcome with the memory of being in the exact same spot just a year earlier.

It was the very spot where Alison had the conversation with John that eventually led her to fall in love with the man.

A nervousness suddenly welled up inside her as Alison realized it was the first time she'd let herself admit she was in love with him. Even to herself. She promptly pushed the thought out of her mind and stared back through the glass at Chris's still figure lying on the examination table. Nervousness was replaced with fear as she watched Kanna lift Chris's eyelids again and note something on a small tablet.

Behind her, the door opened and she turned to see both Lee and Neely enter, joining Tay, Lightfoot, and herself.

"How is he?!"

"We don't know yet."

"What happened?"

"We lost control of the sling trying to get Sally into the

water and she swung back straight into Chris. He flew head first into the winch."

"Jesus." Lee stepped forward toward the glass. After a long silence, he turned back around. "God, please let him be all right."

"Is there anything we can do?"

Alison shook her head, holding back tears. "Just wait, I guess."

Lightfoot, who had been staring at Chris and the doctor, somberly replied. "I don't think there's much you can do here."

"He's right," Tay nodded. "As harsh as it sounds, we need to let Doctor Kanna do what he can." He glanced at his watch. "The clock is ticking."

"I can't just leave him."

Tay and Lightfoot looked at Neely, who stepped closer to Alison. "I think we have to," Neely said softly.

"It's true, Ali," Lee frowned, although also reluctant to leave. "If the situation were reversed, Chris would have to do the same thing. We're all here for a reason and we don't have much time."

"And the faster we finish," added Neely, "the faster we leave…for Chris's sake."

Alison continued staring at the glass. They were right. Although she still didn't want to admit it. She and Chris had been through so much together. He was her best friend. The thought of leaving him alone tore at her heart.

But she had to.

Alison could barely focus. And attempting to don their gear under the rocking of the ship left both her and Neely struggling to keep their balance, even with the help of Tay and his men surrounding them. The light-colored steel deck was covered with a slick sheen of water, making it nearly impossible to stand up for more than a few seconds. After they were geared up, Lightfoot sat down and began putting his own equipment on. Getting into the water was one thing, but getting back out was quite another. It would be Lightfoot's job to help them back up.

Tay slid a thick headband over Alison's forehead and turned on the strip of bright LED lights. "These should last a few hours. The battery on your head is going to feel a little heavy, but once you're in the water, you won't even notice it anymore."

Alison nodded and tested the airflow from her rebreather, ensuring the oxygen mixture was sufficient. She then adjusted the rubber seal of her mask around her eyes into a more comfortable position. Finally, she checked the IMIS unit on her chest to make sure it was powered on. She took a few deep breaths before looking back up at Tay.

He took her hands and helped her to her feet. Together, they waited for the next roll before he quickly passed her to Smitty, who stood along the steel railing. Smitty grabbed her and pulled her across. Beyond the railing, with the help of her headlamp, dozens of dolphins could be seen converging around the stern.

"Are you good?"

Alison nodded.

"Okay. Hold on," he said, before turning to receive Neely.

She stumbled into him with a soft bounce, but managed to latch onto the rail next to Alison. Her fins went on just as quickly and Smitty moved back to Alison.

"Okay!" he yelled. "Let's go to the end." He wrapped his arms around her and they shuffled to the end of the railing together. "We have to wait and go with the roll! When we're as close to the water as possible, you take a step to your right and jump! Don't be afraid if you feel me give you a little push! We have to do it fast!"

When Alison felt the starboard side begin its dip, she stepped nervously to the side while Smitty maintained an iron grip from the back. She was surprised when Smitty launched her forward, sending her head first into the dark ocean with a giant splash.

From between the swells, she watched as Neely stepped to the end of the rail. She wished she could warn her about Smitty and that first step, but only moments later, Neely hit the water next to her. Lastly came Lightfoot, splashing on the opposite side of Alison with a natural grace that reminded her he'd been a semi-professional swimmer before joining the Navy. Even in those conditions, he surfaced as relaxed as anyone she'd ever seen.

"Can you both hear me?"

"Yes," answered the women in unison.

"Good. Any problems?"

"Nope. I'm fine."

"Me too."

"All right," he said. He motioned to Smitty and turned back to both women. His full face mask reflected brightly from their LED strips. "Ms. Shaw, we're all yours."

Alison nodded. "Lee, can you hear me?"

"Loud and clear, Ali."

"Are we ready?"

"Ready as we'll ever be. I've paused the translating on your vest. When I turn it back on, it will only be filtering for Dirk and Sally to begin with."

"Okay." Alison looked to Neely and Lightfoot. "Here we go."

Alison used the button on her scuba BCD to release some of its air and reduce her buoyancy. She began slowly sinking and watched the waterline pass over her mask and head. Together the three continued down, eventually adding enough air to end their descent.

Neely and Lightfoot became silent, marveling at the hundreds of dolphins swirling around them.

"Still there, Lee?"

"Like a bad penny."

She smiled inside her mask. "Let's turn it on."

"Okay. Here goes." Far above them on the ship's bridge, Lee typed a command on his keyboard and hit the enter key. Almost instantly, the lines on his screen began dancing as the microphone was reactivated on Alison's vest and began transmitting wirelessly to the server at Lee's feet.

However, below the surface Alison heard nothing through her earbuds. She waited patiently for almost a minute before finally responding. "Lee?"

"Yes, Ali."

"I'm not hearing anything. Is it working?"

"It's because of the filter. I'm getting an audio feed from your mike, but the server isn't translating any of it. Try calling Dirk or Sally."

"Sally? Dirk? Are you there?"

After a moment, the reassuring mechanical voice of IMIS sounded in Alison's ears.

We here Alison.

They both appeared from out of the darkness and into the bright glow of her lamp.

Behind her, Lightfoot reached out his hand and skimmed the body of several passing dolphins. "My God," he said through his microphone. "I've never seen anything like this. What is this place?"

Neely twisted around to face him. Her LED lamp illuminated him as if he were suspended in space without gravity.

"That's what we're about to find out."

70

Where Chris?

Alison stared blankly at Sally, her mind returning to her friend. She could still see him, lying unconscious in the ship's sick bay.

"He's resting."

Sally did not reply. For a moment, Alison could have sworn a look of doubt passed over the dolphin's face. She cleared her throat and answered Lightfoot's question.

"We originally thought this was a breeding ground, since dolphins tend to seek out protected areas for birthing. But this is different. This," she said, "is literally off the scale."

She turned to Dirk and Sally, still watching her and strangely quiet.

"Sally. Dirk. We've come to see the plants."

Sally surprised Alison with her response.

We know.

Alison began to speak before Sally interrupted.

Follow now.

The abruptness felt strange as she watched the dolphins turn and move smoothly downward with a single thrust of their tails. The motion was clear and Alison turned to the others while letting more air out of her BCD. "Stay close."

The three followed the dolphins in a gradual descent, below the endless field of dolphins and into the darkness, with only a few meters before them lit by their headlamps. They continued until nothing could be seen above them, lacking even the slightest hint of moonlight. One by one, they cleared the pressure from their ears and continued downward until it appeared.

The darkness below them gradually began to lighten, first into a field of gray, and then followed by a subtle, strange green glow of phosphorescence. Finally, the plants began to appear, waving rhythmically in the gentle ocean currents.

"Wow," Neely whispered. "It's beautiful."

For as far as they could see, beyond even their lamps, the faint green glow continued until finally disappearing again into the blackness.

Dirk and Sally slowed, watching as Alison stopped kicking and let her momentum carry her forward. She was now within an arm's reach of a large sea whip, sweeping back and forth in slow motion. The bright light from Alison's lamp washed over the plant, displaying its branches of polyps in a darker green.

She reached out and touched one of the tubes lightly with her fingertips, rubbing it carefully between her thumb and index finger.

Neely and Lightfoot both slowed beside her. "This is incredible."

"How far does it go?"

"Far," answered Alison. "Over a square mile."

"Good God."

Neely propelled herself forward, gliding horizontally over the vegetation and studying it. "I've never seen anything like it."

"I don't think anyone has."

She reached down and brushed her hand over another large plant as it passed silently beneath her. Awash in the bright light, its streaming tendrils resembling long ribbons and changing colors into translucent oranges and pinks.

"Amazing," she whispered.

Behind her, Alison turned back to Dirk and Sally, both still floating effortlessly. "Sally, is something wrong?"

No Alison. No wrong.

"Then what are you doing?"

We wait.

"Waiting? For what?" Alison studied them, waiting for a reply but not getting one. Instead she got an answer, when three shapes emerged from the darkness.

It was three dolphins. Larger and older. The same three she'd met before. Three "heads" as Sally called them. Elders.

As the trio neared, Dirk and Sally faded back slightly.

Alison smiled behind her mask. Perhaps for the first time in all of this, it was exactly what she was expecting.

"Lee, can you hear me?"

"Yes, Ali. I'm here."

"I think it's time to test your new program."

Topside, Lee squinted at his screen, enlarging the smaller video picture from Alison's vest.

"Yes," he replied slowly. "I think you're right."

He switched back to the IMIS control window and typed out a long command. "Cross your fingers." With that, he held his breath and hit the enter key.

His worst fear was realized. The new software didn't work.

Below him, Alison's earplugs screeched with a jumble of high-pitched noise as IMIS listened and tried unsuccessfully to translate hundreds of conversations at once. Sound carried further in water, which meant everything from any dolphin within earshot of Alison was easily picked up by the vest's microphone. All without the video feed, an essential element needed for identifiable translation. The sheer deluge of noise completely overwhelmed both the processors on Alison's vest and those in Lee's small servers.

Alison cringed in pain and immediately yanked the buds out of her ears. "Lee! It's too loud!"

"I know, I know!" He scrambled to lower the sound. "Is that better?" There was no response. "Ali? Ali, can you hear me?"

With one headphone back in, she nodded. "Yes, barely. But I can still hear all the noise. Turn it off!"

A moment later, the background noise was gone and Lee's voice rose again in volume. "Sorry. How's that?"

"Better. What happened?"

"The software doesn't work."

"Crap. Okay, just turn Dirk and Sally back on."

"I can't. The process is hung on the server. I can't stop it without stopping *everything*."

"You mean permanently?"

"No, just until I can reboot the system. Maybe ten minutes."

Alison looked at the dive watch strapped to her left arm. "That doesn't leave much time. We have to surface soon."

"I know, I know. I'm sorry. But we have no choice. The only thing that isn't hung is our radios."

Alison shook her head and peered at Neely and Lightfoot, who were both watching her.

"Fine. Reboot."

71

From their viewpoint, Sally and Dirk were both watching Alison, puzzled. They didn't understand why she was not speaking.

"Why are they no speak?" one of the elders asked.

Dirk peered at Alison. "They talked much before." He drifted in closer and could see Alison's mouth moving inside the glass. He examined the machine on her chest. The small light was on. Dirk circled back toward the other two. Their mouths were also moving. "I don't know."

The three elders continued floating, waiting.

After a long wait, the silence was broken by Alison's translated mechanical voice.

-ally Dirk can hear me?

"Yes, Alison. We hear you now. You are not talking before."

Metal broken. Work now. Sorry.

Sally watched as the three older dolphins glided in closer. "You hear us?"

There was no answer.

"Alison, you are hearing?" repeated Dirk.

Metal broken. Hear Dirk and Sally. No heads.

One elder seemed to understand and spoke through Dirk instead. "Ask her why plants."

"Why do you come back, Alison? For plants?"

Yes. Plants important.

"Yes. You take plants, Alison. We want to talk."

Alison turned and nodded at Neely, who was still hovering beside her.

Neely acknowledged and reached down to retrieve a knife from her leg. She then reached out and cut a small sample from a nearby tendril. She moved forward and took a piece from another plant, continuing until she had several. The dolphins followed her curiously.

What talk?

Dirk turned back to her. "You come back with more friends. Heads want to know how many others."

From inside her face mask, Alison watched as the dolphins spoke to each other. She paused, trying to understand Dirk's translated question. The IMIS system was amazing, but it still had limitations. And the way Alison sounded to them must have been just as challenging.

"How many of us? Um...three."

She watched the elders speak again through Dirk.

Not three. How more?

How more? Alison thought to herself. *How more what?*

"I don't understand."

How more peoples?

"How many people where?"

No. How more peoples there.

Alison still didn't understand. *What did they mean by there? On the boat?*

"I'm not-" she began to speak but stopped. IMIS hadn't caught it. But she suddenly did. They didn't mean there, they meant everywhere!

"You mean how many people are there?"

Yes. How peoples all there?

Alison smiled, briefly gloating over the realization that she'd translated something before IMIS did. Yet her face became dour again as she considered the question. They wanted to know how many humans there were. In total. She suddenly found herself nervous. They understood numbers, but there was no way they could understand *billions*. And if they did, her answer was probably going to scare the hell out of them.

"Many," she replied.

How?

Alison looked to Neely and Lightfoot, both still watching her. She wasn't about to lie, but there was no way the dolphins were ready for the truth of just how many humans there really were. Not by a long shot.

"Many," she repeated. She took a breath. "Like fish."

Their reaction was unreadable. The elders simply stared at her with their dark, soft eyes. It wasn't worth pointing out that not all people were *friends*.

The third elder on the right moved closer. She drifted past Alison's shoulder, examining the scuba gear.

She say stay.

Alison began to reply when she was interrupted by the beeping from her dive computer. They were reaching their nitrogen limit. They needed to get to the surface. "I cannot stay. We must go up."

She motioned to the others and added a brief blast of air to increase her buoyancy. "I'm sorry, we're out of time. We will come back."

They want stay.

"I'm sorry," Alison repeated. "I cannot. But I will come back."

It was the last translation Alison heard before reaching the pod of dolphins above her, where the trio stopped and hovered for a few minutes before finally breaching the surface.

Bobbing among the waves, Alison pulled her mask off and inhaled a lung full of fresh air.

She raised her voice so the others could hear her. "We have to get back aboard!"

Lightfoot nodded and swam forward. Neely followed, leaving Alison floating behind them. Something had struck Alison from the moment they'd reached the bottom, but it didn't register until Dirk mentioned the plants. She suspected neither Neely nor Lightfoot knew enough about phosphorescence to catch it. There was something wrong

357

with what they saw. Bioluminescence caused by the light-emitting pigments and enzymes, luciferin and luciferase, had very distinct hues of green and blue. But what Alison had just seen below was not the same — it was a very different hue of green. One that she'd seen only once before and in a place very far from the ocean. It had been on top of the Acarai Mountains in South America. She didn't notice the first time she'd seen the plants because they were there during the day.

She had to get to a phone. Immediately.

72

The tropical waters from which Alison was being lifted could not have been more different from those in which John Clay now stood. Water had collected at the lowest point of one of the mine's shafts, leaving an ultra-clear basin that was waist-high, stretching over a hundred yards along their path. And unlike the warm Caribbean, this water was ice-cold.

Carrying his bag on one shoulder and holding his phone and flashlight with the opposite hand, Clay could feel his toes growing numb. Which meant it must be even worse for Li Na, who was trailing behind him.

The only consolation was that the second half of the tunnel was relatively free of debris, while in the first half they had encountered a number of small cave-ins. It had slowed their progress considerably, making the icy water a faster, if somewhat painful, change of pace.

They had been underground for hours, far longer than expected. And unless the remainder of the shaft was in better shape than the way they'd came, their chances of finding a way out anytime soon weren't very good.

Clay continued pushing forward through the water, maintaining a slow enough pace to keep the ripples to a minimum. He held his flashlight above his head, allowing him to see the bottom clearly, or at least well enough to spot any surprises. But maintaining a clear view wouldn't be a good trade-off if their slow progress resulted in frostbite.

He paused to look ahead and could hear the chattering of Li Na's teeth.

"Not much farther."

The teenage girl behind him nodded, but said nothing.

The truth was she had no idea what she was doing. She felt sure the man in front was trying to help her, but she didn't know anything about him. She finally spoke to distract herself from the biting pain in her legs and feet.

"Mister Ishmael. W-Why did you come here?"

Clay stopped again, momentarily. He smiled at Li Na under the glow of his light. "My name is not Ishmael. It's John."

She looked at him with a confused expression. "Why did you say it was Ishmael?"

He turned back around and continued. "It's kind of a joke."

"Oh." She didn't understand the joke. "Why did you come here?"

"To find the case you're holding in your arms."

In the dark coldness of the cave, she'd almost forgotten she was carrying it and gripped it tighter. "My father's case?"

"Yes. Did your father tell you what was inside?"

"Not exactly. I wasn't awake the last time he came." After thinking, her expression changed to quizzical. "You didn't know I was here?"

"I did. But only shortly before I arrived."

"I see. So you weren't expecting…all of this."

Clay grinned again but continued moving. "No."

Li Na shrugged and tried to lighten the mood. "Surprise."

Clay chuckled. "Your English is very good."

"My father was a soldier. He told me it was important to learn English, like the Americans. He said someday they would have to learn Chinese."

"Your father sounds like a wise man."

Li Na's voice grew quiet. "He was."

They continued in silence for several minutes before she spoke again. "So what exactly is in this case?"

"I'm afraid it's a long story."

"I think we have time."

"Not enough," Clay responded. He stopped again and shined the light forward. The end was in sight. In the

360

distance, he could see wet soil rising up from the water.

Several minutes later, they made it to dry ground where Clay immediately dropped his things. He focused his light on the bag and unzipped it, retrieving the thermal blanket.

"Here." He moved to Li Na, who had just sat down against the rock wall, wrapping the blanket around her legs and feet. "It'll warm you up faster."

"Thank you."

He stood up. "You're doing great."

"It doesn't feel like it. I can barely stand up. I've been sick."

Clay nodded. "Are you hungry?" He turned back to his bag and pulled out a small package. He cut it open with a knife and handed it to her.

"What is this?" She took the thick, brown plastic bag and turned it over.

"It tastes better than it looks."

"What's an MRE?" she asked, reading the letters off the bag.

"Food. It'll give you some energy."

Clay sat down on the opposite wall and watched Li Na take a bite of an unrecognizable chunk. After chewing, she raised her eyebrows and took another bite.

"Not bad, huh?"

"It's very good."

Clay leaned his head back and closed his eyes. He hadn't slept more than an hour in the past two days and without much food, he was reaching a new level of exhaustion.

"Where are we going?"

He rolled his head from side to side. "I'm not sure yet. First we need to get out of here."

"How much farther do you think it is?"

"Hopefully not far. We're headed back uphill, which is encouraging."

"What does that mean?"

"Encouraging? It means...hopeful. Of course, a little

361

luck wouldn't hurt either."

"Do you believe in luck?"

He grinned and closed his eyes. "I do right now."

Li Na stared at him in the ambient glow of his flashlight. It was the first time she'd gotten a good look at his face. Or at least all of it. He was handsome, for an American. With dark hair and a square jawline, he reminded her of someone she might see on television. He was also tall and very tired.

"Are you in the military? In America?"

"I am."

"Like a soldier?"

"Not anymore. Now I'm more of an investigator."

"What's that?"

"Someone who tries to find things out."

"Oh." She took her last bite and folded up the empty plastic bag. "My father admired the American military."

"Is that right?"

"Yes. He said Americans fight for honor."

"We try to. Usually."

"You don't always?"

"Unfortunately, not."

"My father said that you-" She stopped suddenly when Clay's eyes shot open.

"Shh!" He held his hand up, signaling her to be quiet. His eyes stared at her, unmoving. "Did you hear that?"

"Hear what?"

He angled his head slightly. He heard it again. They both did. A distant thump.

Clay was instantly on his feet. He grabbed Li Na and pulled her up, whipping the blanket from her legs.

"There's someone else in this tunnel!"

"Are you-" Clay cut her off, clamping a hand over her mouth.

"Yes, I'm sure," he whispered. "We have to go! Quietly."

He stuffed the blanket and empty plastic into his bag,

362

hefting it back onto his shoulder. The rest he gathered quickly before stopping and looking at the case in Li Na's hands.

They had traveled almost another quarter mile through the tunnel before Clay suddenly lowered his light and turned it off, plunging them into blackness. He remained still. "Do you feel that?"

"What?"

"A breeze." Clay closed his eyes in the darkness and held his breath. He was sure he felt it. An almost undetectable flow of air. "Come on!" He turned the light back on and surged forward, with Li Na stumbling to hold on.

A hundred yards farther and Clay stopped again. This time when he briefly turned off the light, Li Na didn't need an explanation. She could see a ray of light in the distance.

"Is that the end?"

"I think so."

Clay turned the flashlight back on. Clumps of rocks and dirt littered the floor of the tunnel as they'd seen at the other end. As they neared, the light grew brighter to illuminate the mouth of the tunnel, largely hidden from the outside beneath a curtain of roots and vines.

Clay stopped at the curtain of vegetation and separated several vines. There wasn't much to see. Just a narrow path outside, almost entirely reclaimed by the forest.

Clay powered off the flashlight, tucking both it and the phone into the pocket on the leg of his pants.

"Stay close."

He unslung his HK in a smooth motion, raising it to his cheek. He then took a step forward and let the rifle slowly emerge from between the vines. His eyes searching left, then right.

He stepped out onto the dry groundcover, crunching under his feet, and listened carefully. Clay continued slowly and had made it less than ten feet when he froze, causing Li Na to bump into him.

"What is it?"

Clay didn't answer. Instead, he turned carefully around and stopped, staring over Li Na's head.

Lining the tiny hill above them were over a dozen soldiers, all with their rifles raised and aimed directly at Clay. Off to the side stood Li Qin, with a bandaged right hand, and before him, the terrified teenage boy who had shown them the tunnel.

Clay didn't move. Instead, he stared up as Qin smiled and laid his good hand reassuringly over the young boy's shoulder.

"Drop your gun."

Clay felt Li Na press in behind him as he studied the other soldiers. Very slowly, he lowered his HK to the ground.

Qin motioned to one of the men next to him, who then lowered his own rifle. It was at that moment that Clay removed the phone from his pocket and held it up.

The approaching soldier stopped and studied the phone curiously. He glanced back to Qin, who was doing the same. Together they watched as Clay turned the unit in his hand and began typing a message with his thumb.

Qin's eyes opened wide. He screamed at the soldier who was now within twenty feet. "STOP HIM!"

The man exploded into a run, quickly reaching the end of the incline and launching himself forward.

Clay took the full impact and was thrown to the ground while the phone tumbled out of his reach. The soldier reached it first and brought down the full weight of his boot, smashing the device into several pieces.

73

In Washington, D.C., Will Borger's heart nearly stopped when he read the single word message from Clay on his own phone. He stared, disbelieving, at each of the nine letters displayed on the tiny screen.

"Oh no."

He suddenly jumped when his desk phone rang. He leaned over his desk and looked at the incoming number.

"You have got to be kidding."

Upstairs, Admiral Langford turned away from his window when his office door opened and Will Borger was shown in by his secretary. She closed it behind him, leaving him standing awkwardly and facing Langford.

"You wanted to see me, Admiral."

"I did."

Langford walked back to his desk and sat on the edge, studying Borger. He motioned to a chair. "Have a seat."

Borger nervously stepped forward and eased himself down.

Langford folded his arms. "Anything you'd like to tell me, Will?"

"Um…what do you mean?"

Langford scratched his temple, thinking. "I just had a very interesting conversation. Care to guess with who?"

Borger tried to smile. "Not my mother, I hope."

"Very funny."

Borger's smile disappeared. "Sorry."

"As insightful as a call with your mother might actually be, the person I just hung up with was Alison Shaw."

Borger stared back with genuine surprise. "Alison?"

365

"Yes. Do you know why?"

"Uh...no, sir."

Langford continued studying Borger. "Do you know where she is?"

"Puerto Rico?"

"She's aboard the Pathfinder. Anchored not far from Trinidad."

"I didn't know that."

Langford nodded. "What's surprising to me, however, is why Ms. Shaw called me...asking about *you*."

"Me?"

"That's right."

"I don't understand."

"Well, that makes two of us. You see, not only is Ms. Shaw in the Caribbean on a very important mission, but now she's calling me...and asking that I put you on a flight to Trinidad."

"Trinidad? What for?"

Langford stared down at Borger with steely eyes. "I thought you might tell me."

"I don't know why, sir."

"I see." Langford sighed and stood up. He rounded his desk and sat down heavily in his chair. After some consideration, he pressed his hands together in front of his face. "Ms. Shaw is with Commander Lawton on the Pathfinder investigating what they believe could be a second location for our mysterious plants. Like those found by Clay and Caesare in Guyana."

"What?!" Borger leaned forward in his seat.

"That's right. Another possible location, but this one is underwater." Langford watched as Borger remained frozen, thinking.

There were three things going through Borger's head, each as earth-shattering as the next. And if it weren't automatic, he probably would have forgotten to breathe.

The possibility of a second location was stunning in and

366

of itself. Another source producing what could only be described as an evolutionary miracle. A mutation capable of changing the genetic structure of a living organism, resulting in something mankind had never seen before. But there was a reason. A reason that was both logical, and at the same time, utterly jaw-dropping. The secret which both Alison and Borger already knew.

The Chinese had made the find of the century. A find that had culminated in the attack on a U.S. naval ship by the Chinese in an attempt to flee with every piece of plant they had managed to gather. The rest they'd burned.

But that was only the tip of the iceberg. The Chinese had fled with what they thought was the entire find. But what they didn't know was that the source wasn't the plants at all — the *source* was in the water. Water, highly enriched by something hidden at the top of the mountain. Something extraordinary.

A vault. A vault hidden within the mountain, housing thousands, maybe millions, of perfectly preserved samples from an alien biosphere. And what appeared to be the total sum of another planet's genetic and cellular history encoded in countless protected seeds…and embryos.

It was an amazing discovery that was nearly beyond words. But now the idea of Alison discovering a *second* site left Will Borger completely speechless. Because a second site could answer a pressing question that Borger had been losing sleep over ever since they discovered the vault.

With the sheer amount of materials needed to construct what was hidden in that cliff, Borger was convinced a ship had been used to transport it. From very far away. But the distance involved, along with the speed needed to reach Earth, would have required a level of energy that was formidable on any scale. To Borger, it meant only one thing: a once-way trip. And if he was right, it presented the big question that Will Borger couldn't answer. *Where was the ship?*

But maybe Alison's discovery was the answer to his

367

question…maybe she had found the ship! By matter of simple deduction, the ship would have had to be destroyed or hidden. Perhaps dumped somewhere that no one would find.

How Alison had managed to find it, he couldn't begin to imagine. But the ramifications of *what* she may have discovered was far more important in Borger's opinion than *how*.

"Mr. Borger," Langford said, breaking the silence. "You look like you have something on your mind."

He slowly nodded. "Yes, sir."

"Well?" Langford said, his hands still pressed together in front of him.

Borger wanted to tell him. He'd wanted to since they'd first found it. But together, he, Clay, Caesare, and Alison were afraid to. They knew what unleashing such a discovery could do. To the world.

The power contained in whatever liquid those embryos were floating in was almost beyond comprehension. Especially in a world that fought wars over far less, and in many cases, on lies alone.

They had kept the secret from Langford and everyone else out of the fear of what would be unleashed onto the world.

And *that* was the third thing which had caused Borger to freeze in his chair. It was the realization that only the threat of someone else finding out would make John Clay send Borger the message that he did.

Nine characters. A single message before his satellite phone lost signal permanently.

TELLNGFRD.

74

M0ngol didn't like to be bothered. Not by his colleagues, not by his boss, not even by his friends. As far as he was concerned, his work was too important to be interrupted, which made the surprise visit by two Ministry of State Security agents all that more irritating.

To him, MSS agents were simply thugs, with Qin being a rare exception. He was one of the few who truly understood what someone like M0ngol was capable of and respected his abilities. Others, like the two now escorting the young hacker down an empty hallway, just had no idea. Together, they were taking him through a section of the building he'd never seen before. He had only heard of it.

However, unlike most others, M0ngol was only mildly interested to see the place in person. He had more important things to do than to explain yet again how cyber espionage worked to someone who would never possess the capacity to understand it.

The two thugs on either side of him hadn't said anything since pulling M0ngol out of his chair downstairs. Together they walked briskly to the end of the hall and turned right, following another long section which ended at two faceless double doors. Outside stood two more agents, waiting for them.

When they reached the doors, he watched the four goons exchange looks of importance amongst themselves. Then the door was opened and M0ngol was ushered inside.

The room was large, and unlike the dreariness of the hallways, it was richly decorated — particularly with the giant mahogany conference table and high-back leather chairs filling the space.

Inside sat a lone person. An elderly man looking

outward from the far end of the table. He studied M0ngol carefully before motioning to the table and chair.

"Please sit down."

The young man complied.

"Do you know who I am?"

"Yes," M0ngol replied. "You're Yu Xinzhen, Chairmen of the Politburo Standing Committee. Most people know who you are."

Xinzhen nodded, studying the young man. His tone and posture spoke volumes. He was one of the new generationals, one of the *inflicted*, as many of the elders referred to them. Immature and emblazoned by a sense of rebelliousness. But in the end, little more than children hiding behind a veneer of maturity, with a shroud of gadgets giving them a feeling of importance. And then there were those like this one, swollen with self-importance and undeserved power, granted by an exploitation of technologies their parents didn't understand. That most of the world didn't understand.

He stared at M0ngol with a sense of bemusement. "Do you know why you're here?"

"No."

"You've been working with Qin."

"I have."

"And it seems you have uncovered a great deal."

Xinzhen watched the expression on M0ngol's face begin to change. This wasn't about giving another explanation of what M0ngol was able to do. This was about what he knew…what he had learned. An air of nervousness began to form.

"I have discovered some things, as requested."

Xinzhen nodded. "As requested."

"Yes."

"And by who would that be?"

M0ngol shifted slightly in his chair. Qin had clearly spoken to the old man, but he didn't know what was said

370

between the two. A fleeting thought that left M0ngol wishing he'd recorded Qin's call.

"Qin. He asked me to learn everything I could about General Wei."

"And what have you learned about Wei?"

"Well, we learned that his daughter is alive."

"And."

"And that the general may have hidden something with her."

"And."

M0ngol stopped. His mind was racing. He looked out through the glass door to find the two agents watching him intently. His confidence was melting. "Um…and… an American is trying to reach her first."

To M0ngol's disappointment, the old man's expression did not show the faintest hint of surprise. Instead, he took a deep breath and placed a delicate hand on the table. "What else?"

"W-what do you mean?"

"My dear boy. You think me a fool."

"No! No, sir."

"Then tell me. What *else* have you been learning about?"

M0ngol swallowed. "What else?"

Xinzhen rapped his fingers on the table. *Oh, how quickly they shrink.*

"I know you've been searching for a great many things on General Wei. Surely you've found more interesting facts to share with me."

"Um…I-"

"You've read about our project in South America."

The young man stammered. "A little."

"I think you know more than a little. Indulge me."

M0ngol nodded. "They're searching."

A trace of interest appeared in Xinzhen's eyes. "Who is searching?"

"The Brazilians. Now. They're searching now."

"Searching for what?"

"Traces of the plants. They think there is more there."

Xinzhen's eyes focused intently on M0ngol. "More?"

"Yes. And they're also looking for a primate. A monkey. They think it may have absorbed some of the plant's DNA."

"And they're searching now?"

"Yes, Your Eminence. On the mountain. The Brazilians and a small team from the U.S."

Xinzhen leaned forward in his chair. "The U.S. too?"

"Yes. Friends of the American that came here to find Wei's daughter."

The old man's eyes were now transfixed on M0ngol. He had been told that all traces were wiped clean on the mountain. Destroyed. If the Americans were now there, *and* the Brazilians, they clearly had reason to believe that something remained. And if they found it first, there would be no stopping them.

Qin said he had Wei's daughter and now the case. But it would mean little if the Americans found their own source.

"Have they found anything yet?"

M0ngol shook his head. "I don't think so. Not yet."

Xinzhen stood up immediately and pointed to the door. "Leave me at once."

As the old man watched M0ngol practically run for the exit, he retrieved the phone from his suit's breast pocket and began dialing.

75

Sixty-three minutes later, Xinzhen ended another call and leaned back into his limousine's soft leather seat.

They had no choice. Xinzhen was about to pull the cover off one of China's largest and well-kept secrets.

As controversial as the Spratly Islands were in the South China Sea, and even with the constant surveillance from the United States, they simply had no choice.

The archipelago was composed of over seven hundred islands and reefs, all uninhabited. But it was its strategic value as the region's most important shipping lanes that was the real focus. Shipping lanes which carried a full sixty percent of the world's trade traffic.

However, completely ignoring the heated territorial claims from neighboring countries, what China was doing in the middle of the Spratly Islands was nothing short of astonishing. Instead of fighting over the small, existing island chains, they were *building their own*.

With dozens of dredging ships in the archipelago's shallow waters, China had spent the last two years expanding existing reefs into entirely *new* military islands. It was a level of progress that stunned the rest of the world.

Contrary to what foreign surveillance assumed about Fiery Cross Reef, the base was now entirely functional. And inside its giant hangar rested one of mankind's greatest modern weapons. A weapon hid well within bombing range of nearly every Pacific Rim country.

The fifteen thousand pound, Russian-built thermobaric bomb was the most powerful conventional explosive device ever created. It was far superior to the United States' Massive Ordnance Air Blast weapon, later colloquially called "Mother of All Bombs." But Russia's version was far superior, quadrupling the equivalent TNT and effective blast radius.

And in what was perhaps the greatest irony, Russia's *Father of All Bombs* could not be fitted to a traditionally military bomber. Instead, it had to be dropped from the rear cargo ramp of a larger transport aircraft. A configuration that could be accommodated by China's existing prototype Xian Y-20 aircraft, originally commandeered by one General Wei.

Still in the limousine, Xinzhen peered pensively at his watch. The Y-20 should have just lifted off from Fiery Cross, where it would refuel once in route with the help of an in-flight tanker before the Y-20 headed directly toward South America and the Acarai Mountains.

There was no way to tell whether the Brazilians or the Americans would find any remnants of what the Chinese had taken, but it was not a risk Xinzhen was willing to take.

In mere hours, the entire area would simply "evaporate" under the raw power of a thermobaric blast. Ensuring that if China would not possess the prize of South America's superorganism…then no one would.

76

Standing just over a mile from the Y-20's final target, Steve Caesare scanned downhill into the darkness and a thick patch of trees, looking for any movement. But beyond the gentle swaying branches and rustling leaves, there was none. The area was eerily quiet.

"You sure we're in the right place?"

Tiewater nodded. "Yep. Unfortunately, those idiots scared them all off when they shot at 'em."

"Perfect." Caesare turned around and focused on the shadows of DeeAnn and Dulce several feet behind him. "Anything?"

DeeAnn knelt down next to Dulce. The small gorilla was standing still and peering into the darkness. She wiggled her black nostrils and cocked her head, listening.

Over their headsets, Caesare, Tiewater, and Corso listened to Anderson speaking softly from a lookout behind them. "They're coming."

"How many?"

He followed the first set of headlights through a handheld scope. "Several trucks worth. We'd better find that monkey fast."

"How far away are they?"

"Maybe a mile."

Caesare looked forward again, back down the slope of tall grass. "You guys see anything in the trees?"

"Nope."

Behind them, Dulce turned her head and looked back the way they came. She suddenly ran in that direction and scampered up a small tree, stopping at the top of one of the branches.

"We're out of time," Caesare said.

DeeAnn was about to reply when the speaker on her vest sounded.

That way.

"What way, Dulce?"

There. She pointed up the hill. Back the way they came.

"What do you hear?"

No hear. Smell.

"What do you smell?"

Friend. He there.

She looked at Caesare. "You smell your friend?"

Yes. Dulce quickly dropped to the base of the tree and jumped on the ground excitedly.

Hurry. We go. Friend here.

"Are you sure?"

Hurry.

DeeAnn looked at Caesare, who shook his head and turned to Tiewater and Corso. "I guess we're going back. I'll take Anderson while you two try to lead them away. If we find Dexter, we'll head for base and try to find a way out. Be ready to move."

The men nodded.

"That ridge runs mostly west and should give you some decent cover," said Tiewater. "It's as far away from the road as you can be without snaking around the back of the peak. We'll try to bring them along the road if we can."

"Good." Caesare then spoke into his mike. "Anderson, meet us at the ridge."

"Roger that."

Caesare smiled. "Time to get that exercise, Juan."

"I'm ready."

In the darkness, Corso stepped closer to DeeAnn and peered down at the primate standing next to her. Without warning, he reached out and did something no one was expecting. He petted Dulce's head.

"I guess she's all right."

The gorilla's large teeth were all he could see.

376

77

From her seat in one of the trucks, Becca could barely make out the taillights bouncing in front of them in the darkness. Salazar's Lieutenant Sosa rode in the lead vehicle which, like the others, held dozens of soldiers. All were hanging on tightly as they rocked back and forth over the uneven dirt road.

The convoy came to a stop at a safe distance from the gunfire and all trucks were quickly emptied. Flashlights appeared everywhere as the men organized into three groups. Two large forward teams to comb the area and a third smaller team to assist Becca.

The road led almost due north, through a wide pass between two ridgelines, both visible in the moonlight.

Sosa called his men forward and began an advance with both groups, leaving Becca and her own team to follow. Together, hundreds of boots marched forward, spreading out over a hundred and eighty degrees. All eyes sharply focused with rifles pointed forward.

Approaching from the opposite direction, Dulce ran through the dense foliage with Anderson right behind her. Further behind were DeeAnn and Juan, running through waves of branches and trying to keep up behind Caesare.

Even through the trees, they could make out the glow of bright headlights farther ahead. They slowed, struggling uphill, until an opening provided a brief view — one that caused DeeAnn to gasp. She could now see the lights clearly, with dozens of shadowed figures moving out in front. And some walking directly toward them.

Dulce slowed down further and finally stopped, still

listening. She sniffed the air again and ran several more steps. When she stopped this time, it was at the base of a familiar rocky outcropping. DeeAnn recognized it from earlier near the poacher's camp. This time they were on the other side and Dulce stood motionless, listening intently.

Anderson moved ahead without a sound and disappeared behind a row of tall bushes. When he returned a moment later, he held up a hand and then motioned them forward slowly. They moved in behind him, squinting to see what he was pointing at.

In the distance, part of the poacher's flatbed truck could be seen. On the bed remained several wood cages, each containing a capuchin inside. But what stunned the group was the familiar shape that came into view on the *outside*.

Covered entirely in gray fur, a monkey stood on the bed of the truck, examining one of the cages. Not only was he scrutinizing it, but he also appeared to be fumbling with the latch while those in the cages remained oddly quiet.

The gray capuchin shifted his head from side to side, as if studying the door from different angles, then returned to the latch which he tried to undo again and again.

"Oh my God!" DeeAnn gasped.

"He's trying to get them out."

DeeAnn nodded excitedly at Juan. "It's Dexter!"

As if hearing his name, Dexter suddenly froze on the truck and looked around. Seconds later, one of the cages next to him exploded under a hail of bullets, bounced off the truck and tumbled to the ground. Dexter screamed and disappeared into the tall vegetation.

Caesare and Anderson immediately pushed the others to the ground and raised their own heads, searching. "Where'd he go?!"

"I don't see him."

Their question was answered when the small capuchin erupted from the bush in front of him and hit Anderson square in the chest. The SEAL scrambled to grab him, but

378

Dexter jumped free and continued running.

"Dammit!" Anderson had stood up to chase after the monkey when several bullets tore through the nearby plants and ricocheted off the outcropping behind them.

"Down!"

Anderson dropped back to the ground while Caesare watched Dexter disappear into the darkness.

"Get Juan out of here! We're going after that monkey!"

Anderson scurried back to Juan. "Come with me."

Juan nodded as best he could with his chin still on the dirt.

Next to him, Caesare grabbed DeeAnn and Dulce.

"Stay low!"

With that, he lifted his rifle in front of his chest and pushed them forward into a crouched run.

78

"MOVE IN! MOVE IN!" Lieutenant Sosa screamed over the gunfire.

His men were now running forward, fanning out from the mouth of the small pass as Becca scrambled up a small incline behind them to see what was happening. From several feet up, she could see flashlights combing through a small camp with two vehicles. She gasped when she spotted captured capuchins on the back of the truck. Further away, several men used their lights to pursue something or someone into the foliage.

To her left, there was more shooting and yelling near the base of the ridge.

She jumped down and yelled, running toward the camp. "Hurry!"

Along the ridge, Juan Diaz nearly froze under the onslaught of gunfire until Anderson forced him forward. When his head rose too much, Anderson reached forward and slapped it back down. "Low!"

Keeping on their hands and knees, they scrambled up the incline to a pair of large rocks, where they hid. Anderson twisted back around and peered into the darkness. "Shit. They're coming." There was no other cover for another twenty yards, far too long to be exposed.

"You see those rocks up ahead?"

"Yeah."

"When I tell you, you run like hell and get behind them. Off your knees but stay as low as you can. And when I say run, I mean *run*."

"Okay."

"We need that cover."

"What about you?"

"I'll be right behind you. First, I gotta slow these guys down." He glanced back again. "Okay, you ready?"

"Not really."

"Good. Here we go. On the count of three. One…two…three!"

All at once, Juan sprung to his feet and moved as fast as he could with his head down. He kept his focus on the rocks, reflecting brightly in the moonlight, and hoped there was nothing in the way to trip him.

When Sosa's men reached the rocks, they approached cautiously from both sides, guns ready. The spot was empty.

Caesare paused when he heard the distinct sound of Anderson's HK416 echoing off the walls of the ridge. A dozen shots were heard before the HK fell silent. Then another burst.

He continued moving. More shots from the Brazilians, followed by silence, told him Anderson was reloading.

Several rounds ricocheted near Caesare and he ducked lower. "Get down!" He growled and stepped behind a wide tree trunk to return fire.

He spotted two silhouettes and fired four more rounds. Both shapes disappeared.

"Stay close to me."

When there was no answer, Caesare spun around to find DeeAnn and Dulce both gone.

"Damn it!"

Farther to the north, Corso watched more men descend across the dirt road while Tiewater knelt behind him, wiring several sets of blasting caps as fast as he could. He twisted the blue and yellow wires into small groups and then connected them to their own timing wires.

Anderson's voice came over their radio between shots. "I could use that diversion!"

"We're working on it," Tiewater said. He moved his fingers faster. When finished he double-checked his work, tracing the wires out with his fingertips.

"Good?"

He nodded to Corso. "Good." He set the timer and dropped the first set. Tiewater then turned to see Corso disappear into the brush, dropping a second set before running in the opposite direction and letting another one go every hundred feet.

"Here we go…" Tiewater called into his microphone. He waited for Anderson to stop firing, then set off the first round of caps.

From that distance, they sounded exactly like gunfire.

Sosa and his men stopped and turned toward the sound of shots farther to their right. The blood drained from the lieutenant's face.

"Crossfire! Move back, move back!"

A crossfire was almost impossible to defend against, and his men were now too far out. He had only minutes to pull them back and regroup.

"MOVE BACK!" he yelled again.

It was then that two of his men fell to the ground.

Higher on the ridge, Juan threw himself behind the next cluster of rocks. He waited several seconds for Anderson. When he didn't show, Juan took a deep breath and continued into the darkness.

Almost a hundred yards behind Juan, Anderson grunted and fell to a knee. He gritted his teeth and tried to speak.

"I'm hit!"

He pulled back his jacket and found the wound, just below his left rib cage. A ricochet.

Anderson lost his balance and twisted down onto both knees. He touched the wound, then withdrew his hand. It was covered in blood.

"Shit."

He was bleeding too fast.

"Where are you?!" Caesare called into his ear.

He tried to catch his breath. "On the other side of the camp. Maybe fifty yards." He turned and tried to look up the hill before inhaling again. "Juan is trying to get back-"

He stopped again, suddenly overwhelmed by the searing pain in his stomach and back. He struggled to stay on his knees.

"I'm down," Anderson repeated in a softer voice as he sank to the ground. "I'm down…"

On the opposite side of the pass, near the top of the ridge, Juan reached their base. And in the darkness, he collapsed with relief onto his knees. He fought to catch his breath.

He never noticed the Brazilian soldiers waiting for him.

Slowly, John Clay's eyes opened to find himself kneeling on a cold concrete floor. His arms were outstretched, each tied with a rope, keeping his upper body suspended from something above.

It was the pain in his shoulders that forcibly pulled him back into consciousness. He had no idea how long they had been supporting most of his weight. He rose on his knees, attempting to alleviate the searing agony, and blinked several times to clear his vision.

The place appeared to be a warehouse with concrete walls, matching floor, and wide overhead beams supporting a long metal roof.

He noticed a figure slumped on the floor against a nearby wall. It wasn't until Clay was finally able to focus that he recognized the body of Jin Tang, the man who'd helped him from Hong Kong. Tang's dark eyes stared lifelessly at the ceiling, while a thick line of blood dried on his face. Both of his feet appeared to be twisted in the wrong directions.

A young Chinese soldier stepped into view and noticed Clay's open eyes, then he promptly shouted to someone behind him. A few moments later, the image of Li Qin stepped in front of Clay and peered at him curiously.

Clay stared back for a moment before dropping his head. There was a small pool of blood on the floor beneath him. Drops farther out that indicated he had been bleeding from his head somewhere.

Qin crossed his arms and smiled at Clay. His injured hand had now been professionally dressed. "Finally, you're awake."

Two more soldiers appeared and stood quietly behind Qin.

"I was afraid at first that they'd killed you."

Clay opened his mouth to speak and immediately felt a jolt of pain in his jaw. "Lucky me."

"I guess Navy SEALs come with a certain amount of durability."

Clay didn't answer. Instead he simply watched, weakly, as Qin stepped closer, examining him.

"And a sense of humor. Mister John Clay."

"Where's Li Na?"

"Oh, don't worry. We'll get to her. As you can see," Qin said, stepping to the side and turning to view the body. "We've already gotten to your friend, Tang. Unfortunately, he was not as durable. Or as helpful."

Qin motioned to another soldier who appeared and handed Li Na's metal case to him. He took it and cracked it open, looking inside. "You've come a long way for something so small. But now, as you can see, it's mine." He closed the case again. "I know what you're thinking. You're upset you lost it. It's understandable. But you should be happy. Because this case is now your relief. Your salvation."

Clay's voice was low. "Yippee."

Qin placed it on the floor and put his hands behind his back. "Tell me what it is inside, and I'll make the ending for you…comfortable. If not, we'll all make this the worst exit you can possibly imagine."

Clay struggled to focus on Qin through the pain. He tried to raise one of his knees to stand but groaned and slumped back to the floor. His leg was broken.

"I wouldn't try standing if I were you." He watched Clay drop his head again. "You have to know that this will be your last day alive. There's no way back. And if your own death isn't enough of an incentive for you, let's not forget our young Li Na."

Clay closed his eyes. His breathing was shallow as he tried to think through the pain. The man was right. There was no way out. Even if there were, he could barely move. Tang was dead. And Clay had no link back to Borger. Whatever help he might provide Li Na would have to be through his cooperation.

If Qin didn't understand what was inside the case, he would soon. They would analyze it and figure it out. Unless Qin didn't want to. Analyzing meant relinquishing the case and its contents to someone else. Which meant they too would find out.

Qin clearly wanted to know what was inside, but Clay doubted Qin would even let these two soldiers remain in the room. A secret like that would be hard to keep. If anyone understood that, Clay did. And the best secrets were best kept only when everyone else was dead.

Qin would find out, one way or another. But did the man know that some of it was already in Li Na? It was possible he still hadn't made the connection with Li Na yet. Which would leave him only what was left in the case.

Clay wasn't sure how much Qin knew, but he suspected the man didn't understand exactly what he had stumbled onto. Wei's discovery was one thing. What was *still* in South America was another.

But some secrets were too important to give up. Some were even worth dying for. What General Wei had sent from South America was something everyone would eventually go after. Something millions would kill for, whether they believed in its effects or not. And now, there in the warehouse, the only person standing in the way of all of it…was Clay.

With his eyes closed, he never saw the anger suddenly swell in Qin's eyes nor his step forward driving a boot into Clay's midsection. He only felt the impact when two of his ribs broke.

Clay's eyes shot open and rolled back as he gasped in agony.

"Tell me!" Qin yelled, just inches from his face. "Tell

386

me, or I promise you, this is just the beginning."

Clay fought again to focus through the pain. To focus on Qin and his cold dark eyes. He had to stop it here. It was bigger than Clay. Bigger than Li Na. This was about the future of the human race and a potential level of greed unmatched throughout all of history.

He continued staring at Qin, trying to come to peace with the inevitability of his own death. And the hope that it would serve a bigger purpose. He thought first of Caesare, then Borger and Admiral Langford. They would have to keep the secret safe now.

Finally, as the pain once again began to overwhelm his concentration, Clay's thoughts focused on Alison. A girl unlike any other he'd met.

And the woman he was sure he would have spent the rest of his life with.

80

There was no other way to describe Admiral Langford's face than "frightening." With eyes ablaze and teeth clenched, he stormed down the wide hallway with a look that made several people jump out of his way. His feet marched deliberately over the carpeted floor, heading for a large office with closed doors.

The secretary outside leaped to her feet but was too late. When he reached the double doors, Langford forced them open, slamming them hard against the inside walls.

In the middle of the room, standing next to a large window, CIA Director Andrew Hayes barely looked back over his shoulder.

"You're wasting your time, Langford."

"The hell I am!"

Behind them, Hayes' secretary nervously grabbed both doors and pulled them closed.

The director turned around. "It's not going to happen. You don't have authority over me or this agency and you know it. Besides, you're not the first one to storm in here and start making demands. It didn't work for them and it sure as hell isn't going to work for you. I suggest you turn around and leave with whatever credibility you have left."

"I don't give a damn about credibility! But mark my words, you are going to do this."

Hayes smirked. "Is that so?" He stuffed his hands in his pockets and smugly returned to his desk, which he circled before sitting down. "According to who? You? You barely have the authority to get inside this building. We're everywhere, *Admiral*. We know everything. Including all about the disappearance of your man Clay. And I'm not about to compromise the power of this entire agency, of the entire *country*, to save your boy scout." He picked up a mug from his desk and took a sip. "It's too late anyway."

"You don't know that."

"Neither do you. But we're not going to give everything up for someone who's probably already dead."

Langford leaned angrily onto the desk. "Now you listen and you listen good-"

"No!" interrupted Hayes. He bolted out of his chair and stared icily at Langford. "In case you're not aware, this is a *big* goddamn deal! I told you it's NOT going to happen, and there's not a damn thing you can do about it!"

They both stood, staring at each other in silence, when the phone on Hayes' desk beeped. The voice of his secretary spoke over the intercom.

"Sir, I have an important call for you."

Hayes kept his eyes on Langford. "Take a message."

"Um, I can't, sir."

The director peered down at his phone. "What the hell does that mean?"

She didn't answer. Instead, she simply said, "I'm putting it through."

The next voice was deep and immediately recognizable. "Hayes, it's Carr. Is Langford already there?"

The look on the man's face froze. It took him several seconds to reply and he did so while glaring across his desk at Langford. "Yes, Mr. President...he's here."

"Good. Listen to me very carefully..."

389

81

In 1993, the Department of Defense established a set of directives and reporting protocols designed to allow rapid response to national incidents and emergencies. Three of these directives established a list of emergency flag words capable of activating the highest level of command structure within both the Department of Defense and National Command Authority.

One such flag word, *Pinnacle*, was designed to launch the highest level of military command to immediately preserve the security and national interests of the United States. Another accompanying code known by many was called *Broken Arrow*.

However, unlike the rest of the major military commands, the CIA was not bound by the Department of Defense directives. Instead, the agency maintained a set of its own protocols, designed as emergency responses within its international intelligence network.

Over the years, several such protocols had been activated though limited in scope.

But one had not.

One protocol, known only by the cryptonym of *CLOWER* was the international equivalent of the DoD's "Pinnacle."

And Andrew Hayes would be the first Director in CIA history to invoke it.

Once authorized, CLOWER took less than fifteen minutes to activate. The signals were sent in a fraction of a second, but the logistics were immense. Every warden, ambassador, and CIA agent in the world was on their phone or computer, arranging for the immediate evacuation of thousands of CIA operatives. Agents who had infiltrated nearly every branch of foreign government throughout Central Asia, along with their spouses and children, had less than one hundred and twenty minutes. A mere two hours to make it to an airport or an American embassy where passports and travel documents would be waiting.

Two hours…because once their covers were blown, the ripple effect would be unstoppable.

82

John Clay looked wearily at Qin and finally nodded his head. Immediately, Qin dismissed his soldiers and waited impatiently for them to leave the room.

Through the beatings, he'd watched with satisfaction the precise moment when Clay finally broke. Every man had his limit. Something Qin knew through experience in the MSS. No one could last forever.

He knelt down in front of Clay and pulled his head up by his thick dark hair. "I will show you mercy," he whispered. "You have my word."

He watched as Clay tried to nod again. His lips trembled and his eyes rolled back from the pain. He tried once more but still couldn't respond. The American simply couldn't concentrate through the agony.

Qin exhaled and retrieved a knife from his belt. He then grabbed one of the ropes suspending Clay and began cutting through it. When he severed the last strand, Clay's right side collapsed, swinging sideways. His body now dangled by a single rope.

"Better?"

Clay came to a stop and hung there motionlessly. Only his chest moved while he breathed.

"Now tell me," Qin said, squatting down again. "What is in this case?"

Clay whispered. "A microorganism…stops aging."

Qin's eyes widened. "It stops *aging*?"

Clay nodded weakly.

The MSS agent stared at Clay in disbelief. *That's what Xinzhen was after? An organism that would stop him from aging? That's what it was all about?* He looked back to Clay. "This organism is from the plants in South America?"

"Yes."

An astounded Qin shook his head and stood up. It was more than he had dreamed. And yet it all made sense — why Xinzhen wanted it so badly, why he told him so little about what General Wei was doing, and why Wei tried to hide it after destroying the cargo ship on its way home from Guyana. Xinzhen and Wei had hidden their discovery from nearly everyone, and even murdered the soldiers they forced to excavate it. *God, it all made sense.*

Qin shook himself from his trance and watched Clay's nearly lifeless body as it hung from one arm. His still eyes staring at the floor. He was practically dead already.

Qin withdrew his gun and gripped it carefully in his opposite hand. He was surprised at the man before him. One of the U.S. Navy's legendary SEALs. He was tough, but not as tough as Qin had expected. The man simply did not live up to the reputation. Where was the American arrogance now?

He'd known men, lesser men, who had lasted longer than this American. It was truly emblematic of the waning might of a once great nation. The might of the United States was fading. And the rise of China was just beginning.

He stepped closer to Clay and shook his head in pity. "I gave you my word." With that, he raised his left hand up and pointed the gun.

Hanging by one arm, Clay remained still. The pain was overwhelming, making it hard to think.

His situation was nearly hopeless. Which meant this was no time for bravado. Instead, he had to outwit Qin.

The first priority had been to find a reason for them to be alone. The second was to get Qin as close as possible. And then to get an arm free. What came next was the last thing Qin ever expected.

Almost every part of his body screamed in pain. But Clay

393

was not motionless because he couldn't move.   He was motionless for a very different reason.   He had been quietly testing each muscle to determine just how much strength he had left.

He didn't have enough to get out alive, but he might have enough left in the very last of his reserves for one last effort.

To take Qin with him.

83

What Qin didn't know as he pointed the gun at Clay was that the American was *waiting*. For the right moment. Because when Clay finally moved, it came as a complete surprise.

In one motion, Clay slapped the gun from Qin's hand and suddenly leaped forward on his broken leg. In a blur, his arm rocketed up, gripped the man's throat like a vice and squeezed.

Qin's gun rattled across the concrete floor and his eyes bulged in shock, still trying to comprehend what had happened. But not before he got out the beginning of a scream.

It was a sound that Qin's men heard from the other side of the door.

An already sinking Clay watched them emerge while the last of his energy began to fade. With clenched teeth, he squeezed harder, giving every last ounce of strength he had left. He ignored the soldier sprinting toward him with the butt of his gun raised. Instead, he tried to tighten one last time before his arm was knocked away and he fell back to the floor.

Qin stumbled back, gasping for air. His frantic eyes searched the floor. When he couldn't find his gun, he pointed at Clay and wheezed.

"Shoot him!"

Several feet away, the squad's leader frowned, and kept his eyes fixed on Clay. "We should keep him alive."

"I said *shoot* him!"

"That doesn't seem wise," retorted the soldier, defiantly.

At that moment a sharp tone sounded. All eyes turned to the squad leader who ripped open a secret pocket, pulling out a small electronic pager.

He stared at the code on the tiny screen in stunned disbelief. He read it again carefully before raising his eyes back to Qin.

"What the hell is that?"

The man stared down at Clay for a long moment. Without a word, he raised his gun and pointed it. Not at Clay, or even Qin, but at his own men. He then made a motion with his head. "Guns down."

All six men stared at him in confusion.

"I said guns down!"

They blinked at him, still stunned. But one by one each man dropped his rifle loudly onto the floor.

Qin was just as confused. "What are you doing?"

The squad leader reached out, grabbing Qin by the collar. He threw him, stumbling, into his own men.

"Now back up!"

They each took several steps backward.

It was then that the leader moved closer to Clay, with his barrel still trained on the others. When he spoke, it was in perfect English.

"You, my friend, are one lucky son of a bitch."

They were the last words Clay heard before the blackness took him.

Far over the Pacific, the drogue basket detached from the second plane. Aboard the giant Chinese bomber, the Hose Drum Unit began the slow process of reeling it back in.

The Xian H-6U was a modified version of China's powerful H-6 bomber. The plane was first detected by U.S. spy satellites in 1971, forcing China to reveal that they had already built three dozen of the aircraft, and stunning the world.

Almost fifty years later, several of the aged bombers had been converted from flying fortresses to flying tankers.

Once the drogue basket had fully detached, the much larger and now fully fueled Y-20 cargo plane began its fateful climb.

After several thousand feet, the monstrous Y-20 adjusted its flight path and headed for Venezuelan airspace — the only country left standing between the aircraft and its final target.

Caesare finally reached Anderson and knelt down beside his body — positioned lifelessly on his side with one hand still clutching his rifle. He'd fought right to the end, judging from the numerous bodies of Brazilian soldiers littering the area. Caesare checked his pulse, and finding nothing, gently rolled him back over. He peered up at Corso as Tiewater approached behind them.

"They've got Juan."

Caesare sighed heavily. They could still hear occasional shouts in the distance. The fight hadn't lasted long as the Brazilians were clearly not expecting a SEAL team on the other side. But it wasn't enough to reach Anderson or Juan in time.

"Now what?"

Caesare stood. He took a deep breath and listened to the sounds of Otero's men fortifying their positions. His answer felt unnatural. "We do our job and leave."

Corso frowned in the darkness. "You're joking, right?"

"No. As bad as we want to, our mission is not to take these bastards out. Our mission is still to find that monkey and get the hell out of here."

Tiewater's voice was low and angry. "I say we take them out and then go."

"We can't risk it. Things could go sideways, fast. It's going to be hard enough finding Juan."

"I'll get him," Corso said.

Caesare nodded. "I'll go with you."

"Negative. You'll just slow me down."

Caesare smirked. "I'm not *that* old."

"No offense, sir. But I can get in faster alone."

Tiewater nodded. "He's right. Besides, someone needs

to locate DeeAnn and Dulce. Which is probably you."

Caesare didn't like the way this argument was going. But he couldn't let his emotions get the best of him. "Fine." He nodded at Tiewater. "Corso gets Juan, you find some transportation, and I'll find the others."

"My pleasure."

"With any luck you might be able to give Corso here a nice diversion."

"But wait for my go," Corso said. "Until I find out what condition Juan is in. We might need a ride."

Tiewater smiled.

"When you find something," Caesare said, "head north, down that way. We're taking the other road out of here."

Captain Salazar was livid. He ended another tirade, directed at his lieutenant, and clenched his fists in frustration.

Thirty percent. THIRTY PERCENT! He'd just lost thirty percent of his men in less than an hour! What in God's name happened?

Sosa tried to explain, but it was too late. Salazar wasn't interested in excuses. He wanted answers. Like how such a large force made it up here before they did? He was expecting a few men. But clearly there were more out there. And to make matters worse, his men evidently didn't see a damn thing!

Salazar put his hands on his hips, thinking. "Where's Becca?"

"We don't know. We lost track of her and her detail."

"Jesus," Salazar muttered, rolling his eyes. "Did your men do anything right?"

Sosa's reply was indignant. "We killed one of them."

"Dozens of men lost for only one of theirs. Doesn't exactly make me feel better. Another fight like that and it'll be over." He shook his head and dismissed Sosa. "Go get me some damn answers."

Sosa nodded but didn't bother replying. Instead, he walked away and crossed through several lines of men until he reached the base of a large tree. Sitting on the ground, tied to the trunk, was the dark outline of Juan Diaz.

Sosa took a flashlight from one of his men and approached, shining the beam into the young man's face.

Juan squinted and turned away as Sosa stopped and stared down at him.

"Who are you?"

"M-my name is Juan. Juan Diaz."

"Why are you here?"

Juan resisted, saying nothing. Until he watched Sosa withdraw a handgun and lay it across his knee.

"I-I was asked to come. I'm an engineer."

"An engineer, out here? Why?" Sosa asked. His accent was strong, leaving Juan struggling to understand.

"To fix the computer."

Sosa frowned. *What computer would be out here?* Either the kid was lying or the enemy had equipment he wasn't familiar with.

"Who brought you here?"

Juan hesitated again, long enough to hear the slide action on someone's gun.

"I came with a group…of SEALs."

"SEALs?" Sosa's voice changed. "How many?"

"Two dozen," Juan lied.

Sosa bolted to his feet. As he turned to leave, Sosa's eyes met with Otero's man, Russo, now standing behind him. If Sosa was nervous at the sound of Navy SEALs, Russo looked as though his heart just stopped.

He had been right all along.

Juan sat on the soft ground, frightened and watching the dark figures of Otero's soldiers moving back and forth.

They were talking excitedly in Portuguese, and judging from all the gunfire, it didn't appear as if things were going very well for them. Which gave him at least some trace of satisfaction.

He'd been on the ground for almost an hour and kept trying to change his position to keep the circulation from being cut off, but the tingling in his feet returned. He was losing feeling.

The headlights of another military truck appeared, easing to a stop at the end of the line where several soldiers were waiting. They quickly jumped in and began unloading a number of large crates, followed by an even larger piece of equipment. It was lowered carefully to the ground, and the thick canvas cover was removed to reveal a powerful-looking piece of artillery. Juan watched helplessly as the men disappeared into the darkness with the giant weapon and its remaining pieces.

When the sound of the men faded, Juan suddenly heard a soft crunching sound behind him. He twisted his neck in an attempt to see who, or what, was approaching. There was nothing but a dense wall of bushes and trees covering most of the hill. Then he noticed something move and peered harder into the darkness until he saw two small dots of white. When they blinked, he froze. They were eyes. And they were watching him.

He gasped and turned back around in a panic. In desperation, he dug his feet into the dirt and tried to move around the trunk of the tree. But the ropes were too tight.

"Help!"

There was no response. He had opened his mouth to yell again when a low voice stopped him.

"Shut up!" it growled.

Juan twisted back again and looked closer. The eyes were still there, yet the more he focused, the more he could see the outline of a dark-colored face. A face painted black.

It was Corso, hiding motionlessly in the bushes. "What

the hell are you doing?"

Juan looked back to make sure no one was coming, then whispered loudly to Corso. "I thought you were a wild animal."

"Well, I'm not," Corso retorted. "So shut up." He looked back and forth, examining the area. "Can you walk?"

"I'm losing some feeling, but I think so. What are you going to do?"

Corso shook his head. "I have absolutely no idea."

Several hundred yards away, Tiewater was watching from the front of the line. Further back, he could see a large base being set up, with several soldiers running tripwire.

They had to move quickly. Once a solid perimeter was established, getting in and out would be much harder.

Tiewater watched several men run past the vehicles. The truck in front was the most logical option. It wasn't as big, but it would be the easiest to drive out if he could get it started. It was too new to hotwire which meant he needed to locate the keys. Because unlike the movies, no one kept their keys stashed above the visor.

"Talk to me, Tiewater," Corso's voice whispered in his ear.

"I'm looking for keys." He watched a soldier approach and stop at the vehicle. He opened the back and retrieved a large bag. He hefted it over his shoulder and closed the door before marching back up the hill to the other side. "Hold on. I may have the driver."

Tiewater continued watching as the soldier reached the top and dropped the bag on the ground. After briefly disappearing, the man reappeared and began heading back down toward the truck.

"How fast can you get Juan out?"

"Pretty damn fast. But it has to happen now."

"Okay." Tiewater looked back and forth before stepping

out of the trees. "I'm taking this guy. Get ready."

Corso slid a knife out and gripped it tight in his hand. "I'm ready."

"Ten seconds…"

When the soldier reached the Humvee, he opened the back again and leaned in. Tiewater was already moving. Running low and smooth from the trees, he covered the distance quickly, stopping at the driver's door. He could see the man searching for something beneath the tailgate's overhead light.

Tiewater raised his gun and began to move when he glanced through the side window. Sitting inside, in the center console between the two front seats, were the keys.

"You've got to be kidding," Tiewater muttered to himself.

"What?" Corso replied over the headset.

"Shh!" Tiewater whispered. He remained frozen at the door, waiting until the man behind the truck pulled something else out and reached up to close the gate. Without looking up, he turned and continued back up the hill.

Tiewater quietly opened the driver's door and reached for the keys. He examined them and slid the larger key into the ignition. With a slight turn, the dash lit up. He immediately turned it back off.

"We got wheels! GO!"

With that, he slid into the driver's seat and laid his rifle across on the passenger's side. He pulled the door closed until it made a soft click. He then kept the key in the ignition and slid down in his seat as low as he could.

No sooner had Tiewater given him the go than Corso rushed out of the brush and dropped behind Juan. He worked quickly with the knife, cutting the lines, then peered out over Juan's shoulder. No one was watching.

"Let's move!"

He jumped up and yanked Juan onto his feet, pulling him back into the shadows.

"Stay on my heels!" was all Corso said before darting back the way he came. Juan scrambled and ran after him.

They had made it less than fifty yards before they heard a yell behind them. Neither of them knew what the words meant, but there was no doubt as to the message.

"Hurry!" Corso barked.

Juan ran harder, but in the darkness, he caught his foot on something hard and tumbled. He scrambled to his feet only to be met by bright lights shining up the slope. One of the lights found both him and Corso, followed by more yelling. Then gunfire.

Tiewater lifted his head in the Humvee just enough to see outside. At the top of the small hill, the driver and several other soldiers looked in the direction of the gunfire and ran toward it.

Tiewater placed one hand on the steering wheel and the other on the key.

"Can you make it?"

"I don't know." From his position, Corso rose up and shot into the lights, dropping two of the men. But there were too many. Bullets passed overhead and he threw Juan down before firing another burst.

Back in the truck, Tiewater suddenly noticed movement in the side mirror of the Humvee. Several men were running up the line of vehicles, toward the front. He continued watching as one of them stopped and climbed into a large truck, two vehicles back. The rest of the men continued running and passed the front vehicle before turning back around.

Behind him, Tiewater heard the larger truck roar to life and saw its bright headlights shining out over the dirt road, illuminating the soldiers now waiting for it. It backed up and began edging its way out of line.

"Okay, we may have a problem."

From further down the mountain, Caesare's voice broke in. "What is it?"

"They're moving their trucks. We might be about to get blocked in."

Caesare stopped running and listened. "Corso, how close are you?"

Corso fired off several more rounds and pushed Juan forward, ahead of him. "Not very."

Caesare shook his head in the darkness. "Tiewater, we need those wheels. Get out of there while you still can!"

Tiewater paused. "Corso?"

"Go!" growled Corso. "We'll get there on foot."

Tiewater shook his head. Their situation was deteriorating quickly. He sat straight up in the car and twisted the key hard in the ignition. The soldiers, still standing several yards in front of him, were startled to see the Humvee's lights come on. They stepped forward, trying to peer through the front windshield.

In one motion, Tiewater dropped it into gear and mashed the accelerator down.

Caesare finally stopped and scanned the area around him. A large hill climbed to the right and he caught a glimpse of movement just before he saw the muzzle flashes. Bullets ripped past him and he dove to the ground, rolling behind a group of small trees. He came to a stop on both elbows and fired back between the narrow trunks.

Two more rounds tore into the tree just above his head, after more muzzle flashes. He fired back, estimating where the outline of the shooter would be, and everything fell silent.

DeeAnn stopped when she heard the shots behind her. After it went quiet, she turned and called forward again. "Dulce!" She stumbled forward in the darkness, listening for the gorilla to answer again.

Here. Come.

There was a slight echo, and DeeAnn looked down to realize that she was standing on a pile of rocks. She leaned forward, placing a hand on the slope in front of her. Under the moonlight she could see a dark opening in the wall, eerily resembling a gaping mouth. "Dulce, are you in there?"

Yes. Come.

She stumbled forward to the entrance and found the first several feet into the cave illuminated by the moonlight overhead. She shook her head and mumbled under her breath. "This feels like a really bad idea."

She stepped slowly into the darkness, trying to keep her balance over the uneven ground. Unable to see beyond the glow of her vest, she stopped again and stared forward, letting her eyes adjust.

"Dulce?"

The small gorilla emerged from the darkness in front of her. *Me here.*

She took DeeAnn's hand and pulled her deeper inside. Together, they walked forward, the vest's blue glow giving her an eerie feeling.

"Did you find Dexter?"

Yes. Me find friend.

DeeAnn squinted, still trying to see, as Dulce pulled her deeper into the cave. After perhaps fifty more feet, she stopped when something emerged out of the blackness. She gasped.

Standing in front of them was the small capuchin, covered with bright gray fur. He remained still, watching them in the damp coolness of the cave.

But it was another image that most surprised DeeAnn. Another monkey standing behind Dexter. She stepped forward to get a better look with the tiny vest light, and her eyes suddenly widened. There wasn't just one monkey behind Dexter, there were several. Dozens. All standing together.

Ever so slowly, DeeAnn turned, shining her light in different directions to find more, all sitting calmly along the walls of the cave. All with gray hair and even a few with white.

But it was what she saw next that caused her mouth to fall completely open. Drawn on the inside of the walls were lines...and shapes. Crude, but easily recognizable as circles and lines.

"Oh my God," DeeAnn whispered. Her vest made a loud buzz. She covered her mouth and continued shaking her head in disbelief.

"Oh my God, indeed," a woman's voice said behind her.

DeeAnn whirled around to find three silhouettes standing in the entrance, backlit from the moonlight.

"Who are you?"

407

One of the figures approached. She stepped close enough for the blue light to show her face. Her Portuguese accent was thick. "My name is Marie Becca."

"What do you want?"

Becca ignored the question, her eyes panning the wall, then falling onto Dexter in amazement. "My God, it's true."

DeeAnn stepped between them. "What do you *want*?"

The other woman smiled with an air of condescension. "I'm here for the same reason you are." She then looked past Dexter to the others. "An evolutionary wonder that no one else has ever seen." She shook her head incredulously. "But I never thought it would be true."

DeeAnn's face hardened. "Leave them alone."

Becca nearly laughed. "Leave them alone? Are you serious? Don't you understand what this means?"

"I know exactly what it means. But you're not going to take them. Any of them."

Becca's eyes returned to DeeAnn's as if seeing her for the first time. Hearing another loud buzz, she lowered her gaze and studied the strange vest with the blue light. "What is that?"

DeeAnn instinctively turned it off. "It's none of your business." At once, the light went off, causing them all to disappear into the darkness.

Moments later a red flare burst into light, revealing both men standing behind Becca, one holding the flame over his head. More of the cave came alive, revealing even more capuchins.

Both women gasped nearly in unison. The cave continued for quite a distance, extending deep into the mountain. About twenty yards back, they noticed something remarkable on the floor. It was a large area ringed by stones. In the middle were several small piles of leaves, layered with taller sticks leaning over them. It didn't look like much, but the women studied it with astonishment. The monkeys were trying to create fire with piles similar to those they had seen from humans. They still didn't understand how to make it happen, but they were trying.

Out of the corner of her eye, DeeAnn saw Becca withdraw a small tranquilizer pistol from behind her back and point it at a nearby monkey — one covered in white fur.

"No!" In a split second, her instincts kicked in and she lunged for the other woman, trying to knock the pistol out of her hand. The two fell to the ground, causing the gun to fire, and a dart ricocheted off the cave wall.

DeeAnn clawed for the gun, trying to wrestle it from Becca's hand. But the taller woman fought back, striking DeeAnn in the face with her fist.

Becca rose onto a knee and tried to aim again, but DeeAnn quickly pushed forward, knocking her back down.

Before she could lunge again, one of the soldiers stepped forward and pushed a heavy boot against DeeAnn's back, pinning her in place while Becca returned to her feet. Not bothering to brush herself off, the Brazilian repointed her gun and fired a dart into the chest of the monkey at close range.

The monkey screamed and clawed at the dart, pulling it out. At the same time, the other capuchins surged forward trying to protect him. But within seconds its movements began to slow.

Forcefully, Becca pushed through the troops, grasped one of the monkey's flailing arms and pulled it off its feet. She immediately jumped back behind the two soldiers for protection.

Becca lifted the monkey and examined her prize as it went decidedly limp, dangling from her hand. She looked at DeeAnn on the ground and smiled. "I win."

Those were the last words spoken before Becca, followed by both men, turned back to the mouth of the cave and disappeared into the night.

By the time Steve Caesare arrived, it was too late. His flashlight searched the cave floor and walls until he spotted DeeAnn leaning against a rock. Next to her was Dulce, and both were surrounded by the capuchins. He slowed and studied DeeAnn, who was holding one of her arms.

"You okay?"

"I will be. I had a run-in with our Brazilian friends."

"What happened?"

"I tried to stop them from taking one of the monkeys and lost."

Caesare tucked his light under an arm and bent down to examine her. He checked her arm and it didn't feel broken. He shone his light around them, scanning the inside of the cave. "What is this place?"

Despite her injured arm and some scrapes on her face, she managed to reach down and turn the vest back on. "I'm not sure." Once the blue light appeared, DeeAnn grinned. "What do you say we find out?"

87

Just twenty-five percent below Mach One, the Chinese Y-20 cargo plane thundered over the southeastern border of Venezuela and headed directly for the Acarai Mountains.

At fifteen minutes out, two crewmen began unlatching the straps holding the giant bomb in place. They then used the hold's loading assembly to slowly roll it back to the edge of the aft ramp, securing two heavy chains to each side.

Once in position, one of the crewmen picked up the phone on the wall and spoke loudly over the Y-20's powerful turbofan engines. After a pause, he replaced the phone and closed the metal cover.

It took less than thirty seconds for the bomb's panel to light up and begin its remote programming.

Seven minutes later, the giant aircraft approached the Acarai summit, hidden thousands of feet below in the pitch-black jungle. The plane gently increased its pitch and began a slow upward climb.

Inside, the crewmen attached one final powerful cable to the device, with an electronic release in the middle nearly the size of a bowling ball. They promptly removed the side chains and moved further up the cargo bay's wall, attaching themselves to nylon safety lines.

There they waited, watching the wall until a bright green light signaled their position.

One of the men looked to the other, who nodded back. He then opened the clear cover and slammed his hand down on the giant button.

Overhead, several red flashing lights filled the cargo bay, accompanied by a loud siren, as the ramp door disengaged and began to lower. The bomb slid backward toward the tail of the plane until it was halted by the thick cable.

It took two full minutes for the ramp door to fully open and provide a smooth path out the rear of the plane.

Then at last, when over their target, the strap disconnected. The long, elliptically-shaped bomb abruptly accelerated, leaving the ramp and disappearing into the night.

The Russian thermobaric bomb detonated at one thousand feet above the Acarai peak, releasing a brilliant orange mushroom cloud into the dark sky, along with a supersonic shockwave hot enough to evaporate solid rock.

88

A jolt from the truck's old suspension shook John Clay from his unconscious state. His head rocked side to side from the continual shaking of the bumpy road, making it hard to focus. He could hear rocks pelting the inside of the wheel wells, indicating a rapid speed over a dirt road.

His eyes closed again for a moment before he was able to find the strength to force them back open. As the light began to sharpen, he tilted his head to see what appeared to be the dark shape of the driver against the bright front windshield. A second person was ahead of him in the passenger seat.

His next sensation was the pain. Every part of his body screamed out from under a thick wool blanket which covered all but his face. He tried to move but couldn't. Not anything. Instead, he tried his mouth and managed a slight whisper.

On his third attempt, the passenger turned around and looked down at him.

"You're awake."

Clay fought to make his lips move again.

"Don't talk, save your energy."

The driver glanced over his shoulder at Clay and quickly turned back to the road.

A severe dip sent a wave of pain through Clay's limbs, causing him to moan.

"Hang in there, man. We're all trying to get you out of here."

"W-what happened?" Clay whispered.

The Chinese passenger shrugged. "Hell if we know. Someone at the agency hit the panic button. Instructions are to find you and then get the hell out."

Clay blinked slowly. His memory was a jumble of images and he was struggling to put them in order.

"Where's Li Na?"

The other man looked at the driver before replying. "We don't know. She escaped and disappeared into the forest before we could stop her."

Clay shook his head. He could see the girl's face, frightened and alone. "Stop."

"What?"

"Stop the car."

"Sorry, can't do that. We have to get out of the country. There's a team waiting for us in Huludao."

Clay shook his head. "We have to go back."

The driver abruptly pulled the truck over to a stop. He twisted around in his seat and Clay recognized him from Qin's team. "Look, I don't think you understand what's happened here. A lot of covers just got blown to find you. Agents who can now be traced to a lot of others all over this region."

The second agent in the passenger's seat nodded in agreement. "Our only priorities are you and this case." He held up the metal case.

Clay managed to angle his head and stare at it. "Did you open it?"

The agent lowered it. "Nope. Not authorized."

Clay's memories were coming back. "Check the case."

"Sorry. I can't do it. Our instructions are to get you, and this thing, *out*."

"Listen to me," Clay said louder. "We have to go back."

The driver shook his head and put the truck back into gear. "I think you got hit one too many times in the head."

Clay gritted his teeth in pain and took a deep breath. "If you won't go back, then at least check the goddamn case!"

The agents both looked at each other. The second agent reached down and brought the case back up. After contemplating, he turned it sideways and opened the clasps, pulling the cool metal case open. He stared inside before turning it for the driver to see.

It was empty.

89

By the time the agents turned the truck around, Qin had already landed in Beijing. After being found and freed with the other soldiers, all he had to do was find a phone.

Less than a minute after his helicopter bounced lightly onto the tarmac, the side door was flung open by two airmen outside. Once on the ground, Qin was quickly escorted to a vehicle which sped across the base to a nearby lab.

He ordered the airmen to remain outside while he pushed through the double doors and ran up a flight of stairs. When he reached the room, a single technician was waiting for him with a very confused look on his face.

Unsure, the technician saluted and returned a nervous hand to his side. "You asked to see me, sir?"

Instead of replying, Qin closed the wide door behind him and locked it.

"Listen very carefully. You are not to repeat a single word of this conversation to anyone. Is that clear?"

"Y-yes, sir."

Qin's cold eyes bore into the man. "And any results you find will be erased."

The technician nodded nervously.

With that, a wry grin spread across Qin's face as he reached inside his jacket. He removed a red rag and began unwrapping it. When he uncovered the final layer, he held his hand below and rolled three clear glass tubes into his palm.

Qin waited impatiently. He watched as the young technician removed samples from each tube and used a swab to carefully place them on the ATP meters. Once in the luminometer, they watched the computer screen as the results were captured and displayed.

Qin squinted, trying to understand what he was seeing on the screen. Multiple lines rose and fell across a horizontal list of molecular compounds. It was clear that two of the compounds were in much higher concentrations than the rest. He pointed at them.

"What are those?"

The technician's confusion was growing. "Those are Selenium and Iron." He pointed to the others. "These, however, are all bacterium."

Qin stepped closer, excitedly. "What sort of bacterium?"

"They're called coliform."

Qin paused and turned toward the technician. "You've seen them before?"

"Yes, sir. Many times."

"What do you mean?"

The technician shrugged. "They're common."

Qin froze. *Impossible.* Deep down a sudden panic began to grow. "How common?"

"Very common. We find it in almost all forms of ground water."

The panic was now overtaking Qin. "It's water?"

"Yes. Judging from the Selenium and Iron, I'd guess a water source in close proximity to a mining operation."

The CIA agent stumbled down the rocky path, keeping the flashlight pointed straight ahead. With one hand on the wall, he moved as quickly as he could without tripping over the larger stones.

The damp tunnel continued to descend for several hundred feet before he spotted the glimmering water. The agent hurried to the edge, and without the slightest pause, waded into the icy pool. He forced himself to remain still and scanned each side, until spotting a large boulder nearby. He crept forward and used the light to study a crevice between the boulder and the wall. Wedged into the middle of the crevice was a small drinking canister.

Exactly where Clay said it would be.

The blast was almost beyond comprehension.

As if in slow motion, the orange mushroom cloud had curled under itself, gradually turning red, then violet, then black, before finally dissolving into the night sky.

The impact of the world's largest conventional bomb was devastating. A full thirty meters of the top of the Acarai summit was simply gone. Rocks, trees, everything…vaporized into nothingness, along with every creature within the radius of a quarter mile.

Salazar and his army, along with Otero and Russo. Every living thing was gone. Including Corso and Juan.

Further down the mountain, the shock wave flattened trees for another full mile, setting nearly half of what remained on fire. The rest was left smoldering.

Much further down, and inside the cave, there was no sound. Dirt and rocks covered the floor, while thick wisps of dust were being sucked outside into the hot air.

On the floor, a single spot of dirt finally moved. Several seconds later, it moved again, but this time, growing larger. Slowly, something pushed upward, causing the loose dirt to fall away before taking the shape of an arm. Dirt moved in another area and Steve Caesare's head emerged.

He wiped the dirt from his eyes and looked around, into blackness. He thrust his arms back into the dirt and found his flashlight, pulling it out. It was still lit.

Caesare climbed to his feet and held the light up, looking for the others. He helped the rising shapes of Dulce and DeeAnn, then began searching for monkeys.

"What the hell was that?" DeeAnn coughed.

"A bomb."

Thirty minutes later, they stood at the cave entrance, peering out in shock at the sight before them. Against the moonlight, warm ash fell silently to the ground. Higher up on the mountain, a raging wall of fire ringed what was left of the summit.

A numb DeeAnn stared up at the flames. Tears appeared and ran down her cheeks, creating tracks on her dust-covered face.

Caesare pointed his flashlight at the ground. His voice was somber. "We have to get out of here. That fire can spread."

With Dulce on his back and DeeAnn following behind, Caesare came to a stop and lowered his flashlight. He studied the sight in front of them with curiosity. Almost a hundred yards ahead, something was glowing, and brightly.

He raised his light and continued forward until he realized what the object was. Then he began running.

It was a vehicle, a Humvee, lying on its left side with two wheels in the air. It was pinned beneath two flattened trees, and miraculously, one of the headlights was still functioning.

Caesare reached the small truck and dropped Dulce to the ground. He turned and held up a hand to them. "Stay here."

He circled the front of the vehicle, taking large steps through the flat brush, then stopped and shined his flashlight through the shattered windshield. Behind the myriad of cracks, he could see the barrel of a gun pointing directly at him.

"Tiewater?"

At the sound of his name, the SEAL let his hand fall with a groan.

Even seeing the man's face covered in blood, Caesare couldn't help but smile. He climbed up onto the vehicle's upturned side and peered down through the open window. "Son of a bitch, you're alive!"

Tiewater, unable to move his head, moved his eyes instead. "Good, because this sure as hell doesn't feel like heaven. Somebody nuked us."

"I don't know what it was, but it wasn't a nuke. Can you move?"

Tiewater clenched his teeth and tried. "Not much. I think my legs are broken. And maybe my arm."

Caesare nodded. He looked around the inside at all the silver-colored airbags, now deflated.

"You might be the best commercial yet for the airbag companies."

"Lucky me. Now get me the hell out of here."

"Hold on. Let me figure this out."

"Wait," Tiewater said, straining to look through the window frame. "What about Corso and the kid?"

Caesare frowned and shook his head.

92

Will Borger never saw the explosion. He was instead gripping the sides of his seat, white-knuckled, as the Sea King helicopter reduced its altitude and began to slow. The bright lights of the Pathfinder could be seen less than a mile away, floating eerily on what resembled a sea of blackness.

When the helicopter touched down, he unbuckled and grabbed his bag in one hand. The door was opened from the outside and a young navy officer motioned him down onto a metal stepladder.

When he reached the deck, he noticed several others standing and waiting, carrying something. It was a wire basket stretcher. In it was a man who looked like an unconscious Chris Ramirez.

Borger forgot about his anxiety and watched the team quickly move in behind him, sliding Chris into the helicopter. A doctor climbed in next to him and slammed the door shut.

Only when Borger turned around did he see Alison standing on the deck several feet away, tears in her eyes.

"Alison?"

Slowly, almost reluctantly, she turned to Will.

"What happened?"

"An accident. Chris is being airlifted back to Trinidad."

Before he could ask, Alison choked back sobs and answered his question. "It doesn't look good."

"My God, I'm sorry."

Alison didn't respond. Instead, she merely watched the helicopter as it roared back into the air. She continued watching until the helicopter's lights faded into nothingness before turning back to Borger. Her face was dour. "Did you bring it?"

"I did."

Alison took a deep breath and looked up at the star-filled sky. She couldn't hold it in anymore. The fear was still there, but she had to ask him. She had to ask him the question she was terrified of hearing the answer to.

"How is John?"

She watched the look on Borger's face change. He struggled, staring at her uncomfortably. "Uh…"

"Just tell me," she said. "I know something is wrong. I can feel it. Just tell me the truth."

Borger blinked and remained still, then finally nodded. "The truth is…I don't know." He slowly shook his head. "I don't know how he is, or even where he is right now. Not exactly."

"What does not exactly mean?"

"He's in China. But I've lost contact with him. A rescue team has been sent in…"

Alison pursed her lips together. Borger could see the glistening of tears in her eyes. "A rescue team?"

He nodded, hoping she wouldn't ask who. Explaining that the CIA was trying to find Clay probably wouldn't help matters.

"It must be bad." Alison's chin quivered slightly. "He's usually the one doing the rescuing."

"He did save someone. A young girl. That much, I do know."

She nodded and tried to blink away the tears. "Do you think he's dead?"

"No. I don't."

"Why?"

Borger let a small grin escape. "Because Clay is my friend. And I know that if the situation were reversed, he would never give up on me."

Alison stared at Borger before finally grinning with him. "You're right." She stepped forward and wrapped her arms around him in a hug. "Thank you."

He nodded and looked around at the men waiting nearby. "Now what?"

She took another deep breath. "Neely Lawton is waiting for you upstairs. They'll take you."

"What about you?"

She turned and looked back at Tay and Lightfoot, both waiting patiently. "I have an appointment."

Borger noticed the SCUBA gear behind the men. "What did you find?"

"The plants are the same. Just like we saw on the mountain. But how it happened here, I haven't the slightest idea."

Borger's face became serious. "Then there's something I need to tell you."

Alison. You back.

"I'm back," Alison nodded. "Just like I promised."

We happy for you back.

Alison looked over her shoulder and smiled at Lightfoot floating next to her. "So are we."

You come for plants.

"Not this time." Alison reached down and retrieved a small device from a pocket on her BCD. It was the device Borger brought.

They knew what they were dealing with now. The plants were the same, which suggested the cause had to be the same. Just like at Acarai, something was in the water. Now they just needed to find the source.

The device in her hand came on automatically and glowed with a soft blue light. On the mountain, it had measured the concentration levels of a very special compound, which ultimately led them to the secret vault. Now they were trying to find the second source: *the ship.*

Alison twisted around, studying the display. She kicked forward, traveling twenty yards, but there was no change.

She turned and swam further still, but could not see anything different. Then it hit her.

In the jungle, it was easier. There was a flow of water, and it was one directional.

"What's wrong?" Lightfoot asked.

"It's not working."

"Why not?"

"Because what this is looking for isn't in front of us, or behind us. It's *everywhere.*"

Alison began to call up to Lee, but stopped when she spotted Dirk and Sally, floating patiently in place.

No plants.

"No. Not the plants this time."

Come Alison. Come now. We show.

Both dolphins thrust their tails and moved past her and Lightfoot, who both turned and followed. Together they descended back into the darkness and watched as the green glow eventually reappeared below them. The effect was both eerie and breathtaking.

The dolphins continued downward, pausing to allow Alison and Lightfoot to catch up.

Hold us.

Alison glanced curiously at Lightfoot before wrapping her hand around Sally's dorsal fin. Then he did the same to Dirk. The dolphins continued, diving deeper into the expanse of dense vegetation.

When they reached a small drop-off, the dolphins dropped with it, skimming over the tops of enormous sea plants, all shining brightly under their headlamps. They suddenly ducked beneath long waving tendrils, and saw a dark yet thriving dip in the coral. Leading the way, Dirk slowed and approached the area carefully. Yet when he reached the wall of plants, Dirk didn't stop. Instead he continued forward smoothly, passed through the vegetation, and disappeared inside. Alison barely had time to blink before Sally did the same.

Both human passengers watched incredulously as the underwater growth extended through a small passageway — through coral tight enough that it caused them to bump repeatedly against the sides.

Gigantic green plants billowed before them, brushing their masks and rolling past harmlessly.

Still holding tightly onto Sally, Alison remembered her device, brought it up to her face, and then gasped. The concentrations were off the chart! It was from here that the nourishing compounds were emanating.

The dolphins reached the other side of the passage and emerged into something much larger.

With her mouth open, Alison let go of Sally and slowed. Just several feet ahead, Lightfoot instinctively did the same upon seeing what lay before them.

Neither moved for a long time. Instead they remained, floating still in the water. It was a cavern. And it looked as though the coral had grown over it, sealing the cavity off from above. The area was approximately fifty yards across with thick columns of coral twisting and extending below in places, providing a natural support system.

And as small as the cavern was in width, it extended much deeper below them, covered in even thicker vegetation.

But it was what the vegetation had attached itself to that left Alison and Lightfoot completely speechless.

Enveloped within a vast green glow was something metal. Manufactured. With powerful looking gray walls and a smooth surface, the structure extended less than a hundred feet before it was completely consumed by the vines and tendrils of plant life around it.

Along one side, and partially obscured, were strange markings. Reminiscent of what Alison had seen in the mountains of Guyana.

Lightfoot pushed himself forward, mesmerized. He closed in, studying the wall of metal. "It looks perfect, without a mark on it." He reached forward and gingerly touched a finger to the object. A green glow rippled out in a small circle, then disappeared.

Lightfoot turned and looked back at Alison, hovering just behind him. He then pressed his entire hand against it to see a larger circle ripple out, before fading again.

Alison peered down through the water. The ship's hull descended further than she could see. She reached out and brushed her hand across the surface of the wall, watching as a green trail briefly followed her glove.

Sally and Dirk floated next to them, barely moving their fins.

This you look Alison.

Alison blinked behind her mask and smiled. "Yes. This is what we were looking for." She continued staring in awe. It was unlike anything she had ever seen.

Borger was right.

Two hours later, Langford picked up his ringing cell phone and answered it.

"Langford."

On the other end, Will Borger stared at the phone in the middle of the small table. Sitting in the room with him were Captain Emerson, Neely, and lastly, Alison, sporting wet but neatly brushed hair.

"Admiral, it's Borger. I'm here with Captain Emerson, Alison, and Neely Lawton."

"Good morning. I hope you're calling with good news."

"You could say that." He turned to Neely and nodded.

"Admiral, this is Commander Lawton." She leaned forward, toward the phone. "I've confirmed that the samples we've recovered here on the sea floor contain the same genetic properties as the plants from Guyana."

"You're sure?"

"There are still a few more tests to run when we return,

427

but yes, sir. I'm sure."

"Thank you, Commander. That is good news."

Borger frowned slightly. The admiral's tone sounded more somber than he was expecting. Even for him.

"Is everything all right, sir?"

"Everything is fine," he replied. "Captain Emerson, under the circumstances, I'd like you to hold your position and await further instructions."

"Aye, Admiral."

Borger cleared his voice. "Uh, Admiral. We also have something else to tell you."

"Go ahead."

Borger glanced around the table at the others.

"Sir, for this…I think you're going to want to sit down."

93

The morning sun was barely climbing into the sky as a gray Crown Victoria was waved through the airport's southern gate. It sped past the row of nondescript aircraft hangars, heading directly for the Gulfstream sitting on a private tarmac.

Upon reaching the plane, the car slowed and came to a stop, where one of the rear doors was immediately opened. Secretary of Defense Miller stepped out in full uniform, closing the door behind him. He walked to the metal staircase and climbed briskly to the top, stepping inside the cabin.

Admiral Langford and CIA Director Hayes were already seated inside, waiting. Each sitting on opposite sides of the aisle.

Miller grinned at the obvious tension between the two and sat down, just seconds before the heavy door was closed behind him.

After remaining an independent and self-governing province for nearly four hundred years, the Republic and Canton of Geneva rejoined the Swiss Confederacy in 1815, establishing itself as Switzerland's westernmost region. Surrounded by the lush green hills of France on nearly all sides, the French-speaking canton remained the most metropolitan and wealthiest in the region. And was home to some of the most powerful multinational corporations in the world.

The Gulfstream's flight lasted eight hours before the aircraft circled and began its final approach. After touching down, it taxied to a secure location at the Geneva Airport and slowed to a stop.

In the darkness, two black SUVs stood waiting, surrounded by several CIA agents. The three men descended the stairs and approached their security detail. Hayes then immediately climbed into the first truck, leaving Langford and Miller to the second. Conducting a final scan of the area, the agents opened their own doors and climbed in around them.

The traffic along the route was light, allowing the two-car caravan to reach Vernier in less than thirty minutes. The small municipality was well-known as home to one of the wealthiest offshore drilling companies in the world. A conglomerate with immense power, yet now perhaps one of the most tarnished reputations in the industry. Transocean Limited would forever be known as the owner of the drill rig responsible for the Deepwater Horizon oil spill, and the largest accidental marine spill in petroleum history.

When Langford, Miller, and Hayes were escorted into the lobby of the company's headquarters, a member of the Transocean staff was waiting for them.

"Good morning, gentlemen," an attractive female said pleasantly. With short black hair, she was impeccably dressed in a red and black colorblock skirt suit. "I'm Alessia Bierle. We're privileged to have you here and hope your trip was enjoyable."

"It was fine. Thank you," Langford replied.

"Can I get you anything before heading upstairs?"

"No, thank you."

"Very well. Then please follow me and we'll head up."

The woman led them to the elevator and held it open for their visitors. Once inside, Bierle pushed the button for the top floor and turned to them, smiling. "Our executive team is waiting for you."

"Thank you, Ms. Bierle," Miller nodded. Hayes had yet to speak.

The elevator opened into an elaborate meeting room with

light marble flooring and a modern design, giving it a clean and efficient look. Bierle led them across the room and gestured to the three closest chairs at the table. On the other side sat several men, all in their fifties and sixties, who immediately stood with welcoming yet cautious expressions.

The man in the middle smiled at all three men and extended his hand across the dark table.

"Good morning," he said in a thick French accent. "We are very pleased to meet you."

Admiral Langford shook his hand and quickly selected a chair, signaling his desire to dispense with pleasantries. He sat down, followed by Miller, Hayes, and the rest of the room.

A man named Abel Abegg, the president of Transocean, was dressed impeccably in a dark blue Brioni suit and eased himself down, studying the three Americans. They were clearly not there to waste time.

"What is it that we can help you with, Admiral?"

"We're interested in one of your mobile drill rigs in the Caribbean. The one that you're replacing."

Abegg nodded. "Ah, you're referring to the Nordic. We just put the newer ultra-deepwater unit in place two weeks ago and are running simulation tests." He looked curiously among all three men. "What is it about the Nordic that you'd like to know?"

Miller cleared his throat. "It's not the newer one we're interested in. It's the older rig being removed."

Abegg looked confused. "The old rig? You mean the Valant?"

"Correct," answered Langford.

"I don't understand," Abegg replied, glancing briefly at the rest of his team.

"You *are* removing it?"

"Yes, of course. We must. Regulations mandate all rigs be replaced if they pose a significant structural risk."

At this, Langford grinned. "Regulations haven't exactly

been your strong suit."

His comment caused several eyes to narrow across the table, and the pleasant expression on their president's face disappeared. "You're speaking of the Deepwater accident."

"We've come here with an opportunity, Mr. Abegg."

He stared at Langford. "Is that right? An opportunity for *whom* may I ask?"

Langford met the man's gaze. "For your redemption."

Abegg slowly smiled. "Redemption?"

"That's right."

"Redemption of what, exactly?"

"Redemption for knowing that cutting the wrong corners resulted in the largest oil spill and manmade disaster on record. And an expensive lesson."

"A *very* expensive lesson," Abegg replied.

"Indeed."

"So, what *sort* of redemption are we speaking of?" Abegg asked.

Miller answered. "Another mistake."

"Excuse me?"

"Another mistake," repeated Langford.

"I don't understand."

"The old rig you're bringing back to dismantle. It needs a problem."

"It *needs* a problem?" The president looked again at his officers on either side, then turned back to Langford with a grin. "And this *problem* is supposed to be our redemption?"

"That's right."

Abegg merely stared at Langford. "Exactly what kind of problem do you have in mind?"

"That's up to you. We only care about the location."

94

John Clay awoke and slowly examined the light-colored blanket tucked neatly around him. The high rails on either side told him it was a hospital bed. Without moving his head, he followed the blanket up to his chest, where he found clear tubes running to either side.

The room came into focus quickly. It was sparsely decorated with little more than a service table and a television high on the opposite wall. He moved both hands and felt something soft to his right.

He turned his head to see a chair pulled close to the bed. Curled up uncomfortably and still sleeping was Alison. Her arm extended across the edge of the bed with her hand resting on top of Clay's.

Clay watched her as she slept. Even with tussled hair and her head resting awkwardly on a pillow atop the chair, he smiled at how beautiful she was.

He was overcome with emotion, staring longingly into a face he thought he would never see again. He took a deep breath and smiled.

Alison's eyes fluttered open and stared at him. But only for a moment before jerking upright. "You're awake!"

Clay smiled. Even her voice was beautiful.

Alison leaned forward to hug him gently.

"When did you get here?" he asked.

She smiled and pulled his hand to her cheek. "As soon as I could."

A flood of emotions overwhelmed him and Clay's eyes began to well with tears. "I-I didn't think-"

"It's okay," she whispered. "I'm here now."

He smiled again and nodded.

Alison lowered his hand, then stood up and leaned in

433

closer to kiss him. When she sat back down, it was on the edge of his bed.

"How do you feel?"

"Old."

She chuckled. "That's not what I meant."

"Everything hurts." He grimaced and pulled the blanket to the side, examining the cast he felt on his leg. "What day is it?"

"Saturday, the twelfth."

He peered through the window into a blue sky with soft scattered clouds. "Where are we?"

She grinned. "Honolulu. At the Queen's Medical Center."

"Hawaii?"

"Yep."

He leaned his head back. "Not exactly how I would have wanted to bring you here."

Alison looked down and straightened the blanket across his chest. "I'll take you any way I can get you."

"I'm sorry I couldn't tell you."

"I know. It was probably better you didn't. Besides, I had my own problems."

His eyes narrowed. "What happened?"

She was still looking down at the blanket and pursed her lips tight, but it didn't prevent what was coming. Alison began to tremble and she fell forward, softly into him. "We lost Juan."

Clay was stunned. "What?!"

"We lost Juan," she repeated, sobbing.

"Oh no." He brought her in closer. "I'm so sorry."

Clay didn't need to ask. He knew what Caesare and his team were up against, and he knew how often things went awry, no matter how well-planned. He put his bandaged arm around her, trying to ignore the pain.

After a minute, she looked up and tried to wipe the tears away. "And Chris!"

434

"Chris?!"

Alison nodded. "He's in the hospital. There was an accident aboard the ship. The doctors think he's going to be okay, but we almost lost him too."

He nodded and squeezed her. "What about Steve?"

"He's okay, and DeeAnn and Dulce. But he lost two of his men."

Clay closed his eyes, shaking his head. Nearly everything had gone wrong. Juan, Chris, and now two of Caesare's team.

He reached up and brushed some hair away from Alison's face. "Not our finest moment, was it?"

She stared at him and wiped her eyes. With a sniff she said, "Well, I'm not sure if I'd go that far."

She forced a small smile at Clay's inquisitive look. "We did manage to find something. Something big."

Ten minutes later, there was a knock on the door. Alison got up and walked across the room to open it, finding Caesare there, quiet and somber. He stepped in, wearing an arm sling and a grave face.

Clay had seen that look before. "How you doin'?"

Caesare shook his head. "Not all that great. How are you?"

"Better than I was."

"I bet." He stopped at the foot of the bed. "You hear about Juan, and Corso, and Anderson?"

"I did. I'm really sorry."

Caesare nodded. "Not much went our way. Doesn't look like too much went your way either."

Clay forced a grin. "I guess it depends on how you look at it."

"Well, it *looks* like you got beat up."

"Yeah, but I think I intimidated the hell out of the other guys."

A small smile spread across Caesare's face. "Based on how bad you look, they must have been shaking in their boots."

"I wish you could have been there."

This time, Caesare laughed. "Gee, thanks." He rounded the bed and dropped his large frame into the chair. "So what did happen?"

"I found Wei's daughter, Li Na."

"She was alive then?"

"Yes. Wei saved her life by injecting her with the bacterium from the plants."

"Where is she now?"

Clay stared at him, still trying to piece his memory back together. No doubt made worse by the medication he was on. "I think she escaped."

"Great." Caesare leaned back. The room became silent before he took a breath and spoke again. "It's gone, John. The whole thing is gone."

"The vault?"

Caesare nodded. "They dropped a bomb and melted the whole damn top of that mountain. We survived by luck. And nothing more."

"The Brazilians?"

"No." Caesare shook his head. "The Chinese."

"The *Chinese*?"

Caesare nodded with his eyes transfixed. "I guess if they couldn't have it, they decided no one would."

Clay was shocked. He gazed back out through the window, shaking his head. "How are the others?"

"Alive," Caesare said. "Chris and Tiewater are both in the hospital. DeeAnn's fine, but I'm sure she's out — this time, for good. If she was on the fence before, that fence doesn't even exist anymore."

Clay looked at Alison, now standing at the foot of his bed. "I guess we can't blame her."

"No," Caesare said absently. "No, we can't."

436

Clay noticed Alison glance back at the door. It was the second time she had done it. "What's wrong?"

"Me? Nothing."

He watched Alison glance subtly at Caesare. They knew something he didn't.

"What?"

The Queen's Medical Center, still commonly referred to as Queen's Hospital, was the largest in the state of Hawaii. Long since expanded beyond the hospital's original footprint, the facility had grown to over 500 beds, 3,600 employees, and now served as the largest trauma center in the Pacific Basin.

On the bottom floor, beneath the light-green roof of the hospital's main entrance, two automatic double doors promptly slid open as Admiral Langford and Secretary of Defense Miller strode in out of the warm, humid Hawaiian air. Both were dressed in casual clothes and walked purposefully toward the elevators. Behind them, three more individuals followed.

Langford slowed as he passed the large waiting room, noticing the feed on the giant television. It was an aerial shot of Transocean's rig "Valant" in the mid-Atlantic. Onscreen, words overlaid the live video feed and read "Transocean loses millions to prevent disaster."

With a bemused grin, Langford continued. He had to admit, between their two public relations teams, the story being fed to the public sounded downright heroic. The "disaster" portion was a stretch. The company hadn't actually replaced the rig sooner than planned, nor was there a malfunction forcing the old rig to be stopped where it was. In truth, the incident was little more than a detour on the way to the scrapyard. The important thing was that it allowed the public to praise Transocean Ltd. on being proactive…before promptly forgetting the incident. Even more importantly, it provided the perfect excuse to now position an unused oil rig directly over Alison Shaw's discovery for the next twelve months, accompanied, of course, by the U.S.S. Pathfinder.

It was the same story that had been circulated throughout each of the U.S. military's five service branches.

When the door to Clay's room opened next, he was surprised to see both Langford and Miller walk in, followed by Neely Lawton, Will Borger, and to Caesare's complete shock, a serious-looking DeeAnn Draper.

Together they looked down at Clay with concern, after which Neely exchanged a quick smile with Caesare as Langford began to speak.

"How are you, John?"

"Uh...surprised, sir."

Langford grinned and glanced to his left. "How about you, Steve?"

Next to Clay, Caesare watched Langford with a cautious expression. "I'm fine."

The admiral motioned to the others around him. "I know this is a little unexpected."

"Just a tad."

Langford frowned at Caesare. "I wanted to have you all in the same room. And since Clay isn't going anywhere soon, I decided we could all do with a bit of warm air and sunshine."

Clay gave a playful but questioning look at Alison, who only shrugged and smiled. Both he and Caesare watched Langford with curiosity.

"Let me start by commending you all. You did a hell of a job under the circumstances." Langford glanced at the others. "I'm not sure if I've ever been more impressed with a group of individuals. It's people like you who remind me what this country is supposed to be about. What it used to

438

be about. And perhaps what it might someday be again. But until then, what has happened in the last few weeks, or in the last year, has been nothing short of earth-shaking. I'm sure you would all agree." Langford straightened and put his hands behind himself. "Which is also why it must be protected. At all costs. By all of you."

Both Clay and Caesare raised their eyebrows simultaneously.

"Sir?"

"What I'm about to say may come as a surprise. Yet it's something on which Defense Secretary Miller and I both agree. And that is the decision to form a new classified team, composed of the members in this room. A team that reports exclusively to Secretary Miller and myself, and no one else."

Silence fell over the room as everyone looked back and forth, curiously.

"Sir, I don't understand," said Clay. "Why form a team when the mission is over?"

Langford chuckled. "And what makes you think things are over?"

"Uh, well, the hidden vault is gone, sir. We recovered the last of Wei's infused bacteria, and Alison has found the new source of plants. It seems to me we're largely done. Except for finding Wei's daughter."

Langford glanced at Clay. "I have to admit, I had a similar thought. Until these three decided to enlighten me." He turned again to face Neely, Will, and DeeAnn. "Mr. Borger, perhaps you would like to start?"

Borger slowly nodded and stepped forward, clearing his voice. "Uh…well, it kinda has to do with Alison's discovery near Trinidad. You see, the vault that was on top of the mountain in Guyana had to have been built…by someone. Someone who traveled here." He nodded to Caesare. "I explained to Steve a few weeks ago that coming here to do that likely meant it was a one-way trip. Primarily due to distance, speed, and the amount of energy needed." Borger inhaled and looked around the room. "So when you couple that with all the material involved, it's likely they needed something to make the journey. Like a ship. And that seems to be exactly what Alison has discovered. Which leads us back to the vault."

Caesare furrowed his brow. "The vault was destroyed, Will."

"I know. But I've been thinking." He took another deep breath. "See, if it were me…and I had to travel all that way…I wouldn't just build one."

"What?"

"I said I wouldn't build just one."

"But what does that mean?" Caesare asked.

Borger replied with a hint of excitement. "So, think about it. Whoever it was had to travel an awful long way. Remember, Palin and his people can create portals, but there's a catch. Distance. He explained that the farther the distance, the greater the energy required, becoming exponential. So at a certain distance, the resources available to create enough energy would be exhausted, which is exactly what was happening to them. He told us they were running out."

Caesare nodded. "So if whoever built that vault traveled by ship…"

"It means they were likely coming from much further away, from a distance they simply *couldn't* create a portal from. This is part of why I think it was a one-way trip. But here's the thing, if they *did* travel all that way to create a safe place for their DNA, it means they'd have to be sure it would survive, right?"

"Right."

"Which also means it would have to be on a planet with a climate compatible with their own DNA…"

Clay stared at Borger. "So you're talking about redundancy."

440

"Exactly! If they came all this way, why would they build just one vault?"

Borger continued, faster. "Our planet is covered in tectonic plates which affect everything, including things like volcanos, storms, and tsunamis. You name it. The conditions are constantly changing. So they had to build their vault where it would be safe."

"But given enough time, nothing is safe," Clay replied.

"That's right! Which means you'd need redundancy. Another, in case one was lost. A backup."

"Or a Plan B."

Borger smiled at Caesare. "A Plan B."

"But we're just theorizing at this point."

"Not necessarily," replied Borger. "Think about us humans. We build redundancy into almost everything around us, especially our technology. Even a simple DVD disk arranges data in a way that protects it against damage like scratches. It's called Reed-Solomon and the code is used in a host of other technologies. Like memory sticks. Or electrical circuits. Even our cars all carry a spare tire. Life is unpredictable, and if we know that, then whoever built that vault did too. And it was supposed to be here for a *long* time."

"Okay," Caesare said. "So the argument then changes from could they have built another to…*did* they?"

This time, Borger didn't reply. Instead he turned to the admiral, who in turn looked to Neely. "Commander Lawton?"

With arms folded, she stepped forward. "There's something else." She smiled at Alison. "A little more than a week ago, when Ali told me about what had happened at her lab with that young girl, we took blood samples from Dirk and Sally. What we've noticed has to do with a number of genetic markers that are common between humans and dolphins when it comes to brain makeup.

"In fact, a paper published a few years ago by a

researcher at the Center of Molecular Medicine has identified a commonality among certain large-brained animals called the *big brain trio*. The similarities strongly suggest a convergent evolution among three very specific animals: dolphins, humans, and gorillas. Similarities in brain size and functionality are more than evident when you image them.

"In other words, a long time ago, something appears to have caused our three brains to evolve in a very similar way. Not exactly the same, but similar."

"You mean some kind of intervention." Caesare leaned back again in his chair.

"That's right," smiled Neely. "And given the genetic influence of what we found, both in Guyana and now under the water near Trinidad, this substance could very well be the *catalyst* responsible for our similar brain evolution."

"Hold on," interjected Clay. "If what's in the water really did influence the development of a dolphin's brain, it doesn't necessarily mean it affected either gorillas or humans. The other two-thirds of the big brain trio."

Now DeeAnn stepped forward. "You're right. It wouldn't explain why our brains developed very similarly." She turned to Borger. "Unless…"

"Unless there is a second vault," Borger added.

Clay and Caesare looked at each other. "And where would that be?"

"I don't know," he shrugged. "But if someone came here to build not just one, but two vaults, I'm pretty sure they wouldn't put them next to each other. In fact, I suspect they would put them as far away from one another as possible." Borger smiled. "Maybe even on another continent."

"There's only seven," said DeeAnn. "And one of them, we already know, is where gorillas and humans originated."

"Africa!" whispered Alison.

DeeAnn nodded. "Africa."

The room grew quiet. Finally Langford spoke to Clay.

"As you can see, John, it's not over. Not only do we have a ship to dissect and a bacterium sample to study, but it seems we may also have a second vault to find."

Secretary Miller spoke up in a deep voice. "Hence the need for a very small and very secret team."

Caesare looked at Miller. "Who else would know about this team?"

"No one. Just the admiral and I. There would be no official records and no official funding. Whatever you need, we will find a way to provide it. Which shouldn't be hard given what a mess our current budget is."

"True," Langford replied. "Fortunately, the federal budget is designed for hiding things."

Caesare looked dubious. "If only you two know about this team, what happens when the two of you…retire?"

Miller crossed his arms. "In the event that both of us leave our posts, for whatever reason, it's over. The team dissolves immediately, and Mr. Borger erases every trace."

Caesare nodded and looked at the others. "So I guess the question now is…who's in?"

"I am," answered Neely.

Borger grinned. "Same here."

Caesare looked to DeeAnn. "Dee?"

She took a deep breath. "I'm more surprised than anyone to be saying this, but I'm in. After seeing what they did to that mountain, what the stakes are, I get it. I see just how far some people are willing to go over this."

Caesare was stunned.

She smiled at him. "Besides, I've always wanted to see Africa."

Clay looked up at Alison. "Ali?"

Without a word, she displayed a wide smile.

Epilogue

I

The rusted red steel of the aging oil rig stood in sharp contrast against the Caribbean's emerald-blue water. The Valant, one of the first deep ocean production rigs, was small in comparison to the newer and more powerful mobile rigs. Yet it still dwarfed the Pathfinder, anchored just a quarter mile from the Valant's pillars, which towered high above the ocean surface.

Transocean's skeleton crew had already been evacuated once the rig was securely in place, replaced by an even smaller Navy crew. A crew comprised almost entirely of engineers, most of who were transferred directly from Captain Emerson's ship.

The group of eight stood in line atop the Valant's upper platform. They watched as the Sea King helicopter slowed and approached the helipad in front of them, clearly marked by a bright-red painted circle.

With only a wisp of a breeze, the Sea King landed smoothly with a gentle bounce, followed by the sound of the rotor's decelerating.

The door slid open and a younger man jumped down onto the deck. Beneath the wind from the spinning blades, he trotted across the small pad, wheeled a small set of stairs back to the chopper, and placed them in position. The second person out was older, in his sixties, carrying a black duffle bag in each hand.

He descended the stairs, and upon reaching the bottom, dropped the bags at a safe distance. He continued across the pad to where Captain Emerson was waiting.

Emerson moved forward and extended his hand, which

the man accepted with a firm shake. They spoke briefly, but could not be heard above the helicopter. Instead, they turned toward the men and waited.

"Gentlemen," Emerson finally announced in a loud voice. "I'd like you to meet Mr. Les Gorski. He's one of the best commercial divers on the planet, and the man who is going to do his damndest to turn all of you into bona fide divers. In case you have any doubts, it may help you to know that Mr. Gorski works extensively, training both Delta Force and SEAL teams. He is uniquely suited for this as he not only knows a great deal about deepwater diving, he invented some of the equipment you will be using."

Emerson looked back and forth among the men. "We have very little time, which means that neither does Mr. Gorski. So you can bet he will be pushing you men *hard*. Let me also remind you that this rig and the Pathfinder are both under communication lockdown. Anything you send or receive will be intercepted and heavily scrutinized. So, if you want to get a message through to your loved ones and remain here, I suggest you make it short and sweet. What lies below your feet is not some myth. It's not a conspiracy. It is a bona fide alien spacecraft. And be it luck or fate, you are the men who are going to get the first crack at it. We will take every precaution but make no mistake, this is dangerous business, which is why Mr. Gorski is here. He will teach you how to live and work at depth and if he can, he will also try to keep you from dying."

Several of the men smiled at Emerson's last comment but quickly realized there was no trace of humor on the captain's face. They watched as he turned to Gorski and nodded.

At roughly six feet tall, Les Gorski examined the group of men with his steely eyes, set behind a pair of dark framed glasses. His face was weathered and hardened against years of sun and wind. He kept himself from shaking his head. The men he was used to dealing with were very different from those standing in front of him.

He turned and glanced back at his two seasoned team members, methodically unloading heavy bags of diving equipment. "All right men," he said, turning back. "Listen up!"

II

Lee sat quietly in the observation room, staring at the glass tank as if in a trance. On the other side of the glass, Dirk and Sally were as quiet as he was. They kept moving around the tank with the same slow, dour feeling as Lee and the others.

It had been just over a week since Juan's funeral service, held at the church he'd attended since he was born. His parents were there, listening to the sermon but never really hearing it. His father stared at the floor, unmoving and devastated. But it was Juan's little sister that completely tore Lee's heart out. Her small figure leaned against her mother and never stopped crying.

Even now, Lee could not get the images out of his memory. Back home, he sat in his black computer chair, mourning his friend. A young kid, fresh out of college, who believed in what they were doing at the Center as much as any of them. Someone who was always there to help, every time he was needed.

The room, along with the rest of the building, was virtually silent. The only detectable sound was the soft hum of IMIS's cooling system. Beyond that, Lee wallowed in the solitude. Juan had given everything. He loved the team. He loved their mission. But more than that, he loved his family, and especially his sister.

Lee pressed his lips together, fighting to keep the tears in while he remembered Juan's face. He was such a good friend. And smart. *God, the kid was smart.* But now, now he was gone...forever.

Although there was one thing left.

He looked up when he heard the sound of voices coming from the lobby, on the other side of the large double doors.

He immediately stood up and waited in anticipation. A few minutes later, one of the doors opened and DeeAnn Draper entered. She was followed by three people and then Caesare, who stepped inside and eased the metal door shut.

Juan's parents and his little sister Angelina had come back for a final visit. Each of the three examined the room again with pained expressions, as if seeing Juan himself for the last time.

Lee approached but said nothing.

DeeAnn brushed a short lock of hair back past her ear and bent down.

"Are you okay, Angelina?"

Juan's sister nodded.

"It doesn't feel the same here, does it?"

She shook her head.

"It doesn't feel the same for us either." DeeAnn glanced at her parents. They didn't have to know how much the team knew about their daughter's disease.

"Angelina, I know Juan brought you here a lot to talk to the dolphins. And we brought you here because they wanted to say hello."

Angelina managed a grin and looked to the tank, where Dirk and Sally were waiting at the glass.

DeeAnn knelt down. "Do you like talking to them?"

"Yes."

"Good," she said. She stole a look at Caesare, standing quietly behind them, and to Lee over her shoulder.

"Angelina, how would you like to *swim* with them?"

III

The night was still, without even a hint of a breeze through the large habitat. On a soft bed of grass, Dulce lay quietly on the ground, listening to the sound of Dexter sleeping overhead in a small rosewood tree.

The young gorilla stood up and walked softly to the side wall, stopping at the large clear door. After a moment, she stepped closer and studied the small security keypad that she had seen DeeAnn and the others use many times. She tilted her head, then lifted her hand and pushed the same tiny squares in the way that they did.

Nothing happened.

Dulce tried again, more carefully.

A loud click sounded as the door's lock disengaged. She wrapped her long fingers around the handle and pulled.

She padded quietly down the hallway until reaching the double doors leading into the observation area. She pulled one open and stepped inside, peering around at the darkened room.

On one side stood a row of machines with hundreds of blinking lights and on the other was a floor-to-ceiling wall of water, held back by glass similar to that used around her habitat.

She approached the glass wall and stared into the dark blue water at the two dolphins. One of them opened its eyes and moved gently toward Dulce.

For several minutes, the two mammals stared curiously at one another. Until IMIS detected Dulce in the room. And powered up the monitor and microphone on the desk beside her.

ABOUT THE AUTHOR

Michael Grumley is a self-published writer who lives in Northern California with his wife and two young daughters. His email address is michael@michaelgrumley.com, and his web site is www.michaelgrumley.com.

ABOUT "TIEWATER"

You might be interested to know that SEAL Team member "Tiewater" in this book is based on a real person by the name of Tim Tigner.

Tim served in Soviet Counterintelligence with the Green Berets. He was kind enough to serve as an advisor for several of the military scenes in Catalyst. Tim is a great guy and one heck of a writer in his own right, on par with Tom Clancy and David Baldacci.

Read just one of his thrillers and you'll see what I mean.

MESSAGE FROM THE AUTHOR

I must admit, when I started the Breakthrough story I had no idea of what reaction I might receive. But I *was* hopeful. After all, who doesn't like dolphins? However, the overwhelming response after the first book was published was something I wasn't expecting.

Not only do most people like the story, but the excitement over the idea of connecting with another intelligent species on our own planet seems to resonate far deeper than I had expected.

Moreover, it's not just that people like dolphins, it's more that practically everyone seems to *love* dolphins. There are of course exceptions, but the consensus among the rest of us makes me wonder if there is indeed some innate love for these creatures bubbling beneath the surface.

Perhaps it's why so many of us are fascinated with the idea of extraterrestrials. An idea that we are not alone and that humans just might *not* be the pinnacle of life in the universe.

Nevertheless, I'm glad you've enjoyed this story so far. Of course, it's not over. And if by chance you found yourself disappointed at the absence of Palin or his people in Catalyst, do not despair. Their story is just beginning.

In the meantime, please visit my website at www.michaelgrumley.com to get a FREE copy of "Genesis." It's an unpublished Breakthrough novella, which tells the story of Alison Shaw's run-in with the Navy, how she came to meet Dirk and Sally for the first time, and how the IMIS project was born. I think you'll like it.

And finally, if you could *please* spare a moment and leave a review for Catalyst, or even a post on your favorite social website, I would be very grateful.

As for myself, I'll be working on the next Breakthrough book.

Thank you,
Michael

Click here to write a review for CATALYST.

Books by Michael C. Grumley

BREAKTHROUGH

LEAP

CATALYST

AMID THE SHADOWS

THROUGH THE FOG

THE UNEXPECTED HERO

Made in the USA
Las Vegas, NV
26 January 2025

17024410R00267